"WHAT DO YOU TAKE ME FOR?"

The question was furious, to hide Sarah's rapidly growing urge to let Gallagher hold her as he would.

"A lady. A very lovely, innocent lady who is shocked at herself because she enjoys my touch." Then his thumb moved, so slowly over her breast. It was all Sarah could do to repress a telltale gasp.

"Don't be ashamed, Sarah. It's perfectly natural for you to feel as you do. Let me show you . . ."

"Let me go. Please." Sarah barely managed to get the words out. More than anything in the world she wished she didn't have to say them. Tonight she wanted to surrender her aching, burning flesh to him, let him take her, and feel what it was like to truly be a woman. Just for tonight . . .

"One of the finest, most talented writers of romantic history today."

—Affaire de Coeur

"Ms. Robards [has] the marvelous talent to zero in on the heart of erotic fantasy. She seems to know instinctively our most secret thoughts and then dreams up the perfect scenario to give them free rein. . . . The result is pure magic."

—Romantic Times

KAREN ROBARDS

Dark Torment

WARNER
VISION
BOOKS

NEW YORK   BOSTON

Copyright © 1985 by Karen Robards
All rights reserved. No part of this book may be reproduced in any form or by any electronic or mechanical means, including information storage and retrieval systems, without permission in writing from the publisher, except by a reviewer who may quote brief passages in a review.

Cover design by Diane Luger
Hand lettering by David Gatti
Photograph by Andy Williams/Getty Images

Warner Books

Time Warner Book Group
1271 Avenue of the Americas, New York, NY 10020
Visit our Web site at www.twbookmark.com

Printed in the United States of America

First Printing: August 1985
Reissued: January 1997, December 2004

22 21 20 19 18 17 16 15 14 13 12 11

To my three brothers, Tod Leslie Johnson, Bruce Hodges Johnson, and Brad Hodges Johnson, with love and thanks for never failing to make my life interesting; and as always, to Doug and Peter.

"I don't know what Pa can have been thinking about, telling us to meet him down here!" As Liza Markham stared over the high wheels of the pony trap her sister was driving, she wrinkled her pert, freckled nose at the slovenly looking men and painted women who crowded the plank sidewalks along the packed-earth street. With its motley collection of wool warehouses, saloons, and other establishments of dubious nature, the area would have given pause to a far more intrepid young lady than Liza.

"I imagine he was thinking that it would be simpler for us to come to the docks than for him to haul a wagonload of convicts through town. This trip wasn't for your exclusive benefit, you know. Pa and Mr. Percival had business to attend to. You were the one who insisted on coming. Remember?" Sarah Markham's usually serene voice was acidic as she cast an irritated look at her young stepsister. Liza was slouched dispiritedly against the trap's curved, padded side. The younger girl looked hot, Sarah thought with a niggle of guilt at her own crossness. But then, Sarah reminded herself, so was she. So, probably, was every resident of Melbourne, Australia, on this scorching afternoon in January 1838. The area surrounding Melbourne had been caught in a heatwave for weeks, and there was no respite in sight. Tempers had been flaring as quickly as the grass plains surrounding the town.

"I needed some new slippers."

"You didn't get any!"

"Is it my fault they didn't have the right color?"

Sarah mentally counted to ten at Liza's sulky response. Her hands tightened automatically on the reins. The piebald mare drawing the trap along at a slow trot threw up her head in surprise. One brown eye rolled back to look reproachfully at Sarah.

"Sorry, Clare," Sarah murmured contritely. Liza gave her a burning look. Sarah knew that her habit of talking to animals—dumb beasts, as Liza and her mother, Lydia, characterized them—annoyed her sister. Nearly everything she did, from running the house to taking care of the station's books to keeping a reluctant but necessary eye on Liza, seemed to annoy one or the other of them. But then, they annoyed her, too, Lydia more than Liza, who at sixteen—six years Sarah's junior—had at least her youth to excuse her behavior. But over the seven years since Sarah's father had married Liza's mother, Sarah had learned to ignore the petty irritations that Liza and Lydia subjected her to daily. Ordinarily she would not have been so vexed by Liza's insistence on accompanying their father and his foreman to town, which necessitated her own presence as chaperone. But then, ordinarily a trip to town did not entail spending the better part of five hours being dragged about Melbourne's many seamstresses' and cobblers' establishments in the middle of a heatwave in search of a pair of rose-pink satin dancing slippers, which Sarah had told her sister at the outset were not to be found. But Liza, of course, had refused to listen. Gritting her teeth, Sarah had vowed once again to let experience be Liza's teacher. Liza tended to be willful—Sarah thought that *spoiled* was a better word for it—and over the years Sarah had learned the folly of expecting mere words of caution or advice to carry much weight. Liza learned that a stove was hot only after burning her hand on it, and so it had been with the dancing slippers. Until the very last possible source had been explored and found wanting, she had insisted that the slippers would be found. By then—a scant half-hour ago— Sarah had been hot, thirsty, sweaty, tired, and thoroughly out of temper. A state from which she had not yet begun to recover.

"Oh well, I suppose I shall just have to wear my black ones."

"I suppose so." Sarah's sarcasm was lost on Liza, as Sarah had known it would be. Liza's despised black slippers were less than three months old; to Sarah's certain knowledge, they had never been worn. But Liza was determined to make a splash at her upcoming seventeenth-birthday ball, which would mark her first official appearance in squattocracy society. She had been planning every detail of her apparel for months, including the acquisition of a pair of dancing slippers to match the rose-pink satin ballgown that Melbourne's leading modiste was now making for her. Sarah thought of the price of that gown and barely repressed a sigh. She was afraid that Liza, with her love of finery, would shortly be as big a drain on the station's funds as her mother was. Ordinarily, Lowella was a thriving sheep operation, but the drought had played havoc with profits. Without sufficient water, the sheep that were their primary source of income were dropping like flies.

"There's Mr. Percival." Liza spoke with obvious relief,

as Sarah turned the trap down the narrow street parallel to the wharf, and pointed in a very unladylike manner. Sarah supposed she should reprove her, but at this moment she didn't have the patience or the energy to cope with the quarrel that would inevitably follow. Instead, she followed her sister's gesture with her eyes to where a stocky man in his mid-forties, wearing a wide-brimmed black hat pushed far back on his head, was silhouetted against the tall-masted ships along the wharf.

As usual, Melbourne's wharf was a scene of bustling activity. Provisions and convicts were continually being offloaded and their places on the ships being taken by wool, which was Australia's primary export. The smell of uncured wool lying in bales beneath the broiling sun was nearly overpowering. Combined with the odor of rotting fish, tar, and the salt air of the bay, it assaulted Sarah's nostrils with the force of a bare-knuckled prizefighter. She swallowed, refusing to give in to a sudden surge of queasiness. Determinedly she focused on the sights and sounds: white sails flapping as they were raised or lowered; the gray boards of the wharf groaning as heavy, brass-bound barrels of rum and molasses were wheeled over them; shirtless men with glistening bare backs grunting and cursing as they hefted a variety of items on and off the ships; the raucous cries of red-winged parrots and gaudy cockatoos wheeling in the azure sky and the sudden flutter of their wings as they swooped to snatch a bit of plunder from the wharf. The scene was crude, yet, in the way it spoke of distant lands and travel, exciting. At least, Sarah thought, it would have been exciting were it not for the nauseating odor.

When Liza groaned, Sarah looked over to see her sister pressing a dainty bit of perfumed hanky to her nose. Just like Liza to have one when she needs it, Sarah reflected wryly, knowing that there was no point in searching the pockets of her own serviceable dun-colored skirt for any such item. In the usual run of things, she had no use for such fripperies. But then, in the usual run of things, the world didn't smell so bad, either.

"Let's collect Pa and Mr. Percival and *go*," Liza said with distaste. As Sarah reined the horse near the wharf, she silently concurred. But as the trap drew to a halt, she saw that Pa was nowhere in sight. Percival stood with his back to them, alone, staring into the glaring sun at one of the ships docked nearby. Securing the reins to the small hitch protruding from the front of the trap, Sarah tried to follow his gaze. But with the sun nearly blinding her she could see little more than the dark outline of denuded masts against the endlessly blue sky.

"Why, Miss Sarah, Miss Liza," Percival exclaimed, turning, his attention attracted by the sound of Clare's hooves as she pawed the ground. "Finished your shopping?"

Neither Sarah nor Liza chose to reply to this still-sore point, but Percival didn't wait for an answer. While Sarah was making one last loop in the reins, he stepped off the weathered boards of the wharf and came around the trap to Sarah's side, his boots raising little puffs of dust as he walked. Percival was the only man of European descent working for her father who was not a convict; Sarah knew that this was not the only reason why he had been made overseer, but it was the most important. A former seaman who had, she had gathered from various tidbits he had let drop, grown up in a bucolic English shire, Percival had a deep hankering to be a gentleman. When the merchant ship on which he had been second mate had docked in Melbourne some ten years before, and he had discovered that in Australia, if a man was not a convict or the descendant of convicts and was of European descent he was considered gentry, he had decided to make England's burgeoning penal colony his home. Six years ago he had come to Lowella, and he had never left. A hard worker with a knack for persuading or coercing those who worked under him into being the same, he had been made overseer within a year. Now Edward Markham consulted him on most decisions, and Percival ran the station with an amazing degree of autonomy.

At the moment, dressed in a black frock coat and intricately tied cravat despite the heat, he looked very much the prosperous grazier. A pleased smile split his seamed face as he looked up at Sarah, lending him a geniality he did not always possess. Sarah returned that smile coolly. But her coolness seemed never to penetrate his thick hide. He was determined to court her no matter how clearly she indicated that his attentions were not welcome. Sarah knew that Lydia and her father—and Percival himself—expected her to encourage him. After all, she was, at twenty-two, decidedly on the matrimonial shelf. No other suitor was likely to come along, and she was not getting younger, as Lydia took great pains to remind her. John Percival, being relatively young (forty was not old, said Lydia, who was some years past it), in good health, and not physically repulsive, seemed in her family's view ideal husband material for a prim spinster who was not likely to get another offer. But Sarah determinedly resisted their coercion. If she could not find a man who sparked some degree of warmth in her (Percival sparked nothing but distaste), then she would not marry at all. Which would not bother her in the least!

Liza, however, had none of Sarah's reservations where Percival was concerned. In her newly discovered guise of femme fatale—enhanced, Sarah suspected, by a female impulse to steal her elder sister's only suitor—Liza turned the full force of her sixteen-year-old smile on Percival. Which, Sarah acknowledged to herself, was really quite something to see. Dressed in a flouncy muslin afternoon dress in her favorite rose pink, with her dusky curls pinned high beneath the floppy straw hat designed to protect her creamy olive complexion from the sun, her coffee-brown eyes sparkling, her white teeth gleaming against lips that had been rubbed with rose petals to match the shade of her dress, Liza gave promise of becoming quite a beauty. If her nose was slightly snub, the sparkle in her eyes made up for it. If her chin was a trifle square, the cupid's-bow mouth with its willful pout compensated beautifully. The freckles dusting her nose did not detract but called attention to the smoothness of her skin. And she was petite, as was the fashion; small but voluptuously rounded, sure to appeal to all susceptible males. To Percival's credit, he did not appear to be much affected by Liza's efforts to captivate him. He responded to her dazzling smile with a perfunctory one of his own, and turned his eyes back to Sarah. Sarah could not help feeling a flicker of amusement at Liza's sudden pout. In consequence, Sarah's second smile at Percival was warmer than any she had previously bestowed upon him. Encouraged, he took off his hat, self-consciously shook his head to settle his untidy, coarse brown hair, and held up his hand to her.

"Wouldn't you like to get down for a minute, Miss Sarah, and stretch your limbs? Mr. Markham had to go aboard the *Septimus* there, and he may be some time yet."

"Trouble, Mr. Percival?" Sarah frowned, hesitated, then placed her gloved hand in his large, stubby-fingered one. She knew her father hated the convict ships, and only the most dire necessity would make him set foot on one.

"Nothing you need concern yourself about," he answered as he helped her down. Sarah suspected that, like most men, he disapproved of women bothering their heads with what was men's business, and that her authority and involvement in Lowella's operation irked him.

"You'd better tell me," Sarah said quietly, her eyes

shifting to the bullock dray pulled up close to the wharf just behind him. It was loaded with perhaps half-a-dozen dirty, scrawny, manacled men, the convicts whose acquisition had been the primary purpose of this unusual mid-week trip into Melbourne. Although convicts were generally assigned by the government to serve out their sentences at hard labor for Australia's landowners, Edward Markham had arranged clandestinely, for a fee, to acquire six brawny men direct from the ship's captain, with whom he had dealt before. Percival had come along to stand guard over the men, although there was really no need: there was nowhere for them to go, and if they ran they would be hunted down like dogs. At the moment, Percival stood with his back to the convicts, ignoring them, as if they were the most God-fearing citizens in the world. And with good reason, Sarah thought, looking over the convicts again. After the long voyage from England, made under conditions that Sarah shuddered even to contemplate, not one of them had a thought in his head about anything save the misery of his own body. Weak from months spent chained in a stiflingly hot hold packed with men, half-starved, most suffering from scurvy, newly arrived convicts were rarely a threat to anyone. It would take a week or more of rest and good food before even the hardiest of them was fit to do the back-breaking work of well digging, for which they had been acquired.

Percival still had not replied to Sarah's question. Annoyed, she looked back to find him eyeing her with blatant admiration, and she knew he meant for her to notice it and feel flattered. If it weren't growing so tiresome, Percival's pursuit of her would have been almost funny, Sarah thought, frowning at his cow-eyed look that she guessed was supposed to represent the very ultimate in bedazzlement. He behaved as if smitten by a raving beauty, which she knew perfectly well she wasn't. She didn't even come close. Tall for a woman, in her sleeveless white linen shirtwaist and plain round skirt she was all sharp lines and angles where she knew men preferred a softer, rounder shape. The color of her hair was good—a rich, tawny gold—but it was thick as a horse's tail and almost as straight. Years ago, after countless nights spent tortured by the rag curlers Lydia had insisted she try, Sarah had given up attempting to achieve a fashionable coiffure. Nowadays she contented herself with bundling the wayward mass into a huge, shapeless knot at the nape of her neck. It took nearly two dozen hairpins to secure it, and even then tendrils were always escaping, not to curl charmingly around her face as Liza's did, but to straggle limply down her neck and back, and make her itch. Her face, with its high cheekbones and forehead and pointed chin, was totally lacking in the soft prettiness that characterized her stepmother and sister. Her skin, while fine and smooth, had a distressing tendency to tan, probably because she was always forgetting her hat under the hot Australian sun. Only her eyes had any real claim to beauty. They were as gold as guineas, a gleaming topaz set aslant beneath thick lashes that were dark at the base and as tawny as her hair at the tips. Even Liza and Lydia—the latter grudgingly—agreed that Sarah's eyes were quite out of the ordinary. The only trouble was that, combined with her prominent cheekbones, pointed chin, and too-thin body, they gave her the look of a scrawny cat. And men, Sarah had found, tended to prefer fluffy kittens.

"Mr. Percival," she prompted with an edge to her voice as he continued his perusal. His eyes jerked up to her face, and he had the grace to flush slightly. Sarah returned his look with a level one, and his flush deepened. "You were going to tell me why my father went aboard a convict ship?"

"There was a problem with the convicts." The words were said reluctantly.

"What kind of problem?" Sarah made no effort to hide her irritation. Percival's attempts to keep her in what he considered her proper, female place were maddening. She supposed that if she married him, he would expect her to confine her activities to the running of the house, and to leave to him everything that had to do with the sheep station. Which, she guessed, was why he wanted to marry her in the first place. As Edward Markham's only child, she could reasonably be expected to inherit Lowella in preference to her stepmother and stepsister. Which, Sarah thought with a wry inward smile, only showed how little he really knew her father. Edward was always inclined to take the easy way out of messy situations, and the future disposition of Lowella was potentially a very messy situation indeed. Her father was fond of her, she thought, but no more than that. Certainly he was not so besotted with her as to leave her the station in preference to Lydia, who periodically questioned him with transparent guilelessness about his will. Sarah suspected that she also questioned her father's lawyer, with some success—Lydia was a very attractive woman. And if Lydia were to find out that she had been denied ownership of a vast, profitable sheep station . . . ! Sarah couldn't blame her father; she wouldn't want to be around on that day, either.

"We contracted for six, and paid for them too, in cash, not kind. When we got here, they had six waiting for us, all right. But the bos'n, who's a chum of mine, tipped me off that we were being cheated, in spirit if not in fact. He said one of the men was a rogue, a real troublemaker, and they couldn't get anyone else to take him so they were trying to palm him off on us. But I passed the word along to your da, and he flatly refused to take him. As Mr. Markham said, and I agree, we don't need no troublemakers on Lowella. Not with the way things have been going lately.''

Sarah nodded agreement. With the convicts whose labor was Australia's lifeblood far outnumbering the landowners who worked them, the situation on the cattle and sheep stations on New South Wales was extremely volatile. Lowella had always been peaceful—their convicts were well treated—but their neighbors had not always been so fortunate. There was no sense in bringing in a rogue convict to stir up trouble on Lowella.

"Didn't Pa just tell them we don't want that kind at Lowella?''

Percival grimaced. "Sure he did. But the mate said a deal's a deal. And your da said, the hell—begging your pardon, Miss Sarah—it is. The mate backed down and agreed to take the convict back, but he didn't have the authority to give your da back his money. And you know how Mr. Markham has been lately about money.''

"I do indeed," Sarah said with wry amusement. Edward, whose lineage included a canny Scots grandmother, could be formidable in the pursuit of money he felt was owed him. She had no doubt that whoever was in charge of the ship would return it to him double-quick. "So Pa went aboard the ship to get his money back. Do you think he'll be long?''

Percival pursed his lips, cocking his head as he considered. "He's been gone quite a while already.''

"Sarah, where's Pa? If I don't get out of this heat soon, I'll just die!'' Liza's plaintive cry brought Sarah's attention back to her. The younger girl was perspiring, her cheeks now more red than rose. She had taken off her hat and was feebly waving it in front of her face. As Sarah looked at her, Liza dropped the hat into her lap, as if fanning herself had suddenly become too much work. Sarah frowned. For all her dark hair and olive skin, Liza did tend to feel the heat. Much more than Sarah herself did. Despite Sarah's fair coloring and deceptive slenderness, she was blessed, or cursed, depending on one's point of view, with the constitution of an ox. While Liza, who appeared to be the sturdier of the two, was far more prone to illness and upsets.

"You won't die, Liza," Sarah said firmly. Catering to Liza's love of the melodramatic was always a mistake. Usually it led to a scene complete with tears.

"No wonder you're an old maid, Sarah! You don't have the least sensibility!" Liza burst out. Sarah could not control a sudden, quick flush of embarrassment as she realized that Percival, who stood no more than a pace from her side, must have heard, although he gave no sign. It was one thing to acknowledge privately that at twenty-two she was well past the common age for marriage; it was another to have Liza announce it to the world. Not that Sarah particularly minded being a spinster. Better an old maid than an unhappy wife, she had decided long ago, when Percival had first made her an offer. The laws of the day made a wife her husband's chattel, completely subject to him in all things; Sarah shuddered at the thought of being so much in any man's control. At least she was content as she was. She knew that she would be desperately unhappy as Percival's wife.

"Sarah, my head aches!" Liza's moan brought Sarah out of her musings. She eyed her sister severely, not yet having forgiven her for that humiliating remark in front of Percival. But Liza's white face and the perspiration dotting her forehead convinced Sarah that the younger girl really was in some distress. Sarah moved quickly around the trap to touch Liza's hand. As she had suspected, her skin felt cold and clammy.

"I feel dreadful, Sarah!"

"I know you do, love." Sarah's sympathy was genuine.

Liza could not be allowed to remain any longer in the sun, and there was no shade in sight. Something had to be done, and from long experience Sarah knew that she was the one who would have to do it. She sighed. "I'll go fetch Pa, Liza, and then we can be on our way. You'll feel better once we get away from the wharf."

"Please hurry, Sarah!"

"Miss Sarah, you can't!"

Liza and Percival spoke at the same time, Liza in an anguished undertone and Percival with disapproval. Percival continued, "You can't have thought—you can't go aboard a convict ship! It's not proper for a lady!"

Sarah took a deep breath, and turned away from Liza to meet Percival's eyes with a calm that was beginning to fray. What an awful, awful day this had been from the start! She didn't know how much more aggravation she could take without losing her temper, which was something she rarely did. Living with Lydia and Liza, one rapidly learned control.

"I am well aware of that, Mr. Percival. But I see no alternative—unless you're suggesting that we simply wait here until Liza faints with the heat. She will, you know. I've seen her do it."

"But, Miss Sarah . . ."

"I'm going to go fetch my father, Mr. Percival. There's nothing more to be said."

Despite the finality of her words, he refused to give up. "If you'll permit me, I'll fetch Mr. Markham."

"And leave me here to watch over the convicts?" Sarah shook her head. "I'll go. I won't be long. Liza, did you hear? I'll be back directly. And for goodness' sake, put on your hat!"

Liza moaned again and closed her eyes. She made no move to obey about the hat. Sarah shut her own eyes for a moment in a silent appeal to heaven—why did Liza have to choose this day to be difficult?—then set off briskly for the *Septimus*. The men on the quay eyed her, some curiously, others with emotions she preferred not to recognize. But she passed among them without difficulty, aided, no doubt, she thought with amusement, by her plain appearance. Or maybe they left her alone simply because they were just too tired and dispirited to pursue her. Despite the fact that they were convicts, and backbreaking work under near-intolerable conditions was part of the punishment for their crimes, she could not help pitying them as they were forced to labor without pause under the menacing eyes of overseers armed with whips and rifles, while the sun blazed down mercilessly on their uncovered heads. Then Sarah silently chided herself, wondering what her father would say if he knew of her embryonic emancipist feelings. In Melbourne, as in the rest of Australia, there were basically two classes of residents: the emancipists, who felt that convicts, former convicts, and the offspring of convicts were as good as any other member of Australian society and should be treated as such; and the exclusionists, who considered past and present convicts and their descendants a lower form of life, not to be spoken of in the same breath as decent folk. The emancipists, for obvious reasons, tended to be convicts, former convicts, or the children of convicts, and consequently had difficulty getting the authorities to listen to their pleas for equal treatment. Like most landowners, Edward was staunchly exclusionist, and Sarah had been brought up to consider convicts very much beneath her.

The *Septimus* was tied up close to where Percival waited with the dray. Like many of the convict ships plying the ocean between England and Australia, she looked as if one good-sized wave would capsize her. Her timbers had weathered to a uniformly dull gray, and if she had ever seen a coat of paint there was no longer any evidence of it.

Her middle sagged like that of a swaybacked horse, and her bare masts and halfheartedly furled sails had a shabby look. Making her way up the rickety gangplank, Sarah's attention was briefly caught by the scene before her. Half a dozen tall ships were anchored farther out in the bay, their bare, black masts stretching into the cloudless azure sky. Another ship, her sails useless because there was no wind, was being towed across the water to the dock by a small flotilla of rowboats. The bay itself was beautiful, with the sun glinting like diamonds off water that ranged from palest sea green to emerald to sapphire to near purple.

Sarah was still absorbing the view when she became aware that, while she was alone on the gangplank, there was much activity on the *Septimus's* deck. Squinting against the glare, and trying to ignore the headache that was beginning to throb at her temples, Sarah tried to make out what was happening. A shifting, muttering crowd of men was gathered near the center of the ship, their attention focused on something that was taking place in their midst. Their bared, sweat-streaked, muscular backs prevented her from seeing exactly what that something was. Sarah toyed with the idea of returning to the dock and waiting in the safety of the little group from Lowella for her father to join them, but then the thought of Liza's probable reaction to her retreat spurred her on. Much as she disliked the idea of getting too near that masculine mob, she preferred it to dealing with Liza in hysterics. Swallowing her reservations, Sarah resumed her walk up the swaying ramp. As she drew closer, she became aware of a sharp cracking noise repeated at regular intervals. It slashed with unexpected violence through the other sounds of the dock—the gentle lapping of the sea, the fluttering of sails, the voices of the men before and behind her. Sarah frowned as she set foot on the lightly rocking deck of the *Septimus*, trying to fathom what that sound could be—and what could be happening at the center of the mob to cause the men to focus so much sullen yet fascinated attention toward one spot. Then came a faint whistling sound, inaudible from farther away, followed by another harsh crack. Then—she was almost sure—she heard a man's guttural moan. Sarah's eyes widened with slowly dawning horror.

She moved cautiously around the gathered men toward the far rail of the ship, where the crowd was thinner. No one paid any attention to her, for which she was thankful. Every eye was focused on what was happening at the center of the crowd. The whistling sound that preceded each jolting crack was clearly audible now, and the cracks themselves were so loud that they made her want to flinch. And the moans that followed—Sarah no longer had any doubt that they were made by a man: a man in agony.

Picking her way through coils of rope and dropped tools, Sarah finally reached the rail. From there she could see a little way through the crowd. There was still one man, a tall, thin fellow with bushy fair hair, whose back blocked her view. As if sensing her need, he chose that moment to shift sideways, and she saw past him. Horrified, Sarah wishes he had not.

A tall, black-haired man, clad only in tattered breeches, forcibly embraced the base of the mizzen, his hands stretched high over his head and around the wooden pole, where the shackles linking his wrists were tied to an iron hook set deep into the wood. He hung suspended from this restraint; only his bare toes touched the deck. The tendons and veins in his arms bulged from supporting his weight. Blood trickled down his arms from the iron cuffs encircling his wrists, but those few streaks of crimson were as nothing compared to the river that ran from the two dozen or so bloody lacerations that marred his broad, muscular back. The skin surrounding the gashes appeared to have been peeled from its underlying layer of muscle; strips of flesh hung from the edges of the wounds like bits of tattered fringe amid a sea of welling blood. The bubbling crimson gashes crisscrossed one another, underlined here and there with the stark white of bared tendons; blood ran freely from the gashes to soak into the man's dingy breeches. His black hair, overlong and soaked with sweat, was matted with blood, probably from his back. He looked to be brutishly strong, and yet, in his current straits, pathetic. As Sarah stared, appalled, a many-thonged leather whip with bits of metal knotted into the ends sang through the air to land with another spine-chilling crack against his oozing back. The victim flinched, shuddering, his head reflexively jerking back in agony as he gave another low, guttural groan. With each lash of the whip, blood and bits of flesh were sprayed onto the men standing closest to the scene of the carnage: the man wielding the whip, another man, who was probably, judging from his uniform, the captain—and her own father. Sarah felt her stomach churn as she saw the drops of blood flecking her father's breeches and coat and even the white of his shirt front. She could hardly believe that this man with his arms crossed implacably over his chest, his eyes intent as they watched the suffering of a helpless human being, was really her father.

The whip whistled through the air again, finding its captive target with another sickening crack. The prisoner shuddered and groaned as before. Sarah watched, horrified, as blood from this new set of gashes splattered against her father's buff-colored lapel. He didn't turn a hair; his attention remained fixed on the whip's victim. A nerve twitching at the corner of his mouth was the only evidence of emotion her father betrayed. The convict was writhing now, pulling futilely at his bonds. His head was thrown back in agony. From the corner of her eye, Sarah saw the shirtless, barrel-chested man who wielded the whip begin to shake the leather thongs out once again. The prisoner must have heard the sound. A series of shudders shook his long muscles.

"Stop it!" Before the intention had even crystallized in her mind, Sarah was running forward. That it was not her place to intervene barely occurred to her. She could not, would not, be a silent witness to such brutality. She pushed through the crowd, uncaring that every eye was suddenly riveted on her. Every eye, that is, except those belonging to the man with the whip. Either he had not heard her cry or intended to ignore it. He lifted the whip high over his head.

"I said stop it!" Sarah's voice was shrill with outrage as she thrust herself between the whip and its victim. "Stop it this instant! Do you hear me?"

II

"Sarah!" Her father sounded shocked as he turned to her. Sarah threw him a brief, burning look before her eyes locked with those of the man with the whip. The man's eyes were small, and of so pale a blue as to be almost colorless. They shone with menace as he glared at her. After the brief hesitation caused by her intervention, he was once again beginning to raise the whip.

"Get out of the way, lady," he warned softly.

"I will not!"

"Sarah!" Shaking off the instant of paralysis that had held him frozen in place, her father rushed to her. His fingers dug into her soft flesh as he caught her by the upper arm.

"Rogers!" the captain warned at nearly the same moment, shaking his head in a curt negative at the man with the whip. Those colorless eyes gleamed evilly at Sarah for a moment longer. Then the man looked at his captain and slowly lowered the whip.

"Sarah, what in the name of heaven do you think you're doing? You're interfering with this man's just punishment—as well as Captain Farley's very proper running of his ship!" Edward Markham's mutter, meant for her ears alone, was angry and embarrassed at the same time. Sarah looked at him mutinously. He was not a tall man—he and she were almost of a height—but he was built like a bull terrier, broad and muscular. Even his face with its deeply carved lines reminded her of a bull terrier's. Anger emphasized his florid complexion so that his skin was almost the color of his thinning red hair; his embarrassment at her action made him seem to swell. Sarah met his bulging gray eyes calmly: she was not afraid of her father.

"Pa, how can you be party to such a thing?" she demanded, her voice as low as his—and as angry. "It is barbarous! It must be stopped!"

Her father scowled at her; his bristling, ginger-colored eyebrows almost met over the bridge of his nose. "Of course it seems barbarous to you—it was never meant for your eyes! What are you doing here, anyway? You have no business on a convict ship—and you cannot go about interfering in things that are none of your concern!"

"If you mean this—this atrocity—it is my concern! It is the concern of anyone with the smallest spark of human decency! They will kill him!"

"Very likely." Her father did not seem troubled by the prospect.

"Pa!"

"Sarah, he deserves it: he nearly killed a man this morning, trying to escape. And on the voyage out he did his best to incite the other convicts to mutiny. He's a bad one, daughter, and no mistake. He deserves every lick. He'll cause trouble wherever he goes."

"Mr. Markham, I must ask you to remove this young lady. I take it you are related? Yes? . . . I would like to get this business concluded. I have many other matters to attend to this afternoon.'' Captain Farley, a swarthy man not much taller than her father, came to stand beside Edward Markham. His eyes were cold with disapproval as they moved over Sarah.

"This—business—has gone quite far enough!"Sarah's voice was as icy as the captain's. She glared at him, chin thrust defiantly forward, arms akimbo, her fists planted on her hips. In her unfashionably plain white shirtwaist and dun-colored skirt, with her hair swept back into a dowdy bun, she should have been a negligible figure, easy to dismiss. Only those great golden eyes flashing angrily warned that she was not.

"Mr. Markham!"

"Sarah!" Her father was almost growling with exasperation. His hand on her arm tightened, and for a moment Sarah thought that he meant to pull her out of the way by force.

"Pa, this is the man meant for Lowella, isn't it?" It required little imagination to link the whip's victim to Percival's tale. At her father's reluctant nod, she continued, "Then he is subject to your authority and no one else's. You surely will not allow him to be beaten to death! I would never have believed such a thing of you!"

"Young lady . . ." The captain's tone was ominous. Sarah met his eyes with outrage in her own. He fell silent.

"Sarah, I have renounced all claim to the man. Captain Farley has returned the money I paid for him. And, since I have refused to take him, he remains under Captain Farley's jurisdiction. Under the circumstances, the captain had no choice but to order the man punished, and I cannot feel that the punishment is unjust. I know it seems harsh to you, but it serves as a deterrent to others as well as to the man himself.''

"If he survives it," Sarah muttered. From the corner of

her eye she could see the subject of their argument. He was slumped against the pole, the muscles of his arms threatening to burst through the skin as they bore his whole weight. He hung limply, head down, apparently oblivious to the cessation of the whipping. Blood ran down his arms and welled from his back to soak his breeches, which were so faded and filthy that their original color was impossible to determine. A swarm of green flies, now that the killing lash had been stilled, buzzed around that bloodied back; occasionally one would alight to gorge itself on the oozing pulp. Bare to the waist, bloodied, drenched with sweat, the convict was animalistic in his maleness. Ordinarily Sarah would have been repulsed by such raw masculinity. But the man aroused a fierce protective instinct in her. She was determined to save him.

"Mr. Markham!" Captain Farley sounded furious now. He kept glancing around, and as Sarah followed his eyes she realized that one reason for the rapid increase of his temper was the staring, murmuring crowd of men surrounding them: Captain Farley disliked being made to look a fool. "I must insist that this outrageous situation be resolved at once! If you do not remove this young lady—immediately!—I will do so."

"You will not lay a hand on my daughter." Edward Markham was not the most loving of fathers, but he had never laid a hand on her, and Sarah knew he would allow no one else to do so. "Sarah . . ." His mouth was tight with exasperation as he turned his eyes back to her.

"Give the captain back his money, Pa!"

"Sarah!"

"I mean it, Pa: I'm not moving until you do." Her chin jutted with determination.

"Sarah, you know as well as I do that a man of that stamp is the very last thing we need on Lowella. For God's sake, use your head, girl!"

Sarah met her father's eyes steadily. "I know he's a troublemaker. It makes no difference. No matter what he is or what he has done, he does not deserve to be beaten in such a fashion."

"Sarah . . ."

"Mr. Markham!"

"Oh, for God's sake!" Edward Markham snapped, glaring from Captain Farley's angry face to Sarah's determined one. With a snort, he reached into his coat pocket for his purse. "Have the man cut down, Farley," he growled. Then, turning back to Sarah, he added in the same tone, "You're getting too headstrong, girl. No wonder you haven't got a husband. You'd badger the poor man to his grave."

"Thank you, Pa." Sarah ignored her father's exasperated aside and smiled at him as, wincing, he counted the sum out of his purse and handed it to Captain Farley, who did not appear mollified. Instead of returning her smile, Edward Markham glared at her.

"I've a feeling you'll soon rue this day, daughter, and no doubt I will, too!"

Sarah did not reply. Instead, she turned her attention to the two sailors who were, on Captain Farley's orders, sawing through the thick rope that bound the convict's irons to the hook. When the rope was cut, the man's arms dropped heavily around the pole. For just an instant, as his legs struggled to bear his weight, he stood upright, leaning heavily against the pole. Then his knees buckled. Groaning, he sagged to the deck. Only his arms, which were still shackled around the mast, prevented him from pitching forward onto his face. His forehead resting against the smooth wood of the mizzen, he half-crouched, half-slumped. The flies, which had swarmed upward in alarm at his sudden movement, settled in once more to continue their meal. One broad, bloodied shoulder twitched in silent protest.

Sarah stepped forward, meaning to shoo the flies away, but her father's hand on her arm stayed her.

"Don't get carried away by kindness, daughter. The man's naught but a convict, remember. And dangerous."

"That may be true, Pa, but he's nearly unconscious. And something must be done for his back. We can't possibly transport him to Lowella in that state."

"You've saved his life for him; that's enough. If he'd had the full two hundred lashes Farley had ordered, he would surely have died. I have not the slightest doubt that he'll survive until we can get him back to Lowella and Madeline can tend him. Curse the luck." This last was an irritated mutter, but Sarah heard.

Frowning, she considered. Madeline, an aborigine who had lived on Lowella for as long as Sarah could remember, was a very good nurse. It was she who cared for the convicts when they were ill or injured. Sarah, as the virtual mistress of the station, was almost as well versed in the arts of healing, but she practiced only on her family and the house servants. She had never nursed a man—her father had never been ill a day in his life—and certainly never a convict. Their neighbors would have been scandalized if one of Lowella's ladies had so demeaned herself. But, under the circumstances, the only humane thing to do now was to administer at least rudimentary first aid to that grievously injured back.

"If that man's back isn't cleaned and covered before we set out, you'll have wasted a considerable amount of money. If he doesn't bleed to death, which looks to be entirely possible, those wounds could putrefy. In either case, he'll die."

Edward Markham stared at her for a moment, then turned his eyes to the convict, now sprawled face down on the deck. His expression registered doubt, then disgust. But still he didn't release his hold on Sarah's arm. He turned to look at Captain Farley, who stood several paces away, his arms folded across his chest, disapproval plain in his face as he stared at the convict.

"Farley, give him a dose of the rough-and-ready. My girl's right, we can't take him like this. He's bleeding like a stuck pig."

Farley glanced over his shoulder at them, scowling.

"Going to mollycoddle him, are you?" he said with a snort. "Well, he's your problem now, and if he lives it's your lookout. I won't be giving you your money back a second time, that's certain."

Edward's mouth tightened in response. Farley shrugged, then turned back to the sailors who hovered over the convict.

"Give him a dose of the rough-and-ready, Vickers."

"Aye, Cap'n."

The man called Vickers, a tall, husky, fair-haired fellow who didn't look as if he was yet out of his teens, saluted. Then, turning, he bent to grasp the edge of a bucket that had been placed nearby. With one hand on the bucket's bottom and the other grasping its rim, he flung its contents over the convict's raw back. As the clear liquid splashed over him, the convict stiffened convulsively, and a hoarse cry rose from his throat. He tried to lever himself up off the deck, straightening his arms beneath him so that his head and black-furred chest were clear of the wood by perhaps two feet. His head jerked around; as he stared in their direction, features contorted with pain, Sarah had her first glimpse of his face.

Beneath the coating of grime, and whiskers, she saw that he was fairly young, certainly no older than his mid-thirties. And once he was cleaned up, she thought, he might be passably attractive. His features seemed regular enough. His eyes met hers, and despite their glazing of pain she saw that they were of a blue that was as clear and bright as the endless sky overhead. They seemed far too beautiful to belong to a convicted criminal. Even as Sarah was absorbing their impact, they closed. The sudden burst of pain-induced strength seemed to vanish as quickly as it had come. Shuddering, he collapsed. Sarah stared at that sprawled figure, and winced as Vickers emptied another bucket of clear liquid over the convict's back. This time the convict didn't even move.

"What was in the bucket?" Sarah's lips felt stiff as she asked the question of her father. Now that she had seen his face, and those beautiful eyes, the convict seemed almost as vulnerable as she was herself. Which was ridiculous, she told herself sternly. He was only a convict, after all. Everyone knew that if convicts had feelings, they were only of the coarsest, roughest kind.

"Brine water, ma'am," Vickers answered.

"Brine water!" Sarah could not restrain a shudder. No wonder the poor creature had cried out. It must have burned his back like liquid fire; the salt, seeping into the open wounds, must be burning still.

"It's standard treatment after a flogging," her father said in her ear. Sarah said nothing more, but she felt ill. She would not use a wounded animal so, and she was fairly certain that her father would not, either.

"Captain, I would thank you to have a couple of your crew carry the man down to my dray. He doesn't look capable of making it on his own."

Farley scowled, and for a moment Sarah thought he was going to refuse. Then he shrugged. Sarah guessed that he was remembering the roll of pound notes he had just pocketed. The same two sailors who had freed the convict from the mast lifted him to his feet as Farley gave the order.

"Come, Sarah." Her father's hand on her arm tightened.

"But his back—shouldn't it be bandaged, at the very least? The flies—and the dray will kick up dust. . . ."

"We've no more time to waste on the likes of him. Besides, open air is the best treatment for a wound like that. A bandage would just stick to it."

There was truth to that, Sarah knew. But watching the flies swarm around the convict's torn flesh made her feel ill. If the wounds were left open to every swarming insect and swirling particle of dust between here and Lowella, there was every chance that they would putrefy. And that mode of dying would be even more hideous than being beaten to death. But her father clearly was impatient to be on his way. Nothing would be gained by making another scene, Sarah realized. Besides, she didn't have any bandages with her.

She allowed her father to lead her through the crowd of men, already parted to permit the two sailors to pass with their burden. The convict's arms were around their shoulders; each sailor gripped him with one hand fastened around his wrist and the other clenched on the seat of his breeches. Sarah quickly averted her eyes from that mutilated back, but not before she saw that the convict was at least partially aware of what was happening. He was trying to walk, his knees wavering as his bare feet shuffled weakly across the deck. The sailors had no patience with his puny efforts. They dragged him along between them. Even sagging at the knees as he was, he was taller than either of them. Sarah could see that it was a struggle for the convict even to hold his head upright; he tried, but instants later his head slumped forward in defeat.

In her outrage, Sarah had completely forgotten her reason for going aboard the *Septimus* in the first place. But as soon as their little group approached the dray, her eyes widened with remembrance. Liza! Liza hated the sight of

blood at any time, claiming it made her nauseated. And
with her already feeling ill . . . Sarah broke away from her
father to hurry forward, meaning to warn her sister to turn
away from the distressing sight. But she was too late; even
as she approached the trap where Liza sat, the sailors were
lifting the convict into the dray. His back was presented to
Liza. With her sister, Sarah again absorbed the full impact
of blood welling from more than two dozen open wounds,
of bared tendons and drying crusts of blood and swarming
flies. . . . She turned back to her sister just in time to see
Liza's eyes roll back into her head; she was barely able to
catch the younger girl before, with a little moan, she
slumped over in a dead faint.

From Lowella to Melbourne and back usually took three
days. This time the trip home seemed twice as long. Liza
was ill and had to lie with her head in Sarah's lap as Sarah
drove the trap. The heat was suffocating, even with a
fringed parasol set in a holder to ward off the glare of the
sun. Clare's hooves kicked up whirlwinds of dust that
seemed to seek out every tiny opening in Sarah's clothes
and settle grittily against her sweat-soaked skin. Behind
them, the bullocks drawing the dray raised even worse
clouds of dust; Sarah shuddered to think of what must be
settling into the convict's open wounds as he lay sprawled
flat on the wagon bed. It was useless to hope that any of
the other convicts sitting scrunched together in what was
left of the space would try to keep the worst of the dirt and
flies out of those wounds. They were likely cursing their
mate for crowding them in such heat. Percival, driving the
dray, must be even more hot and miserable than she was
herself. Only Edward, riding astride at the head of the
procession, had any hope of escaping the miseries of the
dust; he could outride it.

For a while their route took them along the banks of the
Yarra Yarra River. There was little more than a trickle of

water left to wend its way through steeply sloped banks of sun-dried mud. Huge eucalyptus trees towering overhead usually provided plentiful shade, but not this day: the sun had left them with only a few small, dry leaves. The red stringybarks, ashes, and slender beech trees had suffered the same fate. Their denuded branches stretched pitifully toward the sky. The ghost gums with their thick gray trunks were just as dry, but their lack of water caused alarm rather than pity: if the heat became too intense, they were likely to explode. Many a brush fire had been started by the spontaneous combustion of a ghost gum in the dry season.

It was nearly dark by the time their little procession pulled into the yard of the inn where they would pass the night. The Markhams were well known at Yancy's place. They nearly always passed the night there on their way to and from Melbourne. In fact, they had spent the previous night there before riding on to Melbourne that morning.

After being shown to the room they would share, Sarah helped Liza to bathe and eat and saw her into bed. By then she wanted nothing so much as a bath and bed herself. The bath she would have, she decided; bed would have to wait a little longer. She would never sleep if she did not do what she could for the injured convict.

With the day's grime washed from her skin, she felt a little better. Winding her hair into its customary knot, she glanced longingly at her nightrail before resolutely donning the clothes that she had packed for the morrow. Not for anything would she wear the filthy garments she had just discarded, but she certainly couldn't parade through a public inn in her night clothes, much as she might long for their soft comfort against her sun- and dust-abraided skin. Liza was soundly asleep in the one large bed; Sarah listened intently to her light breathing for a moment, then bent and blew out the candle. Although she would need a light, she was too much of a grazier's daughter to take a lit candle into a stable. And the stable was where the convicts were bedded down for the night.

Percival and her father would be in the inn's taproom, drinking and spinning yarns with the other men at Yancy's place that night. They would violently disapprove of what she was planning to do, so Sarah had no intention of letting them find her out. Accordingly, she made her way down the stairs past the taproom with extreme caution, her hands clutching the small medical kit that accompanied every bush-wise Australian on journeys of any length. The accidents that could occur in the bush were many and varied, from snakebite to sunstroke to a broken limb. Only fools challenged the unforgiving miles of sun-baked wilderness unprepared.

Sarah was thankful that the moon was up as she crossed the yard toward the stable. Its silvery light made the night almost as light as day, but far cooler. She shivered in her sleeveless dress of tan calico. The garment was as unfashionable as the skirt and shirtwaist she had worn earlier, but it was also as serviceable. Sarah, seeing no reason to emphasize her plainness with fine feathers that could only make her appear ridiculous, chose colors that rarely showed dirt.

The stable was dark with eerily shifting shadows. Sarah hesitated for a moment in the wide, open doorway. The convicts would be securely chained, so, if she was careful, they could do her no harm. But it was always possible that some other, unfettered man lurked in the darkness. . . .

Chiding herself for an overactive imagination that was uncharacteristic of her—she was usually practical to the point where it drove Liza and Lydia to fits of screaming irritation—Sarah resolutely stepped forward. She had come out tonight to do a job, and she would do it.

The first several stalls she passed housed horses. Then

came the bullocks. Companionable beasts, they were penned together, munching contentedly at mangers of straw. In the last two stalls were the convicts. Three in one, chained securely and sleeping, judging by their resonant snores. And in the other, the man she sought: even in the gloom, his bloodied back turned uppermost as he lay sprawled in the straw, his height and clearly defined muscles were unmistakable. Another, smaller man was chained with him, huddled in a ball in a far corner of the stall. From their steady breathing, she knew both men were sound asleep.

Sarah hesitated again before entering the stall, her nerve nearly failing her. The man was a convict, after all, and reputedly a dangerous one. What business did she have even getting near him? Then he moved, and moaned, a piteous sound that tugged at her conscience. He was a human being. And in pain.

Slowly, moving carefully so as not to drop the box she carried and wake the sleeping men, Sarah entered the stall. She knew that the convict would wake when she put the healing unguent on his raw back. But she wanted to delay the moment as long as possible. Which was silly, she told herself. He was not going to hurt her. She had come to help him.

Kneeling beside the convict, Sarah stretched out her hand to touch his arm, meaning to wake him gently and warn him of what she planned to do. His sheer size gave her pause. Despite the leanness that was the inevitable result of his incarceration on the prison ship, he was broad-shouldered and long-limbed. Standing, Sarah guessed that he would top her by nearly a foot. But the beating and the resulting loss of blood would have left him severely weakened. Even if he wished to harm her, she thought he could not. Still, she peered through the darkness for the reassuring glint of iron chains before waking him. Just to make sure.

The irons were there, stretched from ankle to ankle, linking his spread legs, which lay black and heavy against the golden brown straw. Her eyes slid up the length of his body to his hands. The wrist farthest from her was enclosed in iron, she saw, but the chain led upward instead of across to his other wrist. It was secured to a halter ring overhead. Which meant that he had one hand free . . .

Sarah rocked back on her heels, ready to rise and leave the stall just as silently as she had entered. The sudden movement of his hand as it grasped her wrist caught her by surprise. She gasped, trying to jerk her wrist free. His hand, warm and hard, held her fast. Eyes wide with fright, Sarah stared from his large, hard-palmed hand, long-fingered enough to wrap twice around her slender wrist and shades darker than her honey-gold skin despite his months of imprisonment, to the shadowed face of the man whose captive she had suddenly become. A shaft of moonlight touched his features, glinting off his blue eyes. They were open. He was watching her.

III

"What do you want?" His husky whisper was rough with pain and, she thought, hostility.

"I—I came to help you. I have some salve for your back." His lack of any immediately violent movement soothed her fright. What would he gain from harming her, after all? He could not escape, and he must know that if he hurt her he would be killed—probably beaten to death. But for all her reasoning she could not still the little shivers of apprehension and something else that crawled up and down her spine. Never before had she been this close to a half-naked man. The sheer masculinity of his bare back disturbed her more than did the wounds she had come to treat. To say nothing of his hair-matted chest, just visible as he lifted his head to look at her. And the smell of him. Raw and earthy, composed of sweat and blood and a musky scent that defied description. It galvanized her. She tugged at her trapped hand, but he would not release her wrist.

"It's the little Good Samaritan, isn't it?" From the bitter, biting words, Sarah deduced that he had indeed been cognizant this afternoon when she had thrust herself between him and the whip. The knowledge should have made her feel safer. It did not. "Trying to buy your way into heaven with good deeds?" he continued, sneering. "Well, forget it. I don't want your help."

With that, he tossed her wrist back at her and turned his head away. Perversely, now that she was free to go, Sarah stayed where she was, surveying the back of his dark, well-shaped head. His hair was wildly tousled, grown overlong and matted with blood. From the look of it, it had not been combed in months. Or washed, either.

"Whether you want help or not, your back needs attention. I mean to see to it."

Her fear had largely vanished when he released her wrist, though her skin still tingled from the strength of his grip. If he meant to harm her, he would already have done so. His harsh words and tone had aroused her ire, instead. It showed in the tartness of her voice.

"And I have no choice in the matter?" He turned to look at her, his eyes glittering almost silver in the moonlight. "Oh, that's right, you *own* me, don't you? Your papa bought me this afternoon." The sneer was more pronounced; his lip curled at her.

Sarah's lips tightened. "That's right, he did," she agreed coolly.

"Nobody owns me!" The words, despite the soft, Irish-sounding lilt that gave his voice an unexpected attraction, were harshly vehement. Sarah said nothing, just returned him look for look. His lips twisted into what was almost a snarl. The faintest glimmer of white teeth showed between them. "Especially not a scrawny, do-gooding female with about as much feminity as a broomstick! What's the matter, lady, can't you get a man to warm your bed? Are you so frustrated you had to have papa buy you one?"

Sarah's mouth dropped open in shock. But as his words began to sink in she felt anger course hot and swift through her veins.

"Why, you ungrateful swine!" she said. "If it weren't for me, you'd be fish bait in Melbourne's harbor right now! How dare you say such things to me! I'll have you . . ." Her voice trailed off as she realized what, in her unusual burst of temper, she had nearly threatened him with.

"Whipped?" he guessed with deadly accuracy. "Is that how you get your excitement? Watching a man being beaten? Or do you like to do it yourself?"

"If you don't shut your nasty mouth, I'll have someone shut it for you!" Her voice rose as her anger returned in full force. She leaped to her feet, uncaring of the box in her lap, which tumbled to the floor, spilling medical supplies in all directions. "I must have been insane to stop them today! My father was right: you deserved every lick, and more. I wish they had beaten you to death! I . . ."

A spreading pool of golden light stopped her in mid-tirade. Eyes widening, Sarah turned toward the stall door and saw the dark figure of a man looming there, his lantern held high. The sudden bright light blinded her, so she could not make out his features, but she knew it had to be either her father or Percival.

"What the bloody hell?" The angry growl was Percival's. "You little slut, if you—" His words choked off abruptly. The lantern wavered and then was lowered, and Sarah saw his face. He looked horrified as he recognized her. As she met his astonished stare, bright color crept up his neck to his face.

"Miss Sarah, I beg your pardon." He sounded shaken. His eyes as they met hers were both embarrassed and apologetic. ''I thought—that is, I heard a woman's voice in here with the convicts—I thought it—you—were one of the barmaids.''

''That's all right, Mr. Percival.'' Sarah's words were clipped, but her anger was directed at the man lying sprawled at her feet. She could feel the insolence of the convict's eyes as he watched her. No doubt he had enjoyed hearing his version of her character confirmed by Percival's furious denunciation. Keeping her eyes fixed on Percival's face so that she wouldn't have to look at the beast who had so vilely insulted her, Sarah began to move with regal dignity toward the stall door. Percival's face still reflected the horror of having addressed her in such a way; then, as the situation began to assert itself, his lips compressed and his eyes narrowed.

''Miss Sarah, what are you doing in the stable? At night, and alone—with the convicts.'' His tone was condemning. Sarah kept her head high as she continued to move toward him. Not waiting for her answer—it must have been obvious that there was no defensible answer she could give—Percival continued, his voice growing angry, ''Good God, Miss Sarah, what were you thinking of, putting yourself within reach of such scum? You could have been hurt, or killed, or . . . worse!'' Sarah, knowing very well what he meant by ''worse,'' felt a faint blush warming her cheeks. But the fact that for once Percival was in the right did not make her feel any more kindly disposed toward him. The convict was a vile, ungrateful brute, and she was willing to believe him capable of any atrocity, including the one that Percival had so delicately alluded to. No doubt, only her own lack of attraction—possibly coupled with the convict's state of health—was all that had saved her from that hideous fate.

''I came to treat the man's back, Mr. Percival,'' Sarah said evenly, determined not to let her perturbation show as she moved forward. She reached the stall door and waited for him to move away from the other side so that she could open it. When he didn't, but stared at her face and then, beyond her, at the convict, she added, "Please let me pass."

Still he didn't move. His eyes swung back to search her face, then his voice was suddenly sharp as he said, "Why is the medical kit spilled all over the ground? If you came to treat his back, why didn't you? I heard you shouting when I came in—by God, if that blackguard laid a hand on you . . . ! Did he touch you, Sarah? Just tell me if he did, and I'll finish what Farley started today!" He stepped back, swung open the stall door, and started through it. His eyes were fixed on the convict, who lay on his stomach staring up at them. At Percival's violent eruption, he levered himself up on one elbow. Both men's eyes met and clashed in a silent war.

"By God, you bastard, if you touched this lady, you'll be begging me to kill you before I'm through with you!"

"Don't be ridiculous, Mr. Percival." Despite her anger at the convict, Sarah stopped Percival's enraged charge with a hand against his chest. She did not want to see more violence done, no matter how much the brute might deserve it.

"Sarah . . ." He was breathing hard. Fury made the lines in his face seem even deeper. His stocky figure was poised for immediate action, his fists clenched at his sides. His hazel eyes bored into hers, demanding that she step out of his path. Chin lifting slightly, Sarah stood her ground.

"I don't believe I gave you permission to address me by my given name, Mr. Percival." She meant to sidetrack him; to her relief, it worked.

"Don't be absurd, girl," he replied. "There's nothing improper about me calling you Sarah. After all, we'll be man and wife soon; I was talking to your da about it just the other day. You'll soon get used to me calling you by name—and to calling me John.''

Percival's refusal to take no for an answer, added to her rage over the convict's lewd insults, brought her temper near the exploding point again. Ordinarily she was very even-tempered; today she had been goaded into angry outbursts no fewer than three times. Spine stiffening, she stared at Percival coldly, her hand dropping from his chest.

''I have no intention of marrying you, as you well know, Mr. Percival,'' she said, emphasizing the title with icy meaning. ''You and Pa can plan all you like; I'm telling you straight out, I won't do it.''

''Ah, Sarah, girl, you're just shy.'' Percival's indulgent tone, coupled with his continued use of her name after she had requested him not to address her so familiarly, made Sarah grit her teeth. She was on the verge of saying something she knew she would regret when he reached out to catch her arm. Sarah shook him off angrily, and when he looked as though he meant to take hold of her again she backed away. His eyes narrowed, but he made no move to follow her.

''You still haven't told me what that—convict—did to you.'' Percival's eyes shifted from her to the man sprawled in the straw.

Glancing over her shoulder, Sarah saw that, although the man had fallen back to lie flat on his stomach, his head was turned toward them. His eyes met hers. In the warm pool of light from the lantern Percival had hung on a hook beside the stall door she saw that, although his face remained carefully expressionless, his lids flickered once and then were stilled, as if deliberately. Sarah knew he realized that this was her chance to be revenged for the appalling things he had said to her. Since Percival was unable to take out on her his anger at her cold rejection of his advances, he was looking for a scapegoat. If she gave him so much as a hint of an excuse, he would undoubtedly beat the convict mercilessly. And he would revel in doing so.

Technically, only government officials and their agents were allowed to order corporal punishment of convicts. In practice, however, the landowners and their employees treated the convicts as they saw fit. Floggings were commonplace, and deaths resulting from them were not extraordinary. In nearly every case, the government looked the other way. The convicts were common criminals, England's scum deposited on Australia's shores. Who would complain about a few less of them? Besides, if the convicts were not afraid of the men for whom they toiled, how would they ever be persuaded to work?

Although Edward kept Percival's excesses under control on Lowella—only under the most extreme circumstances would Edward permit a convict to be whipped—Percival's authority on the station was such that he could order a beating and Edward would never hear of it. Sarah suspected that he had done so more than once in the past, but the convicts and aborigines alike were deathly afraid of Percival, and would never tell on him out of fear for their own lives.

"Sarah?" Percival reminded her that she still hadn't answered him.

Sarah held those deep blue eyes with her own for a moment longer. The convict's haggard face could have been carved from stone now. Not even by so much as a flicker of an eyelid did he importune her silence. Sarah compressed her lips angrily at the cold insolence of his stare; she remembered what he had called her and the disgusting things he had said. He undoubtedly deserved to be punished most severely.

"Now who's being absurd, Mr. Percival?" Sarah scoffed. "The man did nothing to me, of course."

"What was all the shouting about then?" Percival was determined not to be deprived of his prey without an argument. "And don't tell me that there was no shouting— I heard it distinctly."

Sarah regarded him haughtily. "Though it's really no concern of yours, I will tell you that he did not want his back treated and I was insistent. Now I see that he was in the right of it after all. And that's all I mean to say about the matter."

Percival glowered at her. It was plain that he wanted to answer her harshly—clearly, he felt that she had overstepped her place as a female—but the fact that she was his employer's daughter stopped his tongue. That, and his own intentions toward her. Sarah could read his changing expressions as he decided not to attempt to exert his masculine authority over her now, before he had wooed or coerced her into becoming his wife.

"Very well, Miss Sarah." He stepped once again into the overseer's role, despite his anger, which he couldn't quite hide. Sarah shivered. If she had ever had any doubts about her decision not to marry Percival, they had just been laid to rest. The glint in his eyes told her plainly how her defiance infuriated him; if she had been his wife and subject to him, she would have had good cause to fear the form his retaliation might take.

Sarah held his eyes for a moment longer, determined not to let him see that she was suddenly wary of him. Then she turned, bending, and began to gather up the scattered medical supplies. In the corner, the other convict huddled in a little ball. His very stillness betrayed that he was awake but wanted no part of what was going on. The ungrateful scoundrel whose life she had just saved for the second time that day lay motionless, his free arm curved under his head to act as a pillow, his eyes expressionless as he watched her. After that one quick glance, Sarah didn't look at him again. As far as she was concerned, he would have to look out for himself in the future. He could expect no further assistance from her.

"Let me help." Trying to recoup the ground he must have known he had lost, Percival stooped to scoop up the supplies nearest him and hand them to Sarah. He looked at the injured convict only once, but Sarah intercepted that look. The malevolence in the overseer's eyes as they rested on the convict reinforced her opinion: she would not like to be in his power. She sighed inwardly. As her father's daughter and a free woman, she was not and was never likely to be subject to Percival's retaliation. But the convict was.

"I'll escort you back to the inn."

Sarah had no fault to find with this; it had been a long and difficult day. The best place for her at the moment was in bed, where she could put from her mind the events of the day and the two very different men who had made it so trying. Clasping the medical kit under her arm, she preceded Percival from the stall, and even waited while he retrieved the lantern from the hook. Neither spoke as he accompanied her back to the inn. He made no effort to touch her, and left her with a muttered good-night when they were safely inside. For this Sarah was thankful. Despite her growing aversion to the man, she did not want to make an enemy of him. Lowella needed Percival. Edward could never run the station single-handed. And Europeans of untainted blood were few. Sarah handled the administrative duties, but she could not oversee the men in the fields. The convicts and the itinerant workers who composed most of Lowella's labor force had one thing in common: they were men, and men did not take orders from a woman. Not without a peck of trouble. And Lowella didn't need that.

*   *   *

For the first ten days after the disastrous visit to Melbourne, Sarah was so busy that she scarcely had time to eat. Her father, as always, spent most of his days at the breeding pens, where he was trying to improve his strain of prize merino sheep. This left Sarah to struggle on her own to balance the cash on hand with the far greater amount needed for bills and supplies. In addition, she had the house to run, the new convicts' papers to sort and file, and nursing duties as well. Lydia, being Lydia, had managed to contract catarrh during her husband's and daughters' absence. Liza no sooner came into contact with her mother than she had it too. As the house staff consisted only of Mrs. Abbott, a former convict who had been trained as cook-housekeeper by Sarah's mother, and two aborigine maids, Sarah had also to do considerable fetching and carrying for the pseudo-invalids. Lydia often bewailed the small number of servants, never more so than when she fancied herself ill, but Edward, with his fondness for a dollar, had instructed Sarah that no more were to be engaged. So Sarah turned a deaf ear to Lydia's complaints, but still it grated on her nerves. When, finally, Lydia seemed ready to get better, Sarah decided to leave Liza in the care of the maids for a while and get out of the house. The strain of the past days was beginning to wear her down.

She left the house by the rear door, walking through the kitchen garden where the family's vegetables grew, toward the stable, which was some two hundred yards distant. To her left were the orchards, which provided Lowella with bananas, oranges, lemons, figs, and guavas in season. Dark-skinned aborigines worked among the groves, picking from the leaves the insects that were a constant threat to the crop and crushing them between their fingers before throwing the carcasses to the ground. The trees and the vegetable garden were green, thanks to a newly constructed windmill just beyond the orchards, silhouetted against the blue haze of mountains to the east. Its rhythmic groaning as the broad paddles turned with the wind had become as much a part of the summer as the heat; Sarah was scarcely aware of either anymore. To her right as she walked was ordinarily a flower garden. Now it was a collection of dried stalks protruding forlornly from the earth. In this time of drought, water was too precious to spare for flowers. The normally green lawn had suffered a similar fate. It rustled dryly against Sarah's skirt as she moved.

Sarah shook her head sadly as she glanced back at the house. With its sheltering grove of eucalyptus nearly leafless, the sprawling structure looked almost ugly. Edward and a small band of aborigine workers had built it years ago from sun-dried planks that they had hewed and shaped themselves. Sarah had often wondered if her father had had any kind of a plan when he began, and, if so, what had happened to it. Certainly now, with the additions that had been made through the years, the house looked to have been put together at random, with wings jutting out in odd directions from the original two-story structure. Wide porches had been added to the front and rear when Sarah was a child, and the whole structure had been painted white. Now, exposed to the glare of the sun without the protective canopy of leaves that usually sheltered it, the whitewash was blistering in places. The feather flowers of the wattles on either side of the porch steps drooped sadly; their color and perfume had been baked away by the heat. Without the softening influence of the trees and flowers, the house's imperfections became glaringly obvious. It looked like what it was: a house built by a man in a hurry.

The few horses in the corral by the stable huddled together in the building's shadow, nose to tail as they obligingly twitched at one another's flies. They were feeling the heat too, poor things, Sarah thought as she entered the relative coolness of the stable. Still dazzled by the glare of the sun, Sarah, bestowing an absent pat on Clare's thrusting nose as she passed, could see nothing but shadows as she made her way to the stall where Malahky, her favorite riding horse, nickered a welcome. Despite the heat, she felt like riding. She would go down to the river, where the trees still retained most of their leaves. It would be blessedly cool.

"Saddle Malahky for me, please," Sarah instructed the shadowy figure that she took to be Jagger, the aborigine groom.

"Yes, ma'am," came the reply, almost mocking in its subservience. That was not Jagger! That gravelly voice with the illusive, lilting accent . . .

Her eyes were gradually growing accustomed to the dimness; she squinted at the man who had answered, realizing that he was too tall, too broad, too big altogether to be Jagger. Then his features swam into focus. In the midst of that lean, dark face, she had no trouble at all recognizing the dazzling blue eyes.

IV

"Gallagher." Sarah identified the convict she had hoped never to lay eyes on again after that disastrous night at Yancy's place. What was he doing in the stable? With his injured back, she and her father had agreed that he needed several weeks of Madeline's nursing and rest before being put to work.

"You know my name." Now that she was used to the relative darkness, she could see one jet-black eyebrow winging upward. He looked much better, she thought, eying him with a trepidation that owed as much to his sheer size as to the memory of her previous exchange with him. She had known he would be tall, but she had not expected to be dwarfed by him. Still lean, he was no longer emaciated. His shoulders admirably filled the clean white shirt he wore, and his legs in their sober black breeches looked well muscled. Her gaze had run over his body involuntarily; the overwhelming maleness of him aroused in her a curious unease.

Remembering his obscene suggestions and realizing how he might interpret her interest, she jerked her eyes back up to his face. And there they halted, widening. The brief glimpses she had had of him before, when he was dirty and unshaved and in pain, had not prepared her for this. When she had first seen his features on the *Septimus,* she had thought that under better circumstances he might be reasonably attractive. Now he looked the embodiment of a schoolgirl's dream. His hair had been washed and trimmed; brushed ruthlessly back from his face, it nevertheless tried to curl. It was as black as her father's Sunday boots, and as glossy. The planes and angles of his face were beautifully sculpted. She had never before seen such perfection. His forehead was broad, his cheekbones elegantly carved, his jaw lean and square. Above a determined chin, his mouth twisted up at one corner in a mocking half-smile; the lower lip was fuller than the upper. His nose was straight, high-bridged, and without flaw. The sickly paleness had left his skin, and its natural swarthiness had been darkened even more by exposure to the hot Australian sun. And of course there were his eyes. Set amid thick black lashes that any girl would envy, they were as devastatingly blue as jewels. As she met them, Sarah saw that they were bright with mockery. To her horror, she realized what construction he must be putting on her dumbstruck silence. Suddenly she thought of his insulting remarks the night she had tried to help him; a vision of him as he had looked without a shirt, all corded muscles and black-pelted chest, rose unbidden in her mind's eye. She could even remember the *smell* of him.

Sarah felt herself blushing, which was something she did more than she wished, as she tried frantically to remember what it was that he had said before she had been struck dumb by his looks. Ah, yes, his name.

"I keep the station's records," she said evenly, determined not to let him see how he had affected her. "Your papers are among them. You're Dominic Gallagher, age thirty-two, Irish, no dependents, sentenced to fifteen years for robbery. And I believe I asked you to saddle my horse for me."

His eyes narrowed at her. Sarah was suddenly, overwhelmingly conscious of how alone they were. The stable was deserted; there were only the horses stamping and chomping contentedly in their stalls. Unlike the other time she had been alone with him, his hands and feet were unfettered; once they reached Lowella, convicts were never chained. It made for better morale; besides, there was little chance of their running away. Where would they go? The bush was unforgiving, especially of those unfamiliar with the country, and if they did happen to survive the relentless sun and scarcity of water, they would be hunted down like mad dogs. In the stillness Sarah could hear the drone of a buzzing fly. Through the open stable door, she could see the blinding sunshine. She longed to be out in it, away from the menacing hostility that emanated from this convict like the tangy smell of his sweat. Then, remembering who he was and who she was, she stiffened her spine. She would not be afraid of him; and if she was, a little, she would certainly do her best to make sure that he did not know it.

"Yes, ma'am," he said as he had before. There was no mistaking the mockery this time. Sarah's lips tightened. If they were ever to have the proper servant-mistress relationship, she could not allow the brute's insolence to go unremarked.

"You may address me as Miss Sarah," she instructed as he turned away to open the door to Malahky's stall and lead the gelding out. He was good with the animal, she noted, watching the confident way he handled the big bay.

"Yas'm, Miss Sarah," he said. His words were such an

obvious parody of the aborigines' obsequiousness that Sarah felt her temper begin to heat. What was it about this man that enabled him to anger her so consistently? Ordinarily, in the face of even the most blatant provocation, she reverted to icy hauteur. With him, it was all she could do to keep from exploding like a musket.

"If you'll point out your saddle to me, Miss Sarah, I'll be as quick as I can, Miss Sarah." He was moving away toward the tack room as he spoke, leaving Malahky securely fastened to the halter line. Lips tightened angrily, Sarah followed. In grim silence she pointed out her own sidesaddle, blanket, and hackamore. He was deliberately needling her, Sarah thought, eyeing his broad back as he saddled the bay with controlled movements that spoke of the pain he must still suffer from the beating.

"Where is Jagger?" she asked when she could bear the uneasy silence no longer.

Gallagher glanced at her over his shoulder. His hands—funny how she could still seem to feel the imprint of those long fingers on her wrist—were deft as he tightened the saddle girth with a horseman's competent ease.

"Your fiancé didn't see much sense in having me lying around the bunkhouse eating my head off. He told me to replace—Jagger, is it?—three days ago. Jagger, I assume, is out digging wells in my place. Miss Sarah."

Sarah gritted her teeth. The convict had a positive genius for riling her.

"If you are referring to Mr. Percival, he is not my fiancé," she said coldly.

"So you've said before. But he seems to think you're just shy." He moved toward her as he spoke. Before Sarah had even the slightest inkling of his intention, his hands were closing around her waist and he was lifting her off her feet. She gasped, automatically clasping his bare, hard-muscled forearms for balance as he swung her around, her feet already high off the ground.

She felt ridiculously small as he held her before him. The sense of being helpless in the face of such overpowering male strength was new to her, and she definitely did not like it! The quickened beating of her heart was due solely, she told herself, to angry alarm.

"Put me down! How dare you! What do you think you're doing?" Her eyes were enormous as she glared at him.

"Why, helping you to mount, Miss Sarah," he said, the glint in his eyes taunting her even as she felt her bottom make contact with the smooth leather of the saddle. "What did you think I was doing, Miss Sarah?"

Bright color heated her cheeks as he guided her knee around the pommel so that she was in the correct sidesaddle position. The feel of his hand on her flesh, even through her gray cotton riding skirt and her single petticoat, unnerved her. He was so very male.

"You insolent . . ." she sputtered as he placed the reins in her ungloved hands. She jerked away from his touch; Malahky danced back in alarm. Controlling and soothing the animal took all her attention for a moment. Then she glared fiercely at Gallagher. Seated on Malahky's back, she was head and shoulders above him. That difference in height, plus the strength of the horse beneath her, restored her confidence.

"If you ever do such a thing again, Gallagher, I will have no choice but to bring your behavior to either my father's or Mr. Percival's attention." Her voice was icy, but she had to work to keep it so. Her every instinct urged her to scream at him.

"And they, as I've already discovered, don't subscribe to your particular brand of Christian charity." His voice was hard. His blue eyes met her gold ones with something like hatred. Sarah shrank inwardly from their unsheathed menace. "But do you know," he continued, musing, "I find I prefer even their brutality to your treacly hypocrisy. At least it's honest."

This was the final straw. Sarah's hand tightened around the reins; she lashed out, catching him full across the face with the dangling ends. The sharp crack of leather against flesh rang out. Gallagher staggered back a pace, his hand rising to his cheek. When he withdrew it, it was smeared with blood. More blood beaded in the hair-thin gash in his cheek.

As he looked down at his bloodstained fingers, his mouth contorted furiously. His blue eyes flashed to hers. Before he could take whatever form of retaliation he was considering, Sarah clapped her heel to Malahky's side. Already made nervous by the unaccustomed human tension surrounding him, Malahky bolted. Sarah nearly lost her seat as he lunged past Gallagher and out the door.

Her ride was ruined, of course. Sarah laughed almost hysterically as she considered how that thought bothered her. Her first hour of freedom in nearly two weeks, and the taunting insolence of a convict spoiled it. The laugh died as she thought of the gash her blow had opened in his cheek. He had looked shocked at first, and then furious. She didn't want to speculate on what form his anger might have taken if she hadn't removed herself so precipitously from the vicinity. After all, he was a convicted criminal; she doubted that he was a stranger to violence. From his expression as he had stared at her after she had hit him, she knew he had been contemplating inflicting it on her. Sarah felt sick as she remembered the blood on his fingers and cheek; blood from a blow she had struck deliberately, in anger. She had never done such a thing before; she hoped never to do such a thing again. But something would have to be done about Gallagher. Her father had been right all those days ago on the *Septimus:* the man was dangerous. He was also insolent, and brutish, and . . . She thought of his hands touching her waist, her knee, remembered the heat and hardness of them, and felt her stomach quiver. The reaction she had felt then, and felt again now, remembering, was revulsion, pure and simple. There was nothing else it could be. The man was a convict. Sarah knew that if she gave her father or Percival even the smallest inkling of how he had behaved toward her, Gallagher would be punished. But did she want to be the cause of another beating like the one he had suffered on the *Septimus*? On her behalf, her father would be ruthless, she knew. And Percival would enjoy having Gallagher under the whip. The memory of that earlier beating made her stomach churn alarmingly. In that moment she knew that she could never wittingly expose another human being to such agony. But neither could she live the next fifteen years fearing to go outdoors on the off chance that she might encounter Gallagher and he might take his revenge for the way she had hit him. It was absurd even to think of it. He would have to be got rid of. But how could she manage that without revealing her reasons to her father?

Sarah was so caught up in worrying about the matter that she scarcely noticed when Malahky turned away from the river to head for the grove of eucalyptus that was his favorite munching spot. Sarah let him have his head, knowing that Malahky could be trusted eventually to amble back to the homestead without getting them lost. Which brought her thoughts back full circle to the problem at hand: how was she going to return Malahky to the stable with Gallagher there?

The eucalyptus grove, with its bubbling mineral spring that kept the surrounding foliage green despite the drought, was a lovely spot, but Sarah was in no mood to enjoy it. Even the beauty of the pink and gray galahs that rose from the shaggy tree ferns as Malahky approached failed to distract her from her thoughts. Here where the grass was green, Malahky grazed with relish on the first living blades he had seen in weeks. Sarah sat on his back, hands resting lightly on the pommel, absently listening to the gurgle of the spring and the whistling cry of a rosella in a nearby smoke tree. What was she going to do about—

Hands closing brutally around her waist brought her instantly back to the present. She was being dragged backward from the saddle. Malahky, frightened, reared and ran out from under her. Even as she screamed and had the scream abruptly cut off by a man's hard hand on her mouth, she thought that what she had feared had happened: Gallagher had followed her and meant to take his vengeance on her away from the homestead, where there was no one to come to her aid. Then her skull was rammed painfully against a man's hard shoulder. Swiveling her head around, kicking and squirming in a frantic effort to break free from the arms that bound her, Sarah got her first look at her attacker. The narrow, sunburned face with its grizzled hair and red-rimmed eyes definitely did not belong to Gallagher. Perversely, her terror increased tenfold. Doubling her efforts to escape, Sarah felt her elbow connect sharply with the man's rib cage. He grunted, shifting his hold. She felt the hard heel of her riding boot find his kneecap in a kick that almost brought him to his knees. Cursing, he staggered backward. Taking advantage of the sudden slackening of his hold, she bit down hard on the fingers covering her mouth and twisted furiously at the same time. She did not manage to break away from him, but her mouth at least was free. Another piercing scream escaped before his hand crushed her mouth once more.

As he dragged her back into the brush, Sarah sobbed with terror even as she fought. He was a white man, which meant that in all likelihood he was a convict. And he was not one of Lowella's. Which meant that he was on the run, a rogue. Maybe he was one of those who had burned and pillaged Brickton, Lowella's neighbor to the south, last month. Although Paul Brickton's cruelty to the convicts assigned to his station was notorious, and an uprising there was almost rough justice, Sarah remembered that two of the Bricktons' sons had been killed. . . . She shuddered as she felt the wiry strength of the arms controlling her struggles. Would he kill her?

He had lifted her off her feet when Sarah felt him stagger again. She writhed wildly in an effort to break free. His arms released her without warning. Sarah cried out in surprise as she tumbled to the ground. Thick bracken cushioned her fall, but pain shot through her elbows and bottom, which made the first, hardest contact with the ground. Scrambling to take advantage of her sudden freedom, she cast a scared glance up at her attacker. To her astonishment, he was struggling as frantically as she had earlier against him. A powerful-looking forearm was locked around his neck, strangling all utterance. One arm was twisted behind his back. Her eyes wide, the ringing in her ears subsiding so that she could hear the sound of masculine grunts and the shuffling of two sets of feet on the bracken, Sarah looked over her attacker's head at her rescuer, who towered some inches above him. Dominic Gallagher's handsome face was grim with effort. His eyes, too, were grim above the gash she had opened in his cheek as he tightened his hold on the smaller man's neck.

V

"Hold still, you scurvy bastard, or I'll break your neck."
Gallagher's Irish lilt was more pronounced than usual as
he growled at the man who still struggled fiercely in his
hold. When the man continued to fight, Gallagher's arm
tightened until his prisoner could no longer breathe. Terror
rounded the smaller man's eyes; his mouth opened and
closed like that of a landed fish as he gasped for breath.
Gallagher continued to deny him air until the man was
almost limp. Then, slowly, he loosened his hold.

"Next time there won't be a next time. Understand?"
Gallagher was white about the mouth as he threatened the
other man. At first Sarah thought it was from anger, and
then she noticed the perspiration beading his forehead. The
drops could be from the heat, but she thought that he must
be suffering some pain. His back couldn't have healed
completely in less than two weeks; the exertion required to
subdue her attacker must have cost him dearly. She was
surprised that he bothered. The only possible explanation

for his presence was that he'd followed her, as she had half-feared he might. To take his revenge... Probably he had been as caught by surprise by what had happened as she had been. He had undoubtedly come to her rescue before he'd had time to think the situation through. Because if he had thought about it, he would have seen that fate had handed him the perfect revenge, with no danger to himself. She would have beeen punished, and he couldn't possibly have been held responsible.

"Did he hurt you?" Gallagher asked sharply.

Sarah shook her head, still feeling a trifle dazed. "No."

Gallagher drew a deep breath. His attention shifted back to the man he held. "What do you want me to do with him? Miss Sarah."

She had been staring blindly at the pair of them, but that mocking afterthought of "Miss Sarah" brought her back to awareness in a hurry. Regardless of how ridiculous she must look, glaring at her rescuer from a prickly, precarious seat in the middle of a gorse bush, she frowned at Gallagher. But what could she say? She had told him to call her that, after all. But it was the *way* he did it. He was deliberately being provoking, she knew, but the knowledge didn't help: his insolence enraged her every time.

Gallagher smiled at her, clearly relishing her helpless anger. He looked unbelievably handsome, with the sun slanting down through the eucalyptus leaves to dapple his hair with blue highlights, and his white teeth gleaming in his dark face. Her involuntary reaction to his dazzling good looks only fueled her anger. And the realization that she was furious with her rescuer rather than with her attacker further outraged her.

"Miss Sarah?"

Sarah scrambled to her feet, impatiently thrusting behind her ears the thick mass of tawny hair that had tumbled from its pins during the struggle. She thought with some annoyance that she must be even more unsightly than usual. Her skirt was smudged with dirt, her shirtwaist was torn so that the edge of her plain white cotton chemise was clearly visible, and her maddening hair spilled around her like an overgrown shock of wheat. Unreasonably, the knowledge of her lack of attraction in the face of Gallagher's masculine beauty incensed her more than anything else. With one hand holding her torn shirtwaist in place, and feeling an utter fool, she glared from the man who was eying her fearfully, motionless now in Gallagher's hold, to Gallagher himself. His mocking smile widened, mocking her even more. Battling the urge to throw something, preferably a large stone, straight at those gleaming teeth, she looked at the man who had attacked her.

"It's very likely that he's a runaway convict," she said, ostensibly to Gallagher but without lifting her eyes to his face. "If so, then he'll have to be turned over to the authorities in Melbourne. In any case, we'll have to take him back to Lowella." She frowned suddenly, remembering that Malahky had bolted in the scuffle. "But how?"

"I left a horse back there in the trees," Gallagher said, nodding toward the river. "When I heard you scream, I thought I'd be more effective if I surprised the army that I envisioned had assaulted you." His mocking smile deepened again, revealing a slashing dimple in his left cheek. Sarah tried not to notice it. "I was sure that nothing less than an army could have forced a scream from such a redoubtable lady. Miss Sarah."

The look she sent him should have seared his eyeballs, but before she could think of a way to annihilate him verbally—without losing her dignity in the process—the man Gallagher still held by the neck suddenly went limp. Eyes closed, mouth open, his skin pasty white where it wasn't stubbled with grizzled whiskers, he looked dead.

Only the barely perceptible rise and fall of his scrawny chest indicated that he lived.

"He's fainted." Sarah looked at Gallagher accusingly, glad to have something concrete to berate him about. Gallagher shrugged, patently unconcerned. Sarah came a step nearer, her eyes shifting back to the man dangling from Gallagher's arm. He seemed to be going a little blue around the mouth and nose.

"You'd better let him go," she said, not wanting to be responsible if the man strangled.

"I don't think that's a good idea." There was a finality about the words that told Sarah that Gallagher did not expect to have his judgment questioned. Sarah looked daggers at him. She was getting tired of all the men of her acquaintance automatically assuming an air of superiority. And this one was a convict, yet!

"I said let him go," she repeated, challenging him with her eyes. "Put him down on the ground and let him get his breath back. For goodness' sake, we can't take him back to Lowella like this. If there's only one horse, he's going to have to walk. Unless you want to carry him."

Gallagher regarded her steadily for a moment, then shrugged again. "Anything you say. Miss Sarah."

Sarah ignored that, watching with a small measure of triumph as Gallagher let the man sink to the ground. He lay unmoving, looking so pathetic that Sarah moved closer to get a better look at him. Perhaps he really was ill. Though why she should be concerned, she didn't know, she thought, reminding herself that only moments before he had dragged her off her horse and into the brush with intentions she didn't want to contemplate. If Gallagher hadn't come when he had . . .

"Get back!" The warning was Gallagher's, but it came too late. The man thrust himself up from the ground, his legs bunched under him to give him greater momentum.

He shoved Sarah, who hovered near him, eyes widening with surprise, backward with all his might. She reeled, and would have fallen if Gallagher had not caught her, his arms sliding around her waist. The feel of his hands gripping her rib cage with such intimacy, even though she knew that his action was nothing more than an instinctive response to keep her from falling, caused her to leap away from him. Her sudden, violent recoil sent Gallagher staggering backward. He tripped over a fallen branch and fell heavily, cursing harshly as his back hit the ground. Sarah winced, hurrying to his side as the other man ran off through the trees as fast as his bandy legs would carry him.

"Dammit, woman, see what you've done." Gallagher was glaring up at her. He had turned over and lay flat on his belly in the bracken, his eyes mere slits of pain as he regarded her with acute dislike. "If you're expecting me to go running after him, you can think again. I may not be able to move for months."

"I'm sorry," Sarah said automatically, before she remembered whom she was addressing. Her brows slanted together to form an irritated V over her eyes as she matched glare for glare with the man who lay sprawled at her feet. "Don't you dare swear at me!"

"Why, you ungrateful . . ." Gallagher bit off the next word, then appeared to remember her saying much the same thing to him not many days before. He smiled, reluctantly, wryly. Sarah, who was remembering too, had to smile back. The whole situation was ridiculous. And he looked so funny, lying there on his stomach with a frond of fern decorating his black hair, his big body framed by more feathery protrusions of greenery, a mingling of pain and amusement on his face. It was the first time she had seen him smile without nastiness or mockery; the effect was dazzling. "I beg your pardon. Miss Sarah."

The warmth of his smile did much to rob the deliberate needling of its bite. Sarah extended a hand to help him up. When he made no effort to respond, but merely lay there looking up at her through narrowed eyes, she frowned. Was he hurt more badly than she had imagined, or was he determined to keep their feud going despite its senselessness? Biting her lip, she decided to give him the benefit of the doubt. She crouched beside him, her eyes meeting his with concern.

"Are you in pain?"

One corner of Gallagher's mouth twisted up wryly. "No more than usual. I think I'll just lie here for a while. I have a sinking suspicion that moving is going to hurt like the devil." He paused, shifting a shoulder experimentally, then grimaced. "I suppose our friend is long gone?"

Sarah looked around the copse, devoutly hoping that the man was indeed gone. With Gallagher out of commission, she didn't fancy her chances of dealing with him. But there was no sign of him. All about them the greenery continued undisturbed, and as if to settle the matter a pair of rosellas chose that moment to settle into a nearby tree fern. Besides the flutter of their wings, the only sound was the gurgle of the spring not far away.

"I think so." She hadn't intended to sound so hopeful.

He smiled again, eying her. "Don't worry. If he comes back, I think I can undertake to defend you."

"Why should you?" Sarah didn't mean to say it aloud, but the words escaped before she could stop them. His hand lifted automatically to the gash she had made in his cheek. She winced at the gesture.

"Why did I, do you mean?" He fingered the cut, which had formed a narrow crust. "I don't know. I came after you meaning to pay you back for this with interest, and then head out for the bush country. I can only suppose my innate chivalry overcame my good sense." This last sentence was laced with self-mockery. Then, softly, "Or maybe I just wanted to make us even."

"Even?"

He inclined his head. "You saved me that day on the *Septimus;* now I've saved you. We're quits." There was a curious satisfaction in his words.

Sarah's brows knitted as she looked at him. He had moved so that he was lying more on his side now than his belly, and she had a three-quarter view of his face. She hadn't been mistaken about the satisfaction in his words, she saw; it was there in his face as well. But, try as she would, she could not understand why it should please him so enormously to know that he no longer had to feel himself under any obligation to her. To her knowledge, it had not affected his behavior in the least. No one could accuse him of having been so much as commonly civil to her.

"Well, whatever your reason, I thank you," Sarah said formally. "I shudder to think what that man might have done to me if you hadn't come when you did."

He very slowly levered himself into a sitting position, wincing and flexing his shoulders as he moved. Sitting in the bracken with his knees bent and his bare forearms resting on his knees, his white shirt unbuttoned so that Sarah could not help but notice the soft whorls of black chest hair at the base of his throat, he exuded so much sheer masculinity that Sarah involuntarily drew back. She was still crouching beside him, but it suddenly occurred to her that now that he was sitting up, he was far too close. She stood up abruptly, making a little business of brushing off her skirt with one hand while the other self-consciously clasped together the ripped edges of her shirtwaist.

"Oh, I doubt that he would have done anything much to you," Gallagher said, regarding her with a grin. Sarah was piqued to notice that her nearness seemed not to have bothered him at all, if he had even been aware of it. But of course, she was plain, while he was far, far too attractive. Gallagher continued, "He was most likely after your horse."

Sarah could not stop herself from feeling, and looking, she had no doubt, affronted. "Well, thank you very much," she said before she could stop the words. Gallagher looked up at her, frowning, then as the reason for her obvious indignation occurred to him he laughed.

"Wounded vanity, Miss Sarah?" he jeered softly, rising to his feet with a lithe movement that gave no quarter to the pain she guessed he must be suffering from his half-healed back. Standing up, he was alarmingly tall—a good head taller than she was, while most of the men of her acquaintance were at best just an inch or so above her height—and alarmingly close. She had to tilt her head back to see his expression, and she didn't like the sensation at all. It occurred to her that here was one man whose strength she could come to fear. . . . "Would you prefer to think that he meant to have his dastardly way with your person before murdering you?"

Sarah flushed. It was all she could do not to let her eyes drop. Put that way, it sounded ridiculous, but yes, it did hurt a little to realize that Gallagher thought she was so unattractive that a man could have no other motive for attacking her than her horse.

"Don't be absurd," she said shortly, turning away. To her surprise, she felt his hand close over her arm. His callused palm seemed to burn her bare skin. Stiffening, she looked at him over her shoulder, her expression as off-putting as she could make it. With all that had happened, she had forgotten for a moment that he was a convict and she his mistress. So, apparently, had he. It would never do to allow him to think that this intimacy could continue. He must remember his place, and so, she told herself fiercely, must she.

"Take your hand off me, Gallagher." Her eyes were steady as they met his. He frowned at her, his eyebrows meeting in a thick black line over his incredible blue eyes.

"And if I don't?" he asked silkily.

Sarah half-turned to face him, her eyes widening. Now there was a question, she thought. What would she—could she—do if he elected not to obey her? She was hardly in any position to enforce her commands physically. A ghost of a smile flitted at the corners of her lips as her eyes moved swiftly, involuntarily over him. He was so big, so tall and broad-shouldered with steel-muscled limbs, that the very thought of overpowering him was ridiculous.

"I have no idea," she admitted frankly, her smile still flickering. "But I should think of something, I assure you."

He laughed, looking suddenly relaxed. "I'm sure you would," he said with humor, and his hand released its grip on her arm to finger the gash in his cheek. "The prospect terrifies me."

Her smile vanished. "I'm really very sorry about that," she said, her eyes earnest. "I just lashed out without thinking. I've never done such a thing before."

His hand fell from his cheek. "Don't worry about it," he said curtly. "It's little more than a scratch. I've been hurt more, with less reason."

"Yes," she agreed, remembering his back.

He frowned suddenly, darkly. "Hadn't we better be getting back?" His words were brusque. "I don't know about you, but I have work to do. I doubt that your overseer will be pleased if he comes by the stable and finds I've disappeared. I don't fancy being strung up and beaten again."

His hand was on her arm again, quite unconsciously, she

thought, while he urged her in the direction he wished her to go. Deciding that so small and obviously unthinking a familiarity was not worth angering him with another reprimand, she glanced up at him.

"Don't worry, if any question arises I will tell him that you very likely saved my life," she promised.

His mouth quirked derisively. "Thank you, but I prefer not to shelter behind your petticoats." His response was short. It occurred to Sarah that she was again in danger of forgetting their relative stations in life. He was addressing and handling her as if they were equals—no, rather as if he, as a man, was for that reason entitled to direct her actions. He was clearly used to being very masterful with women. She sighed.

"Gallagher, I don't mean to offend you," she began carefully, meaning what she said. "But you are going to make life difficult for yourself if you don't learn to behave properly."

They had stopped walking; Max, her father's big black stallion—typical of what she had seen so far of Gallagher's character that he should boldly choose the best horse in the stable—was just behind Sarah as she turned to look at Gallagher. The horse was placidly stripping what few leaves he could reach of the eucalyptus branch he was tied to. Gallagher's hand left Sarah's arm as she finished speaking, but not, she realized, because of anything she'd said. He was merely untying the horse.

"Are you listening?" she demanded, impatient. And there it was again: she was addressing him as he had addressed her, as an equal. A state of affairs that she would have to put a stop to, no matter how secretly pleasant she might find it. For his sake, if for no other reason. She shuddered to think of what her father's or Percival's reaction would be if either should witness such familiarity.

"You were telling me I don't behave properly." He led the horse forward as he spoke, then turned back to Sarah with the reins looped casually around one hand. Before she could do more than sputter a protest, he caught her around her narrow waist and lifted her into the saddle as he had once before. Sarah again had to clutch his forearms for balance; involuntarily her fingers spread, absorbing the hard, warm strength of him and the coarse abrasion of the hairs that roughened his skin. Her palms ached to explore further, to stroke the male flesh beneath them. As soon as he sat her in the saddle, she snatched her hands away as if his flesh had suddenly scorched her.

"That's just what I'm talking about!" she exclaimed wrathfully. Anger was the first of the jumble of emotions swirling through her, and she welcomed it. She refused to acknowledge how the feel of his skin under her hands had affected her. . . . Of course, she was still shaken from her recent harrowing experience. Her responses were quite naturally out of kilter. And that, she told herself firmly as she unconsciously clasped her still-tingling hands together, was all there was to it! Certainly she was not physically attracted to a—a convict, be he ever so handsome!

Gallagher lifted one eyebrow at her as she stared down at him in perturbation, then put a booted foot in the stirrup and swung himself up behind her. Alarmed, Sarah lost her balance, nearly sliding sideways off the saddle as she felt the strength of his big body so close behind her. He caught her, his arms encircling her waist and hauling her back into position to sit precariously sideways in the man's saddle, her shoulder butting into his chest, her bottom nestled snugly between the hard muscles of his spread thighs, her legs draped over one steely thigh as both feet dangled to one side. She was practically sitting on his lap! The hem of her skirt had caught on the pommel, revealing her plain white cotton petticoat with the single flounce at the bottom

from the knee down. Hurriedly she bent to free it. The
movement made her even more excruciatingly aware of her
position. His body heat enveloped her, as did his musky
male scent. His strong thighs hugging her derriere unnerved her to the point where she lost her head.

"Let me go! Get down!" she cried, squirming futilely
in his hold. Her frantic movements only made the situation
worse as she felt the enveloping muscles of his arms and
legs tighten to keep her in position. Suddenly her throat
went dry. Her struggles stilled abruptly.

"You prefer to walk back to the stable?" He sounded
totally unmoved by the way she was nestled into him,
Sarah thought bitterly. Which, when she thought about it,
was a very good thing indeed.

"No!"

"Nor do I." With that calm statement, he touched his
heels lightly to Max's sides. Obediently the horse moved
off. Sarah's attempts to hold herself ramrod straight and
away from him went for naught as she felt herself slipping
again, and had to clutch at Gallagher's shirt to save
herself. Beneath the soft linen she could feel the solid wall
of his chest. Hurriedly she released her grip, and immediately began to slide. He obligingly tightened the arm he
had wrapped around her waist, seeming unaware of her
agitation.

"You have to get down. At once! Do you hear me?"
Her voice was shrill. Her fingers clutched at the pommel
for balance so that she would not have to lean so closely
against him. The only trouble was, she had this insane
desire to lean against him. A convict! The knowledge
horrified her.

"If you think that I'm going to walk for miles in this
infernal heat, just because you think you're too good to
suffer my touch—" The hostility was back in his voice.
Looking up at him, taken aback to find his face so close

above hers, she saw that his eyes were narrowed and his mouth was set in a bitter line. Clearly, he had misinterpreted the reason for her agitation—thank the Lord!—and her frantic protests had injured his pride. Sarah cast her eyes to heaven. On top of everything else, to find herself concerned about a convict's pride!

"Gallagher," she said carefully—or as carefully as she could with his arms all around her and his chin grazing her hair and the heat and scent of him enveloping her like a heady perfume. "Whether or not I think I am 'too good' has nothing to do with it. I don't know how you are used to behaving—at least, I do, you're making it fairly obvious—but you're in Australia now. And, like it or not, you're a convict. However much it may go against the grain with you, you're going to have to learn to keep to your place. And not to—to—be so familiar."

"Am I being familiar, Miss Sarah?" The harsh mockery was back in his voice. Glancing up at him again, Sarah saw to her alarm that white lines bracketed his mouth, and his eyes blazed sapphire with anger. They locked with hers; she could feel her own eyes widening and her mouth dropping open. The menace she had sensed in him before was back, too, but she so close to him that it was far more intimidating.

"Not half as familiar as I could be," he continued savagely, pulling Max to a halt. Sarah was shocked to feel his hand tangling in her hair, pulling her head even farther back so that it rested on his shoulder. She was so surprised that she didn't even struggle, merely stared up at him with golden eyes grown huge with apprehension—and, though she refused to acknowledge it, a furtive excitement. He returned her look for a moment, his eyes and mouth hard, cruel. His hand, twisted in her hair, hurt her abominably; with a tiny, inconsequent part of her mind Sarah thought that it would be a mass of rat's tails later. His eyes bored into hers for what seemed an eternity, brightly blue, furious, beautiful. That black head tilted toward her, descending. . . . Sarah could feel her heart begin to pound. Her throat went dry; her eyes, strangely heavy, fluttered shut. He was going to kiss her, she knew. She was suddenly, avidly curious about how he would kiss. . . .

"Let me go. You're hurting me," she ordered tremulously, dragging her eyes back open with an effort and forcing her too-pliant spine to stiffen. To her surprise, he did, his head jerking back as though she had slapped him, his hand releasing its grip on her hair. At the same time, the arm around her waist was lifted. Without his brawny strength to hold her on the saddle, she felt herself slipping.

When, a moment later, they both heard the pounding of horses' hooves, she was safely on the ground, breathing erratically as she smoothed her skirt and then attempted to do the same to her hair. Her eyes were bright with wariness and other emotions she preferred not to analyze as she stared at the man who slid agilely over Max's haunches to stand a few feet away. When Edward, with Percival close behind, came galloping into the copse, faces tense with alarm, horses lathered from such hard riding in the intense heat, Sarah had regained most of her aplomb. She turned to face them with surface calm. Overhead, a kookaburra let loose with a burst of raucous laughter, mocking her efforts.

"Sarah, my God, Sarah, are you all right? What did he do to you?" Percival was off his horse in a flash, rifle in hand and pointed at Gallagher, who looked back at him with a silent taunt. Sarah, taken by surprise, gaped at Percival for a moment.

"Answer the man, daughter," Edward advised, dismounting in a more leisurely fashion. Sarah looked from her father to Percival and back again, anger kindling in her eyes.

"If you mean Gallagher, nothing," she said. That was literally true, but what had almost happened—what she had almost *wanted* to happen—made her flush. She turned to Percival, and spoke sharply in an effort to disguise her embarrassment. "For goodness' sake, put that rifle down. You're being ridiculous."

"You don't look as if he did 'nothing' to you," her father pointed out in a neutral tone, his eyes surveying her.

Sarah, suddenly conscious of how she must look with her riding skirt stained with earth and grass, her shirtwaist torn so that her chemise peeped forth, and her hair tumbling in streaked-gold tangles to her waist, felt herself flushing anew. Self-consciously she clutched the edges of her shirtwaist together again—she was ashamed to remember that she had forgotten all about the revealing tear during her exchanges with Gallagher—and shook her hair back from her face as she met her father's eyes with a calm she did not feel.

VI

"You're right, he did not do 'nothing,' " Sarah said slowly. She met Gallagher's eyes for a moment and saw a faint wariness there. The moment was too brief to allow her to savor her satisfaction in having disconcerted him. Small revenge for the unthinkable feelings he had aroused in her. Percival turned to look at her, his expression belligerent. The sharp click as he cocked the rifle reverberated in the still air. "He very likely saved my life," she finished quickly, spurred by that ominous click. Percival wouldn't need much of an excuse to shoot Gallagher down like a dog, she suspected.

"How so?" her father asked, looking from her to Gallagher and back again. While not as angry as Percival, Edward looked grim, too. "Were you thrown? I wouldn't have thought...But I'll grant you that Malahky was wild-eyed when he came running back to the stable."

"I've never seen you part company with a saddle in all the years I've known you, Sa—Miss Sarah," Percival

interjected harshly. "You're the best damn—ah, danged—
female rider I've ever seen. Don't let your modesty betray
you into protecting a convict." He nodded once in Gallagher's
direction. "It's obvious that he attacked you. That rip in
your dress didn't come from any fall. And look at his
face—he didn't have that scratch on his cheek this morning."

Sarah longed to give Percival a set-down he wouldn't
soon forget for daring to question her, but she didn't want
to exacerbate his anger at Gallagher. Just why she should
feel that way, she wasn't certain; perhaps it was because
the brief glimpses she had had of Gallagher when he
wasn't angry or mocking her had shown her how humanly
vulnerable he could be. Or perhaps—dreadful thought!—it
was because his slightest touch had the unprecedented
power to awaken her physical responses. The notion was
so appalling that she immediately banished it from her
mind. No, she assured herself, her motive was pure
philanthropy. Of course it was!

"If you will give me the chance to speak, Mr. Percival, I
was about to tell you what 'really happened.' " She raked
Percival with an icy stare, then turned to address her
father, who was regarding her closely. He stood a few feet
away, idly holding his reins in one hand while his horse
stood with its head lowered, panting for breath. "Really,
Pa, surely you know me better than to think that my
modesty, to use Mr. Percival's word, would prevent me
from shouting it to the rooftops if indeed Gallagher had
offered me any kind of violence! Yes, I was attacked—by a
runaway convict, I think. He pulled me off Malahky and
was trying to drag me away into the brush when Gallagher
intervened. Gallagher's cheek was hurt in the ensuing
fight. You should thank him instead of standing idly by
while Mr. Percival threatens him with that rifle as if he
were rabid! I told you, he very likely saved my life.
Certainly he saved me from being mauled."

Her father looked at her meditatively for a long moment, his ginger-colored eyebrows knitting as he considered her words, then shifted his gaze to Percival. "Put that rifle down, John." Percival, reluctantly, did as he was bidden. Edward's eyes then moved on to Gallagher. "I do indeed thank you for coming to my daughter's rescue—what is your name?—Gallagher?"

"Yes, sir." If Sarah was surprised to hear the respectful note in Gallagher's voice, she hoped she managed to hide it. At least the man was not stupid, as he would have been had he permitted his pride to make an enemy of her father. "It was my pleasure, sir."

"You . . ." Edward began, but Percival interrupted.

"And just what were you doing out here in the first place?" Percival's voice as he addressed Gallagher was sharp with dislike. "I put you to work in the stable—and I don't recall giving you permission to go pleasure riding, especially on Mr. Markham's best horse."

Gallagher's eyes narrowed on the overseer. Sarah, seeing the anger flash in their blue depths, hurried into speech before Gallagher could condemn himself with his own words. Though why it mattered to her if he did, she couldn't have said; or if, just possibly, she could have hazarded a guess, she refused to allow herself to do so.

"I asked him to accompany me. I believe my orders must take precedence over yours, Mr. Percival?" To her father: "I remembered about the convict uprising over at Brickton last month, and I suddenly felt nervous about riding on my own. And very rightly, as it turned out."

As Sarah was very seldom nervous of anything, and her father knew it, she was not sure that this fabrication would be accepted without skepticism. But, to her relief, it was.

"Yes." Edward nodded. The heated flush in his cheeks was starting to fade, but perspiration still streaked his forehead and darkened his red hair. He had forgotten his hat, Sarah noted, or perhaps had lost it in the rush to come to her aid. In either case, she suddenly thought he did not look well.

"Let's get back to the homestead, Pa. I'm hot and tired and, as you can see, dirty." If she suggested that concern for his health prompted her, he would stubbornly stay out in the heat until nightfall. Edward hated to be fussed over; he thought illness was womanish.

"Good idea. I want to get a party together to catch the man who attacked you. Can't allow a rogue like that to roam free. In the meantime, Sarah, I don't want you riding out alone. You take Gallagher here with you anytime you're further than shouting distance from the homestead. Even walking. I'll tell your sister and mother to do the same. Understand?"

Sarah's eyes widened slightly as she shot a quick, involuntary glance at Gallagher. He was still standing beside Max, one hand on the horse's glistening black rump. Percival's attention had shifted; he was frowning at Edward. Sarah thought she was the only one to catch the faint, taunting smile that twisted the corner of Gallagher's mouth and then was gone as quickly as it had come. She was sure she was the only one to guess that half-smile's significance. He was enjoying himself, the swine, enjoying watching her trapped in the corner into which she had painted herself with her lies on his behalf.

"Yes, Pa," she murmured, inwardly vowing not to set so much as a toe outside the boundary he had prescribed for her until the scoundrel who had attacked her had been caught. Not even for the pleasure of escaping the house for an occasional ride or walk would she put herself in the position of having to endure Gallagher's company. As she had discovered, he could not be trusted to keep to the line;

and she found his refusal to stay in his place unsettling, to say the least.

"If I may say so, Mr. Markham, I don't think Gallagher is the right man to set to escorting the ladies, although I agree they do need an escort. With your permission, I'll undertake the chore myself."

Edward snorted. "Don't be daft, John. You know I need you working the sheep. You can't be spending your days trotting about after the women like a pup on a leash."

Percival pursed his lips. He wore a hat, Sarah saw, but it had not kept his face from being burned a dark red by the sun. The angry color did nothing to improve the appearance of his features, which, in such near proximity to Gallagher's chiseled good looks, barely escaped being ugly. For the first time, Sarah noticed how thick Percival's lips were. Probably because she could not get out of her mind Gallagher's long, hard-looking mouth as it had descended toward hers.

"Still, there are any number of men I could set to the job who would be preferable to this—one." Percival eyed Gallagher with open dislike. Gallagher's face was bland as he met that look. Again, Sarah had to admire his cleverness at dissembling so thoroughly before her father. Edward would never guess that he had just given license to a fox to mind his hens. "Mr. Markham, I think you must be forgetting the circumstances under which we acquired him. The man's a rogue himself. He's not to be trusted."

"I think he's proved that he is by his actions today. Gallagher, do you feel that you could undertake to keep my wife and daughters from coming to harm about the place?" Although Edward shot the question at him like a bullet, Gallagher didn't even blink.

"Yes, sir," he said. Sarah sneaked a glance in his direction, taking care that neither her father nor Percival saw. If Gallagher himself did, he pretended not to.

"That's settled, then. Sarah, you hear?" Sarah had no choice. How could she protest now, without laying bare the whole of her exchanges with Gallagher in explanation? And this she was loath to do. Swallowing a sigh of resignation, she nodded.

"Mr. Markham . . ." Percival was still inclined to argue.

"Say no more on the subject, John. My mind's made up. Even you yourself said that Gallagher was not yet up to doing the kind of work we need him for. He may as well be watching the women as mucking out the stable. Besides, there's no one else we can spare. If we're going to save the rest of the flock, we need every able-bodied man out there digging for water."

This was true, so there was nothing Percival could say. Still frowning, he turned to his horse and mounted without another word. Then, gathering up the chestnut's reins, he addressed Sarah.

"You'd best ride pillion behind me. My horse is a trifle fresher than your father's, I believe."

Sarah lifted her chin as she stared at him with cold eyes.

"Thank you, but I prefer to ride with my father."

Edward glanced from one to the other of them, clearly not liking to see his daughter at loggerheads with the man he thought to acquire for a son-in-law.

"John's in the right of it, girl. We came after you so fast that I damn near killed this plug I'm riding. Can't think how he came to be in our stable in the first place. Not the kind of horseflesh I like. But Max was nowhere to be found, and this sorry bag of bones was the first one to hand."

"You could ride Max, and I could ride behind you. Gallagher can ride your horse."

"I'm not up to handling Max today, daughter." This was so patently a bid to force her to ride with Percival that Sarah almost stamped her foot. Her father never admitted to illness under any circumstances; despite his uncharacteristic lack of vigor, she seriously doubted that he was ill or even feeling poorly. No, his words were nothing more than a shoddy attempt at coercion, and she would not be coerced.

"I'll ride behind Gallagher, then. After all, Max is the freshest of the horses. I wouldn't want to injure Mr. Percival's animal." This last was said with a saccharine smile. If Max were only wearing a sidesaddle, she would ride him herself and let Gallagher walk home!

"My daughter doesn't ride pillion with a convict!" The words were said so sharply that Sarah's eyes widened. Her father suddenly looked angry; unable to help herself, Sarah glanced over at Gallagher. He looked angry, too, although he was controlling it well. Probably only someone who had seen that particular bitter twist to his lips before would guess that he was furious at the slur.

Left with no choice, Sarah reluctantly allowed Percival to mount her pillion behind him. The skirt of his saddle was deep and wide. Sarah clung to that rather than to the man; she was determined not to touch him. By the time they arrived back at Lowella, her fingers ached from holding on so tightly. Since the horses were tired and her father refused to abuse good horseflesh, they kept to a walk. Only this enabled Sarah to maintain her balance without wrapping her arms around Percival's waist. Percival tried once or twice to initiate a conversation with her as they went along, but Sarah affected deafness. As a result, the overseer was fuming; Sarah herself was annoyed at having to put up with his possessiveness. Bringing up the rear of the procession, Gallagher was glowering quite as fiercely as either herself or Percival. Only Edward, riding as usual in the lead, reached the homestead in a fairly sunny humor.

When at long last they drew to a halt in the stable yard, Gallagher dismounted first. Max's reins in hand, he forestalled

Percival, whose own dismount was hampered by Sarah's
presence behind him, and held up his hands to Sarah.
Glowering at him for his presumption, which she did not
dare refuse for fear of arousing her father's and Percival's
curiosity, she placed her hands on the hard width of his
shoulders. She felt the smooth contraction of his muscles
through the damp cotton of his shirt as he placed his hands
on her waist and swung her to the ground. Her fingers—
the traitors!—ached to stroke that broad expanse, to discover for themselves how such perfection of bone and
muscle felt to the touch. Instead, she jerked her hands
away. He released her immediately, stepping back. There
was nothing in his action that even the closest observer
could take exception to. But Sarah felt threatened. She
drew away from him immediately, not even deigning to
look at him. Her palms tingled from the contact with his
hard shoulders, but she ignored the sensation. Leaving the
men to see to the horses, she started for the house.

Liza was on the porch at the back of the house, waiting
for her. This was the first time she had been out of her
room since contracting the catarrh. Sarah felt mildly surprised at seeing her up and around. She could only
suppose that Liza had decided to recover, Sarah's absence
having deprived Liza of her captive nurse; certainly Lydia,
who was as self-centered as her daughter, would not cater
to Liza's incessant demands for more barley water to drink
or for a cool cloth to place across her brow, and Mrs.
Abbott, as a former convict, was barely tolerated by both
mother and daughter. At any rate, the younger girl was
clad in one of the loose white frocks she wore only when
there was no danger of being seen by anyone outside the
family. She was seated in a slat-backed rocker with a
cushioned foot-rest positioned conveniently near. A jug of
lemonade rested on a table by her elbow. But instead of
reclining languidly, as Sarah would have expected—Liza

could usually be counted on to milk a convalescence for all it was worth—her posture was surprisingly alert. Her eyes touched on her sister only briefly; then they moved beyond her, widening and brightening. Nonplussed, Sarah looked over her shoulder. And the reason for Liza's uncharacteristic behavior was immediately in view. Gallagher! He had had the infernal nerve to follow her up to the house!

"What do you think you're doing?" she demanded, forgetting their audience as she whirled to face the man whom she was rapidly coming to think of as her nemesis.

"Why, Miss Sarah!" It was not his voice so much as his bright blue eyes that mocked her. "Surely you don't think I'd follow you up here without a reason? Mr. Markham decided that he didn't want to leave you ladies alone at the house until the man who attacked you is caught. He thought that you could probably find some work for me to do around the house when I'm not accompanying one of you somewhere. After all, as he said, there's no point in keeping a man idle. Is there now, Miss Sarah?"

"Oh, you're a convict." This, uttered in tones of deepest disappointment, came from Liza.

Sarah, mortified, saw a tiny muscle twitch once at the corner of Gallagher's mouth before his expression became impossible to read. She turned to frown at her sister. "Where are your manners, Liza?"

The younger girl's mouth drooped petulantly. She leaned back in the rocker, her attitude evincing her disgust. "I'm sorry." The apology was grudging, given only because Sarah had silently demanded it. Out and out rudeness, even to a convict, was something that Sarah would not tolerate, as Liza—and Lydia—had discovered early on, when they had attempted to set Mrs. Abbott in what they felt was her place. Liza's eyes moved broodingly over Gallagher, then brightened a little. "You're very good-looking, you know. Do you by any chance know how to dance?''

"Liza!"

"Well, my ball is next Friday and I still don't have the steps of that new dance right. I have to practice with someone, and you know Pa dances like a water buffalo!''

"Liza!"

"I'm afraid the kind of dances I'm used to wouldn't be at all suitable for a ball," Gallagher said, and to Sarah's surprise he sounded amused, instead of angry. She glanced over her shoulder at him. He was smiling beguilingly at Liza, looking so handsome that Sarah felt a stab of what she immediately decided was alarm. It was certainly not jealousy of her young sister and a convict! It was just that Liza was young and impressionable. And very, very foolish. To Sarah's certain knowledge, Liza had never seen a man whose looks rivaled Gallagher's; the men and boys of both girls' acquaintance tended toward the salt-of-the-earth type—steady and dependable, but nothing to dazzle a young lady with dreams of romance.

"Liza, behave yourself! Gallagher, if Pa truly sent you up here to work, then you can wait in the office while I change and then I'll find you something to do. Come with me." There was an edge to her voice as she swept up the porch steps, Gallagher obediently following.

"Oh, Sarah, you're such a stick! If you don't stop being so proper all the time, you'll never find a husband!''

Liza's voice, sulky with the embarrassment of being scolded before a stranger—a very handsome, decidedly male stranger, even if he was a convict—floated after Sarah as she entered the kitchen through the back door. Sarah had to stifle an urge to turn around and throttle her. Controlling it with what she considered true nobility, she battled a similar longing with regard to Gallagher as she glanced at him over her shoulder and saw that he was watching her with cool mockery. Before she could give in to that impulse, or another, equally unworthy one, Mrs. Abbott bustled into the room from the long corridor that separated the kitchen from the rest of the house. Designed to spare the house proper from the heat of cooking food, the corridor served that purpose admirably. It meant, however, that the family frequently had to put up with food gone cold between stove and table.

"Why, Miss Sarah, whatever 'ave you done to yourself?" Mrs. Abbott had not lost a syllable of her cockney accent in the fifteen years she had been in Australia. Like most of the women sentenced to transportation, her crime had been prostitution, a fact that had caused Lydia and, following her mother's example, Liza, when they had first come to live at Lowella, to treat Mrs. Abbott as if she carried the plague. Only Sarah's staunch championship of the woman who had, whatever her past transgressions, devotedly nursed her mother, coupled with Edward's slightly grudging recognition that they did indeed owe Mrs. Abbott a debt, had kept her from being sent away as soon as Lydia had come home to Lowella as the second Mrs. Markham. As broad as a barn door and as homely, dressed from neck to toes in a long-sleeved black bombazine that she wore because, despite the heat and Sarah's pleading, she considered it proper attire for a housekeeper, Bess Abbott had lost whatever degree of beauty she must once have possessed. At least, Sarah had always assumed she must once have been at least marginally attractive; wasn't that a requirement for success in Mrs. Abbott's former line of endeavor?

"It's a long story, Mrs. Abbott," Sarah answered, not feeling up to going into the details of what had happened. Gesturing at the man who loomed behind her, she said, "This is Gallagher. He'll be working around the homestead for a while. Gallagher, this is Mrs. Abbott, Lowella's housekeeper and a very good cook. If you're hungry, I'm sure she has something about the kitchen that you could eat. After you finish, you can wait for me in the office. Mrs. Abbott will show you where it is.''

"Be that glad to," Mrs. Abbott said, smiling at Gallagher. "Well, sit, man. I've just cooked up some gingerbread, and there's that, with cream, if you like. Miss Sarah, it wouldn't 'urt you to stop a minute and eat some too; you're barely more than skin and bones as it is.''

"I'm not hungry, Mrs. Abbott.'' Conscious of Gallagher's broadening grin, knowing that he was deriving great amusement from her discomfiture, first at Liza's hands and now at Mrs. Abbott's, Sarah flashed him a darkling look before fleeing the kitchen. He was already, at Mrs. Abbott's urging, seating himself at the scrubbed kitchen table. Sarah had no doubt that Mrs. Abbott would serve him an enormous plate of gingerbread with cream before he could blink an eye. She was positively beaming at him. Well, Sarah told herself with a sigh as she let the kitchen door slam, at least I'm not the only one. He seemed to affect every female with whom he came into contact like catnip affected cats.

On the way to her room, Sarah glanced in through the open door of the large parlor at the front of the house and saw Mary and Tess, the two aborigine maids (Lydia had insisted that their names be anglicized; she claimed that she could never remember their native Australian names, which she thought were heathen anyway), hard at work polishing the teakwood floor in preparation for the dancing that would take place on it during Liza's ball. The rugs and furniture had already been removed and stored in a little-used room at the rear of the house. But the walls still had to be scrubbed and the windows washed, and the enormous chandelier that had traveled with Lydia from England had to be taken down and every separate piece of crystal washed and polished before it could be rehung. All the other rooms, both downstairs and up, had to be brought to their shining best as well. Besides creating many hours of extra work, and much bother for Sarah and the staff, the ball was costing Edward a great deal of money that he could not at the moment afford. But Lydia had insisted that her daughter come out in true English style, and, as usual, Edward had bowed to his wife's wishes.

"Sarah! You look positively unkempt! If I didn't know better, I would think you had been cleaning out the stables!" Lydia was coming down the stairs just as Sarah started up them; her distaste made the frown lines that she was usually careful to avoid crease her forehead. Sarah sighed as she approached her stepmother, who swept her skirt aside as though to avoid contamination when they passed on the stairs. An older, plumper version of Liza, with the same dusky brown hair worn in nearly the same artless style and with her daughter's spaniel eyes, Lydia had never made any secret of the fact that she merely tolerated her husband's daughter. Sarah, for her part, could not summon for Lydia any of the fondness she had learned to feel for her stepsister. The daughter of a minor baron, Lydia's first husband had been a wealthy cit, attracted as much, Sarah suspected, by Lydia's noble connections as by her person. Lydia had come to Australia with the very young Liza in tow when her husband had died and left them, against all her expectations, nearly paupers. Edward had been dazzled by the widow's charming smiles during one of his twice-yearly visits to Canberra, and had married her within the week. Sarah's mother had by then been dead for nearly five years, and although Lydia's and Liza's advent had been something of a shock, Sarah had been prepared to be fond of her new stepmother. Certainly she had admired her. With her dazzling array of bright silk and

satin dresses, her perfumes and lotions and soft femininity,
Lydia had seemed to the fifteen-year-old Sarah the very
epitome of a lady. For months she had tried—futilely—to
emulate her. When, finally, Lydia had driven it home to
her that, with her too-thin body and pointy face and
hopeless hair, the best Sarah could hope for was to be
clean and tidy, Sarah had been crushed. All her secret
longings to be beautiful ruthlessly exposed for the idiocies
they were, Sarah had determined to eschew fashion entirely. Lydia had made it clear in a hundred different ways that
Sarah could never hope to rival her own and her daughter's
looks; Sarah, accepting Lydia's evaluation with the humili-
ty of the young and untried, had never again attempted to
compete.

"I had an accident," she said now, briefly, to her
stepmother. She knew Lydia would not be concerned
enough to press her for details. Quite simply, she was not
interested in what happened to her husband's daughter, as
long as it was not something that would interfere with her
own comfort.

"I would hope so." The faintest suggestion of scorn
was discernible through the British upper-class accent
Lydia carefully cultivated. "I would hate to think that you
had taken to aping the style of a ragamuffin. Although,
now I come to think of it, it wouldn't be much of a
difference."

"Excuse me." Ignoring Lydia's dig, as she had learned
to do over the years, Sarah passed her stepmother and
continued on up the stairs to her room at the back of the
house.

Edward and Lydia shared one of the large bedrooms at
the front of the second story, and Liza had the other.
Sarah's room overlooked the orchard and was adjoined by
a very pretty little sitting room she had converted from an
unused bedroom. Furnished in palest green and peach, her

bedchamber was dominated by the large four-poster that had been her mother's marriage bed and in which she herself had been born. Lydia had banished it from her new husband's bedroom almost as soon as she had hung up her clothes, and Sarah had rescued it from the attic to which it had been ignominiously consigned. What Sarah wanted more than anything just at that moment was to fling herself on it and never leave its soft comfort again; what she did was strip off her ruined clothes, sluice her face and body with water, and tidy her hair before donning a clean dress in a nondescript calico print that, like her other clothes, had the advantage of not showing dirt.

Glancing at herself in the cheval mirror to make certain that her dress was properly buttoned and her hair pinned up securely, Sarah was suddenly struck by a wave of dissatisfaction with her looks such as she had not felt in years. With her hair skinned back from her face into the cumbersome knot at her nape, her face looked all eyes. The gold tone of the dress brought out their color but unfortunately made her skin appear sallow. Buttoned primly to the neck, the looseness of the dress disguised what few curves she possessed. Her bare arms looked as brown as an aborigine's from constant exposure to the sun.

Sarah turned her back on her reflection, disliking it intensely. Why did she have to be so hopelessly plain? And why, suddenly, did it bother her so much? She had thought that she had successfully ridded herself of every last lingering quiver of female vanity years ago. Then, as she forced her mind to turn to the tasks that awaited her downstairs, Sarah realized that the answer to that last question lay there, in a tall, hard-muscled body, a lean, handsome face, and a pair of breathtakingly blue eyes.

VII

Dominic Gallagher flexed his shoulder muscles and grimaced. The pain in his back was almost gone now, but it had been replaced by a lingering stiffness that made it difficult for him to lift his arms above his head and hold them there for any length of time. Not that that scrawny witch could have guessed, of course, when she had set him to washing windows. He would have grimly endured a dozen beatings like the one that had caused his present discomfort before he had confessed any weakness to her—or, for that matter, to anyone. He had never asked for quarter in his life, and he never would—not even if his arms fell off. Which they were clearly threatening to do. Today she had him washing windows, which involved a great deal of reaching and stretching. Yesterday she had set him to whitewashing walls, which called for much the same thing. The day before that, it had been his lot to remove what must have been thousands of tiny pieces of crystal from a chandelier in the front parlor, dip them in soapy water, rinse and polish them, and then rehang them. For someone with no knowledge of his difficulties, she was fiendishly accurate in assigning him jobs that caused him physical discomfort.

He could see her now, through the window he had just finished washing, that bossy mouth moving as she directed the poor, defenseless little aborigine maids to perform some no-doubt impossible task. The maids nodded respectfully, and, armed with feather dusters, attacked the furniture like twin dervishes. *Miss* Sarah—the respectful form of address stuck in his craw like a swallowed chicken bone, although it was no more or less than he would have called any gentlewoman in Ireland or England with whom he was not intimately acquainted; he suspected that it was the enforced servility of his position that made him despise the title so much when it came to *her*—oversaw their efforts for a moment, then left the room. Dominic watched the faint twitch of her skirts as she walked, and scowled. She was skinny, bossy, plain, not his type at all. What was it about her that appealed to him so? He could not for the life of him explain why he should find her attractive— unless it was because, underneath her air of prim propriety, he caught an occasional, tantalizing glimpse of another woman entirely. A staggeringly passionate woman. He had not missed the hungry way she looked at him sometimes, when she thought he wasn't aware of it—damn, sometimes he thought *she* wasn't even aware of the way she looked at him—or the faint tremor in her fingers when she had occasion to touch him. But that kind of reaction was nothing new to him. Without conceit, as matter-of-factly as he knew that the sun would rise in the morning, he accepted that his looks made most women find him attractive. It was alternately awkward, amusing, and useful, depending on his degree of attraction for the female concerned. And he had to admit that *Miss* Sarah attracted him inordinately. He could not fathom the how or the why of it, but the thought of bedding her, of stripping the hideous clothing from her slim body and holding her naked in his arms while he kissed and caressed and possessed her, was keeping him awake nights.

Dominic fingered his cheek where she had struck him with her reins. The narrow cut had healed now, but he could still see the fire in her eyes when she had lashed out at him, hear the rage in her usually quiet, courteous voice. She had surprised him then, as had her temper that first night in the inn's stable. Who ever would have thought that such a do-gooding old maid was capable of such a fine flare-up of fury? Certainly not he. The spitting tigress she had become on both occasions was a fascinating contrast to the dowdy spinster who ordinarily inhabited her body. Maybe that was it: maybe he just wanted to discover which of the two women was the real one. Maybe then this aggravating, unbelievable attraction would disappear.

He hadn't had a woman in months, of course, but that wasn't it. If that had been all it was, he would have been hot for that young stepsister of hers, who was much closer to the kind of woman he usually preferred. The younger girl was round and soft in all the right places, and not afraid to *be* a woman—but he was not in the least attracted to her. And this despite the way she had taken to following him about the place, flirting with him so blatantly that he was hard put sometimes not to laugh, or, when *Miss* Sarah had just finished giving him another order in that uppity way of hers and he was feeling more enraged than usual, box the little minx's ears. Young Liza was clearly ripe for a man. It would be the easiest thing in the world to take what she continually, and none too subtly, offered him. At nearly seventeen, she was old enough, so it wasn't her age that held him back; he would wager the best horse he had owned in Ireland that she was more sexually mature than her prim and proper stepsister. But he could not summon up a single spark of desire for the chit, or for that rapacious bitch of a stepmother, either, whom he had caught eying him once or twice, and who, like her daughter, had suddenly begun taking a "healthful" afternoon walk. With his escort, of course. At least Mrs. Markham was more subtle than her daughter. Only her eyes had told him that she found him attractive. No, the only one of the Markham ladies he could envision in his bed was Sarah—*Miss* Sarah. And he was beginning to be positively haunted by visions of bedding her, if for no other reason than so that he could once again get a decent night's sleep.

"I've brought you some lemonade, Gallagher. You look dreadfully hot." It was Liza, of course. Dominic turned to look at her, dropping the cloth he had been using on the window into the bucket of soapy water at his feet and flexing his shoulders again, which were stiff as a board.

"That was nice of you. Thank you." Ignoring her coy smile, Dominic reached for the glass and downed its contents thirstily. The unaccustomed heat of this infernal country was making him sweat like a chunk of ice near a bonfire; he needed all the liquids he could get. When he was finished, he wiped the back of his hand across his mouth and handed her back the glass. She took it, her eyes fixed on the expanse of chest that showed through his unbuttoned shirt. He would have shed the garment entirely if it hadn't been for the marks on his back; not for anything would he advertise the shame of having been beaten like a dog—or a slave. Which, of course, was exactly what he was.

"You'd better go back inside. You don't want to get your nose sunburned before your ball." The words were a dismissal. No matter that it wasn't for a slave to dismiss a lady of the house. He'd be damned before he'd act the part of humble servant to a seventeen-year-old chit!

"We're in the shade." Her eyes were fixed on his face, and she was batting her eyelashes at him. If he hadn't been so out of humor, he would have been amused at her blatant flirtation. But he was out of humor; being ordered around like a damned lackey by Miss Prunes-and-Prisms Sarah was beginning to set his teeth on edge.

"So we are." He acknowledged the valiant eucalyptus that cast a meager patch of shade over this bit of ground at the side of the house. "But I've finished this window, and the next one is not in the shade."

She sighed impatiently, planting her hands on her hips and looking up at him with a pout that he was sure she must have spent hours practicing in the mirror. The dress she had on, a white dimity strewn with pink rosebuds, left her shoulders and the tops of her breasts bare. He wasn't certain of how things were done in Australia, but in Ireland revealing so much so early in the day would have been considered highly improper. And he suspected that Australia was no different. Today young Liza was gunning for bear.

"I want to go for a walk. Pa said you were to come with me."

Dominic looked her up and down, his eyes guarded. She was posturing prettily, her plump bosoms thrust forward, one hand on a rounded hip while the other fluffed the dark curls that cascaded over her shoulders—in what, he thought, must have been a hellishly hot style. With those sparkling brown eyes and pink cupid's-bow of a mouth, she was a remarkably pretty girl. Why did she arouse in him nothing but the desire to shake her until her teeth rattled?

"Your sister particularly asked me to finish these windows this afternoon. Your walk will have to wait, I'm afraid."

"Oh, bother Sarah! You don't have to do what she tells you—at least, you don't have to mind her any more than you do me. I'm your mistress as much as she is!"

"Now, that may be true. But, you see, she got in her orders first. So you will agree that she has prior claim on my time." The words were another unmistakable dismissal. Liza looked affronted as Dominic bent to pick up the bucket. But before he could complete the action, another voice arrested his attention and brought him upright, the bucket forgotten at his feet.

"Liza, your mother is looking for you. You're to go to her at once." Sarah had rounded the corner of the house and stood frowning at them from the shelter of a wilted wattle some few feet away. Her bare arms were crossed over her small breasts; she looked as cross as he felt. The faded blue gingham dress she wore did nothing for either her face or her figure. Her hair—very nice hair, as he remembered from the one time he had seen it loose—was pulled back into an untidy bun. Her eyes—she had lovely eyes—were marred by the beetling of her brows above them. Next to her lusciously feminine sister, she was about as sexless as a grasshopper. Her very plainness irritated him. How could he possibly be tormented by desire for such an unfeminine female? It went against everything he'd ever known of himself.

"What does she want?" Liza asked, regarding her sister petulantly.

"You'd better go find out, hadn't you? Perhaps your ball dress has arrived at last."

"Oh, do you think so?" Liza squealed with delight. Her demeanor changed, and she looked like what she was—a young girl thrilled at the idea of her first ball. "I must go try it on." With that she picked up her skirts and, despite the heat, ran around the side of the house.

"I want to talk to you," Sarah said evenly when Liza was gone.

Dominic said nothing, merely leaned a shoulder against the frame of the window he had just finished cleaning and waited. She moved closer.

"I want you to stay away from Liza."

He laughed, the sound derisive. She moved another step nearer. With her golden eyes glaring at him, she reminded him suddenly of a lioness he had seen once at a circus in Dublin. He had a sudden urge to bait the lioness, to madden her as she constantly managed to madden him.

"I mean it, Gallagher. She's very young and impressionable. You're not to flirt with her. You're far too old for her, for one thing, and you're a . . ."

She seemed to sense that he hated that word, because she broke off without uttering it.

"Convict?" he finished, too pleasantly, straightening away from the window. "Not fit to wipe your little sister's shoes? Well, maybe I find her attractive—God knows, there's a dearth of attractive women around here."

That riled her, as he had meant it to. She seemed to be inordinately sensitive about her looks. Her eyes flashed angrily at him, and as her mouth tightened, he suddenly noticed how wide and full that mouth was; its softness was unmistakable evidence of her feminity that she could not disguise as she did her body. He found himself wondering, idly, what she would look like if she took more pains with her appearance. Found a softer style for her hair, say, and wore a dress that fitted her instead of looking as if it had been intended to shroud Mrs. Abbott's ample form.

"Are you listening to me?" She was practically right under his nose now, looking as furious as she sounded. Dominic suddenly found that he was enjoying himself. Baiting her was far more entertaining than washing windows.

"You wouldn't be jealous of your pretty sister, now,

would you, Miss Sarah?'' He spoke softly, the Irish lilt rolling through the words. They had all the effect he intended. He could see the temper explode inside her like a firecracker.

''Why, you impertinent jackanapes! As if I would be jealous of Liza over a—a convict!''

''Wouldn't you, *Miss* Sarah?'' He grinned at her tantalizingly, prepared for the furious tensing of her body. What he was not prepared for was the sudden sting of her palm against his cheek. He stopped grinning. His eyes were at once as furious as hers as he lifted a questing hand to his face.

''Violent little thing, aren't you?'' he growled, a savage satisfaction lighting his eyes. ''Well, it's time you learned that violence begets violence, *Miss Sarah!*''

And with that he reached out and hauled her toward him, not caring if his hands bruised the smooth bare flesh of her arms. She gaped up at him, her eyes huge, her lips parted in angry surprise. He bent his head and caught those lips, grinding his own roughly against them as he had dreamed of doing for weeks. Only a single thought penetrated the rage that engulfed him: He had been right about that mouth. It was every bit as soft as it looked.

VIII

At the first touch of Gallagher's mouth on hers, Sarah went rigid, fighting to ignore a frightening excitement in favor of healthy outrage. How dare he do such a thing, she ranted inwardly. He was hurting her, his lips brutal as they crushed hers, forcing her lips hard against her teeth. Focusing on the physical discomfort he was causing her was her best defense against a nearly overwhelming urge to melt in his arms and let him kiss her as he would, she knew. She concentrated . . . then tasted blood from a split lip, and moaned. That small sound seemed to be all he was waiting for. His hands on her upper arms tightened cruelly, his fingers digging into her flesh. But, try as she might, she could not seem to care about the pain that shot through her arms. Instead she was drowningly aware of that hard mouth as it moved harshly on her own; of his tongue as it thrust its way into her mouth.

She moaned again, shuddering, as she felt the intimate invasion. His hands left her arms and came around her, pulling her hard against him. She felt the heat and strength of his body, his unmistakable arousal pressing crudely against her belly. Her arms were crushed between them; with a last, frantic effort at sanity, she tried to use her arms to force a distance between them. She would not, could not let this happen. . . . Her hands encountered the bare skin of his chest, roughened with a thick growth of hair and wet with sweat—and were suddenly still. Her fingers curled of their own volition into that curling mat, her nails scraping his skin. He groaned, the sound guttural, rasping. His hold on her changed, became less brutal although no less tight as he bent her head backward so that it rested against the iron muscles of his upper arm. His breathing quickened. Sarah could feel his heart pounding through his chest against her breasts. His thrusting tongue gentled as it began a hot exploration of the inside of her mouth. Sarah suddenly lost the battle for control of her wayward senses as a gusher of fire shot from their joined mouths all the way to her toes. Her eyes, which had been glaring furiously at him, fluttered shut.

Under the intoxicating influence of his mouth, she forgot that he was a convict and she was a lady. She forgot everything, able to concentrate on nothing except the hot pounding of her blood, the trembling hunger that made her small breasts seem to swell as they pressed against his chest, the wonderful, moist, aching weakness that pulsed to life in that secret, shameful place between her legs.

When his tongue moved again, she responded mindlessly, her own moving fiercely to meet it. He stiffened against her; she could feel every hard muscle and sinew of his body pressing into her yielding flesh, including that one that both excited and embarrassed her even to think about. His lips seared hers; she felt as if she would be reduced to cinders at their touch. Her lips clung to his in convulsive response. If she could have freed them, her arms would have been tight around his neck.

He ended the kiss as abruptly as he had begun it, his hands moving back to her arms and thrusting her away from him without warning. Sarah whimpered a protest, blinking at him bemusedly for an instant, noting even through her daze how his glistening blue-black hair, his hard mouth tight now as he stared grimly at her, and his blue eyes could take her breath away. Then his mouth twisted, and his hands clenched on her arms.

"Someone's coming," he said through his teeth.

The words didn't penetrate at first. He shook her, impatient, in what she took to be rage. As her head snapped back, her reason returned—and with it came growing horror. It showed in her eyes as she stared at him, her hand coming up to press against her suddenly trembling mouth. The voices of the approaching workers seeped through to her consciousness, and she went crimson. If they had seen . . . if anyone had seen . . .

"Let me go," she said, pulling against the hold he still had on her. He hesitated for a moment. Then his hands dropped from her arms. A group of aborigine workers came into view, heading for the orchard. Sarah took that moment to back away, her hand still pressed to her mouth. When she was safely out of his reach, she turned and ran for the house.

The next three days were hectic as preparations for Liza's ball were completed. Sarah had a thousand and one tasks to attend to, and she could not concentrate on any of them. The burning memory of that kiss drove all else from her mind. That she had been kissed by a convict was shameful; the friends and neighbors who were so shortly to be their guests would be scandalized if they knew. But that she had actually returned that kiss. . . . She shuddered every time she remembered how she had responded. Gallagher's mouth on hers had robbed her of her senses; that was the only explanation she could find for behavior that in anyone else she would not have hesitated to condemn. If, for instance, she had caught Liza kissing Gallagher like that, she would have recommended to her father that the girl be shipped off to a convent without delay!

Sarah had been kissed before, of course—twice. The first man to kiss her had been Michael Argers, the son of one of the neighboring station owners; he had had too much to drink at one of the graziers' infrequent get-togethers and had surprised her in a dark hallway. He was seventeen at the time, the same age as she, and clumsy, but if his mouth had not been rancid with whiskey she would have quite enjoyed the experience. He had used his tongue, too—but there all comparison to Gallagher's kiss ended. Not by the largest stretch of the imagination could her reaction to Gallagher's kiss have been described by such a tepid sentiment as "quite enjoyed."

Percival had been the source of her other kiss, when he had begun to lose patience with her refusals of his proposals of marriage. Apparently he had thought to sweep her off her feet with a show of ardor; or perhaps he had merely hoped to drive home the fact that he was a physically superior male, and that she, as a weaker female, should submit to him in all things, including marriage. It hadn't worked. Sarah had found his kiss downright distasteful, and had told him so in words of icy rage when he had at last released her. He had never tried such a thing since. Whether he had decided that such a tactic would not aid his cause, or whether he had simply found their kiss as distasteful as she had, Sarah couldn't say.

She dreaded having any further contact with Gallagher, but as he was constantly around the house during those three days it was impossible to avoid him. Sarah wanted to die of mortification every time her eyes met his. She knew from his expression that he was remembering their kiss just as she was. His eyes mocked her everywhere she went; he seemed constantly to be underfoot. But there was no way to rid herself of him without it being obvious to him how much his kiss had affected her. And she thought he despised her enough without that.

The worst part about it was that he had kissed her in anger, as a means of retaliation for that slap. It had been no more to him than answering the blow she had struck. How he must have laughed inside when she had begun to kiss him back! Because of course he had not felt the same bewildering surge of fire through his body as she had. Long ago she had faced the fact that she was plain. Gallagher himself, on that never-to-be-forgotten night in the stable at Yancy's place, had called her scrawny and said she had about as much feminity as a broomstick. While he, if she had been mentally concocting a portrait of a dream lover, would have fitted it like a glove.

He had made a fool of her—no, she had made a fool of herself, Sarah corrected bitterly. If she had only maintained her poise, had held to a semblance of icy detachment or even righteous fury, she would not now be writhing with humiliation. Instead, she had let a convict kiss her; worse, she had behaved like a wanton in his arms, kissing him back with a fervor that she would have gladly slit her throat to be able to erase from both their minds forever. But the fact was that it was done, she *had* kissed him back in that feverish way, and she must deal with it.

Sarah had determined that, for the sake of what self-respect she had left, Gallagher must have no inkling of how deep her embarrassment was. She would act as if nothing, nothing at all, had happened—after making their relative positions crystal clear to him. . . . When she had run away after that traumatic kiss, she had fled to her room and flung herself on her bed, reliving every shameful nuance of what had happened. Even then, when her mortification threatened to choke her, she had realized that she could not remain in her room forever and would inevitably have to face Gallagher again. He must be made to understand that nothing between them had changed: he was still the servant, she the mistress. She would tolerate not the slightest deviation from that.

The next morning she had mustered every ounce of her courage and summoned him to the station office. As she faced him across the large, scarred desk at which she did the station accounts—she seated; he, in the absence of an invitation from her to sit, standing with his hat in his hand—she had met his blue eyes, which seemed nearly as hostile as she felt despite outward composure. Inwardly she was a mass of nerves, but she was determined that he would never guess. To that end, her tone was severe as she told him that if he ever, ever so far forgot himself again as to lay a hand on her, she would not hesitate to report his behavior to her father, who would undoubtedly mete out the severest punishment. Her manner implied that what had happened was entirely something that he had done to her; her eyes dared him to so much as remember how she had responded to his outrageous act. He stared at her as she spoke, his face as coldly aloof as her own, his big body formidable in the small room, his eyes now unreadable. When she had finished, favoring him with her haughtiest stare, he spoke not a single word by way of a reply. Instead he merely inclined his head arrogantly at her, with more mockery than deference, turned on his heel, and, without permission, left. She had been left staring at the gently closing door, fiercely fighting an impulse to pick up the heavy glass paperweight near her left hand and hurl it after him.

Since then, she had spoken to him as little as possible,

and then only to assign him to some task or another. She had kept her words brief, her manner cool. His replies had been equally brief, and entirely proper—too proper: "Yes, Miss Sarah; No, Miss Sarah," while his lilting Irish voice mocked her and his eyes seemed to laugh.

Maddened, Sarah knew that her only recourse was to go to her father and tell him everything that had transpired between Gallagher and herself, starting with his appalling insolence and ending with his constant refusal to recognize and keep to his place. The trouble with that was that she would have to reveal everything, including that shameful kiss. And that she could not bring herself to do.

The guests began to arrive the day before the ball. Because of the distances between homesteads, some would stay for two or three nights. Everyone would stay at least the night of the ball. Sarah was glad when Tom and Mary Eaton and their three strapping sons arrived, followed shortly by Amos McClintock and his only child, his daughter, Chloe. The single men would share the convicts' bunkhouse, which had been cleaned and furbished especially for the occasion, while the convicts made do with bedrolls in the sheep barns. Tom and Mary Eaton had been given Sarah's own sitting room, which she had converted back to a bedchamber temporarily. Chloe, who was one of Liza's particular friends, would share with Liza, as would Katy Armbruster when she arrived. Sarah had moved out of her own room, which would serve for another of the married couples among the guests, and up into the attic with Mrs. Abbott and the maids. Supposedly, her reason was to make more room for their guests, but really Sarah could not stand the idea of sharing her chamber with several of the young ladies, which she would have to do if she remained. Nearly all of them were closer to Liza's age than to hers, and treated her with the deference due a member of an older generation, combined with the almost unconscious contempt accorded a woman already past marriageable age who had failed to catch a husband. Sarah knew their attitude was not deliberate, but still it hurt. She hated being reminded that she was an old maid, even if it was the truth.

No sooner had the Eatons and the McClintocks been settled than more guests began to arrive. They came in a steady stream throughout the day. For the most part, they were bluff, hearty people, used to hardships and hard travel in this country they had adopted for their own. The heat was a nuisance, but no more. The distance was something one took in stride, even if it meant camping out under the stars for a night or two on the way. Not all were wealthy, though most were well enough to pass. All were graziers, and all, without exception, were staunchly exclusionist. Looking at them, separately and as a group, Sarah shuddered to think how they would titter if they knew that she was caught in the throes of a devastating sexual attraction to a convict.

With guests on hand, Lydia bestirred herself to act as hostess. It was a role she thoroughly enjoyed, sitting in the sparkling parlor that Sarah and the maids had refurbished from floor to ceiling, dispensing tea from the ornate silver service that Sarah had spent hours polishing because the servants were busy with other tasks, making light, witty conversation so that the guests remarked to one another how very charming the second Mrs. Markham was. And beautiful, too. Liza had had a new ball dress for the occasion; Lydia had ordered a whole new wardrobe. Every time Sarah saw her, resplendent in green satin or orange taffeta, she winced, thinking of Lowella's depleted coffers. With the money that had been spent on clothes, food, drink, and renewed hangings and furnishings and linens—

the list was endless—for this one occasion, the sheep could have been kept in grain for a year.

With the house full, Sarah had less time to think of Gallagher, for which she was thankful. Percival had sent him back to the stables while there were so many guests about, and Sarah didn't even have to see him. Which was a relief. When he had been constantly about the house, she had never felt comfortable. She always had the feeling that, even if he was out of sight, he was somehow watching her.

She was surprised, therefore, the day before the ball, to hear his voice as he greeted Mrs. Abbott. Sarah was in the small pantry off the kitchen, checking to see that they had enough jams and jellies and other dainties on hand to feed fifty-odd people determined to have a rollicking good time at Lowella's expense. Mrs. Abbott was in the kitchen, frantically trying to save Liza's birthday cake, which was supposed to be seventeen tiers tall. Two of the layers had failed to rise, and Mrs. Abbott was in despair. Lydia had been most insistent on having a tier for every year of Liza's age.

Sarah stopped what she was doing and stood motionless for what must have been the first time in a week as she heard Gallagher's voice. Then she heard his footsteps approaching, and became suddenly very busy again.

"I need to have a word with you." His voice came from directly behind her, deep and low and full of the lilt that made it different from any other she had ever heard.

"Yes?" she said, turning slowly to face him. Reluctant to do it, she nevertheless made her eyes meet his. Their blueness startled her; she always thought that they could not possibly be as blue as she remembered, and they were always bluer. He was frowning slightly as he stood in the door of the pantry, his head brushing the top of the doorjamb and his big body completely blocking her exit.

He was clad in the loose white shirt and snug black breeches that were standard attire for all the convicts on Lowella.

"I overheard some of your guests getting up a race for this afternoon. They mean to put Max with one of the dunderheads up against another boy with a new horse that he says is the fastest thing for a hundred miles around. It's too damn hot: they'll kill those horses. I want to stop it when they come for Max, but I don't have the authority. I need your permission."

He was looking at her very steadily. Sarah had to fight the impulse to let her eyes drop away from his. It was very, very important that he not guess how nervous she was in his presence.

"Why come to me? Why not my father, or Mr. Percival?"

"Mr. Percival has taken a group of the men shooting. Your father is off somewhere with another group of men showing them his beloved sheep."

"Oh." She dared to look away from him for a moment. It was ridiculous, the way she had to fight to keep her eyes from wandering from his face to his body. That tall, strong body that had felt so hard pressed against hers... "Of course you have my permission. You're right: it's far too hot for a race."

"Thank you." He inclined his head and turned as if to go. Sarah was surprised at how much she hated to see the back of him. Then he looked at her over his shoulder and gave a mocking grin. "You have flour on your nose. Miss Sarah." She gaped at him, astonished at his sudden reversion to his former manner, while her hand flew to her nose. His eyes raked her once, and then he was gone, his booted feet making noises on the stone floor of the kitchen as he let himself out the back door.

*   *   *

The day of the ball dawned as hot and dry as the six weeks preceding it. Sarah, in the attic, which was hotter by several degrees than the lower floors, had slept with her window open; the first thing she did upon arising was to pull back the insect netting shrouding it and lean out, hoping for a breath of cooler air. The hope was futile, of course. The air outside was just as stuffy as the air within.

The windmill groaned in the distance, protesting wearily at the impossibility of its task. Hot gusts of wind blowing down from the mountains to the north kept the paddles turning sluggishly. When the winds ceased, as they inevitably did, Percival had rigged up some sort of contraption with ropes and a wheel, and mules to turn the wheel, that got the windmill going again. Without the windmill, there would be no water for the house and orchards. And probably no water for the horses. Edward was perfectly capable of refusing every creature on the place, except for his sheep, a drop of water if it got scarce enough.

The guests were still sleeping, of course—most of the men, especially, got too few chances to sleep in at home— but the aborigines were already in the orchard, crooning their native songs as they picked insects from the leaves before the day grew too hot. Mrs. Abbott was in the garden, harvesting the vegetables she would need to feed the crowd of guests for the day. Tess was there with her, digging industriously at the potato hills. Sarah started to call to them, but just at that moment a man strode from the stables toward the house. Gallagher. Sarah watched, fascinated at the way the already bright sun picked up shimmering blue highlights in the ebony waves of his hair, at the broadness of his shoulders and narrowness of his hips in comparison, and at the length of his stride as his long legs ate up the short distance. She heard the lilt in his voice as he greeted Mrs. Abbott and Tess, and heard the affection in Mrs. Abbott's answer as she straightened away from the

rows of vegetables and urged him to come into the house
for a bite of breakfast before anyone else was up. Mrs.
Abbott knew as well as Sarah did that no convicts ever ate
in the house; her invitation was a flagrant violation of one
of Edward's unspoken but universally understood rules.
But Sarah would not reprimand Mrs. Abbott for her
transgression. Despite the weight Gallagher had gained
since she had first seen him on the convict ship, and
despite the breadth of his shoulders and the hardness of his
muscles, he was still too thin. He needed feeding up.

Mrs. Abbott was already inside the house, Gallagher a
few paces behind her, when Sarah started to draw her head
back inside. She had meant to go straight down; now she
would have to give Mrs. Abbott time to feed Gallagher
and get him out of the house first, or else, for appearances'
sake, she would have to scold the housekeeper after all.
Her head came into hard, painful contact with the windowsill.
Sarah cried out automatically, clapping a hand to the
injured spot and rubbing tenderly. Three stories below,
Gallagher looked up. His eyes locked with hers for a long
moment, then moved swiftly over every part of her that he
could see, from the childish twin plaits that kept her hair
tidy while she slept, to the expanse of skin left bare by the
skimpy cotton chemise that she had worn in preference to
a nightgown because of the heat. Sarah crimsoned and
immediately withdrew back inside the window. But not
before he had given her one of his nasty, mocking smiles.

For the rest of the day she burned with embarrassment
whenever she thought of that incident. And, as she attended
to the myriad last-minute tasks that were crucial to the
evening's success, she thought of it with maddening fre-
quency. When she directed the maids to give the front
parlors a final sweeping and dusting, it was at the forefront
of her mind. When she helped Mrs. Abbott peel the
mountain of potatoes that would be made into potato cakes

for that night's birthday feast, it hovered beneath the light conversation she was exchanging with the housekeeper. The terrible thing about it, she admitted to herself, was that, while she did not like the idea of Gallagher seeing her in such dishabille, it was not the impropriety of it that bothered her most: it was the knowledge of how unprepossessing she must have looked with her infuriatingly straight hair hanging over the windowsill in braids as thick as his wrist, and her lack of feminine curves readily apparent in the chemise that did nothing to conceal her shape. If he had found her unappealing before, what must he think of her now? And this, to her fury, was the thought that aroused her blushes.

Liza and Lydia, and, for that matter, nearly all the female guests except old Mrs. Grainger, spent the day in their rooms, resting up for the evening's festivities. Mrs. Grainger, a feisty old lady whose husband had been one of the first white men in this part of Australia, could not be left to her own devices. So Sarah, feeling duty-bound, joined her on the front porch, where she listened as patiently as she could to the old woman's reminiscences, which at any other time would have been fascinating. Mrs. Grainger's husband, John, now long deceased, had come to Australia in 1770 on the HMS *Endeavour* under the captainship of Lieutenant James Cook. Her tales of those early pioneering days were vivid, and occasionally spiced with expressions not often heard on the lips of ladies, but which Mrs. Grainger had culled from the vocabulary of her seafaring husband. By the time Sarah was able diplomatically to suggest that it was time that both ladies start dressing for the evening, she was torn between scandalized laughter and a nagging headache that throbbed relentlessly at her temples. The knowledge that she had still to see to a few last-minute details before she herself could retire didn't make her feel any better.

When Sarah at last made it up to the small, airless

cubbyhole that she had taken over for the duration of the guests' stay, she just had time for a quick wash and change of clothing before she had to be downstairs again. Lydia's hostessing did not extend to overseeing the final readying of the food, the allocating of the staff, or the strategic placement of the traveling musicians who had been engaged for the evening so that their music could be heard to best advantage.

She was not able even to have a tub bath; the maids were being run off their feet carrying hot water in cans up to the other women, and Sarah was too hospitable to demand their attention for herself in preference to her guests. And she was too tired to fetch the hot water herself. She contented herself with stripping down to her skin and standing in a basin while she washed herself with soap and a wet cloth. When she was finished, she caught up the pitcher and sluiced the water remaining in it over her body to rinse away the soapsuds. Then, feeling marginally refreshed, she dried herself.

As Sarah surveyed the dress she had laid out on the narrow bed, she wished that she had ordered a new gown for herself when Liza and Lydia had ordered theirs. Just once, she would have liked to look nice. She refused to consider why. If Gallagher's darkly handsome face appeared momentarily in her mind's eye, she resolutely banished it. Anyway, the finest of satin ball gowns in the loveliest of colors wouldn't have transformed the ugly duckling into a swan. The white silk dress that she had worn to every party since she was seventeen would do just fine. Anything else would have been wasted on her.

Sarah pulled on her chemise—as a concession to the nature of the evening she chose one of fine muslin, but it was as unadorned as her everyday cotton ones—and topped it with a single petticoat. It was too hot for any additional undergarments, and if as a result her dress did not have the fashionable full skirt, that was just too bad. What was one more sartorial shortcoming among so many?

The dress itself fitted close around her neckline, framing her throat with a little frill of lace and buttoning clear down past the snug waist with two dozen tiny, silk-covered buttons. The sleeves were short and puffed and likewise ended with a frill of lace; a white satin sash was tied in a big bow at the rear, with the trailing ends of the sash falling girlishly down the back of the skirt. The skirt itself was plain, and cut full for the three petticoats that were supposed to be worn beneath it. With only one, it billowed around her. The effect had always pleased her, because she felt that it must disguise her lack of a rounded derrière and curving, feminine thighs. A pair of white cotton stockings—she had always felt it was absurd to wear silk ones, as Liza and Lydia did, where no one could see—held up by frilly white-satin garters that had belonged to her mother and sensible flat black slippers completed her ensemble. She wore no jewelry—indeed, the only pieces she possessed had belonged to her mother, who had been considered a beauty; they would have been wasted on Jane Markham's plain daughter. She brushed her hair until it crackled, then wound it up into its usual bun. Not even twenty-four hours spent in rag curlers, as she had tried on several occasions when she was younger and more foolish, had sufficed to give her curls. She had learned to be content with herself as she was; and tonight, if, when looking at herself in the slightly wavy mirror on the wall of her attic bedroom before hurrying downstairs, she was somewhat less than content, there was nothing she could do to change either the feeling or her appearance.

By ten o'clock the ball was in full swing. The musicians were scraping a lively tune on their fiddles; couples were kicking up their heels and laughing breathlessly as they romped around the floor. Even Mrs. Grainger was danc-

ing, partnered by one of the Eaton boys, who was crimson
with the indignity of just having been told that he had two
left feet in the old lady's strident voice, which carried to
every corner of the room. His two brothers were more
fortunate: one partnered Liza and the other Chloe. Liza
was entrancing in her rose-pink satin gown, her hair
arranged in a careless pile of curls that Sarah knew had
taken the better part of the day to achieve. She was flirting
madly, shamelessly batting her eyelashes at the boy, who
looked suitably dazzled by his good fortune. Lydia was
dancing with George Banks, a distinguished-looking man
of about fifty with a full head of silver hair, and flirting
quite as openly as Liza. Sarah looked quickly around to
see if her father had noticed. He was partnering Mrs.
Eaton, his expression politely attentive as he piloted that
lady's ample form about the room. If he was aware of his
wife's behavior, he showed no sign of it. Like Sarah
herself, Percival was not dancing. As she looked in his
direction, he started toward her, clearly bent on rectifying
that omission.

"Will you dance, Miss Sarah?"

Percival was looking more attractive than usual in a
brown cutaway coat and yellow breeches. A striped cravat
was tied haphazardly around his neck, giving him an
unaccustomed rakish air. His dark brown hair was already
untidy, straggling over his forehead, although it still bore
marks of the comb that had been dragged through it when
it was wet. His sunburned skin was redder than usual,
flushed with the exertion of having preceded Sarah's father
as Mrs. Eaton's partner. He was smiling at her, his thick
lips parted over teeth that overlapped in front. The smile
was quite absent from his eyes.

"I'd rather not, thank you, Mr. Percival." The reply
and the glance that accompanied it were cool. His *faux*
smile faded, to be replaced by a darkening frown.

"By God, girl, if you don't stop trifling with me . . ." The harsh words, muttered under his breath, broke off at her outraged stiffening; but his eyes stayed angry as they met her icy gaze.

"What will you do, Mr. Percival?" she inquired sweetly, raising her punch cup to her lips and taking a sip as she eyed him with inquiringly lifted brows.

His lips thinned, and he openly glared at her. "I'll school you proper when I get you to wife," he growled. Then, as though aware that he had said too much, he shut his mouth with a sharp click of teeth and turned on his heel, stomping away from her.

Sarah took another sip of punch, hoping that the innocuous orange brew would steady her, hoping that no one standing nearby had overheard the exchange. She glanced surreptitiously about. Mr. and Mrs. Brady were talking animatedly to Lawrence Newcomb, the banker, and young Jared Bledsoe was whispering something to Amy Carruthers, who for once was not being quietly retiring and was actually giggling. They were far too engrossed in their own activities to have spent any time eavesdropping on her. For which Sarah was thankful.

The exchange with Percival had worsened the headache that had plagued her all evening. She took another sip of her punch, then set the glass on a nearby small table, her movements deliberate so that she would not reveal her upset by spilling any. Percival was growing more and more open about his intent—and resorting to more forceful means of expressing it. Thoughts of what he might try in the future alarmed her. There was one very good way by which a man could almost make certain that the woman he wanted would become his wife. She would not put it past Percival to resort to rape—but she meant to make mighty certain that he didn't get the opportunity.

No one noticed Sarah as she slipped away to the kitchen, as she had been doing all evening. Mrs. Abbott had had the monumental task of making sure that the trays of refreshments on the long table at the end of the room were kept filled. At the moment, she was slicing the meat off a leg of mutton. She looked over her shoulder as Sarah entered the kitchen.

"Tired of dancing, lamb?"

When they were alone, Mrs. Abbott sometimes resorted to a cozy familiarity that Sarah knew stemmed both from long years of knowledge and true affection. Sarah smiled at her.

"Just tired." She crossed to watch the older woman as she deftly sliced the meat onto a large platter already filled to overflowing. "You'd think we were feeding an army."

"Dancin's hungry work." Mrs. Abbott's cheeks were flushed from the heat of the kitchen, and perspiration beaded her brow beneath her frazzled, salt-and-pepper topknot. The only concession she made to the heat was that the sleeves of her dress, another high-necked, long-sleeved black bombazine, were rolled up to her elbows. "You there, Mary!" she said sharply over her shoulder. The maid came out of the pantry, an open jar of candied fruit in one hand. "Take this platter on into the parlor. Be careful with it, mind."

With a quick bob, Mary set the jar on the table and obeyed.

"You ought to take something in yourself and watch the dancing for a while. You need a break," Sarah said gently.

Mrs. Abbott snorted. "They'd likely spit on the likes of me."

"Not in this house they wouldn't."

"No, 'cause you wouldn't let them. You're a real lady, Miss Sarah, and I'm not the only one around here that thinks so! You treat people like people, with no never mind about whether they be convicts or not. Them other two . . . ! They're no ladies.''

"Mrs. Abbott . . .''

"I know, I know. I shouldn't be talkin' about them that are my betters. But that's what I think. Can't 'ang a body for thinkin', can they?''

Sarah had to smile at the truculence of the look that accompanied this last. "No, they can't,'' she agreed. Scooping a section of candied orange from the jar Mary had left on the table, Sarah popped it into her mouth.

"I'm going out in the back garden for a breath of fresh air. If anyone comes looking for me, don't tell them.''

Mrs. Abbott said, "Not me, Miss Sarah,'' and shook her head vigorously. Sarah had a feeling that the housekeeper knew all about Percival's attempts to coerce her into marriage; she was very cool toward Lowella's overseer whenever she saw him, which, thankfully for the station's harmony, wasn't too often.

Sarah smiled her thanks and let herself out the back door. With darkness shrouding the shriveled brown grass and the nearly leafless trees, the garden was much more pleasing than during the daytime. Tonight a huge full moon, round and misty white, hovered low over the horizon. It cast a silvery light over everything. A breeze, cool compared to the searing winds that had whipped down from the mountains earlier, set the grasses and leaves to rustling. The scrape of the fiddles, playing at a slower tempo now, wafted clearly to her through the open windows. In the distance a dingo howled. It was a mournful sound, but, because Sarah had been familiar with it from babyhood, it was oddly comforting. The heady fragrance of the wattles mingled with the spicier scents of oranges and lemons as she wandered toward the orchard. Reaching it, she paused to lean against a fig tree, not thinking of anything in particular as she let the peace of the night envelop her. Her headache was almost gone. . . .

"For a minute there I thought you were a ghost. I nearly ran."

Sarah would have recognized that teasing lilt anywhere. She turned her head to find Gallagher standing behind her, a few feet away. The foliage of a banana tree blocked out the moon rays where he stood, so that he appeared to be no more than a tall, dark shadow. Sarah had thought that she would feel more embarrassed than ever the next time she saw him, remembering that morning when he had seen her in nothing but her chemise. But the peace of the night seemed to have infected her. Besides, what harm could come from talking—just talking—to him? She smiled faintly.

"I would like to have seen that."

He moved a couple of steps nearer, drawn perhaps by the unexpected friendliness of her tone. The moonlight poured over him now, highlighting the sculpted bones of his face, the proud curves of cheekbones and chin and forehead, the faintly aquiline nose. It formed a soft, silvery nimbus around his hair, which was darker than the night; the light touched his mouth, the feel of which her lips remembered so well, like a lover's caress.

"Is your sister enjoying her party?"

"I think so. She seems to be. So does everyone." She was talking to him like an equal again, as she seemed to most of the time. But what harm could come from it? Just for tonight . . .

"Except you?"

"What do you mean?" She frowned, trying to read his expression in the shifting pattern of light and shadows.

"You're out here."

"Oh." She smiled and shrugged. "My head ached. And

I didn't feel like dancing. Probably because I'm not very good at it.''

"You should learn. With your natural grace, you would enjoy it.''

She stared at him. He was smiling, just barely, that handsome mouth twisted up slightly at one corner so that it looked almost lopsided.

"Why, thank you." She nearly stuttered, so flustered was she by the compliment. She rarely got compliments; in fact, she couldn't remember the last one. And from Gallagher . . . Did he really think she was graceful? To cover her confusion, she continued lightly, "Maybe I will learn one day. If I can find someone to teach me."

"I will."

"What?" She thought she must have misunderstood him.

"I said, I will teach you. To dance. Miss Sarah." He sounded as if he were laughing at her, but he looked perfectly solemn, except for dancing devils in his eyes.

Sarah looked at him warily. "You told Liza you couldn't dance." It was foolish, but it was the first thing that came into her head. She should be upbraiding him for his impertinence.

"I lied." He moved forward until he stood directly in front of her, towering over her so that she had to tilt her head back to see his face. He was so big—she liked the sensation of being small and fragile she had when she was near him. It made her feel, for once, very feminine. "I'd like to teach you to dance. Will you let me?" He held out his hand as he spoke, clearly waiting for her to put her own into it.

Sarah stared at that brown, long-fingered hand. He was a convict. She would be utterly disgraced if anyone ever learned of it. The explosive reaction his slightest touch seemed able to engender in her made it dangerous . . . too dangerous.

She put her hand in his.

IX

"That didn't hurt, now, did it?" He was smiling. His teeth gleamed white against the darkness of his face.

Quivering with renewed misgivings, Sarah stared up into that face. She should pull away from him now. . . . Her hand trembled in his like a trapped bird. His much larger one enwrapped hers comfortingly, refusing to let it go. In the distance, the fiddlers struck up again. Sarah recognized the tune. It was a new one, from England. A waltz.

"I really don't know how to dance to this." She pulled away her hand, both relieved and disappointed to have the decision taken from her.

"I do. Put your other hand on my shoulder. It's too late to back out now."

"Gallagher . . ."

He reached out and caught her hand, placing it firmly on his shoulder. One arm slid around her waist. He pulled her close to him, not right up against his body but near enough that her skirt brushed his legs.

"Gallagher . . ."

"Relax. You're as stiff as a board. Let me lead you."

He began to move in time to the music, dragging Sarah after him. Being held so close to him, with his arm hard and warm around her waist, sent her senses spinning with mingled pleasure and alarm. This was all wrong, she knew, and she also knew that she would bitterly regret it in the morning. But just for tonight . . .

"That's better. You're doing fine. One-two-three, one-two-three, one-two-three-four . . ." He counted off the rhythm, molding her body into a pattern of intoxicating dips and sways and turns.

When Sarah became more comfortable with the steps, he increased the tempo until he had her twirling breathlessly, laughing. She felt so strange, unlike herself. It was as if the beauty of the night and the feel of him holding her, his hard legs brushing hers with every step, had cast a spell over her. Looking up at him, watching that chiseled mouth quirk with honest amusement, seeing the blue eyes twinkling down at her out of that darkly handsome face, feeling the height and breadth of him against her, the strength of his muscles beneath her hand and against her legs, she was in danger of forgetting who she was. Who he was. The silvery spill of moonlight washing over them as they danced among the trees, the warm, perfumed air, the haunting lilt of the music drifting from the house, each carried its own brand of magic. As did he. He was enchanting her, he and the night and the music together, conspiring. Sarah felt it happening but could do nothing about it. She was already bewitched.

The fiddles reached a climax, and Gallagher spun her around, then dipped her over his arm so that her head fell back toward the ground. She clutched frantically at his shoulder for balance, laughing up at him, feeling her hair slipping from its pins to hang thick and heavy behind her, but not caring. At that moment, in his arms, she felt herself everything she had always wanted to be: beautiful, feminine, the kind of woman whom a man like Gallagher could look at and desire. . . .

"Where did you learn to dance like that?" she asked as the music ceased and he pulled her upright but did not release her. Sarah was supremely conscious of the warmth of his hand clasping hers, of the strength of the arm around her waist as he grinned a little mockingly at the honest admiration in her question.

"When I was a boy, I lived in a castle. A very big castle with battlements and turrets, made of stone as black as the devil's heart. There, among many other useless accomplishments, I was taught to dance. Much good that it ever did me."

"You're making that up!" Sarah accused, laughing again. Then, when he said nothing, just looked down at her with a whimsical expression, she added with a touch of uncertainty, "Aren't you?"

He shook his head, then grinned tantalizingly. "What do you think?"

Sarah considered the matter for an instant. "I think you are," she decided.

"Then I must be." He was looking down at her, his mouth twisted up in a half-smile. The expression in his eyes was unreadable.

"Your hair fell down."

Self-consciously Sarah lifted the hand that had rested almost forgotten on his shoulder and tried to tame the wayward mass. But she needed both hands for that, and he would not release the other one.

"Leave it. It becomes you."

She looked up at him uncertainly. Was he teasing her? He seemed perfectly serious. With the moonlight illuminating his face she could see that he was no longer smiling. His eyes had changed from bright blue to a darker, smoky sapphire. . . . Something about the way he was looking at her made her suddenly, achingly aware of how close he was, of the way he was holding her.

"The music has stopped. You can let me go now." She tried to pull away, suddenly very self-conscious. She was enjoying his touch too much. It was time she remembered who, and what, they both were.

"I don't want to." His voice was husky. Sarah looked up at him, her eyes widening, her breath catching in her throat. His hand released hers to capture her chin.

"Gallagher..." His name was both a plea and a warning.

"Miss Sarah." He was mocking her, but the mockery sounded oddly gentle. "I think I'm going to have to kiss you again. Miss Sarah."

"Gallagher!" Before Sarah could do more than gasp out his name in strangled protest, he was bending his head. Sarah could only watch, mesmerized, as that handsome mouth descended so very slowly toward hers. He was not holding her so tightly that she could not have evaded his kiss if she had wanted to. But she didn't want to. She was horrified to discover that, more than she had ever wanted anything in her life, she wanted him to kiss her.

When his mouth touched hers in a gentle, butterfly kiss, the shock of it made her shudder. She closed her eyes helplessly, pressing close to him, her lips fluttering apart as she sighed her surrender. She did not make even a token protest. This was what she had wanted since that other time when he had kissed her. But she had not realized the depth of her own need—until now. Her mouth opened to him, her lips trembling beneath the heated encroachment of his. His tongue was hot and spicy-tasting as it explored the wet sweet cave of her mouth, licking over her lips and the smooth surface of her teeth before venturing further to stroke the ridges at the top of her mouth, the soft skin of the insides of her cheeks, and then, finally, her tongue. She trembled against him. Shyly at first, and then with increasing boldness, her tongue moved to meet his, to learn the inside of his mouth as he was renewing his discovery of her own. She loved the taste of him, the passion. Her arms crept around his neck, her fingers tangling in his thick black hair. It curled around them seductively, as cool as the moonlight and as soft as raw silk. The back of his neck felt hard and warm in contrast.

To her surprise, as he felt her surrender he seemed to shudder, too. His arms went hard around her waist, pulling her even tighter against him. Sarah felt the heat and strength of him with every centimeter of her skin. Her fingers clenched on his hair.

"Gallagher," she sighed against his mouth. He broke off the kiss, lifting his head a little away from her. Sarah moaned a protest, clutching at the back of his neck, her eyes opening to look at him in dazed reproach. His eyes seemed lit by tiny, raw flames. His answering whisper was hoarse.

"Dominic. My name is Dominic. Say it."

"Dominic," she responded obediently. She would say anything, do anything, if only he would kiss her again.

"Sarah." Her name was a mutter of satisfaction as his mouth came down on hers again, not gently this time, but demanding and receiving her response. Sarah clung to him with all her strength, on fire for him, letting his lips and tongue teach hers all she didn't know about kissing. She felt as if she were melting in his arms.

One arm left her waist to slide between them. His hand crept up the silk covering her rib cage to close over the slight curve of her breast. At the feel of his hand warm and intimate against her, Sarah went rigid with shock and an excitement that she immediately strove not to recognize. Her eyes flew open; her hands slid from around his neck to shove frantically at his wide shoulders. He was going too far. He had to stop. Her insistent pushes brought results at last: his eyes opened, to gaze down into hers with smoldering intensity. His mouth continued to hold hers captive; his hand stayed cupped around her breast, which to her horror seemed to swell against his palm. She shoved at him again, harder this time. Her urgency finally communicated itself to him. He lifted his head—but not his hand.

"Sarah?" It was a husky question.

"Please—let me go." Her words were disjointed. Her hands were braced against his shoulders, holding him off as best she could. She had no illusions that she could maintain the slight distance between them if he wanted to force the issue. But, curiously, she did not think he would do that.

"Has no one ever touched you like this before?" He sounded almost detached—except for the huskiness that deepened his voice to a rasp. As if to underline his question, his hand tightened over her breast, squeezing gently. To her distress, Sarah felt every nerve she possessed quiver and tighten in response.

"No! What do you take me for?" The question was furious, to hide her rapidly growing urge to close her mouth and let him hold her as he would. She had never dreamed that, by the simple act of covering her breast with his hand, a man could rouse in her such feverish confusion.

"A lady. A very lovely, innocent lady who is shocked at herself because she enjoys my touch." The words were very low, a velvety growl that caressed her ears even as his hand caressed her breast. He kneaded the small, silk-covered mound very gently—and then his thumb moved, so slowly, over the sensitive crest. Sarah felt the shock of it clear down to her toes. It was all she could do to repress a gasp. She thanked the Lord for the darkness that hid the sudden, mortified crimsoning of her cheeks as she felt her nipple stiffen under his hand. But the darkness could not hide the rise and fall of her chest as her breathing quickened.

"Don't be ashamed, Sarah. It's perfectly natural for you to feel as you do. Let me show you. . . ."

"Let me go. Please." Sarah barely managed to get the words out. More than anything in the world she wished she didn't have to say them. She wanted him to show her what it felt like to be a woman. Oh, how she wanted that! The touch of his mouth and hand had ignited a fire in her that threatened to consume her.

"If you want me to." But he leaned closer, his mouth descending again until it was a scant inch from her own. Sarah looked up into his eyes and felt as if she were drowning in their shadowed depths. There was a curious roaring in her ears, and her knees felt as if they could no longer support her weight. His thumb moved across her nipple once more, and then back. She moaned involuntarily, her eyes fluttering shut. She forced them open again, knowing that if she closed them she was lost. . . . But the sheer, overpowering attraction of his face so close to her own made her head spin. She bit down hard on her lower lip, trying to muster her spinning senses, trying to fight him—and herself.

"Do you want me to let you go, Sarah?" He was whispering in her ear, his breath warm, teasing. His thumb moved again, finding the hardened bud that quivered at his caress. His hand shifted; he caught her nipple between his thumb and forefinger and gently squeezed it. Sarah felt another shaft of fire shoot through her body like a lightning bolt.

"Yes," she moaned, forcing the word out. She was swaying in his hold, her head thrown back so that the tumbled masses of her hair cascaded over his arm toward the ground. Her eyelids were fluttering first closed, then open as her body warred with her mind. He started to remove his hand, slowly. She felt the withdrawal of that tingling warmth like a physical pain. Her flesh ached for the return of his touch. . . . "No," she whispered, surrendering.

Before she could stop herself, her hand caught his where it hovered just over her breast without touching it, and pressed it wantonly back against her starving flesh. At the indescribable pleasure of that possessing hand, she sucked in her breath. Her eyes closed momentarily; her knees felt weak, and she swayed closer to the solid strength of him. He made no move; even his hand was still on her breast. Her eyes opened again to find that he was watching her, his eyes narrowed. She stared up at him, her own eyes glazed, watching him watch her, knowing that her behavior was utterly shameless but too drunk with passion to care. Tonight she was just a woman like any other woman, and he was just a man. Her woman's body craved the maleness of him like a thirsty man craved water in the desert. And of its own volition her body was letting him know of her need. Her nipple was pebble-hard against the cupped palm of his hand; she knew he had to feel it, know the eagerness it signaled. He also could not miss the quick, hot indrawing of her breath, or the trembling of her limbs, or the sultry glow of passion that she knew must be suffusing her face, lighting her eyes. . . . He was still watching her, unmoving. With a wordless whimper, her hand left his and, with its fellow, crept around his neck. Blindly she lifted her face toward his, seeking his kiss, her eyes closed. For once she would let her senses, not reason, rule her. For once she would allow herself to be weak and silly and feminine—all the things she usually despised. Gallagher's arms around her, his mouth on hers, his hand on her body made her a traitor to the self she had always known. It was as if someone totally different inhabited her body—just for tonight.

"Are you sure, Sarah?" Sarah quivered at the tenderness she thought she heard in his voice. She kept her eyes tightly shut; to open them would be to invite an end to the rapture that held her in thrall. She was no longer a plain, prim old maid, but a woman, desired and desiring—just for tonight.

She lifted her face to his again in silent assent. He needed no further invitation. His mouth came down on hers again, not roughly but possessively, as though he meant to make it his. She surrendered her lips to him, opened her mouth to him, moaned at the caress of his lips on hers, at the hot wet invasion of his tongue. . . .

His hand no longer held her breast. Sarah arched her back, missing that delicious pressing warmth, moaning shamelessly as she pleaded without words for its return. She heard the quickened thud of his heart against her, felt the world spin as she was picked up off her feet and lowered to the ground. . . . The dry grass made little scratching sounds against the silk of her dress; it prickled against her bare arms. But she could have been lying on the softest of feather beds, for all the notice she took of her surroundings. All she knew was the devastating heat of Gallagher's mouth on hers.

His hand was at her throat. She felt it, vaguely, as it moved down the front of her bodice. The night air caressed her skin in its wake. He was opening her buttons. She should stop him—the thought surfaced again—and for a moment she was on the verge of struggling back into her everyday skin. But then his mouth left hers to trace a burning path down the side of her throat, and she was lost again. In fire and wonder.

"Gallagher." She breathed his name into his hair as he bent his head further, his tongue seeking the throbbing hollow of her throat while his hand continued to free her buttons. His head lifted.

"Dominic," he corrected once more, his voice a hoarse whisper against her mouth. Sarah parted her lips in eager invitation to the warmth hovering so near. When he did not take her mouth, she strained upward, shamelessly seeking his kiss. "Dominic," he whispered again, insistently.

"Dominic," she said, moaning, and was rewarded by the sweet brand of his kiss.

His hand was beneath her now, tugging at the ends of her sash. Then it returned to her throat, parting the silk he had so recently unfastened, baring the skin of her shoulders and the fine white muslin of her chemise. Sarah moved then, finally, catching at his hand in a final, obligatory protest. He bent over her, his breath hot and moist against her cheek.

"Let me take your dress off, Sarah."

The soft words coupled with the husky passion that thickened them made her quiver all over. She *wanted* him to take off her dress. She wet her lips, staring up at him, unable to say the words that would push her irretrievably over the edge. But she let go of his hand. . . . He brushed a quick, soft kiss on her trembling lips, and then his hands returned to their work. Sarah did nothing to hinder him as he pulled the dress off her shoulders and down over her arms. The coolness of the night air against her bare skin was quickly replaced by the scorching heat of his mouth. He pressed tiny kisses along her collar bone and then back across her chest until at last he was kissing just above the prim edge of her chemise where the upper slopes of her breasts rose in gentle swells. Soft sobs of pleasure floated in the air around them; Sarah was vaguely surprised to discover that they came from her own throat. Her eyes stayed tightly shut as he knelt to pull her dress completely off. Through her thin petticoat she felt the material slither

down her thighs. Then his hands were encircling her slim
ankles, lifting her feet. The touch of his fingers on her
insteps as he loosened first one and then the other of the
ribbon bows that held her shoes made her skin tingle.
When he came back to her, it was to press his mouth to
one small, high breast through the fine muslin of her
chemise. Sarah felt the moist heat of his mouth, felt the
rhythmic tugging as he suckled her like a babe through the
thin material, and groaned. Then she couldn't stop. Wanton
little cries of delight rippled from her throat of their own
volition. Her hands clutched at his black hair; her back
arched as she pressed herself to him, on fire with need.
When next he pulled the chemise from her shoulders,
baring her breasts, she quivered with fear and longing
combined, but made no protest. Her hunger for him far
outweighed her instinctive fear. Fiercely, shockingly, she
wanted him to make her naked, to look at her, and touch
her, and love her. . . .

The night air caressed her pink-tipped flesh, teasing the
aching nipples, then was replaced by the blaze of his
mouth. Her arms were around his shoulders, her hands in
his hair, pressing his head tightly against her breasts as he
lay half on, half beside her, his mouth with its lazy
suckling driving her wild. She could feel the weight of his
chest against her bare rib cage. The coarse linen of his
shirt felt slightly abrasive to her skin. She loved the
sensation. Through her haze of pleasure she felt his hands
moving at her waist. Then he was lifting himself away
from her. She moaned, clutching at him, but he put her
hands aside. Quickly, efficiently he stripped away her
petticoat and tossed it aside. With aching satisfaction she
realized that at last she was naked except for the chemise
twisted around her middle and the wisps of her stockings.
The knowledge made her tremble all over. He saw her
convulsive shiver and stroked his hand lightly over her

thighs and then her belly, gentling her, soothing her. She only shivered all the more, loving the hot abrasion of his work-hardened hand. Then he slid the chemise over her hips and down her legs, and she was left wearing only her stockings and lacy white garters. He was kneeling near her feet, the shimmering moon high overhead making him look big and dark and faintly unreal as he sucked in his breath, the sound harsh, ragged against the gentle noises of the night, and his eyes scorched over her breasts and belly and thighs.... Demon lover, she thought before her eyes fluttered shut. He had come to her out of the shadows of the night, and was no more real. Tonight she could surrender her aching, burning flesh to him, let him love her and take her and make her truly a woman. Just for tonight...

Wordlessly she lifted her arms to him, her eyes still tightly closed. He moved then, answering her silent invitation, his large body covering her much slighter one like a blanket of fire. His mouth took hers, ravenous in its passion, blistering her with its heat. His hands were on her breasts, kneading them, caressing the nipples, which stood quivering beneath his touch. Her arms went around his neck as she answered his kiss with sweet, wild desire. His weight was crushing her into the ground. It should have hurt, but the hard heaviness of him was exactly what her body craved. She felt the rasp of his chest hair against her breasts, felt the abrasion of his hair-roughened legs through the fine cotton of her stockings as one knee nudged her thighs apart so that he could lie between them—and only then did she realize that he was naked too. His skin was fiery hot against her, burning her up, incinerating her—and she loved it. She writhed against him in helpless rapture, her legs instinctively parting even more, her breasts pressing boldly up into the thick mat of hair covering his chest. Her hands clenched in his hair as he seared her throat with his lips.

His hand was between their bodies, stroking her breasts, then sliding down to the silky skin of her belly and below, stroking the curling thatch of hair briefly before insinuating itself even farther between her thighs. He touched her then where no one had ever touched her, where she was shy to touch herself, even when she bathed. His fingers slid moistly against her, finding all her unimagined pleasure points, trailing fire in their wake and sending quickening spirals of ecstasy like red-hot whirlwinds over her skin. She arched against those fingers, burning, pulsating, spinning away into a netherworld of shooting flames and bursts of black smoke and red sparks glowing like eyes. . . .

Her head thrashed from side to side, unconscious of the hard ground that pillowed it or the twigs and bits of grass and leaves that tangled in her hair. Her legs were opened wide, slender and pale in their thin white stockings as he lay between them, his thighs burning hers, his hand working its unbelievable magic. Her eyes were closed tightly, her arms locked around the neck of the man who was carrying her away with him. . . . His lips left her throat to take her mouth, and she sighed with ecstasy, drinking in the taste of him. Then his hand that was causing her such exquisite torment left her, to be replaced a scant instant later by a hard, hot shaft that felt enormous and alien and tremendously exciting. . . .

It found her softness, entered her just a little, then stopped. Sarah moaned and writhed at this wonderful new sensation, quivering from head to toe at this slow invasion that was the culmination of every heated caress that had gone before. When it ceased, when he no longer thrust against her in the way that every nerve and bone and sinew told her that he should, she surged to find him, arching shamelessly in the arms which held her clamped to the inferno that was his body.

"God." The word was a ragged prayer, nearly lost in

the rustling of the leaves and grass beneath them and in their ragged breathing. But Sarah heard it, heard the blistering passion it conveyed, and arched again, thrusting her hips against his, pleading with her body for him to answer. He did, gasping, thrusting into her with a surging force that made her cry out.

"Ohhh!" It hurt. There was a sharp stinging between her legs as he filled her, imbedding himself deep inside her. She stiffened, and her eyes flew open. He was not moving now, but lay heavily across her while his breathing sounded like a dying man's in her ears. For a long moment he lay like that while her hands clutched at his sweat-damp shoulders, and she tried to decide whether to push him away; but then he braced himself up on his arms, lifting his head so that he could look down at her. His face was flushed, his eyes dark with passion. A faint tremor shook those bracing arms.

"Are you—all right?" It was a husky whisper.

Sarah stared up into that handsome face, saw the concern mixed with the heady desire in his midnight-blue eyes, felt the effort that he was exerting to hold his need in check. Her hands moved then, of their own volition, to caress and then clutch his shoulders.

"Yes," she whispered. She could feel the part of him that still possessed her throbbing and burning inside her, and didn't know if she was lying or telling the truth. All she knew was that, having come so far, she could not stop. Not now.

"Ahhh, Sarah." The words were almost a groan.

Sarah stared into that dark face and felt something hot and urgent begin to clamor again inside her. Her hands slid from his shoulders over the sweat-dampened pelt of hair on his chest, rubbing over his flat nipples with a kind of sensual delight before suddenly, fiercely digging into the rigid wall of muscle that was his chest.

"Sweet Jesus!" He stiffened for an instant, his eyes closing, his lips clenching as if in pain. Then, as if he couldn't help himself, he began to move. He lowered himself upon her, his mouth finding hers and taking it with hot, drugging urgency while she clung to him and trembled and quaked.

The hot, slick strokes that made her his were like nothing she had ever experienced. The pain was gone now, and there was nothing but pleasure, a dark, secret pleasure such as she had never felt before, had never dreamed she could feel. She wanted it to go on and on and on. . . . He was arching over her, his hips moving in and out in a hot, urgent rhythm, and she was moving with him, her arms and legs clutching him, her hips undulating in an answering rhythm that seemed to drive him wild. His arms were tight around her, crushing her to him in a hold that should have hurt but didn't because she was beyond feeling it, was beyond feeling anything but the fiery bursting ecstasy that was exploding inside her.

"Oh, Dominic, oh, oh, oh, Dominic!" The cry and the accompanying stiffening of her body seemed to drive him to a sudden frenzy. He plunged into her fiercely, grinding her into the unyielding ground as he panted and groaned above her and his sweat fused them like red-hot lava. She clung to him, shuddering, as he found his own ecstasy. Finally he groaned, thrusting into her savagely one last time, holding himself inside her as he stiffened and shuddered. Then he too was still.

For long minutes they lay fused together, unmoving, the ragged tempo of their breathing as it evened and slowed the only sounds they made. Slowly, reluctantly, Sarah became aware again. Aware of the feel of the prickly ground beneath her bare backside, aware of the sound of the wind in the leaves overhead, aware of the cold white face of the moon that stared down at her with such icy disdain. Even more reluctantly, she acknowledged the fact that she was naked, lying sprawled upon the ground with a sweaty, still-panting man lying heavily across her. A naked man who still possessed her body. A *convict* . . .

Sarah felt sudden nausea rise in her throat. She lay staring up sightlessly at the star-studded sky, while sick horror began to clutch at her stomach and make her shiver.

"Dear God." The words replayed themselves over and over again in her brain in an endless litany of regret. "Oh, dear God, what have I done?"

X

"You're crushing me." Sarah managed to force out the words a long time later. He still lay sprawled across her, crushing her as she had said, his body hot and wet and abrasive against hers, his breath searing her neck. The part of him that had caused first her pleasure and then her shame still possessed her; she could feel it slowly ebbing between her thighs. His arms were hard around her and his black head was buried in the curve between her shoulder and her neck. She shuddered with distaste.

He didn't move for a long moment after she had spoken; then, at last, he lifted his head. Sarah wanted to close her eyes in shame as his raked her face. But proudly she met his gaze with a bitter stare. He frowned, looking down at her. His arms shifted, and one hand came up to smooth the tangled strands of her hair away from her face. She jerked away from his touch.

"Take your hands off me!"

His frown deepened. His blue eyes darkened and turned

cloudy. Despite her words, his hand returned to her face to be joined by its fellow as he cupped her cheeks, his expression grave as he stared down at her face, studying it.

"Sarah . . ."

"Don't call me that! I'm *Miss* Sarah to you! Oh, will you let me up?" She was suddenly, ragingly angry at him. Sarah welcomed the feeling as an antidote to the utter shame that threatened to overwhelm her. What had she done? How could she have allowed him to . . . to . . . ? The strength returned to her arms. She shoved furiously at the wide shoulders that loomed over her, blocking out the moon.

"Certainly. *Miss* Sarah."

He rolled away from her, coming easily to his feet, standing with his legs apart and his hands balled into fists on his hips as he towered above her. He was naked, the moonlight silvering the hard planes and muscles of his body, hiding nothing. Before, Sarah had been too caught up in her dream world to notice how he looked naked. Now, she could not look away. Her stomach heaved as she absorbed the broad shoulders and powerful chest, the narrow waist and hips, the abdomen that she knew was as hard and unyielding as a board, the long, well-muscled legs—and that *thing* that hung between them. It still looked huge, even semilimp. . . . Sarah shuddered. Everything about him repulsed her now, from the thick black whorls of hair that formed a wedge on his chest and tapered down to trail across his belly before widening again to form a bushy nest around that obscene proof of his maleness, to the muscles bulging in his arms as they angled away from his body, even to the too-beautiful face. Like the rest of him, it was too uncompromisingly male. It made her sick to her stomach. . . .

With a start, she realized that his eyes were moving over her body just as hers had moved over his. She looked hastily down at herself, feeling fiery color creep up her neck as she realized how very wanton she must look, long, slim, pale legs, still clad in her white stockings and garters, sprawled apart, tawny strands of hair cascading down over her shoulders past her waist to tangle with the only slightly darker triangle of curls between her thighs, her belly and the small, tip-tilted mounds of her breasts glistening with his sweat. She scrambled into a crouching position, swinging her hair forward, intent on hiding as much as she could from him as she groped for the clothes that he had flung aside as he had pulled them from her body. Her chemise was crumpled and stained with earth, but she pulled it thankfully over her head as soon as it came to hand. Then she reached for her petticoat, only to find his hand there before hers, snatching it out of her reach.

"Look at me." His voice was ominous.

Sarah, still crouching, feeling almost as indecent in her near-transparent chemise as she had moments earlier when she had been naked, needed no encouragement to glare at him. His unabashed nakedness as he stood there glowering down at her, her white petticoat dangling from his hand, made her cringe.

"For God's sake, put on your clothes," she muttered, averting her eyes.

He swore, the oath succinct and so profane that it fairly blistered Sarah's ears. Then her petticoat came fluttering into her line of vision as he flung it to the ground. Before she could register his intention, he was crouching before her, his hand rough as it caught her chin and jerked her face around so that her eyes met his.

"I'll be damned before I'll apologize." He sounded as angry as she felt.

She matched him glare for glare, refusing to shrink away as her every instinct urged her to. He had stripped her of every vestige of virtue she had felt she possessed; she would not let him steal what few tatters remained of her pride.

"Have I asked you to? Take your hand off me!"

His eyes narrowed. "It's a little late for that now, isn't it?" The words were a cruel taunt. Inwardly Sarah flinched; outwardly her eyes flashed at him, golden with scorn.

"I said take your hand off me!" The words were hissed from between her teeth, deadly with the cold superiority of a mistress to her servant. As it registered, his eyes narrowed until they were mere slits, and his mouth compressed into a savage line.

"Don't take that tone with me, you haughty little bitch! You wanted my hand on you badly enough earlier, remember? You wanted everything I did to you! You were hot for it, you liked it—so what the hell's the matter with you now?"

He was speaking through his teeth just as she was, rage darkening his face so that he really did resemble the devil. Her fingers itched to slap him with every bit of strength she possessed; but instinctively she knew that if she did, it would snap the tight rein that kept his temper under control. He was far bigger than she, far stronger. . . . Clutching at the shreds of her dignity, Sarah met the fire in his eyes with ice in her own.

"I made a mistake."

Rage flared brighter in his eyes. The hand holding her chin tightened painfully. Sarah tried to pull away, but he held her fast.

"You sure as hell did, lady. Now that I've scratched your itch for you, you've remembered that I'm a *convict*. That's what this little farce is all about, isn't it?"

She winced, both from his deliberate crudeness and the accuracy of his guess, and refused to answer; her eyes wavered and fell before the savage light in his.

He swore again, his expression ugly, and practically threw her chin away from him. Standing, he snatched up her clothes and flung them at her.

"Get dressed and get out of my sight," he growled.

Sarah thought about snapping that she didn't take orders from him, but his words coincided so exactly with her own desires that she quickly scrambled into her clothes. Her fingers were clumsy as she knotted the ties to her petticoat; they fumbled as she tried to do up the buttons of her dress, only to find when she was done that she had missed one and had to go back and do it over again. Hopping from one foot to the other as she slid her slippers on her feet, she started to move away almost before the second sole hit the ground. Gallagher's hand on her arm stopped her. She whirled to face him, her hand flying up to knock his away. He had made no move to don his own clothes, she saw. His unabashed nakedness made bile rise in her throat.

"Your hair." The words were thick with dislike.

"Don't you dare put your hand on me again, you . . . !" she raged, too angry to listen to his words, or to come up with an epithet to adequately describe how she loathed him. He grabbed her arm again, his grip cruel. She tried futilely to pull away from him, wincing at the force with which his fingers dug into her soft flesh.

"Put up your damned hair: you look like you've been rolling around on the ground with a man—which, of course, you have."

"What do you care?"

"I think we'd both agree that what happened out here tonight is best kept between ourselves. Sweet Jesus, do you want everyone in there to know you lost your virtue— *to a convict*?" He bit the last words out at her.

"I'll go up the back stairs: no one will see me." Sarah ignored the savage taunt, wild to get away from him before her rage reverted again to shame and she disgraced herself

by breaking down completely. She could feel hysterical
tears dangerously near the surface.

"I'm not willing to take that chance," he said. Hauling
her to him by his hand on her arm, he raked his fingers
through the tangled thickness of her hair, not caring that he
was hurting her, oblivious to the tears that stood in her
eyes as he searched for the hairpins that still clung to the
heavy strands. When he had several between his teeth, he
turned her so that her back was to him. He had to let go of
her arm to gather up her hair. It was a task that needed
both hands. Sarah immediately lunged forward, desperate
to escape. He caught her by her hair, jerking brutally to
bring her back to where he wanted her.

"Stand still," he growled at her. Then, as she made one
final, abortive movement, he jerked at her hair again.
"Stand still, damn you, or..."

He never said what he would do, but Sarah found that
she didn't want to know. Fury emanated from him in
waves, reminding her suddenly that, despite what had
transpired between them tonight, she didn't know him at
all. Except for the fact that he was a convict. She could
well believe him guilty of the most vicious of crimes, she
thought, shuddering. Deadly menace was in his hands and
his voice as he twisted her hair into its customary knot at
her nape. The one glimpse she had had of his eyes
frightened her. He looked on the verge of violence.

"Now get out of my sight," he muttered when he was
done.

Sarah wasted no time in obeying him. She flew through
the trees toward the house as fast as her feet would carry
her, running as though the devil himself were at her heels.
All around her moonlight shimmered, and the hot wind
caressed her skin as his hands had earlier. Sarah shuddered
at the comparison, forcing herself to slow her headlong
pace as she neared the house. Every window was lit,

reminding her of the party still in progress. Voices floated to her ears, and laughter, and the clink of glasses. Music swirled out to surround her. The haunting strains made her catch her breath. With a choked little laugh, she recognized the lilting melody that, just an hour before, had so betrayed her.

XI

Dominic watched her go, watched the tall slim shape of her skimming over the rough ground like a ghost as her white dress billowed behind her and shimmered in the moonlight. He cursed again, viciously. What the sweet bloody hell had happened? He'd taken the little bitch with more tenderness and care than he had ever before lavished on a woman, given her a woman's supreme pleasure—he knew damned well he had!—and as soon as the throes of rapture had passed she had been sick to death with shame because she considered him so far beneath her. She *owned* him, he reminded himself with savage mockery. And tonight she had gotten her money's worth with a vengeance. His performance had been pretty damned good for a paid stud, if he did say so himself. He had given her ecstasy, only to have her treat him afterward like a leper. She had *used* him. The thought made him grind his teeth. Usually it was he who used women—he had never expected the tables to be turned as they were now. Maybe it was rough justice, but he didn't like it one damned bit.

Tonight, when he had first seen Sarah standing in the moonlight, it had entered his mind that this might be the best chance he would ever get to make love to her. He'd known that persuading her into it would not be all that difficult, despite the maddening air of prim propriety that she wore like a cloak. Enough women had been attracted to him over the years for him to recognize the signs. She wanted him, no matter how hard she tried to disguise the fact. Tonight he had simply decided that, if he could, he would give her what she wanted.

Three days ago, when he had first kissed her, he had been astounded at the shaft of desire that had hardened all his muscles, but he had decided that it was an aberration. He couldn't possibly be taken with a female shaped more like a boy than a woman, with an adder's tongue to boot and a damned uppity way about her that made him long to strangle her at least half the time. No woman had ever given him orders before, or spoken to him like a servant and eyed him with condescension mixed with, yes, dammit, with pity. It enraged him. He had not yet gotten used to having come so far down in the world. Tonight he had meant to turn the tables on her, to make himself her master, to reduce her to a clinging supplicant in his arms. He had thought he could take her body and walk away triumphant, knowing that she had been humbled as she had been part of his humiliation. But, from the beginning, everything had gone wrong.

To start with, she was no prim old maid. When they had danced and she had laughed and her hair had tumbled down, she had charmed him utterly. When he had kissed her, the strength of his own wanting had caught him by surprise. And then, when he'd done more, he had discovered to his bedazzled enjoyment that beneath that proper manner, those unattractive clothes and that awful bun, was a woman as wild as any he'd bedded. She had been on fire for him, quivering in his arms, begging him to take her with her mouth and body and hands... until he had obliged. He had hesitated even then, feeling some faint inkling through the throbbing lust that drove him that something was not right, he was being drawn in too deep, deeper than he had ever been before. When he had felt her maidenhead, he had almost pulled back. Now he wished to God he had.

He had found her lovely. Dominic laughed harshly. Was it possible that, all unknowing, he preferred boys? he asked himself sardonically. Every woman he had had before had been lushly endowed, flauntingly female with full white breasts and an ample behind. Yet, none of their bodies had fired his senses as Sarah's had tonight. Her slim body, gleaming pale in the moonlight, had been so sleek and supple under his hands; her small breasts with their dusky rose nipples so enticingly virginal; her hips so slight, her bottom so firm and round, as taut and smooth as any boy's. Her long, slender, curving legs and tiny waist were the only truly feminine things about her. Except, of course, for the satin of her skin; the softness of her mouth; her huge golden eyes; the silken masses of sun-shot hair... and her passion. That was all woman, and it had shaken him to the core.

His possession of her body had, at the end, been frenzied. He had meant to spin it out, to bring her to that ecstasy again and again and again before succumbing to his own pleasure. But, to his amazement, he hadn't been able to wait. He had been so damned hot for her.... Unwillingly he remembered how she had felt beneath him, how soft yet resilient her body was, how sweet her breasts had tasted, how hot and wet that woman part of her had been for him, and felt himself hardening again. He muttered a single, succinct profanity, then forced the memory from his mind. But her face as it had looked afterward, pale and sick with shame, would not be banished. Those huge golden eyes filled with loathing as they stared at him would, he feared, haunt him to his grave.

Of course, she was ashamed. Leaving aside the fact that he was a convict, she had just given up her virginity outside the bonds of matrimony. Reluctantly he acknowledged that, for a lady such as Sarah, that was bound to be traumatic. But he knew too that a good part of her distress was due to the fact that she considered him so far beneath her. That thought still enraged him. But now, as the first hot blast of his temper cooled, he realized that that was a fact of his life that he would have to accept—at least for the present. He didn't like Sarah's reaction, but losing his temper and frightening her had not helped the situation. He should have expected and tried to reason away her distress, soothing her shame and revulsion with soft words and softer kisses. He would have done that as a common courtesy with any virgin he took; in such cases, a certain amount of agitation was expected. But with Sarah . . . Dammit, why was his reaction to her so different from his reaction to any other woman? What was it about her?

The cream of the jest was that, by taking her, he had meant to turn the tables, to own her where she had previously owned him. What he had not counted on was that, by the very act of possessing her, she had in some unfathomable way managed equally to possess him.

When he had first been arrested and tossed into jail, he had not been able to believe that they could make the charge stick. When they had, first to his fury and then to his fright, he had vowed that he would be a prisoner only for as long as it would take him to escape. Learning that he had been sentenced to transportation to Australia, of all ungodly places, to serve fifteen years—fifteen years!—at hard labor for a crime he had not committed, he had been stunned. But then it had occurred to him that it would be even easier to escape from a prison without walls. He would be back, he vowed, to confront those who had declared themselves his enemy. And soon. But that was before he had endured those eight hellish months on the prison ship, before he had been chained and starved and beaten. . . .

When the ship had docked in Melbourne and the convicts had been herded up on deck to be washed down with buckets of sea water thrown over their heads so that their filth would not disgust their new owners, he had been able to stand it no longer. After all those weeks cooped up in a dark hold filled with men more sick than well and their sweat, their vomit, their excrement; the brilliant sunlight glinting off the sea; the warm, fresh air, after months of being damp and cold; even the birds wheeling overhead, beautiful birds, red-winged parrots, lorikeets in a rainbow of colors, yellow-crested cockatoos—how he had envied them!—had driven him temporarily out of his head. He had throttled the guard nearest him, not caring if he killed the man, and run for the side, meaning to dive over, into the sea. They had caught him, of course; but, since a landowner had paid good money for him and they didn't want to damage the merchandise, he had thought that despite everything he would be let off with just a few kicks and blows. But then Edward Markham had refused to take him. . . . Deprived of his double profit, Captain Farley had turned nasty. There was not the slightest doubt in his mind that the captain would at that point have honored the terms of his original agreement with those in England who wished Dominic Gallagher ill. He had not been meant to survive the voyage, Dominic knew. He shuddered, remembering how they had stripped off his shirt and bound him to the mast, recalling in excruciating detail the soul-destroying agony of the blows. . . .

Sarah had saved his life. He had been only half-conscious, but he had heard that soft voice, unmistakably female, as she came to his rescue, placing herself between him and the whip with a courage that had fascinated him at the time—most females would have screamed, or swooned, and turned away from the horror instead of defying an entire crew of hardened sea-dogs for the sake of a wretched stranger. When they had, at her insistence, cut him free, he had wanted to go down on his knees to her to thank her for saving his life, which he had been surprised to discover that, despite everything, he still valued. And he had hated her for making him feel that way. Nearly all his growing-up years he had been beholden to someone who begrudged even the food he ate. When he had reached sixteen, he had vowed that he would never again allow anyone to put him in a position where he was in their debt. Sarah had; and it galled him every time he thought about it.

Despite the fact that he owed Sarah his life, even as he was being half-carried, half-dragged from the *Septimus* he was already promising himself that he would escape as soon as he could. He would not spend the next fifteen years of his life as a slave! The idea unnerved him far more than the little speech that Sarah's damned overseer had made to him and the other newly arrived convicts about the consequences of trying to run. Regardless of how many men or dogs they put on his trail, run he would—but first he had to wait until his back healed and he had regained his strength enough that he could survive off the land in a country he did not know. And if he gave the appearance of docility for the first month or two, he calculated, they would be less likely to suspect when he did run, and that lack of suspicion might buy him time.

But then there was Sarah. She had attracted him from the beginning, first by the spirit he could only admire, by the very self-possession that had maddened him at the same time as it attracted him. Then, when he had seen past the dowdy clothes and hairstyle and old-maid manner, by the elusive beauty that was absent far more often than it was present. From the beginning, he had been conscious of a desire to strip away the layers of propriety in which she buried herself to see if the woman beneath could possibly be as fascinating as he half-hoped, half-feared she would be.

He might as well face facts, Dominic told himself grimly. For some days now he had felt well enough to run. They were no longer watching him so closely, and living off the land was not going to get any easier for being put off. But, despite his growing hunger for freedom, he had stayed at Lowella, doing Sarah's bidding although her bossy ways annoyed him, simply because he was not yet ready to see the last of her. Tonight, even, he had been thinking about leaving, just walking away. There was nothing to stop him, and with so many guests he doubted that he would even be missed before late tomorrow. But then he had seen Sarah standing under the trees. . . .

He could go now, he thought, reluctant to recognize the opportunity. Then he thought of Sarah, naked, passionate, clinging, of the priceless gift she had offered him and that he had taken, and of her anger—and her shame. And he knew that he would not go yet.

Sarah awoke slowly the next morning in her attic bed-room. Something lingered at the edge of her mind, some-thing that she knew she would have to face with the coming of the day. Something so unpleasant that she was doing her very best to block it from her consciousness. Then, there it was. Last night she had allowed Gallagher to make love to her. Remembering, Sarah felt her stomach heave. For a moment she was afraid that she might actually vomit. Then, slowly, her stomach settled—but her mind did not. It tormented her with graphic images of her degradation.

He was a convict. That fact stood out above all the others. Far, far better that she had given herself to Percival, or to young Michael Argers all those years ago, or to anyone—but a convict. She shuddered at the thought. She had shamed herself beyond redemption. How could she have done such a thing? To have let him take her virginity— she must have been mad. She thought of herself naked in his arms, allowing him—no, begging him—to do things to her body that made her go crimson with mortification even now, remembering. Just for tonight, she had thought. Well, morning had dawned with a vengeance. And brought with it a terrible price.

Would he tell anyone? Sarah was ashamed that this was one of her main concerns, but she couldn't help it. She would want to die if anyone knew. She thought of Lydia's malicious enjoyment, Liza's shock, her father's horror, Percival's rage—at least, she thought with a hysterical laugh, it was unlikely that he would still want to marry her, if he knew—the disgust of her friends and neighbors; she knew she wouldn't be able to bear it. Her father would be within his rights to cast her out, though she didn't think he would. But she would go, nonetheless. She wouldn't be able to endure the humiliation.

But then Sarah realized that it would be as much as his life was worth to betray her. She would face public scorn if what had happened between them should ever become common knowledge; he would face far worse. She had not a doubt that her father would have him killed if he knew the truth. And Gallagher—she seemed to hear her own voice calling him Dominic and felt the bile rise again in her throat—must know it, too.

That worry reduced to nothing more than a niggle, she was left with another, major one: How could she ever face Gallagher again? Sarah thought of what he had done to her, what she had allowed him to do, wanted him to do, and reveled in the doing—and had her answer: she couldn't.

But she would have to. There was no way around that. At least not for a while. Later, if the situation became as intolerable as she feared it might, she likely could talk her father into trading Gallagher to some other grazier. Unless Gallagher objected—all he would have to do was to threaten to talk, and her hand would be stayed. Which he would be a fool to do—but once he was out from under her father's authority, what would prevent him from saying anything he pleased? He could blacken her name for the sheer vindictiveness of it, and get off scot-free.

Sarah reluctantly concluded that Gallagher would have to remain on Lowella. Only then could she be certain that he would keep their guilty secret to himself. Which left her with the prospect of living in close proximity to him for the next fifteen years, seeing his intimate knowledge of her in his eyes every time he looked at her, having to stomach his insolence, or whatever else he might care to inflict on her, for fear that he would talk.

It did not bear thinking about. Agitated, Sarah swung her legs over the side of the narrow bed and stood up. If she did not put it out of her mind, for just a little while at least, she really would go mad. What had happened was like a nightmare come true.

Sarah walked toward the bowl and pitcher that stood in one corner of the room, meaning to splash her face with

cold water in hopes that it would rid her stomach of the
horrible queasiness that still threatened. She had reached
the basin when her eye fell on a crumpled heap of white
silk peeking out from beneath the bed. Her dress—last
night she had stripped it off with shaking hands and
kicked it and her underclothes away, wanting never to see
them again, even as scraps for the rag bag; she would
throw them away. And with the dress, nearly hidden by
the folds of white silk that still glistened virginally, was
the towel she had used to clean her virgin's blood from
her thighs. She could see the brown stains clearly. . . . Sarah
barely managed to snatch up the basin before she
vomited.

A long time later, she dragged herself up from the floor
and made herself wash and dress. It would do no good to
dwell on her shame. It had happened, and it was over. She
would do her best to put it out of her mind. If Gallagher
had to be faced down, then she would face him. And she
would act as though nothing had happened. Her humiliation would be increased tenfold if he were to realize how
very sickened she was by her own behavior. And it was
her own behavior that made her feel so ill. He had done
nothing more or less than she should have expected. He
was a man, after all, and a convict; what moral standards
could he have? But she—before last night, she would have
called herself a lady.

Sarah felt her stomach heave again, and resolutely
forced herself to concentrate on getting dressed. If she
chose her most unattractive dress—a pale gray poplin that
was almost four years old and had faded to a noncolor
from repeated washings—it was simply because it was the
nearest to hand in the tall wardrobe. If she scraped her hair
back from her face so severely that it tugged at the edges
of her scalp, and wound it into a bun so tight that it would
take a whirlwind to blast it free, it was simply because the

heat made meandering strands uncomfortable. And if there were dark circles under her eyes, making them look huge and almost bruised, and if her skin was pale and drawn so that her cheekbones were emphasized by the hollows beneath them, well, she was not getting any younger. It was no more than that.

Sarah winced a little as she descended the stairs, not expecting the soreness between her thighs. She felt as she had once, long ago, when she had been learning to ride and had unwisely ridden for miles. It was that same kind of tenderness. And from a similar cause, she thought bitterly. Only this time, instead of being the rider, she had been the mount. . . . She banished that thought from her mind almost as soon as it appeared. Forcing herself to walk normally despite the discomfort, she entered the kitchen.

Tess and Mary were washing and drying the many dirty dishes stacked on the kitchen table. Mrs. Abbott was nowhere in sight, but Sarah knew, from the savory smells emanating from the bubbling kettles atop the iron stove, that she was not far away. The two girls smiled at Sarah and bobbed a greeting, too shy despite their several years' service on Lowella to speak without cause. Sarah smiled back, though it cost her an effort; she was determined to behave as naturally as if last night had never happened. She was helping herself to a piece of what was left of Liza's birthday cake when Mrs. Abbott bustled in from the door leading into the garden, her apron filled with vegetables.

"G' morning, Miss Sarah," Mrs. Abbott said comfortably, emptying her burden on a cleared space at the far end of the table and sorting through the tumbled vegetables with her hands. "Last night's carryings-on must have tired you out. I've never known you to sleep so late."

Sarah tensed, giving the older woman a wide-eyed look, afraid of the meaning that might be hidden in the seemingly innocuous words. But Mrs. Abbott was examining her vegetables with a frown, serenely unconscious of having caused Sarah any distress.

"I was tired," Sarah acknowledged, hoping that her voice did not sound as thin to Mrs. Abbott as it did to her own ears. "Where—where is everyone?"

Is Gallagher around? she was screaming inside. But of course he wouldn't be. Percival had sent him to tend the horses—something that he showed marked aptitude for—while Lowella had guests. He would have no business up at the house—unless Mrs. Abbott meant to slip him in for a bite of breakfast. But of course it was long past time for breakfast.

"Well," Mrs. Abbott said, tapping her forefinger against her front tooth thoughtfully, her attention still focused on the vegetables, "Mr. Percival came by a couple of hours ago to get your pa. Seems that somebody set a fire in one of the fields; the men working there got it out all right, but Mr. Percival thought your pa should have a look at it anyways. Mrs. Markham is still abed, so far as I know. Leastways, I 'aven't seen her. Miss Liza is, too, and so are the other ladies, except for Mrs. Grainger and Mrs. Eaton, who are sittin' on the front porch; I'm to take them some tea presently. The Taylors and the Crowells 'ave already started for 'ome; asked me to make their good-byes for them; said you'd all understand, since they 'ave a long way to go." She looked up then, smiling broadly. "Did I leave anybody out?"

Sarah shook her head, smiling too. "I don't think so." Where's Gallagher? she wanted to demand, but she couldn't. The last thing she wanted was to create curiosity where none existed.

"What are you wantin' for breakfast?" Mrs. Abbott inquired, pulling a chair up to the table and sitting down, paring knife in hand, to start on the vegetables. "There's porridge left, and some cold mutton—I could fry it up for you. Or there's some fig jelly left, and fresh bread.''

Sarah shook her head. "I've already eaten a piece of Liza's cake. I don't want anything else.''

Mrs. Abbott frowned. "Miss Sarah . . .''

"I know, I know, I'm too thin, I should eat. But I'm not hungry. I think I'll go for a ride.'' And with that she escaped out the door into the garden. Just at the moment, she didn't think she could tolerate Mrs. Abbott's well-meant criticism of her appearance.

Going for a ride had been the furthest thing from her mind when she said it; it had merely been an excuse to leave the kitchen before the thin shell of her composure cracked and she snapped at Mrs. Abbott, or the maids, or anyone else who ventured near, as a means of releasing the tension that still had her stomach tied up in knots. But, thinking about how wonderful it would feel to get away from the homestead for a while, to put aside her troubles in the sheer joy of having a horse beneath her and the endless miles of bush spread out before her, she suddenly longed to ride. Before the drought, she had been used to riding every day. The heat had made her think of Malahky's well-being before her own enjoyment, and she had stopped riding so frequently. But the urge was back, and she would answer it—except for one difficulty. Gallagher would be in the stable. She winced at the thought of coming face to face with him so soon. Later, when she had had time to put what had happened out of her mind . . . But would waiting really make any difference? Sarah asked herself. The truth was that she never wanted to see Gallagher again. And equally true was the fact that she would not be able to avoid it. How she dreaded the encounter! She knew the dread wasn't likely to go away. It would haunt her constantly, limiting her movements for fear that she would run into Gallagher. She couldn't live like that, constantly on edge. Sarah knew it, and, reluctantly, came to the conclusion that there was only one thing to do about it. She would have to face Gallagher as soon as possible and get it behind her. The longer she put it off, the harder it would get, until she became a prisoner of her own embarrassment.

Now was always the best time for doing something distasteful. Her father had said that many times. Sarah grimaced, the words replaying in her brain, as she stopped momentarily at the edge of the kitchen garden and stared at the whitewashed walls of the stable as David might once have stared at Goliath. She had to battle a strong impulse to return to the house. But the ordeal would not get any easier for postponing it. Squaring her shoulders, she walked deliberately toward the stable. She would lay the groundwork for her future relationship with Gallagher by behaving as though nothing, absolutely nothing, had happened between them. She was the mistress of Lowella, he a convict laborer. It was time to get that clear between them.

It was dark in the stable after the brilliance of the light outside. Sarah hesitated in the wide doorway, one hand on the edge of the open door. Try as she would, she could not make out Gallagher's tall form. . . .

"Goin' for a ride, Miss Sarah?" The voice was not Gallagher's. Sarah nearly fainted with relief. She had not realized how flimsy her courage was, or how much effort it had cost her to summon it for this confrontation, until she found that she no longer needed it. She let out her breath in a long, shaky sigh. Her knees trembled. Percival must have decided that Gallagher was now well enough to do the labor he had originally been meant to do and assigned him to one of the convict work gangs that were digging for water on the range.

"Yes, Jagger, I am. Would you please saddle Malahky

for me?'' Her voice sounded almost gay, she was so giddy with relief.

"Sure thing, Miss Sarah." Jagger's dark face creased in a broad grin as he hurried to do her bidding. He had lived and worked on Lowella for as long as Sarah could remember. Like most of the other aborigines, he would occasionally disappear for a few months—"gone walkabout"— they called it, but he always came back. The aborigines had trouble staying in one place for too long, but Lowella was his home.

"Uh—what happened to the convict who was taking care of the horses while you helped with the digging?" She hadn't meant to ask that, but the words forced themselves to the surface. She had to know if she was safe from running into Gallagher for hours, or days, or even weeks, if Percival had sent him out to join the men digging on the farthest edge of the property. This part of Australia required approximately one acre to support each sheep, and Lowella had thirty thousand sheep. If Gallagher was working near the station's perimeter, he would be camping out with the others because it took too much time to ride back and forth each day. She might not set eyes on him for quite some time. No matter what she had told herself about the virtues of getting unpleasant tasks out of the way, she could not suppress the bubbling sense of having been reprieved.

"Oh, he's . . ." Jagger began.

"Here, Miss Sarah," Gallagher said with an edge of mockery.

Sarah felt as if a huge fist had just made contact with her stomach. Turning slowly in the direction of that distinctive lilt—it had come from one of the stalls—Sarah found to her dismay that her courage had quite deserted her. He stood in the stall beside Master, a big roan, pitchfork in hand and sweat glistening on the bronze planes of his face. His black hair was wildly mussed; it formed deep waves all over his head. His mouth was set in a controlled line, and his eyes—she was almost afraid to meet those blue eyes—were unreadable. Sarah stared at him, unspeaking. She had not been prepared for this. She felt sick, dizzy. To her horror, she was completely unable to speak.

"Did you want me for something, Miss Sarah?" Despite the glint in his eyes, the words were respectful, Sarah supposed for Jagger's benefit. The smaller man was in the process of saddling Malahky. His cocoa-brown eyes, flickering from one to the other of them, were only casually interested. Sarah knew that she would have to get hold of herself before his interest became more than casual. The aborigines loved to gossip.

"Not—really." Sarah forced the words out. "I just wondered where you were. You can go back to work now, Gallagher."

Instead of taking her words as dismissal, Gallagher opened the stall door and stepped out. His height and breadth were intimidating. Sarah gritted her teeth and put up her chin. This was far, far worse than she had expected. All she wanted was to find a hole and crawl into it and quietly die of mortification. The memory of this man's hands and mouth on her body made her want to cringe. But she looked at him steadily, hoping he couldn't read her feelings in her eyes.

"Thank you, Jagger." Malahky was ready, and Jagger had chosen that moment to lead him forward. Sarah could have kissed his frizzy hair. Not looking at Gallagher, she put her foot in Jagger's cupped hands as he stood half-stooped, waiting to help her mount.

"If you'll hold there a moment, Miss Sarah, I'll saddle Max as quickly as I can." Gallagher's tone was still as respectful as she could have wished. Sarah eyed him as he deliberately set the pitchfork, tines up, against a wall and moved to the tack room, where he extracted a saddle and bridle, slinging the bridle over his shoulder and carrying the heavy saddle negligently with one arm. While his back was to her, Sarah noticed that the white linen between his shoulder blades was wet with sweat. She shuddered. The sight was so rawly masculine that it made her stomach quiver.

"There's no need for that." Sarah tried to speak crisply as he led Max from his stall. Jagger had handed her her reins and was adjusting her stirrup for her. Inwardly Sarah screamed for him to hurry. She had to get away from Gallagher, or disgrace herself by being sick. . . . "I don't need you to accompany me. You can go back to whatever work you were doing."

"Your father asked me to keep an eye on you when you're away from the house. It'll just take a moment for me to be ready. Miss Sarah." He didn't even look at her as he spoke.

"I tell you it's not necessary. I am quite accustomed to riding alone. Isn't that so, Jagger?" He was fiddling with the stirrup strap, raising it one notch and then another, so slowly that Sarah had to fight an urge to kick him.

"Yes, miss, it sure is. Miss Sarah is one bruisin' rider." This was addressed to Gallagher, who didn't even bother to grunt in reply. He had tossed the saddle on Max's back and was reaching under the horse's belly for the girth. As he had promised, it would be no time at all before he was ready to go.

Sarah panicked. She slipped her foot into the stirrup, not caring whether it was the right length, and gestured at Jagger to stand back. He did. Sarah touched her heel to Malahky's side, and the animal trotted out of the stable. Behind her she heard Gallagher's angry shout. Thus spurred, she put her heel to Malahky's side again and urged him into a fast canter despite the heat. She rode straight for the orchard, knowing that once the trees stood between her and the stable there was no way Gallagher could follow her. He was not familiar with the countryside and would have no idea which way she had gone.

By the time an hour had passed, it occurred to Sarah that she had only delayed the inevitable. Gallagher would still be waiting in the stable when she returned. It was ridiculous to feel nervous at the idea of confronting a convict, but she did. Nervous and embarrassed and so on edge that she wanted to scream from tension.

When two hours had passed, Sarah knew that she could delay no longer: she had to go back. Malahky was flagging, and it wasn't in her to be unkind to a horse. And it would be unkind to keep him out much longer in the baking heat. Besides, she couldn't stay out indefinitely. Sooner or later she would have to return to the stable. And face Gallagher.

Her heart was pounding as, a scant quarter-hour later, she rode Malahky back through the stable door. It was late afternoon by then, but the heat had not lessened. She was perspiring, and her hair was straggling down her neck. It itched, and she scratched at it dispiritedly. She was still scratching when she felt hard hands grab her around the waist and haul her from the saddle in an unsettling repeat of the attack on her days earlier. Malahky, alarmed, skittered into his open stall. Sarah kicked frantically until her feet touched solid ground.

"Take your hands off me!" Those were the first words out of her mouth as she slewed around to face Gallagher, who was glaring at her as angrily as she was at him. His hands had left her waist before the words were out of her mouth. Sarah bit her lip, looking furtively around for Jagger. The angry command had revealed an intimacy between the two of them completely out of keeping with their mistress-servant relationship. But Jagger was nowhere in sight, as she should have guessed as soon as she felt Gallagher dragging her from the saddle. He would be careful; he could not be more anxious to advertise their hateful familiarity than she was.

"You stupid little bitch." Gallagher bit the words out, his hands clenched at his sides as he obviously struggled to keep them off her. Sarah's eyes widened in angry amazement at his temerity in speaking so to her.

"Don't you dare speak to me like that!" Her voice trembled with anger. It was all she could do not to launch herself at him, tearing at that handsome face with her nails, savaging him with her teeth. She wanted to lash out at him so badly that she ached. . . . In the one part of her mind not wholly given over to fury, Sarah marveled at the strength of the rage that shook her. Before meeting Gallagher, she had prided herself on her self-control.

"I'll speak to you any bloody way I please." He was still biting off the words, looking as if he wanted to throttle her. "I don't give a damn if you blush all the way down to your prim little toes every time you look at me. From now on, when you go riding, I go with you. Understand?"

Sarah fairly quivered with temper. "Who do you think you are to give me orders? Just because—just because . . ." His eyes darkened, and she abruptly abandoned that line of reasoning. "You don't give the orders around here, Gallagher. I do!"

She was shouting. Gallagher's hands fastened on her arms in a grip that would have made her wince if she hadn't been so angry. His eyes narrowed to gleaming blue slits.

"You heard about that fire in the west field? It was set, Sarah! This morning, maybe by a gang of runaway convicts like the one who attacked you, maybe by someone else. Nobody knows. But whoever set that fire was on the

station *this morning,* and they haven't been caught and
there've been no signs that they've left. What if you'd run
into them? What do you suppose they'd have done to you,
you stupid female? You were shamed by what I did to you
last night? You should bloody well try rape for comparison!"

"You're disgusting!" Sarah felt her cheeks crimson
with rage and mortification. Her hands clenched into fists.
She jerked free of his hold and swung a fist at him with all
her strength. It never connected. He caught it in his hand,
squeezing it cruelly, making her wince.

"I warned you before about violence," he snarled.
Before Sarah had time to do more than gasp, he yanked
her against him, his arms locking her to his body in a
bone-crushing embrace. His grim mouth descended. . . .

The kiss was brief, hard, and brutal. Sarah kept her
mouth closed until his hand reached up to clamp around
her jaw, forcing her teeth apart. Then his tongue invaded,
conquering territory that had surrendered the night before,
forcing her to accept that, in physical strength at least, he
was her master. Sarah could not fight him; he held her too
closely. She chose the next best course, standing rigid in
his arms, refusing to concede him an inch of ground.
Whatever he had from her, he would have to take.

Finally, with an ugly oath, he lifted his head, thrusting
her away from him with such force that Sarah nearly fell.
Recovering her balance, she backed away from him toward
the stable door, her face contorted with rage.

"You dirty *convict,*" she hissed, choosing the one word
that she knew would infuriate him more than any other.
"How dare you manhandle me! I'll make you sorry you
were ever born!"

Jaws clenched, Gallagher took a step toward her. Sarah's
bravado vanished. Whirling, she gathered up her skirts and
ran for the house. As she bolted through the stable door,

she sped past Liza, who ducked around the corner out of sight. Sarah did not even notice her.

It was long past midnight, and Dominic was lying awake in his hard, narrow bunk in the long shed that housed all the convicts and a few of the aborigines, who kept together at the far end. All about him came the sounds of men asleep. Phipps, in the bunk to his right, a burly footpad as tall as Dominic himself, whimpered like a child as he slept. He would keep up the keening off and on all night, just as he had every night since Dominic had arrived. Dominic had learned to ignore the ragged sounds. Brady, on the opposite side, a short, thick, good-humored Yorkshire man, slept like an innocent babe. Which only showed how little one could rely on the quality of a man's sleep as a way of gauging character, Dominic thought. Phipps, who despite his thieving ways had never harmed anyone, cried in his sleep. Brady, on the other hand, a professional smuggler who had murdered, with a hunting knife, his wife and her two young children when he caught her being unfaithful to him, slept like an angel from the time they turned in at night until they were booted awake by the convict trustees who oversaw their labor during the day.

Dominic himself could not sleep. He lay on his back with his arms crossed beneath his head, staring at the velvety black sky through the cracks between the ceiling boards, cursing himself steadily for his handling of Sarah. He had meant to be gentle with her when next they'd met, but first she'd scared him by going off alone, and then she'd made him so damned mad. . . .

The thud of booted feet on the rickety porch outside caught his attention. Dominic looked toward the door as it opened and three men entered. In the darkness it was impossible to recognize them. He watched with wary interest as they passed down the rows of sleeping men. One of them held a lantern; he shone it discreetly on each of the sleepers in turn. Some sort of bed check, Dominic surmised, and wondered what had made it necessary. When they got to him, he blinked into the light, waiting for them to pass on. But they stayed where they were, surrounding his bed. The lantern was blown out. Instinctively all his muscles stiffened in alarm. He started up.

"Take him," one of them said.

XII

Gallagher had run away. Sarah was surprised at how that knowledge troubled her. He was a greenhorn, and the bush country was deadly to greenhorns. He should have known that, should have had more sense. Within hours of their arrival on Lowella, Percival always made new convicts aware of the hopelessness of running. Like others before him, Gallagher had clearly chosen not to believe Percival. Most of those who left perished in the miles of desolation around them; with the drought drying up most sources of water, Gallagher's eventual fate would be even more certain. And if he came back to Lowella, as a few did, staggering with exhaustion and defeat, he would be whipped. But however severe the beating, surely it would be better than dying of thirst and exposure to the raging sun. Surely he would come back.... But a week passed, then two, then four. Sarah had to face the truth: Gallagher was very likely dead, his long, hard body lying out on the parched tundra, the flesh stripped from his bones by carrion eaters so that soon only a bleached skeleton would remain to attest that a man had lived and died. . . . The dingoes would carry off even the bones, Sarah realized with a shudder; nothing would be left of Gallagher at all. The thought haunted Sarah; she was preoccupied by day and unable to sleep at night.

"Have you had any luck finding that convict Gallagher?" She could contain the question no longer. The family, plus Percival, who usually joined them, was at dinner, gathered around the large mahogany table. Candles provided illumination in preference to oil lamps, at Lydia's insistence. Crystal and silver gleamed, while the dishes were of fine china imported from England and the white tablecloth was made of the best damask and lace. Dinner, Lydia said, was going to be civilized, even if nothing else was in this crude country. Edward sat at the head of the table, his black cutaway coat and white silk stock an uncomfortable concession to his wife's badgering. Only Sarah, who remembered how her father had refused ever to wear a coat no matter what the occasion, recognized his donning of such apparel for the sacrifice it was. Lydia, resplendent in white silk and pearls, with a great deal of her bounteous charms on display, sat at the foot. Sarah and Liza, in beige muslin and yellow silk, respectively, sat on one side of the table. Percival, who was attired even more correctly than Edward, was directly opposite Sarah. Mary, the quieter and less clumsy of the maids, waited on table. Mrs. Abbott rarely appeared in the dining room; Lydia said that the sight of a convict while she was eating was enough to put her off her food.

Edward shrugged in answer to Sarah's question, glancing over at Percival, who picked up his wineglass and swirled the red liquid slowly.

"Haven't tried," Percival replied indifferently, his eyes on the candlelight shining through the wine to form a red shadow on the tablecloth. "The man's no loss; he was a troublemaker from the start, as I told you he would be."

Liza giggled. "I think Sarah liked him," she suggested slyly.

Sarah could feel herself turning pink even as she struggled to reply to Liza with the scorn the remark should have merited.

"Don't be silly," she said, and was pardonably pleased with the crispness of her voice. The fact that all eyes except her father's were focused on her made her hope fervently that the color she knew was in her cheeks would be hidden by the dimness of the candlelight.

"He was a very handsome man," Lydia observed, her languid tone masking the glitter in her eyes from everyone but Sarah. Sarah was too familiar with that look to miss it. She felt her stomach begin to tense as she waited for Lydia to home in for the kill. "I for one wouldn't blame dear Sarah if he turned her head just a little bit. She has so few opportunities. . . . Oh, I'm sorry. Don't mind me, Sarah. You know my wretched tongue. Of course, we have all learned to value you for your sterling character, and not give your looks a thought."

This was accompanied by such a poisonously sweet smile that Sarah glanced instinctively at her father, thinking that this time surely he would be able to see the hostility behind the pretense of affection. But he was spearing a chunk of mutton with his fork; Sarah doubted that he had even heard. And even if he had, he wouldn't come to her defense. She had learned that long ago. He detested being made uncomfortable, and Lydia, if she got into a snit with him because of his championship of his daughter, was more than capable of making his life very uncomfortable indeed.

"Of course you have," she managed unconcernedly,

knowing that to affect indifference was the best way to handle Lydia's barbs. She spread some butter made from ewe's milk on one of Mrs. Abbott's caraway-seed rolls and bit into it with every appearance of pleasure. Her eyes met Lydia's for the barest second. Both ladies smiled.

"Found out anything more about that fire in the west field, John?" Edward asked placidly, changing the subject. He did that nearly every time Lydia launched one of her attacks; Sarah suspected that it was deliberate, aimed at diverting his wife's attention from her, but she could never be sure. Her father was never interested for long in any conversation that did not deal with the station, and through it, directly or indirectly, his beloved merinos.

"You know it was set." Percival's tone was suddenly brusque as he seemed to come to attention. Edward nodded, while the ladies listened in silence, Lydia and Liza clearly bored, Sarah attentive. "It could be that same group of convicts that burned Paul Brickton out a couple of months back. Or it could be a single convict. Or even an aborigine or a group of aborigines, though they don't usually do anything like that. I don't know. I do know that they won't get a chance to do it again. I've got guards stationed in all the fields and outbuildings. If whoever did it comes back, they're in for a nasty surprise."

"Good thinking, John," Edward said absently. Percival inclined his head in silent acknowledgment.

Lydia leaned forward so that the candlelight gleamed on the smooth white slopes of her full bosoms, exposed almost to the nipples by the dipping neckline of her dress. "To you, John Percival," she purred, lifting her wineglass toward Percival in salute. The smile that accompanied the gesture was meant to be provocative.

Sarah, watching her stepmother as she flirted under her husband's nose, wondered at her temerity. After seven years of marriage, Lydia still did not know her husband as well as she obviously thought she did. Usually her father was mild-mannered, largely because he was almost always preoccupied with his sheep. But if Lydia actually carried through on what her flirting promised, and her father found out, Sarah had not a doubt that Lydia would discover Edward Markham's temper with a vengeance.

"What would we do without you?" Lydia continued. Her smile had changed, becoming nothing more than polite now that her husband's eyes were on her as he too raised his glass. Liza and Sarah, the latter reluctantly, followed suit. "May you soon become a permanent member of the family!"

Sarah, in the process of taking the required sip of wine, nearly choked. There was no mistaking Lydia's meaning. Her father was smiling at her, and Liza was suppressing giggles, while Percival looked smugly pleased.

"I look forward to it as soon as Miss Sarah sets the date," Percival replied as if their marriage were a settled thing.

Sarah decided then to make it quite clear, before the whole family so that there could no longer be any doubt, that she would not marry Percival. "I have no intention, ever, of setting a date for our wedding, Mr. Percival," she said evenly, looking at him across the table with steady eyes as she set down her wineglass deliberately. "As you know, for I have told you many times, I have no wish to marry you." The words were calm, and even fairly polite, but their effect on the company was electric. Percival stiffened, glowering at her, while her father eyed her with dismayed disapproval. Lydia was smiling, pleased at the furor she had created, while Liza was staring first at Sarah, then at Percival.

"Sarah!" Edward remonstrated. Then, to Percival: "Forgive her, John. Every lass likes a little courting, eh? She'll come round in time."

Her father's connivance wounded Sarah to the heart. Although why it should, she didn't know. He had never listened to her, never really cared for her, at least not enough to protect her from Lydia and, now, Percival. For the good of his beloved sheep, he was prepared to hand her over to Percival lock, stock, and barrel.

"Excuse me," she said, standing abruptly. Before anyone could reply, she put her napkin on the table and walked from the room.

Sarah spent the rest of the evening in her bedroom, defiantly reading a very lurid and very enjoyable novel. It was so seldom that she had time to read that she felt guilty, but she continued nonetheless, hoping that the plot's melodramatic twists and turns would take her mind off the many things that troubled her. It did; for a couple of hours Sarah forgot Gallagher, Percival, Lydia, her father, the breeding papers she should be going over, the mending that needed to be done. . . . She read until at last, thankfully, she felt sleepy. Then she washed her face and hands and put on her nightrail, a plain, prim affair of sleeveless white cotton. It buttoned clear up to her neck, but in deference to the heat Sarah left the top two buttons undone so that what little breeze there was could reach her throat. She brushed her hair and braided it in a single thick plait, which she secured with a bit of yellow ribbon before twisting the braid into a loose coil on the top of her head. The night seemed even hotter than usual; only the merest suggestion of a breeze stirred the lengths of peach silk that draped the sides of the open windows. Sarah blew out the lamp, then crossed to stand by one of the windows, looking out over the garden without really seeing it. She was remembering the morning in the attic when she had leaned out another window, clad even more skimpily than she was tonight. Even from a distance of three stories, Gallagher's eyes as they had raked over her body had been incredibly blue. . . . Sarah shivered, wrapping her arms around herself, suddenly feeling cold despite the heat. Why Gallagher's disappearance should so upset her she did not know.

Sarah was turning away from the window when an orange glow caught her eye. She turned back, her eyes widening as she saw flames, vivid and pulsing as they burst forth, reaching for the black velvet of the night sky. The stable!

"Fire!" The scream tore out of her mouth. Whirling, she barely paused to snatch up her wrapper before flying from the room. "Fire!"

She ran along the hall to her father's and Lydia's bedroom and hammered wildly on their closed door.

"Pa, Pa, come quick! The stable's on fire!" she screamed. She heard his answering shout, and didn't wait for anything else.

Dragging on her wrapper as she ran, not even conscious of her bare feet, she tore down the stairs and out the back door. Dried stalks of grass cut into the tender soles of her feet as she went; she could feel the heat of the fire on her face before she was halfway there. The screams of the horses trapped inside mingled with the roar and crackle of the flames.

Men were pouring out of buildings all around her; free men, convicts, and aborigines alike rushed to fight an enemy all understood: fire. Sarah rushed toward the stable, the smell of burning acrid in her nostrils, feeling the terror of the horses as if it were her own. They had to be gotten out: Malahky, Clare, Max, and the others. . . .

"My God, the breeding barns!" The hoarse cry, in what Sarah barely recognized as her father's voice, came from

behind her. Automatically Sarah glanced to the west, in
the direction of the breeding barns, as she ran. More
seething flames raged in the distance. The sheep barns
were burning, too.

"Leave the stable! Get to those barns! My sheep!" Her
father was shrieking, beside himself with dread, as he
mustered the men. With the horses all trapped in the
stable, and the bullocks rolling their eyes and lunging
against the fence in a nearby paddock too slow, the men,
following her father's urgent call, began to run. Under
Percival's hoarse direction, they grabbed up buckets and
blankets and shovels and pitchforks.

"What about the horses?" Sarah was screaming at
their departing backs. The horses were shrieking; the
terrified cries tore at Sarah's heart. They would all
perish. . . .

They would not! She would save as many as she
could. Tearing off her wrapper, Sarah ran to the stable
door. It was closed; the wood felt hot against her
tugging hands. It would not budge. She nearly despaired,
then she felt the door give. Other hands added their
strength to hers.

"Mrs. Abbott!" Sarah cried, looking around to see the
woman's plump, determined face. Mrs. Abbott's nightcap
was wildly askew, and her voluminous nightgown flapped
behind her in the breeze that showered them both with
sparks. In the background, Sarah could see Liza and Lydia
huddled together on the porch, watching.

"Let's get them horses!" Mrs. Abbott yelled.

Sarah had no time to speculate on the gallantry of this
woman who would risk her life for animals that belonged
to a man who had done nothing to prevent his wife from
openly scorning her. She rushed through the open door,
her wrapper still clutched in her hand. The tremendous
outpouring of thick black smoke nearly sent her reeling

back. Ducking low to the ground, she forced herself forward. Already she knew that, with only the two of them, they would not be able to save all the horses. Clare's was the first stall. Sarah opened it, and the terrified mare lunged past her and bolted out the stable door.

"Open the stall doors! Maybe some of the others will run out on their own!" she called to Mrs. Abbott, barely getting the words out for the smoke that threatened to choke her. But Mrs. Abbott heard, and obeyed. Coughing, Sarah ran down the opposite row of stalls, throwing doors wide. Some of the horses bolted past her, running for safety. Others reared and plunged, trumpeting their fear, but were too terrified to leave their stalls.

Max—Max was out. Sparks were dropping on Sarah from the roof, which was now almost fully ablaze, as the big horse galloped by, nostrils flaring, eyes rolling, mane and tail flying, hooves pawing the earth. There was no way to know how many horses remained. Some did; panicked screams told her that.

"We've got to get out!" Sarah shrieked at Mrs. Abbott, who had just reached the end of her line of stalls. Mrs. Abbott lifted an arm to show Sarah she understood. Sarah could barely see her for the thick smoke that was stinging her eyes, making them water, choking her. . . . Overhead, the roof gave an ominous creak. There was no time to do any more. The roof could collapse at any time. She was not foolish enough to stay any longer.

Malahky! Sarah saw the bay rear and lunge in the corner of his stall as, crouched low, she ran past. Her wrapper, which she now had wrapped around her mouth and nose, was the only thing that kept her from suffocating on the thickening smoke. She could not leave Malahky. Sarah stopped, trembling with fear as the roof gave another warning creak. Sparks showered all around her, along with charred bits of wood and ash. She waited until Malahky was down on all four legs, then darted into the stall, praying that he wouldn't rear again before she could grab his halter. She made it just in time. She could feel the great strength of him as he tried to go back on his hind feet. Practically swinging from the halter, Sarah held him down. He backed and plunged, whinnying frantically. If he chose to run for it now, he would trample her.

He did not. Sides heaving, he stood still while she tore the wrapper from around her own nose and mouth and wrapped it around his eyes. Coughing, she led him from the stall.

The smoke was denser now, the heat more intense. Sarah had been holding her breath. She could do without air no longer; her lungs felt as if they would burst. Taking a deep, shuddering breath without volition, she felt the hot, thick, malodorous vapors swirl into her lungs and gagged. Her head began to spin. Sarah knew that she was going to faint.

With the last remaining bit of her strength, she heaved herself up on Malahky's back. Leaning forward, she whipped the wrapper from around his eyes and clapped her heels hard to his sides at the same time. She could only pray that he would run for his life.

Sarah felt him sweating and trembling beneath her as he plunged for the open door. Her hands clung to his mane and her knees locked into his sides as she leaned low over his neck.

Sarah was barely conscious, her whole being focused on keeping her seat on that slippery back, as Malahky leaped forward. No sooner had they cleared the door than she heard the crash of the roof collapsing behind them. Immediately they were awash in a rain of sparks and flying, burning debris. Panic-stricken, Malahky lunged out of the stable yard for the dark mystery of the scrubland to the east; clinging to his back, Sarah's last coherent thought was how very human were the sounds of horses' screams.

XIII

There were rifle shots to the west, in the direction of the sheep barns. Sarah heard the sharp, staccato bursts and surmised that whoever had set the fires—there were too many for them to have started accidentally—had encountered the guards Percival had posted. It sounded like a small war. For an instant, Sarah considered riding over to see if she could be of help, but then her common sense told her that she was more likely to be in the way. Her best course of action would be to return to the house.

She was a few miles from home. Malahky, crazed with terror, had run until he could run no more. Finally he had slowed his headlong gallop to a canter, then a trot, and then a walk before stopping altogether. He stood now with his head down as he drew in great gulps of air; his sides heaved with the aftermath of exertion, and he was trembling. Sarah, still astride with her nightrail hiked up around her thighs so that most of her long, slim legs were bare, leaned over to pat his reddish-brown neck soothingly.

He shuddered in response; his eyes rolled wildly, showing the whites. Sarah knew that he was still terrified; horses feared fire more than anything. Only exhaustion had made him stop running. If she had been wearing shoes, she would have walked him back to Lowella. But the rocky ground with its sharp sticks and razorlike blades of dried grass would crucify the soft skin of her bare feet. She would ride Malahky back, but very, very slowly.

They were in the middle of the bush, with great, eerily bare ghost gums rising up out of the sun-cracked earth to tower overhead. Sarah remembered that the aborigines wouldn't pass a grove of ghost gums at night, and shivered. They believed that the souls of the dead occupied the trees, and that it was this that accounted for the trees' distinctive gray-white color. This was very easy to dismiss as nonsense— during the day. At night, without another human for miles around . . . Sarah listened to the soft groans of the branches swaying in the wind and resolutely forced her mind to more mundane matters.

Without a bridle, it was difficult to pull Malahky's head up. Sarah pondered the problem for a moment, then reached down and tore off the small flounce that edged the hem of her nightrail. Securing each end of the strip to either side of the halter, she made a crude hackamore. Then she hauled Malahky's head up, and, kicking him lightly in the sides, pointed him toward home. Sweat-soaked sides heaving, he obeyed her command, walking slowly forward. Sarah rewarded him with a whispered word of praise in his ear and another pat on his neck.

Sarah guessed that it was nearly an hour before they passed the dried-up gorge from which the homestead was just over the next rise. The night was spookily silent; the gunshots had ceased some time before. Instead of being allowed to roam freely as they generally were, the sheep had been herded into pens and barns so that they could be watered more easily during the drought; Sarah missed their incessant baaing, which had been part of her life for as long as she could remember. The birds slept at night, so their cries were silenced too. The only sound was the distant, echoing howls of a pack of dingoes on the hunt. The moon, mistily white, floated near the horizon behind her. The hot wind blew small particles of dust with it.

Before they topped the rise that would bring the homestead into sight, Sarah became aware of the acrid smell of burning. Along with the more familiar pungent scent of charred wood and ashes was another, stronger odor that Sarah could not immediately place. The stink was nauseating. Malahky's head was up now; his eyes were rolling again, and he was tossing his head from side to side as he sidled, refusing to go forward. Sarah had to fight him for a moment before he gave in. Only then did she realize what the smell was: cremated horseflesh. Her stomach twisted violently, and she gagged.

Malahky was misbehaving again, and Sarah had to concentrate on controlling him. He gave every evidence of wanting to flee back the way they had come. It was only as they reached the crest of the rise and Lowella lay spread before them like a miniature city that Sarah realized they were no longer alone. To her right, some little distance away, surged a dark tide of men, some holding blazing torches, some carrying shovels and pick axes, a few shouldering rifles. Sarah pulled Malahky to a halt, staring. It was a veritable army, and it was headed down the rise toward Lowella. The only sound she heard was the thud of dozens of marching feet; the men's very silence was ominous.

An uprising! Sarah felt her breath stop as the only possible explanation popped into her mind. As had happened on Brickton, Lowella's convicts had taken up arms and meant to wreak bloody vengeance on their masters. But there were too many of them to be just from Lowella; the station had only about three dozen. Neither Percival nor her father particularly liked employing convicts. They maintained that they were dangerous. Instead, they preferred to hire on the bands of itinerant workers roaming the countryside. And now Sarah saw how right they had been: if this mob made it to Lowella unhindered, her family wouldn't stand a chance.

No sooner had the thought occurred to Sarah than she clapped her heels hard to Malahky's sides. The horse was exhausted, but she had to ride, to warn the station. . . . Malahky neighed a protest even as he leaped forward. Heart thudding, Sarah looked over her shoulder to see if she had been spotted. She had! The torches were turning in her direction; the faces beneath them were ugly. Angry muttering rose from the mob as they stared at her. A few individuals broke into a run. Suddenly more were running, toward her—and Lowella. . . . Sarah clapped her heels to Malahky's sides again, wrenching her attention away from the threatening horde and forcing herself to concentrate instead on reaching the homestead, which was peaceful now in the aftermath of the fire. As Malahky stretched out beneath her, his sides heaving, Sarah felt fear constrict her throat. If that mob should catch her . . . But of course they wouldn't catch her: she was mounted, while they were on foot.

The pounding of Malahky's hooves echoed in her ears. Only a little farther now, and she could scream a warning. . . . Suddenly Sarah realized that the thudding hoofbeats did not all belong to Malahky. There were too many. . . . Turning around, she saw that three riders were bearing down on her from behind, formless black shapes swooping like bats out of hell.

"Go, Malahky!" Sarah screamed, kicking the horse again and lashing at him with her makeshift reins. The big bay responded with a truly heroic effort; he surged forward, flying over the uneven ground, galloping toward the homestead and safety while the three dark riders pounded close behind.

"Uprising!" Sarah shrieked as Malahky sped toward the house. The stable had burned to the ground, she saw; only a single wall remained standing amid the blackened ruins. She was afraid to look behind her, afraid the riders were right on her tail. Leaning low over the horse's neck, she screamed her warning again. Malahky, panicked anew by the terror in her voice and by the horses closing in behind him, leaped forward wildly, out of control. Sarah didn't care. It was the only chance she had of warning the homestead.

"Uprising!" She was nearly in the yard now; she dared a glance over her shoulder. The riders were almost upon her. Behind them she could see the mob surging down the rise toward Lowella, their sputtering torches trailing dark streams of smoke as they ran. They were no longer silent; the clash of metal from their makeshift weapons mingled with hoarse shouts and the thud of running feet. Sarah kicked Malahky one more time, and felt his muscles bunching beneath her as he gave her all he had.

"Uprising!" The house was strangely dark, Sarah noticed, puzzling at it. Surely, in the aftermath of the fire, they would be prepared for trouble. Then the dreadful thought occurred: What if the men had not yet returned from the sheep barns, and the women were alone in the house? Horrified at the implications, as she hurtled through the yard she screamed the warning at the top of her lungs. It should not have been necessary now. The roars of the mob behind her reverberated like thunder.

Without warning, men seemed to burst from the house and the outbuildings. Rifles at the ready, they ran to form an uneven line between the buildings and the oncoming mob. Sarah practically cheered—and wondered why they waited to open fire. . . .

"Get out of the way, Sarah!" her father bellowed from near the house. And Sarah knew why they were waiting. She couldn't have stopped Malahky if she had tried, and she wasn't trying. Now she hauled hard on the reins, dragging his head to the right. . . . Suddenly they were no longer between Lowella's defenders and the mob. Malahky was still running as the defenders opened fire.

Safe at last, Sarah began to saw rhythmically on the makeshift reins, trying to convey to Malahky that the danger was past. Gradually he responded, slowing.

Suddenly behind her a hard arm swooped around her waist and lifted her clear up off Malahky's back. Sarah screamed as she was flung face down across the saddle of another galloping horse, one that raced right by Malahky and kept going.

XIV

They galloped into the night for what seemed like hours. To Sarah, who was held ruthlessly across the saddle bow by a man's hand bunched in the loose folds of her nightrail, the nightmarish ride was endless. At first she fought, kicking and screaming in an effort to writhe free. That earned her nothing but her own exhaustion; her captor continued to ride as if she were no more than a squirming pup. Finally she surrendered to the inevitable and lay still. At least, her body was still. Her mind seethed with fright and fury. Fortunately, the indignity of her position, to say nothing of the pain of it, gave fury the upper hand. How she would like to get her hands on the vile creature who dared to use her in such a way, she fumed. She would get a great deal of satisfaction from clawing out his eyes.

Focusing her anger on her silent captor helped to keep her mind off the exigencies of her situation. Sprawled uncomfortably across his saddle, with his hard thighs pressing into her hip and shoulder, she was very much at the nameless marauder's mercy, and she knew it. Sarah preferred not to think of the spectacle she must present, her masses of tawny hair dragged from its braid by the wind to stream against the man's knee and the horse's dark side, her long bare legs and white-clad arms jouncing ludicrously as the horse galloped over the uneven ground, her nightrail twisted tightly around her body by the man's fist. She also refused to think about how very nearly naked she was. Except for the thin nightrail—rendered almost useless as a covering by her captor's grip on it—she was unclothed. With her new knowledge of men and their lusts, Sarah was conscious of a pang of terror at inciting such an emotion in the man—men—who had abducted her. Would he—they—rape her? She shuddered at the very word. The act itself—she could hardly bear to think about it. It had been shameful enough with Gallagher, who at least, as much as she hated to admit it, had appealed to her senses and given her pleasure. With strangers—hard, uncaring strangers who would glory in her degradation and find their enjoyment in brutalizing and humiliating her—it would be unspeakably horrible. She had felt the hardness of this man's hand when he had shifted her position by clasping her backside through the thin layer of cloth that was all that shielded her skin from his touch. Was he even now plotting how he would use her when at last they stopped? Sarah felt sickened at the thought. Resolutely she forced it from her mind. It was possible that she would be raped, and just as possible that she would be killed. Giving way to panic would do her no good. She had to think, use her wits to save herself. Undoubtedly the man who held her captive expected his poor little female victim to be mindless with terror. Well, she would not be. She would wait for the opportunity, and when it came she would do whatever she had to to escape. And if her chances were remote, well, she wouldn't dwell on that either. She would escape, because she had to.

When at last the horse slowed to a trot, then a walk, and finally stopped, Sarah would have breathed a sigh of relief, if she hadn't been so frightened. What would happen to her now? Her captor dismounted, swinging easily down from the saddle and reaching up to catch her around her waist and drag her down too. Sarah's every instinct screamed for her to attack him, to fight, to claw and kick and bite in a desperate bid for freedom. But she forced herself to go limp, feigning a faint. Maybe, if he thought she had fainted, he would put her down on the ground and leave her alone. . . . He pulled her off the saddle, one hard arm sliding under her waist to support her as she drooped forward, her hair and fingers and toes brushing the ground. Grunting, he shifted her from one arm to the other, then turned her so that she was facing upward. Sarah concentrated on being a dead weight, on keeping her eyes closed and her breathing regular, but shallow and fast as Liza's was when she had swooned. A long-fingered, callused-palmed hand closed over one small breast. Sarah shot upright, her eyes flying open, her arms flailing as she knocked away the too-intimate hand.

"You . . . !" She gasped out a string of insults, not even aware of what she was saying as she went for him, teeth bared, fingers curved into claws. His hands closed over her upper arms, pushing her away from him before she had inflicted any but minor damage. Sarah glared her hatred at the grimy bandanna that concealed the lower part of his face while darkness veiled the rest of him as he towered over her. His hands tightened ruthlessly, painfully, around the soft flesh of her upper arms. Sarah moaned and abruptly quit fighting. His grip on her arms eased, but he did not release her.

"Best tie the vixen up. Or strangle her," one of her captor's companions suggested, not without a touch of enjoyment. Sarah saw that the two other riders were masked like the man whose hands still held her prisoner. Only one man remained mounted. It was he who had spoken, tossing her captor a coiled length of rope as he did so. The grip on one of her arms was abruptly released as her captor lifted a hand to catch the rope; then he was holding her again, turning her. . . .

Sarah struggled, but without any real expectation of success. His grip on her arms tightened again, not hurting her this time but reminding her that he could if he wished. Facing outward, Sarah saw that the moon had risen high overhead, a perfect semicircle against the darkness of the sky, occasionally veiled by a drifting wisp of cloud. The barren, pockmarked landscape stretched flat around them, broken only by a solitary ghost gum and a few isolated outcroppings of brush. The land, bathed in shimmering moonlight, was deserted except for herself and the three men. There was no help to be had; Sarah could not even help herself as her hands were deftly tied behind her back.

"Ahh." It was a satisfied sound from the other man on the ground. Sarah frowned, trying to puzzle out what had occasioned it, as her captor put his hands on her shoulders and turned her around to face him. Then the bleating sound of sheep floated to her from the way they had come. Sarah twisted to look over her shoulder. A pale, shifting blur in the distance resolved itself into more riders driving what could only be a herd of her father's prized merinos. As the milling flock approached, the sounds grew louder.

"Rustlers!" Sarah gasped, understanding suddenly what had lain behind tonight's unprecedented attack on Lowella. Bushrangers—the bandits who terrorized this part of New

South Wales—had evidently banded together to make off with her father's prize sheep. The unprecedented convict uprising—there had never been such a thing before on Lowella—had doubtless been carefully orchestrated by the bushrangers to provide a diversion. That would explain why some had been mounted, while the majority had been on foot. The convicts who had attacked the homestead armed with shovels and torches and pick axes had been left behind to be slaughtered while this small group of outlaws made off with their booty.

"Keep her quiet!" growled the man who had spoken before. Sarah could not discern his expression, but his tone was angry.

Her captor ignored the other man; his hands slid from her arms to fasten around her waist preparatory to lifting her into the saddle. With her hands tied behind her, to say nothing of the raw power of the tall male body looming so menacingly close, struggling would have been useless. Sarah permitted him to lift her off the ground because she could think of no alternative that would not worsen her present situation, and obediently straddled the saddle, trying not to think of the length of slender pale leg left bare by her immodest posture. Her captor was swinging himself into the saddle behind her when it occurred to her that he had not, during the entire operation, said a word. Was he mute, or merely taciturn, or . . . ? The lithe movements, the height and breadth of him, and the hard muscular strength of the body now settling close behind her in the saddle struck a hideous chord of familiarity. Eyes widening, Sarah turned around in the saddle just as the horse surged into an effortless canter in the wake of the others, who had moved out to join the band herding the sheep. The grimy kerchief still obscured his features, and a dusty, wide-brimmed black hat was pulled low over his forehead, hiding his hair, but even in the moonshot darkness there was no mistaking the Irish blue eyes.

"Gallagher!" Sarah stared at him, unable to believe what she was seeing. His eyes glinted tauntingly down at her.

"You sound surprised. Did you think I was dead?" Despite the muffling mask, she would have recognized that distinctive lilt anywhere. No wonder he hadn't spoken! She would have known him at once.

"Yes," Sarah answered, because she had thought he was dead. His eyes narrowed, grew hard. The arm around her waist tightened, holding her in place in the saddle.

"Nasty little bitch, aren't you?" he remarked almost casually.

Sarah stared at him, taken aback by his hostility. Upon discovering his identity, she had felt a tremendous sense of relief as it occurred to her that either or both of the dreadful fates she had feared were extremely unlikely to befall her. But now, suddenly, she wasn't so sure. He sounded as if he hated her, though why, Sarah couldn't fathom. She had done nothing to him. Indeed, it was the other way around.

"Are you any kin to the black widow spider, I wonder?" he continued, the laziness of his voice failing to mask its hard undertone. "They devour their lovers after a single mating, you know. But, unlike you, at least they have the courage to do their own dirty work."

"What are you talking about?" Sarah looked at him uncomprehendingly. His eyes seemed to lance into her soul.

"You know damned well what I'm talking about," he said tightly. "You may as well forget about playing innocent. I won't believe it—and you're liable to make me angry."

"You're mad!" Sarah said with conviction, still twisted around so that she could see him. "I don't know why you should get angry—you're the one in the wrong. *You* ran away, *you* abducted me, and *you* are helping to steal my father's sheep."

"And *you* ran squalling to your papa. Tell me something, *Miss* Sarah: Just how did you explain our lovemaking? Did you tell him that I forced myself on you, or were you honest enough to admit that you asked for everything you got? Your overseer—a hard man with a whip, that—never said, and I wasn't in a position to do any asking."

"I don't know what you're talking about. I never told my father anything." At his blatant reference to what had taken place between them, Sarah's eyes dropped away from his. She didn't realize it, but her downcast eyes made her look the picture of guilt. His breath hissed through his teeth and his eyes grew harder.

"Then why did he send that lout of an overseer and two other men to drag me from the bunkhouse and string me up in one of the barns? Did you know that I hung there for two days, *Miss* Sarah, after they beat me, with the flies buzzing around the wounds they left and my waste on the floor, without a bite to eat or a drop of water? Did you know that they meant to leave me there until I died? Does the thought of it turn your stomach, *Miss* Sarah? Believe me, experiencing it did far more than that to mine."

"My father had you beaten?" she whispered, appalled. Impossible to believe . . .

He laughed, the sound without humor. "What did you think he would do? Shake his finger under my nose while he scolded me for being a bad boy?" He bent his head so that his mouth was almost touching her ear. His near-whisper sent chills down her spine: "Do you know what it's like to be totally helpless, totally at the mercy of

someone who has no mercy?'' She shuddered. His voice
grew even softer as his breath seared her skin. ''Believe
me, *Miss* Sarah, you will.''

''Gallagher...'' she began, her eyes wide as she searched
his face. She could find no hint of softening in his
expression. His eyes over the bandanna were hard and
fierce, implacable. She shivered as she began to compre-
hend what had happened to him, what he thought she had
done . . . what he might do to her in revenge. They were no
longer mistress and servant, he bound to obey her commands while she had the power of life and death over him,
however little inclined to use it she might be. The tables
had turned with a vengeance.

''Gallagher...'' The word was a hoarse croak.

She saw the sudden snarl in his eyes before she heard it
in his voice. The arm around her waist tightened until it
felt like an iron band locking her against him. Beneath
them, the horse rocked in its easy canter, the motion oddly
soothing.

''In view of our relationship—our new relationship—it
might behoove you to call me Dominic, however much
that might offend your notion of what's right and proper.''

''What do you mean, our new relationship?'' she asked,
faltering, dreading the answer.

''Why, I'm your master now, Sarah. And you'll do just
exactly as I tell you. Whatever I tell you, whenever I tell
you to do it.'' The silky raspiness of his voice sent a shiver
down her spine. Pressed close against her, the hard strength
of his body was nearly as intimidating as his tone.

''And if I don't?'' The question was pure bravado.
Sarah sensed that it would be fatal to allow Gallagher to
suspect how much she was beginning to fear him. The
terror at her plight, which had begun to abate when she
recognized Gallagher, was returning in full force. He
hated her, blamed her for what he had suffered. Dimly,

she felt that he also blamed her in some way because he was forced to serve her and her family until the expiration of his sentence. He was angry and he needed a scapegoat—that much was overwhelmingly clear. And she was to be that scapegoat. Sarah chewed her lower lip. The thought of being helpless in his hands made her throat go dry.

"If you don't?" He sounded thoughtful. The very lack of threat in his voice was somehow more alarming than any blustering he could have done. With a gesture he indicated the panorama around them, the masked riders as graceful as wraiths in the darkness as they wove efficiently among the tide of bleating sheep, driving them toward the horizon where the moon now rode low. "Why, I won't do a thing, Sarah. Nothing at all."

He smiled as he said it. She could tell by the narrowing of his eyes. His eyes also told her that it was not a pleasant smile. Sarah did not understand what he was threatening her with, but she had a feeling that she would rather not know.

Sarah was still puzzling uneasily over Gallagher's answer when he touched his heels to the horse's sides, urging the animal into a gallop to chase after a wayward sheep. Only his arm around her held her in the saddle. Sarah was forced to turn so that she was facing forward, giving her attention to clinging to the saddle with her thighs and knees so that she would not fall off the horse. There was no more time to ponder Gallagher's meaning—now.

By the time the sun was high in the sky, Sarah was leaning back limply against Gallagher's solid form, the enmity between them pushed aside as she strove to find what ease she could. She had never been so physically uncomfortable in her life. Her bare legs, which had grown colder and colder as they had ridden through the night, were now being broiled to a bright red by the blazing sun. The soft insides of her knees and thighs had been chafed by the leather saddle until they felt raw. Her hands, which were still bound behind her, had lost all feeling, and her lips were dry from the sun and lack of water. To add to her misery, a fine coating of dust covered her skin and the unbound, tangled mass of her hair. The wind had blown grit into her eyes so often that she now kept them shut. Not that this was any hardship. Every time she chanced to open them, it was to find one or another of the men's eyes upon her, staring, with an avidity that made her quiver with fear, at the pale length of her legs left bare by the nightrail hiked up around her thighs and at the slight curves of her body, so inadequately concealed by the thin cloth. Held tightly before Gallagher in the saddle, she felt ruthlessly, totally exposed. She tried not to speculate on how much worse her situation could get. If the looks in those men's eyes were any indication, the answer was, much worse. But worrying about it would do no good, and Sarah was almost too tired and miserable to care.

The horses and sheep were walking now. No other gait was possible in the enervating heat. A thick cloud of dust hovered over them as they went, making breathing almost impossible. Without even her hands to cover her mouth and nose, Sarah inhaled as shallowly as she could, not wanting to choke on the dust that inevitably found its way into her nose and mouth and from there to her lungs. Finally she gave up. Her head lolled limply back against Gallagher's shoulder as she drew a deep, shuddering breath, then immediately began to cough. If she continued with only the tiny, unsatisfying sips of air she had been taking into her starved lungs, she would have suffocated. But now, as she coughed and wheezed and coughed some more, she feared she might choke to death.

"Christ," Gallagher growled in her ear, the first word

he had spoken to her for hours. She felt him draw rein, bringing the horse to a halt beside the plodding sheep. As he started to dismount, Sarah swayed, and would have toppled sideways out of the saddle if he had not caught her around the waist and lifted her down with him. Even then, when the bare soles of her feet made contact with the hot, sun-cracked earth just barely covered by a shriveled mat of brown grass, she could not find the strength to hold herself upright. Her knees buckled; she would have fallen if he had not supported her as he lowered her with surprising gentleness to the ground.

"Problems, mate?" One of the other riders had reined in beside them and was staring down at Sarah's prone form with something more than idle concern. Sarah had opened her eyes as Gallagher lifted her from the saddle, but now she squeezed them shut. She felt threatened by the expression on the man's face. All she could do was shut it out.

"Nothing I can't handle," Gallagher replied.

There was a brief silence, then Sarah heard the jingle of stirrups and the rhythmic thud of hooves as the rider moved on again. Still she didn't open her eyes. She was too exhausted. Even the pain of lying on her bound hands could not rouse her.

"What in the name of all the saints ails you?" She had never heard him sound so very Irish. Sheer surprise sent her lids flickering open to find that he was down on one knee beside her, glaring at her with annoyance and, she thought, a touch of concern.

Sarah had to run her tongue over her lips before she could speak, but annoyance at his annoyance spurred her into making the effort. "I'm dying of thirst, my nose and throat are so full of grit I can hardly breathe, much less speak, I think my hands fell off long ago, I'm sunburnt, and . . ."

"Half-naked," he finished for her, his eyes sweeping

over her body with what she was sure was disapproval. He had pulled down his bandanna so that it rested around his neck. Its color, she saw, had once been blue. The faded cloth made his eyes look even brighter in contrast. The ancient red shirt he wore, obviously scrounged up after he had left Lowella, was tight across his shoulders and chest. To ease the fit, he had left several buttons undone, and the black tangle of curls on his chest was clearly visible. Sarah averted her eyes from the sight, and in the process discovered that he still wore his convict-issue black breeches and sturdy boots. "What the devil were you doing, anyway, out riding in your shimmy at midnight?" He sounded genuinely puzzled.

Sarah found the strength to glare at him. "Having fun," she muttered, the words heavy with sarcasm. His eyes narrowed. "Does it matter?" she continued. "You can take my word for it, I didn't plan it. Could you please untie my hands?—if they're still there. I'm hardly likely to be a threat to you. You're much bigger than I."

He didn't like her tone, she could tell by the ominous tightening of his mouth, but he didn't say anything, just rolled her onto her side so that he could get at her hands. What he saw made him swear under his breath. His hands were oddly gentle as they worked the knots loose.

When her hands were free, Sarah rolled back onto her back, bringing her hands in front of her with an effort that sent needles through her arms and shoulders. She shook her hands, gingerly, until she felt the blood flowing back into her fingertips. Then she brought her hands together, rubbing her raw wrists.

He didn't say a word, but his expression was stony as he stared at the raw bands of flesh encircling her wrists. For a moment Sarah thought he might apologize for having bound her so tightly, and she looked up at him, thinking that if he did it would be a good sign. But he did not. He got to his feet, moved to where the horse stood with its head lowered, trying vainly to find a blade of green among the brown, and untied a chamois pouch from behind the saddle.

"You have water," she croaked accusingly, thinking of the hours she had just passed dreaming of just a drop to wet her parched lips.

His eyes raked her as she lay limply in the small circle of shade cast by a solitary smoke tree, her tawny hair fallen around her pointed face to form a tangled lion's mane, her golden eyes huge and faintly unfocused as she tried to glare, her soft, full lips cracked and coated with dust. Sarah felt his eyes on the uncovered length of her legs, and made an instinctive attempt to pull down the torn hem of her dust- and perspiration-streaked nightrail. But the movement required too much effort. Her hand fell limply back to rest beside her.

"A little late for modesty now," he said caustically, coming down on one knee beside her again and sliding a hand behind her head, lifting it slightly while he held the contoured nozzle of the pouch to her lips. Sarah drank thirstily, until he pulled the pouch away.

"Drink too much and you'll be ill," he told her. Sarah had lived in the bush country long enough to know that, and had even said it herself more than once. But she had never before realized how one could crave water, lust for it, need it with an intensity that defied all reason. She made a halfhearted grab for the soft pouch, but he pulled it farther out of her reach. "You can have more later."

He stood up, his big body blocking the sun, and took a brief swallow from the water pouch. As he tilted his head back, the clean lines of his throat and chin were exposed. His skin was bronzed, she saw, far darker than it had been when he had disappeared from Lowella a month ago. A night's stubble of black whiskers toughened his appearance, making him look more like a bandit than the seasoned bushrangers. He had filled out some, his shoulders in the snug-fitting red shirt so broad that they gave her pause, his waist and hips and legs still lean but tautly muscled.

He turned away to refasten the water pouch to the saddle. The thought of gathering her slowly returning strength and using this opportunity to flee occurred to Sarah, to be savored and then, reluctantly, dismissed. He would catch her in seconds. And he wouldn't even need the horse to do it.

"Here." He was back, kneeling beside her again, dropping a blanket to the ground nearby. The bandanna was no longer tied around his neck, she saw as he bent over her, but was in his hand, darkened where he had moistened it with a little of the precious water. "You should have told me what bad shape you were in."

Sarah met his gaze, relieved at the touch of the cool cloth on her burning skin even though she tried to glare at him. "I had no reason to believe you would have been concerned."

His face hardened. "Unlike you, I don't take pleasure from causing gratuitous suffering. I have no wish for you to be uncomfortable. The punishment I have in mind for you won't cause you any pain. At least, not as long as you're a good girl and do as you're told." His hand, which had been wiping her face with the cloth, moved down to slide the blessed coolness over her neck. Then, to her horror, she felt him slip his hand beneath the prim neckline of her nightrail and swish the cloth casually between and beneath her breasts, his knuckles brushing the soft crests, accidentally, she thought. But it was no accident the way her nipples suddenly sprang to attention. Galvanized into action, Sarah struggled into a sitting position, thrusting his hand away.

"Get your hands off me!"

He rocked back on his heels, a slow smile stretching his taut lips. It was not a pleasant smile.

"I don't think you understand what I've been telling you, Sarah. Our positions have been reversed. You no longer give the orders. I do. And it would behoove you to keep that in mind."

"I won't have you pawing me anytime you feel like it!" Shock at her reaction to his touch had made her foolish. She knew better than to challenge him now, before she had had time to analyze the situation, but the words could not be rescinded. Her breasts felt as if they were on fire where his hand had so casually brushed them. After what had happened between them—the shameful things that he had done to her naked body, the even more shameful things he had caused her to do and to feel, the horrible humiliation that had overcome her afterward—she had thought that she had been cured forever of the cursed attraction he had held for her from the beginning. Now it appeared that, while her mind might have recovered, the message had not yet gotten through to her traitorous body. And he knew it, the swine. She could tell by the mocking gleam in his eyes as he stared at the rigid nubs of her nipples, clearly visible as they pressed wantonly against her thin cotton nightrail.

"I won't paw you again—until you ask me nicely," he said with a nasty smile.

Sarah should have felt relieved by his mild response to her ill-advised challenge—she knew very well that, whatever he chose to do to her, she had no means of stopping him—but the twin demons in his blue eyes gave her pause. He was not picking up the gauntlet she had flung at his feet because he felt no need to. The knowledge worried her.

He bent to scoop up the blanket he had dropped beside her. Sarah watched him, her mind working furiously, as he extracted a wicked-looking, curved-blade knife from the scabbard attached to his belt. Holding the blanket in one hand, he pierced it with the knife, making a small slit in the center and then another one, perpendicular to the first.

"Gallagher," she began carefully as he returned the knife to its scabbard. At his hard look, she hastily amended her unintentional error. "Dominic." He inclined his head, approving the change. "Why did you abduct me? To pay my father back for having you beaten, or . . . ?"

"Not your father. You. I mean to pay *you* back, *Miss* Sarah."

"I tell you I didn't tell anyone about—about what happened! As if I would! You must see that I had as much to lose as you."

"Not quite as much. I nearly lost my life."

"Not because of me!" His shuttered face told her that she was wasting her time and her breath—and making him angry to boot. She tried a new tack. "When a runaway convict is caught—and most are—they are usually hanged. If Percival—if my father had you beaten, I can see why you ran. But if you were to go back now, taking me with you, I could say that you saved me from the bushrangers, and you wouldn't be punished at all. I could even get my father to try to get your sentence reduced, as a reward. Wouldn't that be better than spending the rest of your life running?"

"Mmmm." He shook out the blanket, making the dust rise around them in a swirling cloud. Sarah coughed, managing just in time not to glare at him. If she had any hope of persuading him to take her home, she had best not anger him. "Hold still." He dropped the blanket over her head as he spoke. Sarah jumped, surprised as she was enveloped in the stifling folds; then as he pulled the slit down over her head she realized that he had fashioned her a rough poncho. The gray blanket with its black diamond pattern was wool, hand-woven by an aborigine sometime in the distant past, and it was faded and dusty, but it

covered her far more adequately than did her tattered
nightrail. She guessed that when she was standing, the
blanket would hang past her knees, so that her nightrail
would show only from the middle of her slim calves to her
ankles. With her bare feet, filthy now, protruding, and her
hair hanging to her waist in a tangle of hopeless snarls,
Sarah knew that she must look ludicrous. But at least she
was decently covered.

"Ga— Dominic," she said, striving to contain her
impatience as he hacked off two corners of the blanket
poncho and, gathering up the rope he had used to bind her
wrists, moved down to crouch at her feet. Still he had not
replied to her proposal. Sarah allowed herself the luxury of
darting a glance at the top of his dusty black hat as he bent
his head, studying her feet. When he picked up one of her
feet and fitted a piece of blanket to her sole, wrapping the
ends around her toes and ankle, she jiggled her captive
foot to get his attention. "Dominic!"

"Hold still." He looked up, frowning, then removed the
piece of blanket around her foot and pierced it in several
places with his knife. After cutting the rope in half, he
again returned the knife to the scabbard at his waist.

"Did you hear me?" Sarah could not stifle the exasperation she felt. It was plain in her voice. He was fitting the
blanket around her foot again, then using the rope to lace it
into a crude sandal. At her words, he glanced up.

"Oh, I heard you." His voice was dry. "I may be a
convict, Sarah, but I am not a fool. Why should I put my
life in your hands? I have only your word that you would
do as you say, and frankly, me darlin', I don't trust you an
inch. You should feel fortunate that I don't take a whip to
you just to show you how it feels. After all, you had me
whipped when I did nothing more than make love to
you—with your cooperation. What would you consider
suitable punishment for abduction, and, uh, everything

else, I wonder?'' He shook his head. ''I'm not inclined to find out.''

''I did not have you whipped!''

He was fitting the second piece of blanket around her other foot and lacing it in place. The brim of his hat shielded his face from her eyes. ''You may not have given the express order, but you must have known damned well what would happen when you went sobbing to Papa about what I'd done to you.''

''I tell you I didn't.''

''It doesn't matter.'' His voice suddenly was weary. ''I'm not going to argue with you, Sarah. Here you are, and here you stay, and that's an end to it.''

''Won't you at least consider . . . ?''

''No, I won't.'' He looked up at her then, his expression suddenly brutal. ''I've had enough of being the next thing to a slave. I'm not going back, and you're not either. At least, not for the present.''

''Dominic . . .''

''Be silent.'' He stood up abruptly, reaching down a hand to grasp her arm and haul her to her feet when she just sat there gaping at him. ''I've made up my mind, and there's an end to it.'' He slipped his hat from his head as he spoke and plopped it down on her tangled mane. ''Here. I don't want you getting sun stroke. And you'll need this, too.''

''This'' was the dirty, still-damp bandanna, which he tied over her nose and mouth. Sarah stared at him over the edge of the cloth when he turned her back around after tying the kerchief behind her head.

''What about you?'' The question was muffled by the mask.

He stood there looking at her, the sun burning down on his bare head, bringing out the blue-black lights in his ebony waves. His eyes were very blue in his dark face as he surveyed her without expression.

"I think I can stand the heat better than you," was all he said before he clasped her waist and lifted her back into the saddle, turning her sideways this time so that the leather would not chafe the tender skin on the insides of her thighs.

XV

It was nearly dusk when they drove the sheep through a grove of ghost gums to the tiny trickle of water that was all that was left of a stream that, judging from the wide, sun-dried banks, had once been bountiful. Sarah stared hard at it. Noting the position of the slowly sinking sun and recalling as best she could the way they had come, she decided that it must be Kerry's Creek, which ran along the northern edge of the station before veering off toward the mountain range known as the Australian Alps. The creek eventually—she could not be sure of her distances—emptied into the Murrumbidgee River near the town of Wagga Wagga. If she could manage to escape, her one hope would be to follow the creek to safety. The trek would be arduous, to say the least, but not, she thought, impossible, now that she knew in what direction to head and had the creek to provide her with water. It would never do simply to run away whenever the opportunity presented itself without some kind of plan. If she did, without some notion of where she was and where she was going, she risked getting lost in the bush. And getting lost in the bush meant quick death.

Sarah had given up trying to hold herself stiffly erect. The heat and the miles they had traveled had robbed her even of that last prideful gesture. She sat sideways, slumped back against Dominic's sweat-soaked chest, her head lolling against one broad shoulder, her legs trailing over one of his as she practically sat in his lap in the saddle. The arm holding the reins was around her back, supporting her. In such close contact with him, his body heat was almost tangible. She could feel the steely hardness of his muscles, hear the rhythmic beat of his heart, smell the musky, perspiration-tinged scent that reminded her constantly that she was being held close by a man. With the heavy wool blanket enveloping her, she felt as if she were being roasted alive. But the alternative was to ride once again with only the thin nightrail to shield her from the curious eyes of the men. And this she refused to do.

The hat and kerchief had been a blessing throughout the sweltering afternoon. The sun had been relentless; the clouds of dust had reduced Dominic, who had no protection from them, to sporadic fits of coughing. Sarah had not offered to return either his hat or his bandanna to him, and to her surprise, given his present hostility toward her, he had not suggested it. Not even when his face began to burn to a deep, dark red and the coughing got so bad that it shook his body. If he wanted to be chivalrous, *she* would not object, Sarah thought caustically. Evidently it hadn't occurred to him that, as a native Australian, she was probably less susceptible to the conditions than he, who came from a country noted for its cool mists and gentle rains. Or, if it had occurred to him, he was stubbornly refusing to admit it. If she felt an occasional twinge of concern when his coughing shook his chest, she squelched it with the reminder that, thanks to him, she was physically miserable and worried about her family's being worried about her. They would have no way of knowing that she had been abducted by Lowella's runaway convict. And even if they did, Sarah thought, it would provide them no comfort. They could not guess that, whatever other emotions he might generate inside her, she was not frightened of him. Although, she thought, casting a darkling look back at him, perhaps she should be.

The smell of the water had apparently reached the sheep, because they were bleating frantically, nearly running as they struggled toward the creek. The horses were affected too. The one they were riding, an Appaloosa with dark gray haunches fading to near white with gray spots toward the withers, picked up its pace, tossing its head and whinnying in anticipation. When the sheep reached the creek, they milled around in the water, spreading out endlessly until they were chest deep in muddy water for as far as the eye could see. Dominic made no attempt to hold back his horse. It splashed into the stream, which came to just past its knees, nudging aside a sheep and lowering its head to drink thirstily. The other riders, seven in all, were likewise watering their horses. There was no fear of the sheep straying now that they had found the stream.

Eventually Dominic pulled up the horse's head, to its obvious displeasure. It snorted and sidestepped dramatically, tossing its head and pawing at the water. He controlled it seemingly without effort, reinforcing Sarah's earlier impression that he was at home with horses. With shouts and swings of the long whip that had been tied to the skirt of the saddle, he began to force the sheep out of the water before they could drink themselves to death. The other riders were doing the same. With Dominic's arm no longer available to support her, Sarah was forced to put her arms around his waist and cling tightly to keep from sliding from the saddle. Pressed so tightly against him, she grew ever more aware of the hard male contours of his body, of his scent, and of the crisp, damp hairs that curled on his chest, on which her cheek was forced to rest. As she felt his body move, heard his lilting voice shouting at the recalcitrant sheep, and felt his thighs shifting beneath her own, Sarah realized to her horror that her body was responding blindly to his nearness. Having once learned the secret joys of being female, her body was reacting automatically to the overwhelming presence of the man who had schooled it.

It was dark by the time the sheep were at last herded together some little way from the creek. The men would watch them in shifts; a rider went from man to man, informing each of which shift he would be expected to take. When he got to Dominic, he eyed Sarah hungrily throughout the terse conversation. Sarah, inwardly shuddering at the thick-featured, unshaven face with its two rotten teeth that were clearly visible as he spoke, pressed her face against Dominic's chest and refused to look at him. It had just occurred to her that she was the only woman, and a helpless captive at that, among eight men, every one of whom, besides the man she was now cringing against, was eying her with some degree of speculation. Sarah had an uneasy suspicion that they were assuming that she would provide the evening's entertainment. . . .

"I'll take care of it, Darby," Dominic said sharply, terminating the conversation. Sarah realized the man called Darby had spun his words out simply so that he could ogle her longer. Before Darby could launch another series of detailed instructions, Dominic wheeled the horse away, heading toward where the men who were not on first watch had already built a fire and were setting up billycans for tea.

"Steady," Dominic said as he pulled up the horse and

Sarah swayed against him. She looked up at that, meeting his eyes briefly before looking away over the dark plain.

"Can you get down?" he asked, sounding faintly impatient as she sat there staring stonily away from him.

Sarah nodded once, the motion jerky, and slid awkwardly from the saddle. To her humiliation, when her feet touched the ground her legs refused to support her. After nearly twenty-four hours of nonstop riding, her knees were like quivering masses of jelly. They folded beneath her, depositing her in a crumpled sitting position on the ground. Dominic looked down at her briefly, then swung one long leg over the saddle and dismounted.

"All right?" he asked, his expression hooded as he looked at her.

"Fine," Sarah answered curtly, belying her exhausted posture. To her annoyance, her voice was a hoarse croak. To make up for its weakness, she glared at him.

He ignored her, reaching beneath the horse to unhitch the girth and then slide the saddle and blanket from the animal's back. He dropped the gear near the base of a thick gray gum a little distance away, then returned to slip off the bridle and tether the horse to the hitching line to which three of the other horses were already tied. The animals greeted one another with soft nickers, while Dominic turned back to Sarah.

"What's his name, anyway?" she asked idly, indicating the Appaloosa, which looked to be far too fine an animal to belong to bushrangers. More than likely stolen, she thought, and sniffed.

"I call him Kilkenny," he said, eying her as if he could not place what had prompted that disdainful sniff.

"Why?" Sarah asked, looking up at him, suddenly interested.

For a moment she thought he wasn't going to answer, but then he shrugged, as if he had decided to humor her.

"Because when I first saw him, when he was rearing and lunging and refusing to let anyone near him, he reminded me of a place called Kilkenny in Ireland: wild and beautiful, and dangerous to the unwary."

"Kilkenny," Sarah repeated softly, suddenly liking the name. "Is that where you're from?"

"Near enough," he answered shortly, and terminated the conversation by reaching down a hand to haul her to her feet. With his arm around her, he led her toward the campfire. Sarah took one look at the unyielding lines of his profile and said nothing further.

They each ate a plate of beans flavored with a bit of bacon and drank strong, bitter tea from tin cups. Each man carried his own utensils, which meant that Sarah had to share Dominic's. She found it strangely unsettling to eat from his plate, although she had sole use of his spoon, while he ate with the knife he carried at his belt—with considerable skill, she noted with surprise, watching him expertly scoop beans onto the long flat blade. Sharing his cup was worse; she went to considerable effort to avoid placing her lips in the spot where his had been. She felt that he noticed her avoidance, but he said nothing about it. When supper was finished, he left her sitting by the fire while he went to rinse the utensils in the creek. Left alone, Sarah slowly became aware of the thickening silence around her. Looking up from the cup of tea she was nursing, she was alarmed to find herself the cynosure of three pairs of male eyes.

Sarah hastily lowered her eyes back to her cup, wishing vainly that the hat that dangled from its string down her back was still atop her head so that its brim could shield her face from prying eyes. But she was aware of the man who got slowly to his feet and began walking around the fire toward where she sat with her back against a fallen tree. As she felt rather than saw his approach, all her senses leaped in alarm. Where was Dominic? she wondered frantically, then wondered at herself. What made her think that he would protect her?

"Walll, little sheila, you gonna set over here by your lonesome all night? Me and the boys has been lookin' forward all day to makin' your better acquaintance."

Sarah said nothing for a moment, but as the booted feet planted firmly in front of her showed no sign of moving away, she lifted her eyes slowly up the dusty, water-splotched herder's garb to his face. It was broad and seamed with years of exposure to the sun, homely but not actually repulsive as had been the face of the man called Darby. A bushy red beard obscured his mouth and jaw; his nose was bulbous, his eyes a pale, sun-faded blue, beneath a fringe of hair the same shade as his beard.

"Pray excuse me. I am very tired." The words were as cool and steady as she could make them. Her eyes met his without, she hoped, any sign of the fear that was making her heart palpitate.

"Ehhh, listen to her talk! We got ourselves a lady," he chortled to the men across the fire, then turned back to Sarah. "That's all right, little sheila. The kind of acquaintance we has in mind involves a lot of laying—flat on your back." He chuckled again at Sarah's appalled expression, then reached out to take a clumsy grip on her arm. "Come on, sheila. There's four of us for now, and four more for later, so you'd best be gettin' a move on. Else you won't be gettin' no sleep at all tonight."

Sarah stiffened, all her muscles bracing for a fight to the death. She would not submit to these—these animals! But before she could do anything, Dominic's tall form materialized out of the darkness. He strolled toward her with infuriating unconcern, his head cocked a little to one side as he took in the situation. Sarah felt temper at his nonchalance begin to churn in her veins—until she noted the long rifle cradled negligently in his arm.

"Now, Minger, the lady doesn't look too excited about the prospect of sharing a bedroll with the three of you. Maybe somebody told her about your fleas."

Minger, who had been scratching at his beard, stopped, looking self-conscious. Across the fire, the other three roared with laughter. Dominic himself was grinning as Minger glared at him.

"Dammit, Gallagher, we saved your hide. Are you gonna stand between us and a little fun? We won't hurt the lady none. She won't be nothin' more than a little sore, come mornin'."

"But what about your fleas, Minger?" Dominic prodded gently, coming to a halt beside Sarah. She stood up, moving close to his side. He didn't so much as look at her, but his solid presence beside her was immensely reassuring. "You can't expect me to share a horse tomorrow with a lady infected with your fleas."

More guffaws from the men who watched and listened with increasing enjoyment from the other side of the fire made Minger's face redden until it was almost the color of his beard.

"Sheila can share my horse," he muttered truculently.

"Now there's an idea," Gallagher said with seeming approval. "But maybe we'd better ask the lady her preference. What about it, sheila?"

The mocking way he called her sheila—a too-familiar Australian name for any young female—made her long to kick him in the shin, but prudence kept her feet planted firmly at her side. She looked up—she didn't think she'd ever get used to having to bend her neck so far to look into a man's face—and met his gaze. His eyes were sending her a message. Be careful, they said. Play it light.

"Why, I thank you for your kind offer, Mr. Minger."

Sarah smiled politely at the perspiring man who was only a couple of inches above her own height. "But I'm deathly allergic to fleas. So I guess I'll just have to forgo the pleasure of riding with such a handsome man in favor of Mr. Gallagher here. He may not be as good to look at, but he won't make me itch, either."

The men across the fire roared again at her response. Minger eyed her, then Dominic, his face growing even redder. For a moment the issue hung in the balance. Then he joined rather halfheartedly in his mates' chuckles and retreated.

"Very good," Dominic whispered in her ear when Minger was once again on the other side of the fire, parrying the inevitable jokes with what grace he could muster. "I didn't know you had a sense of humor, *Miss* Sarah. Surprising, all the talents you manage to hide under that old-maid exterior."

"I am not an old maid!" Sarah snapped without thinking, stung by the slur. He looked down at her, smiling suddenly, a very charming smile such as she had never before seen him wear. It made his blue eyes twinkle in the handsome, sun-baked bronze of his face; his mouth tilted up lopsidedly, while a lone dimple creased his right cheek. Sarah stared, dazzled.

"No, you're not, are you," he said, his hand coming up to tug unexpectedly at a tangled lock of her hair. "Like the proverbial wolf in sheep's clothing, you merely pretend to be. When something happens to shake you out of your prim ways, you become quite a woman."

Sarah could find nothing to say to this, which was, she thought, in the nature of a compliment. But maybe not. He might have some ulterior meaning that she, in her naïveté, could not even guess at. He might even be alluding to that night when he had taken her virginity. . . . He must have read her thoughts in the golden eyes that she had fastened on his, and made his own associations, because abruptly his face hardened as his smile vanished.

"Come with me." He turned his back, speaking over his shoulder as he walked away from her. "I think it's best if we let our friends cool down a little." He nodded toward the trio who were now swigging rum as they swapped stories and stared into the flickering fire. Sarah quickly fell into step behind him. She didn't want to be left on her own with them again. Next time, Dominic might not appear so fortuitously—or he might take it into his head not to intervene.

"How did you get hooked up with them, anyway?" she asked, hurrying to catch up with him. His long stride was carrying him rapidly into the darkness of the denser part of the gum grove.

"Sorry they saved my life?" The snarl was ugly. He didn't even look at her as he continued his rapid pace. Sarah winced, sorry that she had asked the question. It had inevitably reminded him of her supposed perfidy—if he had needed reminding.

"Not at all," she answered stiffly.

His eyes gleamed in the darkness as he turned his head to look at her. "I stumbled upon their camp about three days after I managed to escape from your father's idea of vengeance. They were getting ready to ride on, and I was half-dead. I think they would have left me to die if they hadn't realized that I had come from the general direction of Lowella. They asked me if that was where I was from, and when I answered a cautious yes, they took one look at my back and guessed the rest—or the important parts, anyway. They offered to give me a horse and let me ride with them, on one condition: that I help them plan a raid on your father's sheep. Not having any particular love for your home, I accepted. And here I am."

"You helped them set fire to the barns, and the stable—

do you know that some of the horses died in that fire? Mrs. Abbott and I were the only ones left to rescue them, and we couldn't get them all out. You killed them, and stole our sheep, and sent a mob to attack the homestead!'' Sarah's voice was shaky by the time she finished her accusations.

He shrugged, looking faintly satisfied at her impotent anger. ''I did what I had to to stay alive. They would have raided Lowella with or without my help, in any case. Besides, why should you expect any different? *You* did your damnedest to have me killed.''

''I did not!''

''Don't lie to me, Sarah. I don't like it.''

''I—'' She broke off abruptly. He had stopped, and was in the process of unbuttoning the few buttons that remained closed on his shirt. ''What are you doing?''

He smiled tauntingly at the horror in her voice. ''What does it look like? I'm taking off my clothes. So are you. Starting now.''

''What?''

''You heard me, Sarah. Strip.''

''I will not! Will you *stop*?''

He had removed his shirt and tossed it over a nearby branch. Hopping from one foot to the other, he pulled off his boots and set them aside. Then his hand moved to the fastenings of his breeches. Sarah whirled so that her back was to him, closing her eyes tightly in horror. She would have run away, but his arm sliding around her waist stopped her.

''Do you remember the little discussion we had earlier today, Sarah?'' He was close behind her, bending down to whisper in her ear. Sarah quivered and tried to pull free of him, but he held her fast. ''When I told you that you were going to do just exactly what I said, when I said? I meant it. So take off your clothes. Now.''

"No!"

"If you don't—if you don't . . ." His voice was silky now, his breath warm against her ear. "I'll do nothing, Sarah, just like I promised. I'll hand you over to Minger and the others and just walk away. It's your choice." She made a single abortive movement, and his arm tightened fractionally around her waist. "And don't try to get out of this by running, Sarah. I'll just fetch you back."

Sarah said nothing, merely stood there with her eyes tightly closed and her arms wrapped around her body. What could she do? She had no doubt that the swine meant every word he said. He *would* turn her over to Minger without a qualm, no doubt feeling that multiple rape was scant return for what she supposedly had done to him. But almost as unthinkable was the alternative—letting Dominic use her body in that animalistic way he had once before. Because of course that was why he wanted her to take off her clothes. There could be no other reason. Against her will, the memory of the glorious feelings he had coaxed from her body surfaced from the place where she had thought it safely locked away. If she was honest, a tiny voice whispered, she would admit that being "forced" to experience his particular kind of ecstasy again would be, in a vast understatement, no hardship. *No!* her mind asserted vehemently, even as her body began to react to the thought. She shuddered inwardly. She could not so demean herself again.

"Make up your mind, Sarah. Me or the others." His arm dropped away from her waist as he spoke, and he stepped back, leaving her to decide.

There was really no choice, as Sarah had known from the beginning. Lifting her chin in a characteristic prideful gesture, Sarah opened her eyes, dropped her hands to her sides, and turned to face him. He was naked. She swallowed, unable to look away. Her eyes ran once, involuntarily, over his body before snapping up to his face. But even that brief glimpse left burned in her mind the image of broad, bronzed shoulders, a wide, hair-roughened chest, taut-muscled belly and hips, and long, hard-looking legs. . . . About what protruded obscenely between those legs, huge and alert in a nest of curling black hair, she refused to allow herself to think. Or remember.

"So I'm to decide between rape in the plural or the singular?" she gritted, hating him. "You know you leave me no choice: I choose you."

"I thought you would." He was grinning, his arms crossing over his chest as he stepped back a pace, his head cocking to one side as he ran his eyes with slow purpose over her body. "Take off your clothes, Sarah."

Still she hesitated. Then, knowing that there was no help for it, she clenched her teeth so hard that her jaw ached and slowly lifted her arms to the string around her throat, which attached to the hat. She removed the hat carefully, turning to hang it on a branch. When that was done she bent to remove her makeshift shoes. Then, with her back to Dominic, moving as slowly as she dared, she began to lift the hem of the poncho.

"Oh no you don't. Turn around, Sarah. I want to see you."

"I must have been out of my mind that day on the ship," she said bitterly. But if she had hoped to jolt him out of his mocking enjoyment of his revenge, she failed. His expression remained unchanging as she turned back to face him.

There was no way out. Sarah lifted the poncho over her head, wishing that she could hide forever under its stifling folds. But she could not. It was off, and when she had finished securing it to a branch there was only her thin nightrail left between her body and his eyes.

She hesitated. To deliberately take off her clothes in

front of a man . . . She shuddered at the degradation of it. No matter that he had seen her naked once before. That night had been a time apart, something unreal, which she had blocked out of her mind. Until now. Now the shaming memories were pressing on her, unbidden.

"That, too." His voice was low as he indicated her nightrail. Sarah looked at him silently for a long moment. Then, doing her best not to think of anything at all, she caught the hem of her nightrail and pulled it over head. When it was off, she didn't bother to hang it with the rest of her clothes but instead let it flutter to land in a crumpled heap on the dark ground. It was too late now to play for time.

She felt his eyes on her. Her every instinct screamed at her to cringe, to cover herself, to hide as much of her body from him as she could. But she fought the impulse. She would not give him the satisfaction of knowing how truly successful was his revenge. Naked, she faced him, her head thrown proudly back so that her hair tumbled down her back to her hips, disdaining even to try to hide behind its tangled thickness. Her hands were uncurled at her sides, making no attempt to shield her body. But, for all her bravado, Sarah could not look at him. She was too ashamed. Instead, her eyes focused on the shadowy forms of a pair of kookaburras nestled for the night high in the branches of a gum not far away. The birds reminded her poignantly of the woods at Lowella. Would she ever see them again? She swallowed, forcing her eyes to shift downward to a rustling thicket of gorse. The sound of the dry branches rubbing together was oddly soothing. Sarah concentrated on that, refusing to allow herself to face the fact that she was naked, not three feet away from a naked man who would undoubtedly soon lay his hands on her, possess her body, and in doing so degrade her abysmally even as he wrung from her cries of shameful delight, while the wind played with her hair and trailed teasing fingers over skin dappled with goosebumps despite the heat. Overhead the moon was silent witness to her humiliation, a thin crescent illuminating her with its iridescent glimmer. Until—she felt it distinctly—the cool moonlight was replaced by the heat of his eyes.

"Look at me, Sarah." His voice was husky.

Shivering, Sarah fought the impulse to close her eyes in a childlike hope that when she opened them again she would be back safe in her own bed and this would all have been a fantastic nightmare. But it was real, she knew, and she also knew that she had no choice but to do as he told her. He had the means to compel her without compelling her at all. . . . She looked at him. His eyes were moving down her body, touching on her small, high breasts with their rosy tips hardening now against her will, her slim waist, the delicate curve of her hips. His eyes slid down the length of her legs, making no effort to hide the desire in their depths. Then, suddenly, they met hers.

"Come here, Sarah," The words were a hoarse whisper. Sarah stared at him, her eyes unconsciously pleading. His expression was implacable.

"Sarah."

Jerkily she moved forward, until she was so close she could feel the heat of his body. She was shivering, her teeth tightly clenched, wanting to flee and never stop but knowing that he would catch her if she did.

"Put your arms around my neck."

Slowly, reluctantly, Sarah did as she was told. His skin was burning hot against the smoothness of her arms. Her hands, locking behind his neck, could not help but be aware of the strength of him, under control now but soon to be unleashed. The already sensitized tips of her breasts brushed the curling mat on his chest. An electric tingle ran through her body. Mortified, her eyes flew to his to find that he was looking down at her, his eyes darkened to a midnight blue as impenetrable as the night sky. She was sore afraid that he knew what she was feeling, what she could not help but feel.

"Close your eyes, Sarah."

His head was bending, his beautiful mouth descending toward hers. Sarah could not stop herself from remembering his kisses. They had set her on fire. . . . She shut her eyes and waited, trembling, for the touch of his lips. In her heart of hearts, she knew that she wanted him to kiss her, to hold her, caress her, love her—and she could hardly bear the knowledge. She shivered with shame and fear and desire combined as his arms slid around her, under her shoulders and hips. He was lifting her, carrying her. . . .

Sarah's head was flung back against his shoulder, her thick hair acting as a cushion between his hard muscles and her skull before cascading over his arm toward the ground. Her eyes were shut, her mouth soft and trembling, waiting. Her body was supine in his arms. It was useless to struggle, she told herself, rationalizing her quivery acquiescence. He was carrying her away with him, to lay her down in the prickly grass as he had once before and take his pleasure of her body. And she could not stop him. Did not want to stop him.

Sarah heard a faint splash of water. She frowned, trying to place the sound. She couldn't. Her eyes opened, first to touch on his face—an odd smile flickered around his mouth—and then to look down. He was wading into the creek; the water was already up to his knees. Feeling befuddled, Sarah looked down at the moon's reflection in the dark, sluggishly moving surface of the water. Why was he crossing the creek? She looked back to his face. He was watching her, his eyes narrowed.

"What are you doing?" Her voice was faint, almost

breathless. She felt as if she had been a long, long way away and was struggling to come back.

His mouth tilted up at one corner. Sarah could clearly see the white gleam of his teeth through his parted lips.

"Giving you a bath, *Miss* Sarah," he said, grinning openly now. Before she could do more than gape at him, his arms were dropping away from her body and she was falling. . . . Sarah hit the water with a splash and sank like a stone. It couldn't have been more than an instant before her behind made bruising contact with the pebbled creek bottom. She surfaced, spluttering and coughing as her lungs tried to rid themselves of the water she had inadvertently swallowed.

"Why, you . . . you . . . !" She clawed at the wet mass of her hair, trying to pull it away from her eyes so that she could see him. At last she succeeded, to find that he was standing over her, unabashedly naked, his head thrown back as he laughed uproariously.

XVI

"You filthy, no-good *swine!*" Sarah choked, spluttering.

Dominic thought that if looks could kill he would drop dead on the spot. Her great golden eyes, their thick tawny lashes darkened into spiky clumps by the water that beaded them and ran down her face, were fixed on his with a feral stare. Her mouth—that soft mouth that he had had to fight the desire to kiss—was working furiously. With that thick mane of gold-shot hair tumbling wetly over her shoulders and her small nostrils flared with rage, she looked like a lioness that had received a dunking and didn't like it—and was getting ready to let everybody know her displeasure. Words like *swine* and *beast* fell from her mouth, intended, he was sure, to hurt him. Dominic couldn't help it—he started laughing again. The image of the prim, proper *Miss* Sarah, naked, soaking wet, and furious but not knowing the right words to express her outrage, tickled him.

"Remind me to teach you some swear words," he said, chuckling, as he sat down in the creek; when his long legs

219

were stretched out along the rocky bottom, the water came halfway up his chest.

"Of course you would know them all!" she spat in reply. He was perhaps three feet away from her. Her eyes, with their savage brilliance, never left his face. "You just wait until I get home again! I'll have them chase you down like a dog! I . . ."

"Unwise to threaten a man when you're in his power," Dominic observed mildly, scooping up a handful of sand from the bottom of the creek and proceeding to scrub lazily at his chest.

"I'll threaten you anytime I like! And carry through on it, too, you . . . !" Sarah yelled.

Dominic watched her, delighted at the reaction he had provoked. Prim, proper *Miss* Sarah had vanished again with a vengeance, to be replaced this time by a shrill-voiced virago who intrigued him as much as did her predecessors. To think that each personality—the convention-bound spinster, the courageous young lady, the charming dancer, the passionate lover, and now the shrew—was a different aspect of the same woman was fascinating. Dominic knew just what it was that was making her so mad—she had thought he would make love to her again, and, while she had professed not to want it, she was now, in the irrational way of women, furious that he had not—and he could not resist teasing her a little more. Sarah enraged was delicious.

"What are you so mad about?" he questioned, lifting a bewildered eyebrow at her. In response, she scooped up a handful of water and threw it at him, looking as if she wished it were something with a good deal more heft.

"You deliberately humiliated me, you beast!" she hissed, lips drawn back from her teeth in a way that made her look ferocious. At her choice of insults, Dominic snorted with hilarity. Seeing *Miss* Sarah turn into a proper spitfire—

though one with very ladylike language even when she was beside herself with rage—was enormously entertaining. "Scumbag! Don't you dare to laugh at me!"

"Sc-scumbag?" Dominic repeated unsteadily, collapsing back in the water with the force of his laughter. "My God, Sarah, where did you ever hear a word like that?"

Her only reply was a howl of rage. Then she launched herself at him, her fingers curved into claws that went for his eyes, her pearly little teeth snapping at his throat, her knees aiming for his groin. Dominic, caught by surprise, barely managed to fend her off. His hands closed around her wrists before her nails could make contact with his face, but, hampered by the water, his legs were slower to react. Her knee missed its primary target—thank the Lord— but got close enough to cause him considerable pain.

"Stop that!" he said, annoyed, wrapping one leg around hers to still them and holding her, hands pinioned by one of his, tight against his chest so that she could barely move.

"Let me go, you . . ." She seemed to have run out of words, so Dominic helpfully supplied one. A very filthy one. Her eyes snapped up to his. She stared at him, shocked and—momentarily at least—silenced.

"That's disgusting," she said.

"But effective," he replied.

Dominic was growing all too aware of the warmth and softness and curves of her woman's body pressed so close against him. Despite himself, he could not control the rising evidence of the effect she was having on him. He rolled so that he was sitting up with her half-lying across one thigh, still safely imprisoned against him but out of the way, he hoped, of that physical sign that he could not for the life of him control. She shifted against him, her silky thigh brushing his much harder one. The sudden passion that shot through his groin made him grit his teeth to keep from groaning.

"You would know words like that," she said, scathing, the force of her fury apparently having been cooled by the filthy word that he had picked up in the stables of the big house where he had grown up. She wriggled, trying to pull away. "Let me go."

Dominic could feel the firmness of her small breasts brushing against his chest and the resilient roundness of her bottom rubbing against his thigh. Another fierce stab of desire pierced him. He was conscious of a sudden, almost irresistible urge to kiss her, make love to her, possess her body here, in the stream. . . . She would make only token protests, he knew. But to do so would make things too easy for her. She could hate him if he took her body that way, and her hatred would wipe out any remorse she might feel for having betrayed him before. If he ever made love to her again—and he was honest enough to admit that that "if" was more window dressing than reality—it would be only when she had finally admitted that she wanted it as much as he did, when she begged him; the next time there would be no question that she did not know exactly what she was doing. He would rub her nose in her desire before he gave her what she wanted. And sooner or later she would admit to wanting him—he meant to see to that.

"Let me go," she said again, squirming. Dominic held her a little away from him. But he thought he could feel the soft thatch of hair between her legs brush against his hip.

" 'Please, Dominic,' " he instructed. His hand tightened around her wrists; he knew that he had to let her go, but he wanted to make sure first that she understood just who was in charge and how he expected to be treated. She was a bossy little witch most of the time, and if he didn't seize and keep the upper hand, no doubt she would soon be trying to tell him what to do. But he could not hold her much longer without doing something that would ruin his plan almost before it had begun.

"Please, Dominic," she said, to his relief, and he obligingly let her go.

She swam a short distance away, then turned back to look at him with an expression he could not read. Sitting again on the creek bottom, she moved her arms slowly back and forth in front of her as she sought to keep herself in place against the force of the current. Her long hair floated around her like twining strands of seaweed. Moonlight picked up gold threads in her water-dark hair and gleamed off the smoke-ringed sulfur of her eyes. Beads of water trickled down the satiny-pale skin from her high, sculpted cheekbones to her small, pointed chin. Her tawny eyebrows winged upward, and her nostrils flared like a cat's. Her wide lips were softly parted, and he saw just a glimpse of her tongue as it flicked over her dewy lips. Her slender neck and fragile shoulders were just visible above the dark surface of the water. She looked to him like an illusive enchantress, born of the moon and the water and the warm night air. As mercurial and changeable as the moon itself...

"Bathe," he said tersely, turning a shoulder toward her and scooping up another handful of sand.

"The water's dirty," she objected. Dominic didn't look at her; instead, he concentrated on scrubbing himself clean.

"Not as dirty as you are," he said. Out of the corner of his eye he could see her making a face at him, but then she followed his example, washing first her face and then her body with the sand. Dominic finished his bath, dunking down beneath the water to rinse away the sand, and surfaced to find that she was wringing out her hair, twisting the thick mass in a long coil like a rope as the water streamed from it.

"Come on." He stood up, indicating that their bath was finished. She looked hastily away from him, and if there had been more light Dominic was positive that he would have seen a blush color her cheeks. "Time to get out."

"You go ahead. I—uh—I'm not quite done." He was walking toward her through the knee-deep water. Still seated, she continued to wring out her hair; nervous, she kept her eyes carefully averted. Reaching her side, Dominic bent to catch her elbow and hauled her to her feet.

"Let go!" She tried to pull away from him, but he refused to release her. At last her eyes met his, as she leaned away from him in an effort to break free, and the moonlight silvered her body. . . .

In his effort to enforce his authority, Dominic realized that he had made a tactical error. The sight of her gleaming wet body, naked and endlessly alluring, set his pulses to pounding. He wanted her; God, he wanted her. . . . He knew he should let her go, should turn away from her now, before he could no longer control his surging need to possess. . . . But to turn away might reveal to her his weakness. And she would hone in on any weakness like a spider on a fly.

"Out," he said gruffly, propelling her toward shore. If he could just control himself for a moment longer, she would never know. . . .

Then she stumbled. Instinctively Dominic reached out to catch her, to save her before she fell. Then automatically he pulled her tight against his body. She had twisted, trying to save herself as she fell. The soft warmth of her naked breasts met the hardness of his chest with the impact of a searing brand.

His arms were around her slim waist; he should release her, he knew, but his arms refused to obey the dictates of his mind. Instead, they tightened. . . . She looked up at him, her hair slicked back against her head revealing the beauty of her bone structure, her eyes wide with alarm and, yes, he wasn't mistaken, a reluctant wanting that was yet as insistent as his own, those soft pink lips parted. . . .

Dominic couldn't help himself. He bent his head and kissed her.

XVII

Sarah felt his mouth close on hers like a bolt of fire that jolted her clear down to her toes. His lips were warm and firm, soft at first and then hardening. . . . She pushed at his shoulders, her hands slipping on his wet skin. He didn't budge. His arms were tight around her waist, hugging her so close that she could feel every hair and sinew. She felt the hot, throbbing maleness of him against her belly, and pushed harder, frantic to get free before her traitorous body could surrender to the clamorous urge to respond.

He didn't release her. His arms tightened, his hands sliding up her back, leaving little frissons of heat in their wake. Then his hands slid down, caressing the small of her back, running over the curve of her bottom to cup each buttock in a callused palm. He pulled her up on her toes, pressing her hard against him, letting her feel him, feeling her body against his. . . . His kiss changed, grew suddenly fiercer. Sarah gasped. The flutter of her lips under his allowed his tongue to enter her mouth. The hot wet strength of it sliding past her teeth to touch her tongue made her shudder. Seemingly of their own volition, her hands stopped shoving at his shoulders; instead they crept up around his neck, clinging. Her eyes closed. She allowed him to pull her body closer as she kissed him back, her mouth open and hot with desire. . . .

Before, when she had been innocent of the demands a man could make on a woman's body, she had been surprised, almost shocked by the things his mouth did to hers. Now she reveled in it, reveled in the devouring force of his lips, the slick exploration of his tongue. And she responded, her nails digging into the back of his neck as she ran her tongue with mindless hunger around the chiseled perfection of his mouth, caught his lower lip between her teeth and bit down until he groaned and twisted her so that her head was forced back against his shoulder, and he was again taking control of the kiss, dominating it—and her.

Sarah was trembling from head to toe. She felt as if she were aflame, burning up with a passion that she had never wanted to feel again, the same helpless burning passion as he had engendered in her mindless body before; she couldn't seem to focus on the shame of it, the degradation. Now her body was in control, weak and wanton as it stifled the screaming protests of her mind. . . .

She wanted him, God help her. Wanted him with a fierce passion that was utterly foreign to her nature. Wanted him despite the muddy water that lapped around their legs and beaded their skin. Wanted him without regard for morality or pride or even the humiliation he had made her suffer just moments earlier. She wanted him— and this time she knew that it had nothing to do with the moonlight, the soft scent of fruit trees in the warm air, or the seductive lilt of music. She wanted *him*—Dominic

Gallagher, convict, thief, abductor, man. She wanted him with a passion that she had thought only men could feel, or whores. . . .

Against her breasts she felt the pounding of his heart. The hardness of him was pressing urgently into her belly. He was leaning over her, his arms holding her close to the heat and strength of his body as the thick mat of hair on his chest abraded her nipples, and the steely muscles of one hair-roughened thigh parted her legs. "Sweet Jesus, Sarah," he muttered thickly into her mouth. Just that one husky whisper sent her senses reeling. She kissed him frantically, as fiercely as he was kissing her, their tongues alternately warring then soothing each other with soft caresses.

One hand was no longer cupping her buttock. She felt it sliding over her damp skin, his fingers trailing fire in the valley separating the soft hills. Then that roaming hand insinuated itself intimately between her parted thighs.

"Oh!" Sarah gasped as he found her, his fingers stroking her softness until her knees would no longer support her and he had to hold her up with one arm around her.

"Oh!" she gasped again, softer this time as his fingers did magic things to her, touching her in ways that sent arrows of fire shooting along her thighs. She felt a flood of heat as his hand slid forward to cup the soft mound of hair, pressing his palm hard against the triangle's apex. Then his hand was sliding between her legs again, his fingers searching for and finding the secret place that he had claimed once before.

She felt her toes curl as one finger found its way inside her, moving to restake his claim in a shocking, wonderful rhythm. . . . Do people really make love like this? Sarah wondered heatedly just before she was caught up and rendered mindless once again by the tight, pulsing coil that started deep in her belly and radiated outward.

"I want you, Sarah," he whispered huskily in her ear, pulling a little away from her.

Her eyes fluttered open to find that his bright blue gaze was smoldering now as it ran over her body, touching on her breasts and belly and thighs. She felt as if she might melt from the blistering heat of his eyes.

She whimpered a protest at the cessation of the marvelous things his fingers had been doing to her, and clung to him convulsively, trying to force him back to her with her strength that was nothing compared with his. He laughed; at least she thought it was a laugh, although it sounded more like a rasping groan.

"I'm not going anywhere," he promised softly, and swung her up in his arms.

Sarah was scarely aware of anything but the quivering intensity of her feelings as he carried her toward the bank of the creek. She spread her fingers behind his head, lifting her mouth to meet his as it descended. She was on fire for him, wanting him more than she had ever wanted anything in her life.

He lowered her to the ground just beyond the creek, his mouth fastened to hers, his arms cradling her as if she was the most precious thing he had ever held. Sarah's eyes were closed as she felt the prickle of fallen leaves and twigs and dried grass against the soft skin of her back and buttocks; the warm wind blew over her breasts, caressing her small, rigid nipples. But the wind's caress was not the one she wanted. Dominic held himself away from her, his hands braced on either side of her head, his muscular legs just brushing her soft inner thighs as they lay between them. Sarah could feel the touch of his eyes on her face, her body. But she wanted more. She whimpered, and when that didn't work she opened her eyes to find him staring down at her, tiny raw flames blazing at the backs of his eyes.

"Dominic," she said hoarsely, lifting her arms as she reached for him. Her hands were on his shoulders, stroking the damp skin, sliding over the hard muscles to lock behind his head and pull him down to her. Still he resisted. She frowned, tugging. "Dominic."

It wasn't she who was calling to him, but that woman he had made her once before, the one who was beautiful, desirable, and desired. That woman felt free to express her desires, to call on her lover to fulfill them. That woman did not know or care who or what he was; she knew only that he was a man, and beautiful. And that she wanted him.

"You're lovely, Sarah," he whispered. His eyes were smoldering on her face and then her body as he spoke.

Sarah heard his words clearly. In her normal state she would have scorned the compliment, disbelieving it, wondering what had prompted him to utter it, what he wanted from her. But now, naked beneath him, seeing the fire in his eyes that was there just for her, she *felt* lovely. That other woman, the one who was inhabiting her skin, *was* lovely. She had transformed plain spinster Sarah into Sarah the beautiful, Sarah the seductress. . . .

"Your hair is wonderful, thick and silky and the color of a palomino mare I had once. Your eyes—they're as bright and shining as twin suns. Your mouth makes me want to kiss it every time I look at it. Your chin—I love your stubborn little chin. It suits you, Sarah. Your neck is lovely, long and slender and tasting of warm honey. Your breasts— ahh, your breasts . . ." His voice thickened, trailed off as his eyes, which had been following along with his litany, fastened on the small, pink-tipped mounds that seemed to swell beneath the heat of his gaze. "They're perfect, exquisite, so beautiful. . . ."

Sarah's mouth opened in dazed anticipation as he bent his head to press a tiny, soft kiss to first one throbbing nipple and then the other. Her nails sank deep into his neck; her back arched as flames shot along her nerve endings. Her breath came in ragged little pants as he bent his head again, this time capturing one nipple and holding it prisoner. She moaned his name, clutching at him as his tongue rasped circles around the quivering bud, tantalizing it, claiming it, making it his. When he moved to the other breast, soft kisses were no longer enough. He drew the whole breast into his mouth, then released it to concentrate on the aching tip. His teeth caught the straining nipple, punishing it with a gentle nip before guiding it deeper into his mouth so that he could suckle it like a babe.

Sarah gasped at the red-hot spirals of sensation that radiated from the captured nipple. The sight of his black-haired head nestled so intimately against the pale skin of her breasts made her ache with desire. Her eyes fluttered shut as her back arched again and her hands spread across the back of his head, pulling him tightly against her. In response, his mouth tugged harder at her breast, ravishing it. She could not be still beneath the intoxicating onslaught. Her whole body writhed, mindless now with need, wanting him . . . wanting the ecstasy he had given her once before.

Her legs rubbed against the hair-roughened surface of his, coaxing them, pleading with them, seducing them. Her hips undulated against the heat of his, still held just a little away from her so that she was nearly out of her mind with frustration. Between her legs she could feel the hard, throbbing heat of him.

Her hands could not be still. They caressed the back of his head, delighting in the rough silk of his hair as it curled around her fingers, in the warm, strong neck, in the satin-over-steel shoulders and the broad back. . . . Her caressing fingers faltered as they encountered the raised,

uneven surface of scars. From the beatings . . . The movements of her body ceased as her hands lingered over the
weals. They reminded her, suddenly, shatteringly, of who
he was and who she was, of what she was letting him do,
of reality—and of shame. . . .

Her eyes opened to find that his body had frozen, too,
poised over hers, his head lifted so that he could stare
down into her eyes. She saw the same reality as that
which had just been forcibly brought home to her surface in his eyes. The dark, smoldering embers solidi-
fied, hardened. . . . The muscles of his arms quivered as
he lifted himself away from her, holding himself above
her for a timeless moment as he stared at her with bitter
anger. Then he was rolling away from her, getting to his
feet, muttering a string of oaths so foul that Sarah winced
to hear them as he found his breeches and dragged them
on.

"Get up."

Sarah needed no second urging to scramble to her feet,
conscious of his eyes on her every second. She was
appalled at what had happened between them, at what she
had so nearly let him do, if she was honest had wanted him to
do. . . . Moon madness. Sarah glanced up with agonized reproach at the slender witch floating high overhead. The silvery
crescent seemed to mock her. Twice now she had succumbed
to him under its seductive spell. Never again, Sarah vowed
fiercely, cringing as she thought of what would have
happened in just instants if he had not stopped. She would
have experienced once again the ecstasy of his possession—
and the shame.

"Get dressed." He flung her clothes at her.

Sarah, standing with her arms around herself to shield
her naked body from his eyes, could scarcely bear to
look at him. He seemed no more eager to look at her,
turning his back to her as he jerked on his shirt and then

sat on a nearby stump to pull on his boots. The very rigidity of his back bespoke his anger. In the moonlight, the crisscrossing scars gleamed pale against the teak brown of his skin. Sarah stared at them as she scrambled into her clothes.

"Come on. We're going back to camp."

His terse order flayed her overstretched nerves. Head flung back as she struggled to adjust the blanket-poncho so that it provided maximum coverage, she whirled on him, her eyes flashing fire.

"Don't give me orders!" she snapped, glaring at him.

"I'll give you orders any damned time I please. And you'll obey them. Get your behind moving. Now!" He turned his back on her again and marched away toward the camp.

"No!" Sarah shouted, nearly beside herself with anger.

Her eyes found what they had unconsciously been searching for. A rock! Snatching it up, she flung it with all her strength at his retreating back. It struck one broad shoulder with a satisfying thud before bouncing aside. His stride faltered; he hesitated for a moment, his back rigid. Sarah held her breath. How would he retaliate? Physically? Would he beat her, or . . . ? Her imagination ran riot as she balanced on her toes, poised to flee. To her astonishment, he didn't even turn. After that one brief pause he just kept walking steadily until the trees hid him from sight.

Sarah stared after him with fury stabbed through with triumph. She had gotten rid of him—and it had been so easy! Now she was free to follow the creek to safety, to make her way home. . . .

In the distance, a dingo howled, then another, and another. The moon stared down at her with a malicious grin on its sly face. Now that she had the chance, she knew with a rush of blind rage that she could not take it: it would be foolish beyond belief to hare off on her own, to attempt to walk back to Lowella or anywhere else without proper preparations. They must have come twenty miles or more since the night before. It was at least that far, she thought, to any place where she might find help. Without food or proper shoes or clothing, and with the sun beating down on her and one mile of bush looking exactly like every other mile, she would be insane to attempt it. She could easily die—people died in the bush all the time. Sarah gritted her teeth, uttering the same oath that had made her cringe when Dominic had used it just moments before. It fell from her lips with a very satisfying sound; for the first time, Sarah understood why men used bad language. There were times when nothing else would do. Kneeling to fasten her makeshift sandals, Sarah said it again. Then she straightened, squared her shoulders, and with fury in her heart trailed slowly, reluctantly, but inevitably in Dominic's wake.

Minger and the others who were not on watch had bedded down near the campfire, Sarah saw as she approached the periphery of the camp. Dominic stood beneath a towering gum, his saddle near its trunk while he spread a blanket beside it. Sitting on the edge of the blanket, he removed his boots, then lay back with his head on the saddle and his eyes on the fire. His rifle was within easy reach. Still Sarah hesitated, of half a mind just to wait there at the edge of the camp until morning. But the thought of the other men, the ones who were on watch and didn't know that Dominic had earlier placed her under his protection, dissuaded her. She would be easy prey. Besides, unless she wanted to be left behind, she would have to face him in the morning.

His eyes were closed when Sarah stopped beside him,

but she sensed—how, she didn't know—that he was aware of her presence and that he had expected no less. A smug satisfaction seemed to radiate from him. Sarah glared at his prone form, working to restrain the urge to kick him. She loathed every millimeter of that hard body, from the booted feet and long legs stretched so negligently over the nubby gray blanket that was nearly identical to the one she was wearing, to the arms crossed in relaxation over the broad chest, to the thick, curling black eyelashes that rested without a flicker on that maddeningly handsome face, to the glossy black hair still disordered from where her hands had run through it. Sarah waited, glaring, for him to open his eyes, to speak, somehow to acknowledge her presence. Gradually it dawned on her that he was not going to. He was not even going to offer to share his blanket! Not that she wanted to sleep with him, but . . .

Sarah glanced warily around the camp. The three other men appeared fast asleep, but they could awaken at any time. And there were the others to consider, too. She did not dare be left behind when Dominic took his turn watching the sheep. All she had to do was ask, she knew, and he would let her huddle at his side, under the mantle of his protection, however grudgingly he might now be offering it. But every vestige of her pride rebelled at humbling herself to that extent. She would not!

Glaring furiously at him, mouthing that oath again—silently, so that he would not hear it and take satisfaction from the straits to which he had reduced her—she stalked to the side of the tree and sank down against it, her back against the trunk. She did not dare go to sleep. It would be just like the unprincipled swine to leave her behind if she did. Arms locked around her knees beneath the enveloping poncho, head resting back against the rough bark, her back already aching as she sought to find a reasonably shaped section against which to brace it, Sarah directed one final, killing glare at Dominic's supremely comfortable-looking form. Doggedly forcing her eyes to remain open, she then settled in for what she knew would be an uncomfortable night.

XVIII

"If you would let me use one of those other horses, I could ride by myself."

It was mid-afternoon of the following day. Sarah was once again leaning back exhaustedly against Dominic's hard chest, her legs almost on top of his as she rode sideways before him in the saddle. One of his arms was around her waist; the other rested lightly on his thigh. Sarah could feel his chin just brushing the top of her hair, which today she had woven into a single thick braid without the use of either brush or comb and secured with a bit of cloth ripped from the increasingly tattered edge of her nightrail. Any observer, seeing the slender, supple woman resting so completely back against the much taller, broader man who was, to all intents and purposes, embracing her in the saddle, might easily have concluded that the two were on the easiest of terms. But then, an observer would have had no way of guessing at the hostility that charged the very air around them.

"Getting tired of my company? You enjoyed it well enough last night," Dominic jeered in reply.

Sarah clenched her teeth. Ever since he had made her practically beg him to take her with him when he went on watch the night before, Dominic had missed no opportunity to throw her behavior by the creek in her face. Sarah wanted to rant and rave at him, to turn around and box his ears until they were as red as the shirt he wore. But she did not. To do so would be to let him know how successfully he was managing to get under her skin.

"Riding tandem can't be any more comfortable for you than it is for me," she pointed out in a carefully neutral voice.

"It isn't," he promptly agreed in a growly undertone. "But as you know very well, both spare horses are loaded with supplies. To let you ride one would mean leaving half our provisions behind. Tell me, if put to the test, which do you think our fellow bandits would choose: you or a side of bacon? I know which I would."

"Don't lump me in with the rest of you miscreants," Sarah muttered nastily. "You're thieves, marauders, and kidnappers. I'm merely your innocent victim."

"Innocent?"

This snide remark, a clear reference to her lost virginity, nearly sent all Sarah's self-control flying. But she managed—barely—to hold onto her temper.

"I had no hand in my kidnapping. Or in setting fire to the stable and barns. Or in stealing my father's sheep," she pointed out virtuously, refusing to acknowledge that she had gotten the point of his latest hit.

"If you don't quit talking, I'm going to have a hand on your backside," he threatened.

Sarah smiled triumphantly at having come out the victor in this encounter. The name of the game seemed to be for each to goad the other into losing his or her temper, and so far the honors were about even. But this last exchange left her slightly ahead, Sarah reckoned.

"Temper, temper," she chided with enjoyment, and didn't even wince at the foul curse he muttered in her ear. During the course of the night and day, she had heard much worse from him.

Now that victory was hers, Sarah lapsed back into brooding silence, pulling the bandanna back up over her mouth and tilting the hat farther forward on her head to shield her nose. Despite their mutual animosity, Dominic had not repossessed his gear. Sarah supposed that some remnant of chivalry must be restraining him, or that he was so intent on scoring off her that he would not admit that he needed the protection of a hat and kerchief, while she did. Whatever the reason, she greatly enjoyed the notion that he was suffering in the broiling heat.

The sheep were on the move again, being driven through the dry bush country parallel to the creek. They would maintain this course for as long as possible, Sarah knew. To move away from a sure source of water before it was absolutely necessary would be lunacy. In this drought, even long-established water holes might be dry. No one had told her so, but Sarah guessed that they were headed for Sydney. Disposing of the sheep to an unwary or unscrupulous buyer would be fairly easy in that bustling port. But there were many miles between here and there. Once away from the water, unless more was found on a regular basis, the sheep would soon start dropping like flies. Sarah was torn between hope and dread that by the time they reached their destination the bushrangers would be left with nothing to sell.

It was after dark when they stopped for the night. This time, Dominic had first watch, and Sarah went with him. The sheep, having been allowed to drink their fill and having found a few blades of green grass on which to munch, bleated contentedly, taking comfort from being so close to their fellows.

Like the three other riders, Dominic patrolled the perimeter of the herd until well past midnight. When at last someone came to relieve him, Sarah was not even aware of it. She had fallen asleep hours before, lulled despite her dislike of him by the rhythmic beat of his heart and the secure feeling of being held in his arms. A rough hand on her shoulder shook her awake; blinking sleepily, Sarah saw that they had returned to the camp.

Before she was fully awake, Dominic swung from the saddle and dragged her down with him. Almost swaying with exhaustion, Sarah stood by as he removed Kilkenny's tack and tethered the horse before lugging the gear to a spot near the dying fire. Then, with a nervous look at the other riders who had followed them in, Sarah trailed after him. Dominic was obnoxious, hateful, and cruel. But the others were even worse. As she looked at his tall form bending to arrange the saddle and blanket, Sarah recalled the saying: "Better the devil you know than the devil you don't." But, she thought venomously, not much better.

To her surprise, instead of going over to the iron cookpot suspended over the fire and dishing out their meal, Dominic lowered himself to the blanket and sprawled back lazily, his arms crossed under his head, which rested on the saddle.

"Pull off my boots," he instructed, looking at her with malice.

"Pull off your own damned boots!" Sarah was exhausted, filthy, hot, and ravenous. She was definitely not in the mood to mince words. Before her life had been turned upside down by this despicable *convict*, she would never have dreamed of uttering an expletive. But lately they seemed to be coming with increasing ease to her lips. *His* influence, she thought, glaring at him.

"*What* did you say, Miss Sarah?" He raised a black eyebrow at her, feigning shocked disapproval. "I can't believe I heard a naughty word fall from your pristine lips."

Sarah thought about replying with several even naughtier words—all of which she had learned from him—but managed to refrain. He had undermined her morals, ruined her reputation by kidnapping her—even if she had been as pure as the driven snow, no one who mattered would ever believe it after she had spent days, maybe even weeks, in the enforced company of a band of escaped convicts and bushrangers—and utterly destroyed her calm and controlled disposition. She would be damned—darned!—before she would let him reduce her to using filthy language. Damn him!

"I'm not going to tell you again, Sarah: pull off my boots."

Sarah straightened her tired spine and glowered at him. With his boots and black breeches so covered with dust that they were practically indistinguishable from his once-red shirt, his face sunburned to a dark sepia making his eyes seem even bluer in contrast, his black hair waving wildly around his head, his long, hard-muscled limbs inelegantly sprawled, he was still so handsome that it made her sick. Her knowledge of her own appearance did not make her feel any better: she too was covered with dust, her face streaked with it, her hair in its long braid dulled by it. Her clothes filthy, her nightrail so stained with sweat and dirt so that she longed to tear it from her body, and her makeshift poncho so begrimed that it was nearly as dark as the black hat that hung from its string down her back. His dishevelment served only to emphasize his blatant maleness; hers, she thought, blotted out any claim to attractiveness she might once have possessed.

"Pull off your own boots," she snarled, the deliberate

absence of the shameful expletive in no way mitigating the venom that infused every word. He smiled up at her lazily. That particular curving of his lips was something she had learned to mistrust.

"Would you rather I turned you over to Minger?"

The soft question infuriated her. Sarah longed to tell him to do it and be damned—darned!—but she didn't dare. He just might take her at her word. He was capable of it, the swine. Clenching her hands into fists under the cover of her poncho—she refused to let him see how he maddened her—she made her way to his feet. Bending, gritting her teeth to keep back the vocabulary of expletives that he had taught her by example, she picked up one of his feet and tugged at the dirt-caked boot. Nothing happened—except that her hands immediately got as filthy as the rest of her. Unable to stop herself, Sarah shot him a hateful look. He chuckled. Sarah felt her rage building dangerously. Her look grew even deadlier, but she managed—barely—to keep a rein on her temper. If she gave way to temptation and told him in satisfying detail exactly what he could do with himself and his boots, she would only fuel his amusement. Because, karen the threat of Minger and his cohorts hanging over her head, she had no choice but to depend on him for protection. But oh, when she got him back to Lowella—she had not the slightest doubt that, sooner or late, he would be recaptured and returned to face her father's vengeance—she would make him pay. It would not be Edward's wrath he would have to worry about; it would be her own!

"Not that way. Turn around," he told her, enjoyment plain in his voice.

Sarah's lips tightened—she hoped not visibly—but she did as he told her.

"Now straddle my leg and pick up the boot."

With poor grace Sarah did that too, wishing she were

strong enough to break the dirty-leather-encased ankle between her hands.

"Hold on."

To Sarah's amazed fury, the words were scarcely out of his mouth before he was lifting his other foot and placing it squarely against her backside. Before she could react, he pushed—and she went stumbling forward, minus the boot.

"I told you to hold on. Now come back here and let's try it again."

Sarah straightened and glared at him—and obeyed. All he had to do was cast a single, significant look with those blue eyes at where Minger and the others were interestedly watching this byplay from across the fire. She turned, bent, picked up that filthy boot again—all the while giving free mental rein to her new vocabulary—and acquiesced while he placed his other boot familiarly against her backside and pushed. This time the boot came off. Sarah stared at it for a moment as she held it in her hands, having to battle against the urge to hurl it straight at that grinning face. But prudence won—for the moment.

"Now the other one."

The operation was repeated, with Sarah no happier than before. When both boots had been removed, Sarah placed them side by side, with infinite care, by the edge of the bedroll.

"Anything else, master?" The words were meant to be sarcastic—indeed, from her tone he could have had no doubt of her intent—but he took them at face value just to torment her, Sarah suspected.

"Now you can go fetch my meal."

Sarah stared at him sprawled like a pasha while he ordered her to wait on him. She knew that if she refused, it would give him great pleasure to compel her. And, if she had to do as he said, there was far more dignity in seeming not to mind than in putting up a battle that she was sure to lose.

Without a word she dug the tin plate and cup and utensils out of one saddlebag and carried them to where the cookpot and billycans were steaming over the fire. Filling the plate with the brown mess that she thought was meant to be meat stew, she had an awful urge to spit right on top of the glutinous mound. But, she reminded herself sternly, despite the extremes that that *convict* had reduced her to, she was still a lady. And ladies definitely did not spit into food.

Balancing the plate, the cup filled to the brim with hot tea, and the knife and spoon was no easy task, but she managed it. Dominic sat up as she approached, mockery plain in his dark face. Sarah ignored it. She handed him the food and stood watching as he dug into it. Her anger grew as he ate with apparent enjoyment without ever offering her so much as a bite. She was hungry too, dammit, and tired and dirty! She certainly wasn't going to stand there and watch him devour her meal as well as his!

"If you've quite finished gorging yourself, I might point out that you are about to consume my dinner as well as your own." Her voice was icy. Her hands-on-hips stance and belligerent glare were a little less cool.

"Miss Sarah's back, is she?" he said, barely bothering to glance up.

This reference to the deliberate precision of her language— she absolutely refused to let herself slip down to his level again!—made her eyes flash angrily. But she would not allow herself to be drawn. That was his intention, she knew.

"You can eat when I'm done," he continued, his tone condescending. "That's when all good slaves eat, isn't it? After their masters?"

"You would know more about that than I," she replied

with malice. His answering glance was rapier sharp. But Sarah wasn't about to back down now. If he grew angry, then that was just too bad.

"Yes, I would, wouldn't I?" The very smoothness of his words told her how much she had annoyed him. Sarah smiled. She *loved* annoying him.

"Be careful I don't decide to teach you your place the same way you tried to have me taught mine. Whipping slaves is quite an acceptable practice, I understand."

Sarah sighed, no longer as angry. "I did not have you whipped," she said for what must have been the dozenth time.

His answering sneer was equally familiar. "So you keep saying. I wonder why I don't believe you."

"Because you're a stupid, stubborn, braying *jackass*!" she yelled, losing her temper with a vengeance.

From across the fire, Minger and the others, who could not have missed hearing that bellow even if they hadn't been intently watching and listening, let loose a series of knee-slapping guffaws. Dominic, his face reddening angrily, set the plate aside and rose with awful slowness. Sarah, all too conscious of how angry he must be, nevertheless bravely stood her ground. She would not turn and flee like a coward. Even if she had wanted to, there was no place for her to run.

"I ought to beat hell out of you for that," he told her in a growl audible to her ears alone. He had gripped her shoulders when he stood up. Now his hands tightened punishingly.

"Why don't you?" she taunted, temper making her reckless.

"I'll do even better," he promised through clenched teeth. "I'll..."

"Hey, Gallagher, it don't look like you can handle her!

You need a *man* to show you how to tame a she-cat like that!''

Dominic's hands clenched even tighter around her shoulders, making Sarah wince. Her hands came up to catch his wrists, tugging at them beseechingly. She looked up to find that his eyes were fixed on the group across the fire. His expression was grim; she doubted that he was even aware of the strength of his grip on her.

''Aye, mate, we're gettin' awful tired of you bein' the only one with a woman. The only fair thing to do is share her!''

''That's right! How'd he get the lass anyways? I don't recall doin' any votin'!''

The chorus of voices from the other side of the fire made her back stiffen in alarm. They were baying like a pack of dogs with a hare in sight—and she was the hare. And this time, from the sound of them, they would not be distracted by a few jokes.

''Damn you, see what you've done?'' he growled for her ears alone.

''Me!'' Sarah shot back angrily, before the ridiculousness of fighting with him—her only protector!—occurred to her.

''You gonna be generous, Gallagher? Or do we have to make you?''

Staring up at him wide-eyed, Sarah saw his jaw clench at the challenge. His hands clenched too, reflexively, she thought, but even as she was wincing he released her.

''Stay out of the way,'' he told her through his teeth, and put her to one side.

Freed of his grip, Sarah turned to find that Minger, Darby, and the third man, whose name she didn't know, were advancing around the fire. Sarah stepped back a pace, then another.

''Stay back,'' Dominic warned them in a voice that

would have stopped Sarah in her tracks. The men just kept coming.

"We mean to have her, Gallagher. Why don't you make it easy on all of us? I told you before—we won't hurt her none. Just take what woman is made for takin'." As Minger spoke, the three men gained the other side of the fire and began to spread out.

Dominic was taller and more muscular than any of them, Sarah thought, frantically weighing their chances. Despite Minger's bull-like build, Darby's rat-meanness, and the nameless other's hulking shoulders and long arms, she would have been confident of Dominic's victory over any one of them—individually. But they were clearly determined not to abide by the Queensberry Rules. Obviously, they subscribed to the doctrine that there was strength in numbers, and meant to take him three on one.

Sarah watched, her heart in her throat, as they closed on Dominic—and was unable to suppress a gasp as, with a roar, Minger charged with his head down and his arms spread as though to butt the larger man to the ground. Dominic stopped him with the quickest, hardest punch Sarah ever seen. She gaped as Minger dropped like a stone to the ground. Maybe the battle would not be as one-sided as she had expected, she thought hopefully. Then, to her horror, as Dominic turned on the other two men, she saw Darby grope at his belt. In an instant a wicked-looking knife glittered in his outstretched hand. The other man, following suit, pulled his knife. Dominic jumped back as Darby lunged, and grabbed his own knife before whirling to meet the next charge. Sarah hysterically thanked God that the rifles were with the men's saddles. The rifles . . .

"No need to make this a killin' matter, Gallagher," Darby wheedled softly. "Give us the woman and we'll forget all about it."

"Come and get her," Dominic invited, half-crouched as

he brandished his knife before him. The firelight glinted off the honed steel blade. Waving the knife and his other arm in the air, Dominic challenged all comers. Darby crouched too, in a replica of Dominic's posture, as he slowly advanced. The other man, knife in hand, began to move out and around. When Dominic was between them, waving his knife threateningly at first one and then the other, the two began to close on him. On the ground, Minger groaned and sat up. Rubbing his jaw, he took a moment to absorb what was happening around him. Then he got slowly, lumberingly to his feet and, like the others, reached for his knife.

"I'm gonna cut your gizzard out for that, Gallagher, and then lay your lady-friend on top of it," he snarled, and took a menacing step toward where Dominic waited to challenge the three of them.

"Don't make another move!"

All four men ignored Sarah's order. She jerked the rifle to her shoulder and fired a warning shot over Minger's head—but not very far over. The breeze of it must have tickled his scalp as it whizzed by. He yelped, ducking and clapping a hand to his head to assure himself that it was still in one piece. The others—Dominic included—stopped in their tracks, turning to stare at her.

"Drop those knives. Now!"

They didn't move, just stood there gaping at her, nearly identical expressions of incredulity on their faces. Clearly, they had dismissed her as a negligible entity in so masculine an undertaking as a fight. She, a woman, was supposed to wait cringing in fear until claimed by the victor as the spoils. Well, this time the spoils was doing a little fighting of her own.

"Believe me, I know how to use this thing, and I will," she said calmly, aiming the rifle right between Darby's bulging eyes. "I said drop those knives!"

Darby dropped his knife. Minger and the other man did too. Dominic, grinning, moved to pick them up. The men glared at him as he threw the three blades into the bush.

"I'll get the horses," Dominic said as he passed her, chuckling. "You keep holding them off. You're doing a hell of a job."

Sarah didn't reply, just kept the rifle trained on the three glowering men. Not one of them made a move. Apparently the thought of a woman with her finger on the trigger unnerved them to the point of caution.

"Let's go, Sarah." Dominic, astride Kilkenny, drew up beside her, leading Minger's big roan. "I've got things under control."

Glancing up, Sarah saw that he had another rifle trained on the men. Looking hastily at the bulging saddlebags as she mounted—no easy task, straddling a man's saddle with her nightrail to hamper her—she concluded approvingly that he had taken most of the provisions.

"I'm afraid the other horses have—uh—run off. You should be able to catch up with them in a day or two. But I left you some food—and your rifles. So count your blessings." Dominic saluted the three, who watched sullen-faced as he nudged Sarah's horse into a canter with his foot and then wheeled his own to follow.

"You left them their rifles?" Sarah asked disapprovingly when they were out of sight of the camp. The rifle she had extracted from Dominic's gear lay across her saddle bow; he had restored the one he had taken to the holster strapped to one side.

"Why not?" he said, grinning. When Sarah spluttered, trying to burst forth with a dozen reasons at once, he leaned over to pat a bulging saddlebag. "I took the bullets."

They rode in silence for a little while before Dominic chuckled.

"What's funny?" She glanced at him without much favor.

He chuckled again, shaking his head. "You are, my girl. Not one female in ten thousand would have done what you did tonight. Most would have had hysterics or swooned. But you—you took stock of the situation and did what you could to correct it. My practical Sarah! Lord, did you see the look on Minger's face when you nearly scalped him with that bullet?" He chuckled again, clearly enjoying the memory. "They'll never get over it, being caught off guard by a mere slip of a girl!"

"Will you?"

He looked over at her, still grinning. "What did you say?"

"I said, will you—ever get over being caught off guard by a mere slip of a girl?" She mimicked his words. His grin slowly began to fade as, with a widening smile, she lifted the rifle from her saddle bow and pointed it squarely at his midsection. "Start heading west. We're going back to Lowella, Gallagher."

XIX

"Dammit, Sarah . . ."

"*Miss* Sarah," she corrected, enjoying herself hugely as anger built in his face. It was long past midnight; she had had an exhausting day and little sleep the night before. She should have felt dreadful, but having *Gallagher* at her mercy again sent energy bursting through her.

"You wouldn't use that." He was looking at her from beneath frowning black brows.

Sarah smiled at him. "Try me." The words were a soft challenge. The rifle never wavered as she pointed it at his belly. Then, slowly, she brought the barrel up a little, changing its target. "But not to kill. I think I'd put a bullet right through your elbow. You would probably lose the use of that arm for life. Now pass your rifle over here. And your knife. Carefully."

He stared at her, clearly pondering whether to chance it. Something in her expression must have warned him not to try. The way she was feeling right now, she would love nothing more than to put a bullet through him. He passed the rifle and the knife. Carefully.

"Head that way." Sarah stored his rifle in the empty saddle holster and tucked the knife in the bedroll behind her.

Then she gestured with her rifle in the direction she meant.

He glared at her, his expression clearly visible in the flood of moonlight that silvered the vast wilderness around them. "Lowella's the other way."

Sarah snorted impatiently. "You must think I'm awfully green. I can tell direction from the stars as well as anyone. It's a useful thing to learn, here in the bush. Kerry's Creek is to the west, and so is Lowella. All we have to do is follow the creek."

"I'm telling you it's the other way."

Sarah didn't bother to reply. Instead, she gestured with the rifle. With a long, hard look at her, Gallagher reined Kilkenny in the direction she had indicated. Careful to keep about two horse's lengths behind him, Sarah followed. They rode in silence until they reached the creek, which was exactly where Sarah had said it would be. Dominic said nothing as they turned to follow its meandering course. His dark face was shuttered, his thoughts hidden from her. But Sarah had a very good idea of how he must feel—furious, frustrated, and frightened, just as she had for the past three days.

"You know they're probably going to hang you," Sarah told him with enjoyment. "If my father lets you live that long. He'll have had people out scouring the bush for me. He won't take kindly to having his daughter kidnapped and abused."

"I don't imagine he'll take kindly to having the whole world know that he has a daughter who's so all fired anxious to take off her clothes and lie down for a convict, either," Dominic said softly, his eyes filled with malice as he looked at her over his shoulder. "And don't think I won't tell him—and anyone else who cares to listen— what a hot little piece he's sired. Why shouldn't I? As you say, they're going to hang me anyway. Why shouldn't I barter his daughter's honor for my life? Think of how many people I could tell about his man-starved old-maid daughter before they actually got me to the gallows."

Sarah's teeth clicked audibly as she clenched them with rage. "If you say another word, just one more, I swear to you I'll shoot you right now. And enjoy doing it."

He laughed, the sound mocking, but he didn't say anything. For which Sarah was thankful. She was so angry that she might really have shot him, and she had a dreadful feeling that she would regret that as soon as she had done it. In truth, Gallagher posed a terrible dilemma. Just the thought of his being hanged made her uneasy. He might deserve it, unprincipled swine that he was, but she suspected already that she wasn't going to be able to carry through on her threat to take him back to Lowella to face the punishment that awaited him. And she had another, equally lowering suspicion that she wasn't going to be able to shoot him, either, if the situation deteriorated to that pass. Not that she was squeamish. Under similar circumstances, with a different kidnapper, she could have shot the man without a qualm if he had given her cause. But despite the fact that she was presently furious with him, Dominic— *Gallagher*—had carved his own niche in her heart. She actually liked him, when she wasn't furious at him. And sometimes . . . sometimes he could make her feel things that she had never dreamed she could feel, beginning with a hot, thick passion. . . . Sarah cast the broad back swaying so easily ahead of her a look of acute dislike. He deserved shooting, or hanging, for that if for no other reason. He

had shown her exactly how barren was her spinsterish life.
And at the same time, by taking her virginity, he had
practically guaranteed that she would never be able to
marry to try to fill that emptiness. How could she
explain her lack of virginity to her husband on their
wedding night? She certainly couldn't tell him the truth—
that she had allowed herself to be seduced by a handsome convict. Because the truth was the one thing that
was totally unforgivable. Not that she had to worry
about it overmuch, she thought. Eligible suitors weren't
exactly beating a path up Lowella's front steps to offer
for her hand. And she would be damned—darned!—if
she would have Percival. Sarah shot Dominic another
castigating look. She would probably have to guard her
tongue for the rest of her life, lest some swear word
should slip out.

They rode without stopping through the night and the
next morning, following the creek as they headed toward
Lowella. Exactly what would happen when they reached
the station's boundaries Sarah wasn't sure, but she had
come to one reluctant conclusion: she could not turn
Dominic over to be hanged, or even whipped. She would
probably be forced to let him ride away scot-free—she
winced as she considered what he would make of that! But
at least she could give him a scare first. Letting him think
that she meant to turn him over for punishment would
serve him right.

Sarah calculated that it was shortly after noon when
Gallagher abruptly reined in. Sarah stopped too, warily
staying some paces back.

"This is ridiculous, Sarah." He turned around in his
saddle to direct a black frown at her. "You're practically
falling out of the saddle with exhaustion, and so am I. We
can't ride all the way back to Lowella without stopping.
We both need rest."

Sarah sneered—she was getting very good at that, she thought, from watching him. "And just how am I supposed to keep the rifle on you while we rest? Oh no you don't, Gallagher. I'm not that stupid."

He sighed. Sarah thought resentfully that he looked handsome even with four days' growth of beard roughening his jaw and his eyes bloodshot from lack of sleep. She eyed his dark face with disfavor, refusing to think how her appearance must suffer in comparison.

"I don't think you're stupid, Sarah." His tone was patient, probably meant to lull her suspicions, Sarah decided. "But you're not thinking straight. Look at you! You can hardly focus your eyes! And I'm not in much better shape."

"We're not stopping," Sarah said determinedly. "Ride on!" Then, when he just sat there staring at her, she lifted the rifle from her saddle bow and pointed it at him. "I said ride on!"

"Bloody little bitch," he growled, looking murderous. Sarah pulled back the hammer. He kicked Kilkenny onward.

As the sun rose to glare relentlessly down at them, the day grew hotter and hotter. Shimmering waves of heat rose from the miles of dusty earth pocked with holes and tiny scrub bushes. The creek to their left had narrowed until it was no more than a thin trickle. Overhead, heat-straggled eucalyptus trees did little to protect them from the sun. Often Sarah would glance over and see animals drinking from the creek. A pair of kangaroos, one with a baby in its pocket, waded against the current, stirring up eddies of mud with their long, comical feet; a hairy-feathered emu pecked thirstily at the muddy brown water; three koala bears ran along on all fours through the stream, looking up at Sarah and Gallagher with their shiny black eyes before scampering up a nearby tree. Ordinarily Sarah would have been charmed by the animals and their antics. Today she was just too tired.

An hour passed, then another. Suddenly Dominic reined in again and dismounted. Gathering her exhaustion-befuddled wits, Sarah fumbled with the rifle and pointed it at him. He gave her a single disgusted look and began to walk away into the bush.

"Hold it right there! Where do you think you're going?"

"Unlike you, I occasionally have to answer nature's call. You're welcome to come along with me, if you like."

Sarah felt scarlet color wash into her face as she watched his retreating back. What could she do? She couldn't shoot him, and she couldn't do as he mockingly suggested and follow him, either.

"If you're not back in a couple of minutes, I'll take Kilkenny and ride off without you. Without a horse or any provisions out here in the bush, you'll die just as surely as if they hang you. You can take your choice." The words were pure bravado. Sarah didn't think she could leave him stranded in the bush, but he couldn't know that. And she fervidly hoped he wouldn't put it to the test.

To her relief, he returned shortly. She kept the rifle trained on him as he approached, aware that this would be an ideal opportunity for him to attempt to overpower her. But he didn't even approach her, just stood looking at her for a moment with one hand on Kilkenny's shiny neck.

"I'll hold the rifle for you, if you have a similar problem," he offered, with a taunting smile. He had more energy than she, Sarah thought crossly, if he could still smile.

"I told you before, I'm not stupid," she snapped, waving the rifle at him. "Get on your horse. I want to reach Lowella tonight."

"Yes, ma'am." He saluted her mockingly, then turned to fit his foot into the stirrup and swing himself into the saddle. Without another word, he set Kilkenny in motion again.

By the time the sun began to sink in a vivid swirl of red over the horizon, Sarah knew they weren't going to make it. It was still more than half a day's ride to Lowella, and she could barely keep her eyes open. Soon she would be falling asleep in the saddle, and that would give Gallagher just the opening he wanted. She had to order a rest stop now, before tiredness fuddled her thinking completely. As for Gallagher, she would have to deal with him as best she could.

"Gallagher, stop!" she called out imperiously. He looked over his shoulder at her, then swung Kilkenny around so that the horse blocked the narrow path and he was facing her.

"What's the matter?" His voice was sharp.

"We're going to make camp. I want you to dismount, unsaddle Kilkenny, and carry your gear over under that tree. And watch yourself. I would hate to have to shoot you."

"Not as much as I would hate for you to," he observed dryly. With surprising efficiency, considering that he had had no more sleep than she, he carried out her instructions.

"Now come unsaddle my horse," Sarah ordered when he had finished. She dismounted, careful to keep the rifle trained on him, and stood to one side as he obeyed. When her gear was stowed under the tree along with his, she had him water the horses, then tether them near a bush with a few remaining green leaves so that they could eat, following along behind him all the while. Finally she ordered him to build a fire.

"Now lie down on your stomach," she instructed when

that was done. He was squatting before the small fire. At her words, he got slowly to his feet. Sarah refused to allow herself to be intimidated by the height and breadth of him, but she did take a step backward. It would be foolish to allow him to get too close.

"Planning to ravish me, are you?" he asked sardonically. "You'll need me on my back for that. But then, you do lack experience, don't you?"

"Close your filthy mouth and lie down!"

He looked at her for a long moment, in which the issue hung in the balance. Sarah kept the rifle aimed steadily at him, her eyes determined as they met his. At last he grimaced, and dropped first to his knees and then to his belly.

"Now put your hands behind your back." Triumph gave Sarah her second wind. It was amazing how much difference a loaded rifle could make; the feeling of power it gave her was intoxicating, and it intensified as he obediently put his hands behind his back.

He was lying between the dropped saddles and the fire. Sarah walked over to the gear, careful to keep a wary eye on her prisoner, and extracted a rope. Then, rope in hand, she approached where he lay sprawled in the dust, his face turned so that he could watch her every move, his long legs spraddled, his hands resting one on top of the other in the small of his back. His eyes were a deep obsidian blue as he stared at her. The expression in them made her that much more careful.

"I'm going to put this rifle against the back of your neck and then I'm going to tie your hands," she said carefully. "It's loaded, and cocked, so if I were you I wouldn't so much as breathe hard. Unless you want a hole in your neck the size of Melbourne, that is."

"Listen, Sarah . . ."

"Don't talk!" she said, warily approaching. "You're

not going to get me to change my mind with your damn—darned!—Irish blarney. But you're liable to make me angry, and with a rifle against your neck I wouldn't want that to happen. Would you?''

He didn't reply. Sarah watched him for a moment, then decided that it was now or never. She could barely keep her eyes open as it was. Pointing the rifle directly at his head, she moved toward him until the mouth of the barrel rested against the back of his neck.

"Turn your face away. Carefully!" This was so that he couldn't watch her all the time. If he watched, he was bound to see her concentration slip from the rifle to his hands. And then it would be very easy to surprise her with a sudden quick move.

He obeyed, the movement sullen. Sarah hesitated, then propped the rifle—which she had stealthily uncocked in case of an accident—against her hip, and bent to tie his hands. When they were secured to her satisfaction, she stepped back hastily, the rifle swinging to her shoulder once more.

"Now stand up."

"Sarah . . ."

"*Miss* Sarah. And I said stand up!"

He stood, his movements awkward because of his bound hands. She gestured him over to the tree and ordered him to sit with his back against it. He did, but with obvious reluctance.

"Hold still." She had come up with an ingenious plan for ensuring that he didn't get the opportunity to attack her while she was tying him to the tree. First she passed the rope around his throat and the tree trunk and tied it tightly. With the rope threatening to cut off his breath if he moved, and his hands bound securely behind his back, she didn't think there was a chance of him overpowering her while she trussed him up. Her plan worked like a charm. He did

nothing more than sit there glowering at her as she passed
the rope around and around his body before tying it in a
series of knots in the back.

"What are you going to do if our bushranger friends
find us? Or some other, equally nefarious characters?"
He was taunting her as she stood admiring her handi-
work.

"I am an excellent shot, thank you. I believe I can take
care of myself." She refused to seriously consider such a
possibility. Her luck couldn't be that bad—she hoped.

"How am I supposed to sleep like this?" he complained.

"You're not. I am."

Satisfied that he was tied securely, she moved away to
open her bedroll. His knife gleamed up at her; tucking it
with the rest of the gear, she sank down on the blankets
with a sigh. Her eyelids felt as if they were attached to
lead weights. . . .

"Don't I even get a meal?"

Sarah roused herself to glare at him. "Don't you ever
shut up?"

"I'm hungry."

"What a shame." She had meant to prepare a simple
meal, but she was simply too tired. They could eat when
she woke. Her eyelids fluttered shut.

"Dammit to hell, Sarah, at least put out the fire before
you fall asleep. We could be roasted alive! As dry as this
brush is, all it would take is one spark to set the whole
countryside ablaze."

There was sense in what he said, she knew. She had
meant to fix tea and beans over the fire, not to let it burn
all night. Struggling to her feet, she stumbled to the fire
and scooped handfuls of dust over it until not a single
ember glowed. Then she just managed to make it back
to her blanket before collapsing. Her eyes closed as
soon as her head found the saddle. Her last conscious

thought was of the malevolent glare in Dominic's eyes as he watched her curl up in the bedroll. She mistrusted the look in his eyes. . . . Her hand reached out to clutch the rifle nestled beside her before she fell deeply asleep.

The sun bright against her eyelids teased them open the next morning. Blinking, staring straight up at the scraggly eucalyptus branches overhead, it took her a moment to remember where she was and what had happened. Then it all came back to her with a rush. She turned her head, and her eyes found Dominic. He was leaning back against the tree, his head slumped sideways as far as it could go with the rope around his neck, his eyes shut. The coils of rope still bound him securely to the tree. Sarah first felt relief that he had not managed to work himself loose, and then a stab of compunction at his posture, which looked extremely uncomfortable. But last night she had not been able to think of any other way to secure him so that she might get some sleep.

Picking up the rifle, she stood up, stretching her muscles painfully. With a quick glance at Dominic, who hadn't moved so much as an eyelash as far as she could tell, she pulled the poncho off her head—she had been too tired and too wary to remove it the night before, although she had managed to take off her hat before falling asleep—and shook it vigorously. The resulting cloud of dust made her cough and close her eyes.

"You'll find some clothes in one of my saddlebags. I took Darby's extras when I was gathering up the gear. I would have told you about them earlier, but you didn't give me a chance."

Sarah cast him a startled glance, to find that his blue eyes were raking her body, which was covered only by the thin rag that was all that was left of her nightrail. Blushing, she immediately turned her back to him and pulled the poncho back over her head. She was embarrassed that he should see her so scantily clad, but along with the embarrassment was another feeling, a curious tingling that ran all the way down to her toes. Sarah felt her nipples hardening, and silently said another of those words with which Dominic had enriched her vocabulary. Why did he have to be so handsome? she asked herself despairingly. Just the sight of him was enough to make her body throb and burn, despite every reprehensible thing he had done to her. She could not even quell the achy feeling by reminding her hungry flesh that he was a convict and probably despised her, to boot.

"You'd get a big laugh out of seeing me tricked out in men's clothes, wouldn't you?" she accused, turning, suddenly inordinately angry.

He shrugged. "Wear what you want. If you enjoy being filthy, then by all means, don't change."

Sarah looked at him for a long moment, undecided. Then cleanliness won out. She would change, no matter how ridiculous or scandalous the clothes might make her look. And she would take a moment to bathe, too. With a haughty lift to her chin, she bent and began to rummage in Dominic's saddlebags. A pair of dark breeches and a gaudy blue shirt came immediately to hand. They were of poor materials, and coarsely sewn, but they were relatively clean. And since Darby had been on the thin side and she was tall, they shouldn't be too terrible a fit.

"Where are you going?" Dominic called after her as she headed for the creek, clothes in hand.

"To bathe, " she called back, grinning despite herself as she heard him groan, "Can't you at least untie me first?"

By the time she returned to their camp, she felt infinitely better. She had sat in the middle of the stream and scrubbed every inch of her body, including her nails, each of which to her shame had managed to collect a tiny crescent of grime. Then she had submerged her whole body, lying on her back on the rocky streambed while she scrubbed her hair with sand. When at last she emerged, she dried herself on the inside of the nightrail—having been next to her skin, it had stayed comparatively clean—before donning her new garb and rebraiding her hair. The breeches were a trifle loose and had to be rolled up at the bottom so that she could walk; the shirt was even looser, with long sleeves that she pushed above her elbows. The dark blue of the breeches was unexceptionable—if one could call a lady dressed in breeches unexceptionable—but the brilliant cobalt of the shirt made her feel like a peacock on the strut. She had never in her life worn such a bright color, and it made her uneasy.

Sarah retraced her steps very slowly, feeling more uncomfortable by the moment at the thought of Dominic's seeing her dressed as she was. She didn't know if she was bothered more by the impropriety of his seeing her clad in breeches, or by the unbecomingly revealing clothes. To her dismay, she suspected it was the latter, and fiercely castigated herself for always wishing to appear attractive to him.

To her surprise, he made no comment about her appearance—she had expected barbed jibes at her expense. Indeed, although she watched him carefully as she approached, she could discern no reaction except for a slight hardening of his eyes. Still feeling uneasy, she got the fire started and quickly set up a billycan for tea. That done, she fried bacon in an iron pan that he had also brought. When it was crispy, she ate a portion and swallowed a cup of scalding, bitter tea, all under his eagle eyes.

"Going to starve me to death?" he inquired nastily as she filled the cup a second time.

"It's a thought," she replied, carrying the cup and the pan with the remaining bacon over to where he sat. "But I think I'd rather watch you hang," she added, setting the food aside and pointing the rifle, which had never left her side, at him. He stared first at it, then at her. She thought his expression looked sullen, and smiled with delight at having so thoroughly gotten the best of him.

"I'm going to untie you. Don't make any sudden moves." She held the rifle on him for a moment longer, savoring his helplessness, then walked around the tree and began to work on the knots. It took her considerably longer than she had expected; she congratulated herself on having tied such knots when she was physically exhausted. But at last he was free. She gathered up the rope, then moved around to stand in front of him again, gesturing him to stand with the rifle. Then she had him move away from the tree and lie on the ground, and repeated the previous day's procedure for untying his hands. She had to work at those knots, too, and when at last they were loose she winced inwardly at the chafed marks on his wrists. She had not realized that she had bound him so tightly.

"All right, get up."

He stood again. Sarah stood over him with the rifle while he ate the food she had saved for him, then oversaw his activities as he packed their gear and loaded it on the two horses. When at last the animals were saddled, she motioned him to mount first, then swung herself into the saddle. He obeyed her every instruction without argument. Sarah didn't know whether to congratulate herself on his docility or to be wary of it. In the end she decided to be wary. She was as cautious as she could be, keeping her horse well behind his and her eyes trained on his back.

Two hours later he made the move she had been half-expecting. They had just passed a dilapidated shepherd's hut, the first building—though the sagging wooden shack could not really be dignified with such a name—they had seen in days. Lowella's western boundary could not have been more than a couple of miles distant. To reach the homestead itself would be about a six-hour ride. Soon she would have to make a final judgment on what to do about Dominic, though secretly she knew that the matter had already been decided. She would never be able to live with herself if she did not let him go. But not quite yet...

"Why are you stopping?" she demanded as he reined in without warning. He said not a word, but deliberately swung a leg over his saddle and dismounted. Sarah's eyes widened in alarm. She swung the rifle up and aimed it at him. He ignored it, walking slowly toward her.

"What are you doing? Get back on that horse!"

"Get down, Sarah. I want to talk to you."

He was alarmingly close. Sarah kept the rifle aimed at his heart. He didn't even hesitate.

"What do you think you're doing? Stop! I'll shoot!" Her voice was shrill.

"Will you, now? Shoot then, for I'm not stopping."

"Damn you, Dominic Gallagher, I will shoot you!" Sarah cried.

When he didn't stop, she hesitated for a moment. But he was only a few feet from being able to catch her horse's bridle. She could ride away, but he would come after her. If she was going to stop him, it had to be now.... But she couldn't bring herself to shoot him. She could see hard triumph in his eyes. He was reaching for her reins. Sarah jerked the rifle up to her shoulder and quickly aimed it between his feet. She would show him she meant business!

She pulled the trigger, bracing herself not to wince from the expected boom. She did not wince, because there was no need. All that emerged from the rifle was a sharp click. Dumbfounded, she pulled the trigger again, thinking the weapon must have misfired. There was another empty click.

"Lose something?" He was holding her horse's bridle now; the animal was docile under his hand. As he spoke, he thrust his hand into his breeches pocket and pulled it out again. When he opened his fist and extended his hand toward her, she saw that he held several rifle shells. The truth dawned on her with a sickening flash. Somehow, somewhere, he had managed to unload the rifle! He grinned maliciously at her stunned expression, his hand leaving her bridle as he took a step forward and reached for her.

"You Irish blasphemer! You no-good, filthy, rotten . . . !" Beside herself with rage at having been duped, Sarah reversed the rifle and clapped her heels to her horse's sides at the same time. The animal bounded forward, but Dominic grabbed at the reins, caught them, and hauled the whinny-ing horse's head around. Sarah swung the rifle butt at Dominic's head, murder in her heart. He ducked in the nick of time, catching the blow on his shoulder instead. He cursed, vividly, but didn't release his grip on her reins. Sarah swung again, wildly. He caught the rifle in his free hand and wrested it from her grasp. Then, despite her struggles, he was pulling her down.

"Let me go, you . . ." She was inundating him with the swear words she had learned from him, and he was laughing. Enraged, she began to beat at his head and shoulders with her fists as he held her tight against him. He caught her hands in his with ridiculous ease and held them pinioned behind her back. Still she fought, kicking and screeching, her head thrashing wildly as she hurled abuse at him. Finally he reached up, catching her long braid in his free hand, and hauled her head back. She glared at him with hate-filled golden eyes. Drawing back her foot, she kicked him hard on the shin, not caring that his hard bone did more damage to her foot than vice-versa.

"Enough, Sarah," he growled. And when she opened her lips to heap more abuse on him, he crammed her words back into her throat with his mouth.

XX

That hard kiss robbed her first of her breath, then of her anger, and finally of her will. Sarah surrendered to him utterly after little more than a token resistance, twining her hands around his neck to clutch with shaking fingers at the rough silk of his hair, pressing her body eagerly against his as he pulled her closer. She could feel the heat and strength and growing desire of him with her every nerve ending. His mouth was hungry as it took hers, his lips and tongue hard and urgent. The force of the kiss should have hurt her, but it didn't. She reveled in his fierceness, returning it with a spiraling passion of her own. There was nothing in all the world for her but his mouth, his hands running up and down the slight curves of her body, the feel of him against her. . . . She was trembling in his arms, on fire for him, wanting the kiss to go on forever, wanting to savor the red-hot desire that rose in her like the sudden awakening of a long-dormant volcano. She opened her mouth to him endlessly, her head thrown back

against his shoulder, her eyes closed. She loved the
sensation of fragility she got in his arms. His kiss made
her dizzy.

When she felt his fingers at her throat, slightly unsteady
as they worked loose first one and then another and
another of the buttons fastening her shirt down the front,
she whimpered into his mouth but refused to open her
eyes. She did not want to see the sun blazing at her over
his shoulder, or the dusty, pockmarked landscape, or the
stamping horses. She did not want to be reminded in any
way of reality, of what had happened before and would
likely happen after. She wanted only to be a woman in the
arms of a man, her man. . . . Sarah quivered helplessly at
the thought. He was her man; her body had recognized
him from the first. The lover she had spent her nights
dreaming of, her life waiting for . . .

His hand slid beneath the opened shirt to close over
one small, high breast. Sarah groaned as she felt his
callused palm cup her sensitive flesh. The erotic sound
shocked her; knowing that it had come from her own
throat shocked her more. But she could not stop the
wordless whimpers that were swallowed by his mouth as
he abraded her aching nipples with the palm of his hand,
brushing it over first one, then the other, then the first
again, before finally, with agonizing slowness, his hand
slid down her belly to the loose waistband of the too-big
breeches. She felt his long fingers and hard palm creep
beneath the waistband over the silky skin of her belly,
pausing only momentarily to explore the indention of her
navel before covering the triangle of hair that he had
claimed before.

"Dominic . . ." His name was a prayer on her lips. She
didn't know if she was begging him to stop or not to stop,
but when he removed his hand to work unsteadily at the
button at her waist, she felt bereft. Her nails dug punishingly

into his neck; her mouth shook beneath the heady passion of his.

One-handed, his other arm still holding her clamped against him, he unfastened the buttons securing her breeches until the garment fell over her hips and thighs to the ground. Underneath she was naked. He slid the shirt from her shoulders, letting it lie where it fell, bending to loosen her sandals before straightening to lift her so that the breeches and sandals were left behind on the sandy ground. Sarah felt the sleeve of his rough cotton shirt against the bare backs of her thighs as he swung her around, felt the tingling rays of the sun on her back and buttocks as he lowered her again, felt the rasp of his clothing and the heat of his body beneath it as she slid, naked and trembling, down the hard length of him.

"Sarah." Her name was husky as he spoke it against her mouth. His hands had moved to clasp her waist; he pushed her a little away from him. Whimpering, Sarah clung with all her might. With her lips she felt his mouth twist in a smile. "Oh, Sarah. Open your eyes, Sarah."

She refused until he lifted his head, breaking off the butterfly contact of their mouths. Then, resentful at the interruption, her eyes flickered open. Her hands were still clasped behind his neck, her naked body pressed to his fully clothed one. The lean brown face with its frame of midnight-black hair was so handsome as it loomed above her that she could scarcely breathe; her lips quivered as her eyes sought and found the beautifully shaped mouth, twisted up at one corner as he took in her dazed expression. Then her eyes met his; the passion she saw in the endless blue depths dazzled her.

"Do you have any idea of what you do to me, Sarah?" His voice sounded rueful despite its huskiness. He reached up and caught her right hand in his and pulled it from around his neck, guiding it down until at last he pressed it against the straining bulge in his breeches. Sarah felt the hard, throbbing outline of him through the coarse material, and snatched her fingers away as if from an open fire. He made no move to recapture her hand, but after a moment curiosity got the better of her. Slowly, cautiously, her fingers returned to explore that most intimate part of him. She touched him, hesitantly at first, and then as he showed no reaction except for a tensing of his muscles she grew bolder. Her fingers measured the width and length and strength of him, alternately squeezing and stroking until he gasped and reached down to catch her hand and pull it away from him, holding it tightly for an instant before lifting it to his mouth and pressing a heated kiss to her knuckles.

"Sweet Jesus, Sarah," he said, groaning. "Much more of that and you'll unman me." Gently, carefully, he replaced her hand on his shoulder.

Her eyes, huge as they gazed into his, asked a question; hard as she might find it to believe, she could think of the answering expression in his eyes only as tender. She stared up at him, lips parted, golden eyes wide, wanting yet not quite daring to believe what she thought she saw. "I burn for you, Sarah," he continued, bending his head so that his mouth brushed the top of her ear as he spoke. She felt a shiver run up and down her spine at the gentle touch of his lips on her ear. "I only have to look at you and I'm as hot as a young boy. I want to make love to you for hours, days, without stopping. I want to touch you all over, to kiss every inch of your skin and make it mine. . . ." He took a deep, shaky breath. Sarah felt a faint quiver in the hard muscles of his arms as they held her. "And I'm going to, Sarah. Right now, this minute, unless you tell me not to."

His head lifted again; he was looking down at her, his

eyes asking a question now. Sarah could no more have denied him than she could have denied herself. She wanted him—she was too shy to say the words, but her eyes said them for her. She felt his hands tremble where they clasped her waist. Her whole body shook in answer. But it seemed that he wanted the words as well.

"Shall I make love to you, Sarah?"

Sarah could only stare up at him, her mouth trembling as she fought one last battle with her common sense. The hard male beauty of the face bent over hers, the soft yet firm mouth scant inches away from her own, the blue eyes with their soul-shaking mixture of passion and tenderness defeated her before the battle had even been joined.

"Yes, please, Dominic," she whispered.

He laughed in a curiously shaken way. "My beautiful, feisty Sarah. I'll make it good for you, I promise."

He let her go, turning away to untie the bedroll from behind Kilkenny's saddle and spread it on the ground. Sarah watched, arms wrapped around her nakedness, second thoughts running riot through her mind. What was she doing, giving herself to him—a convict—again? Hadn't she learned?

Before she could change her mind entirely, he came back to her, taking her into his arms, pulling her against him so that she could feel the hard, warm muscles beneath his clothes. At his touch, her doubts wavered and then vanished. Her body seemed to catch fire. Trembling, she rose on her toes to find his mouth as he lowered his head. Their lips met with an explosion of passion. Her hands tightened around his neck, straining him to her as he lifted her and laid her down. Sarah felt the rough wool of the blanket beneath her bare back, felt the sharpness of a trio of tiny pebbles as they dug through the coarsely woven material into the soft skin of her buttocks, felt the scratchy limbs of a small, crushed shrub poking through somewhere in the vicinity of her waist, and didn't care. She wanted Dominic too badly.

He was taking off his clothes, his movements lacking their usual deftness because of the tremor of his long brown fingers. Staring up at him from her prone position on the ground, her eyes narrowed against the sun beating down on them, Sarah felt her mouth go dry as he quickly stripped off his shirt to reveal the wide, bronzed shoulders and the wedge of curling black hair on his chest. Still standing over her, his eyes never leaving her body, he pulled off his boots. Barefoot, he lifted his hands to the buttons securing his breeches. . . . Sarah was barely conscious of her legs shifting restlessly as she watched him unfasten his breeches and push them down, revealing lean hips and flanks and long, hard-muscled legs. Stepping out of his breeches and dropping them needlessly to one side, Dominic stood motionless for a long moment, just looking at her. His eyes on the most intimate parts of her body were as fiery hot as the sun overhead.

Sarah was no longer conscious of her surroundings; she did not hear the jingle of the stirrups as the horses, trained to stay in place as long as their reins trailed the ground, shuffled their feet impatiently; she did not see the sable-skinned platypus who waddled from the creek, took one look at the naked humans and stamping horses, and promptly waddled back again; she did not feel the penetrating heat of the sun-baked ground through the blanket. She was conscious only of Dominic, of his blue eyes and the waving thickness of his silky, blue-black hair, of his broad, bronzed shoulders and hard-muscled arms and legs roughened by the same curling black hair that grew luxuriantly on his wide chest, and of the way that thick pelt narrowed into an ebony trail down his muscle-ridged abdomen only to widen again around the tangible evidence of his desire. Once there, Sarah could not drag her eyes away. She stared at that part of him with fascination and trepidation as the enormity of what she was about to do came home to her with a vengeance. This time, there could be no excuse of moonlight and music. This time, of her own free will, she was making the conscious decision to go against every precept she had ever been taught and willfully take a lover—a convict lover. . . .

"Dominic . . ." Sudden doubts made her lift her eyes frantically to his.

His eyes shifted from their searing contemplation of her nakedness to meet her beseeching gaze. He must have read the uncertainty there, because he drew in his breath thickly and dropped to one knee beside her, his hand reaching out to trail a gentle finger across the tips of both breasts. Her nipples hardened and tightened in instant response to his touch. Sarah stared down the length of her slim pale body, mesmerized by the contrast between his hard brown hand and her small, creamy-skinned breasts with their tiny rosebud nipples standing rigidly at attention as that finger softly caressed them.

"It will be all right, Sarah. I'll take care of you." The hoarse words were a promise. He was bending over her, the dark beauty of his face blocking out her ability to think, or remember, or do anything but feel, as his hand slid from her breasts over the silken skin of her belly to the tawny thicket of hair between her thighs. She arched against that hand, returning his kiss feverishly as her legs parted and his hand slipped between them.

Her arms were locked around his head as she kissed him with fierce abandon. Gently he broke her hold, catching her hands in his and prying them from around his neck as he slid down her body, his lips gliding hotly across her neck to nibble with tiny erotic bites on first her collar bone and then, devastatingly, her breasts. Sarah moaned, her eyes closed tight against the fierce heat of the sun and the even fiercer heat that his hungry mouth was stoking in her body. Her hands found his head again, to twine with mindless need in the thick strands of his hair. She felt a shaft of liquid fire shoot along her veins as he suckled at her quivering nipples, and whimpered when at last his mouth left her breasts to forge a moist trail across her flat belly to the curling triangle of hair below. He pressed a hard, hot kiss to the soft mound; Sarah felt the shock of it clear down to her toes. Her eyes fluttered open. They widened at seeing his black head nestling cozily between the slender white gleam of her parted thighs.

"Dominic, no!" she protested raggedly as he pressed torrid kisses to the dampening heat of her. She tried to close her thighs and her senses against the unthinkable thing he was doing to her; her fingers tugged sharply on his hair. "Dominic!"

He lifted his head at the frantic plea in her voice. Unable to help herself, she moved her hips in silent protest at the cessation of the fiery torment of his lips on the most secret, shameful part of her. At her involuntary movement his eyes narrowed with passion. His breath caught in a harsh sigh.

"You taste so good—like honey and spice," he muttered gutturally as he slid slowly back up her body. "Sweet Jesus, Sarah, I want you!"

His lips claimed hers in a fierce, savage possession. Sarah gasped and shuddered into his mouth. She could taste herself on his lips; the notion both shocked and excited her unbearably. Her arms came up to lock around his neck, pulling him to her. She pressed her body to his as he ground himself against her, groaning. With her satiny inner thigh she could feel the fiery hardness of him as he sought her softness. But even as she returned his kiss with passionate abandon, undulating her body against his, rejoicing in the rasp of his chest hair against her straining breasts, in the steely strength of his muscles as he locked her to his body, in the sheer overwhelming maleness of him, he was pulling away, arms trembling as he propped himself above her on his elbows.

"Dominic!" His name left her lips in a drugged protest. Her eyes opened to blink dazedly at him. Her nails dug into the back of his neck with feline savagery. Beneath the crushing weight of his hips, her pelvis arched instinctively, pressing her soft female parts against the hardness of his masculinity. Why had he stopped? She couldn't bear it if he stopped. She was on fire for him. . . . But, despite her wordless pleading, still he held himself away.

"Not yet," he murmured, his arms loosening their hold on her body so that one hand could slide between them to find and caress the soft triangle of hair—and beyond. "Not yet, Sarah. Let me make it even better. . . ."

His fingers were doing wondrous things to her, touching off that same secret wellspring of spiraling madness that he had tapped before, making her writhe and groan until she was wild under his hand, her head thrashing helplessly in the tangled nest of brown-gold hair, loosened from its braid by her frenzied movements. When at last his hand was replaced by that hot, throbbing part of him she craved, she was sobbing with passion, her nails digging deep into his shoulders, her legs winding around his waist. When he found her, and plunged inside as if he could not wait an instant longer, she cried out with boundless pleasure. He was huge, and hard, and fiery hot, and quite the most wonderful thing she had ever felt. At first he barely moved inside her, gentling her, driving her crazy with his very control. Finally she could stand it no longer. Her hips began to undulate in an age-old, instinctive rhythm that made him gasp, moving faster and faster, on fire for that ecstasy he had given her before. The sensation of her body swallowing him only to free him and swallow him again was exquisite. She clutched him tighter, calling his name.

"Christ, Sarah, you're driving me out of my mind." The guttural mutter was labored. Then, suddenly, he was taking control again, moving harder and faster until at last he was pounding into her, rushing her away with him on a fierce, never-ending ride. . . .

"Sarah, my Sarah." He was moaning her name into her neck as his mouth pressed into her heated skin and his arms clasped her to him.

Her hands clasped his back now, frantically caressing his shoulders before raking them and the wealed flesh lower down with her nails. This time she didn't even notice the scars; if she hurt him, he made no sign. He was breathing thickly and heavily into the curve between her neck and shoulder, his body coming into hers again and again and again. . . .

"Dominic, Dominic, Dominic, Dominic, *Dominic*." The cry was wrenched from Sarah's throat as at last the hot, escalating spiral of need inside her exploded without warning into a maelstrom of fiery rapture. As she sobbed out his name Dominic stiffened, poised above her, then plunged deep inside her with a hoarse groan. He shuddered, holding her clamped against him, then slowly, very slowly, their bodies ceased their wild quaking and they clung limply together.

It was an endless eternity later when Dominic propped himself on his elbows again, his body still joined to hers, and looked down at her. Sarah, slowly coming back from the drifting fog he had lost her in, felt him looking at her, but she couldn't bring herself to open her eyes. She felt suddenly, hideously exposed. In his arms, she had again shed her ladylike skin and been as wanton as a street woman. She felt herself color with embarrassment as the memory of what had just passed ran through her mind in a series of vivid vignettes. He had done dreadful, shameful things to her and she had reveled in them. . . . Would he mock her? Would he laugh?

"Sarah." She was not mistaken: there was an undertone of laughter in that lilting voice. Cringing inwardly, she kept her eyes tightly shut, refusing to admit daylight and reality. "Come on, Sarah, you have to open your eyes sometime. I won't go away just because you refuse to look at me."

Bowing to the inevitable, Sarah forced open her eyes. She was shocked to find his face so close—and mortified to see the smile tugging at the corners of his mouth.

"Don't laugh at me!" Her voice was slightly wobbly, but sharp.

He smoothed her tangled hair away from her face. Sarah jerked away from the touch of those long, strong fingers, but he caught her face firmly with his hands on either side of it so that she could not look away from him. Unwillingly she met his eyes. What she saw there confused her: his bright blue gaze was rueful, amused—and tender.

"I'm not laughing at you, Sarah. I'm laughing at me, at us, at this entire ridiculous situation. There you were, spitting mad at me, threatening to have me hanged and doing your damnedest to shoot me, and clubbing me with a rifle butt, but all I could think of was how lovely you were without your clothes. I was frustrated as hell because I wanted to make love to you and there wasn't any place. And now here we are, on a blanket in the dirt. . . ." He broke off, laughing a little. Sarah stared bemusedly up into his lean brown face. "Never before have I wanted a woman enough to risk a sunburned behind and a terminal case of flea bites."

Sarah's eyes searched his for a long moment. Then,

slowly, cautiously, she smiled, a mere tentative curving of her lips, but one he rewarded with a kiss. Her lips fluttered under the brief, warm touch; her hands, which had been resting beside her on the blanket, fingers burrowing into the wool, came up to touch his arms, rubbing almost unconsciously over the hard, bulging muscles.

''You're heavy.'' The words were a halfhearted protest, made because she thought she should. In truth, despite the odd little niggling discomforts that were beginning to make themselves felt along her body as he pressed her into the blanket, she never wanted to move again in her life. She loved the feel of him, the rasp of his body hair against her, the rivulets of sweat fusing their naked bodies. And that other, fused part of them . . . Sarah could feel him, still inside her, but softer now and smaller, and slowly slipping away.

''Am I now?'' He rolled obligingly to one side, propping his head on one hand and imprisoning her on the blanket with his other arm lying heavily across her waist.

''We should get up.'' She felt very self-conscious lying there stark naked, with the glaring sunlight playing over her, exposing every deficiency of her too-slim body. And it didn't help that he was openly staring at her, from her small breasts with their crests now rosy-soft to her tiny waist and narrow pelvis to the long, slender curves of her pale legs. His eyes traced caressingly back up the length of those legs to linger on the dampened patch of gold curls between her thighs. Galvanized, Sarah struggled to sit up. He held her easily in place with that arm around her waist.

''Oh no you don't. If I let you up, you'll probably have the bullets out of my pocket and the rifle aimed on me in a trice. And, while I must admit I enjoyed watching you hold the beast at bay, I'd rather rest my weary bones awhile longer. And the sand fleas be damned.''

Sarah eyes flickered up to meet his, shy and uncertain

yet quite liking being kept so close to his naked body. Her own nakedness, and the feminine deficiencies revealed by the shimmering sunlight, she did not know quite how to deal with, so she refused to think of them any longer. He was grinning warmly at her, a teasing light in his eyes. Staring bedazzled into that handsome face, Sarah felt her heart begin to beat in slow, uneven strokes.

"How did you manage to unload the rifle?" she asked, seeking to focus on something other than the way he was making her feel. Besides, that point still mystified her. His hand slid from her waist to absently cup and then caress her right breast, which immediately responded by swelling into his hand. Sarah sucked in her breath, fighting the urge to turn to him. It was an effort, but she managed to force her eyes away from that large brown hand on her pale skin and up to his eyes.

He grinned. "A priest I once knew in Ireland—an old rapscallion if there ever was one, despite his holy calling— shared his various methods for avoiding a Protestant jail with me when I was a young boy. One of his less-nefarious tricks was to grab a loop of the rope being used to tie him up and twist it around his hand. When the loop is released, the rope is loosened. That's what I did when you were tying my hands—very clever you were about it, too; your resourcefulness never ceases to amaze me. Then, when you were sound asleep, it was not difficult to work my hands free. And once they were free, well . . ."

"You untied yourself, took the rifle from my side, unloaded it, tied yourself up again—no wonder those knots were so tight!"

"I must admit, tying myself up again was more difficult than I had anticipated. Fortunately, you were more concerned with the ropes around the tree than the ones on my hands."

"And you let me order you around all day as if I could

really shoot you if you didn't do as I said!'' she said with a rush of indignation as she glared at him. His grin widened, revealing even white teeth gleaming in the sun. Sarah refused to allow herself to be sidetracked by the memory of how smooth those teeth felt against her tongue. . . .

"You were having so much fun," he explained, trying and failing dismally to sound apologetic.

"You—you . . . !" she sputtered, unable to force out the very uncomplimentary word she had in mind.

"Swine? Beast?" he supplied helpfully.

"No," she said, and before she could stop it, out popped the filthy sobriquet he had supplied her with once before.

His eyes widened with mock horror, and then he dissolved into laughter, rolling onto his back and dragging her, willy-nilly, with him. "Oh, Sarah," he said when at last he could speak again, his eyes gleaming at her with amusement and something else as she lay sprawled inelegantly—and unwillingly!—across his chest. "You are a delight. I keep having difficulty getting past the way you look—so much a lady, my own, even when you're riding astride in your nightrail, or dressed in too-big men's breeches—to the way you really are."

"And how am I?" She was pushing against his chest, embarrassed by her posture almost as much as by the profanity she had uttered. Her hair was tumbling over her shoulders to mix with the dark mat on his chest before trailing against the gray wool of the blanket. She used it to shield her face, knowing that she was blushing.

"A woman," he said softly, suddenly sounding serious. "A real, live, honest-to-Jesus woman, with enough fire beneath the cold surface to keep me constantly aflame."

Shaken by the sober note in his voice, her eyes came out

of hiding and rose to search his face. He was no longer smiling.

"Dominic . . ." His name was all she got out before his hand was burrowing through her hair to clasp the back of her head and pull her mouth down to his. She went willingly, a fine trembling in all her limbs. As her mouth met his, she moaned. To her surprise, his body responded promptly to the heated union of their mouths. Even before the kiss ended, he was ready for her. Sarah felt the evidence of his desire against her bottom as he pushed her into a sitting position straddling his abdomen, his hands on her waist. Her eyes widened to huge golden pools as she looked down at him with amazement. Was this lovemaking something that people did so often? Animals, she knew, mated only once or twice a season. She turned beet red at the thought.

"Don't be embarrassed, Sarah." The thickness of his voice made her heart pound. "You're so beautiful, it's only natural for me to want you again—and again—and again. . . ."

"Do you really think I'm—beautiful, Dominic?" The question was humble despite the tremors that shook her legs and her arms, which were braced with hands palms-down against the damp pelt on his chest. Her eyes as she met his darkening ones were vulnerable.

"Yes," he answered without hesitation, his eyes moving over her face. "The shape of your face, an almost perfect oval with those high cheekbones and that smooth round forehead and determined little chin, is beautiful. Your hair, so thick and soft, the color of honey with glistening gold threads running all through it, is beautiful. Your eyes, as golden as the sun up there beneath those funny winged brows, are beautiful. Your mouth, so full and pink, is beautiful. . . ."

"Dominic . . ." she interrupted, half-laughing, touched

to the heart by his soft, seductive words. His hands tightened on her waist; his eyes, midnight blue now with passion, frowned a warning at her.

"I'm not finished," he said severely, his eyes sliding down over her body. "As I was saying, your neck, so long and elegant, is beautiful. Your shoulders and arms are beautiful. Your breasts—they're beautiful: soft and white with little pink nipples that taste of strawberries, just the right size to fit into the palm of my hand. Your tiny waist, which would be the envy of many a fashionable young lady in Dublin, is beautiful. Your silky little belly is beautiful; your behind—you have no idea what that round little bottom does to me!—is beautiful. Your long, lovely legs and everything that's between them is beautiful. But the most beautiful thing about you, Sarah..." He paused, making her wait. "The most beautiful thing about you, Sarah, is you. You're brave and funny and kind, and beneath your very proper exterior lurks a woman who can make me shake with terror or passion—depending upon the circumstances—clear to my toes. Oh yes, Sarah, never doubt it: you're beautiful."

"Oh, Dominic!" She felt moisture rise to her eyes and determinedly blinked it away. How absurd, to be moved to tears by his teasing. She shook her head at him, her long hair moving seductively across his chest. "I fear you've a bad touch of the Blarney stone, Mr. Gallagher."

Her attempt to ape his distinctive lilt made him smile. "No, I don't," he denied, his eyes caressing. "But if I did—there's an old Irish custom says that a dreadful fate will befall a maid who sees the Blarney stone but doesn't kiss it."

"Is there now?" she said softly, letting him pull her down.

"Aye," he confirmed against her mouth, his brogue deliberately exaggerated. With her lips just brushing his, she felt his smile widen. ''And I'm afraid, my Sarah, that you're about to meet it.''

''Am I now?'' she whispered just before her lips surrendered to his.

XXI

It was much, much later when Dominic opened his eyes to survey with lazy satisfaction the form of the sleeping woman sprawled naked across him. He had not meant to let what had happened happen. When he had dragged her down off her horse he had meant only to give her a good scare before sending her on her way to Lowella alone. But, writhing and struggling in his arms, her small fists beating at him and his own colorful curses falling furiously from her lips, she had lighted a fire in him that had prompted him to taste her lips one more time—the last time, he had promised himself. He hadn't foreseen that she would go wild in his arms—or that a single kiss could make the fire in him blaze up until it raged wildly out of control. After that, everything that had followed had been inevitable. He had wanted her with a greedy craving that swept all before it. He smiled with some amusement at himself, his hand coming up to gently stroke a strand of shot-gold hair that trailed across his chest. Who would have guessed that he,

Dominic Gallagher, long addicted to the charms of lushly endowed beauties, veteran of more beds than he could remember, would be so violently attracted to a skinny, bossy, viper-tongued old maid? If any of his former skirt-chasing companions could know, they would think it the biggest joke of the year. Because of course they wouldn't see Sarah as he had come to see her. Her quiet, fine-boned beauty was not readily apparent at first glance. One had to look again and again. But rig her out in some fashionable, becoming clothes and teach her to style her hair, and he wagered that she would turn heads. She would be an elegant, cool-mannered lady—with the soul of a virago. Dominic didn't know which side of her appealed to him most.

He was inclined to forgive her for her betrayal of him and the subsequent beating, he mused, his hand leaving her hair to wander lightly over an exposed white shoulder. She must have been shocked and shamed by what had happened between them that night in the orchard, and disgusted with him. A very natural reaction, he saw now, to her first experience with lovemaking—especially under the circumstances. And he had not helped matters the next morning by shouting at her and forcing a kiss on her. She must have been convinced that he would be forever trying to get under her skirts. The thought made him grin. She had not been far wrong. He had wanted to make love to her again almost as soon as he had finished doing it the first time; her disgusted reaction had hurt as well as angered him. Then and there he had vowed to teach her a lesson, but the beating and his escape had robbed him of the opportunity. He had thought never to see her again; when she had come flying down the hill in front of him the night he had abducted her, riding like a Valkyrie with her long slim legs gleaming bare against the horse's dark sides and her acres of hair, gilded by moonlight, flying behind her like a banner, it had been as if fate was giving him another chance. Despite the beating she had cost him, or perhaps even because of it, his sexual attraction for her had burned hotter than ever. Here, he had thought, was a chance to quench the flames, and incidentally to pay Miss Propriety back in the kind of coin she could understand. He had chased her down and caught her, carrying her off with him in what was, now that he thought about it, really a most romantic fashion. Wasn't there some poem circulating through Dublin's drawing rooms about a fellow called young Lochinvar who rode off with a maid across his saddle bow? And weren't the ladies always swooning over it and carrying on about how romantic it was? Only Sarah, practical Sarah, had quite obviously not thought it at all romantic. Before she had discovered his identity, she had been frightened. Though she had tried not to let it show, he had known it, and at the time it had afforded him considerable satisfaction. Later, when she had recognized him, she had been first shocked, then furious. Dominic grinned, remembering the way she had stood up to him, a runaway convict, a desperado, sassing him as pertly as if she had been safe in her papa's drawing room. That was his Sarah, all right, grit to the backbone. Yes, he decided, still grinning, he would forgive her for running to Papa with her tale. It didn't matter anyway. Not now—now that he had captured that frightened, vengeful Sarah and made her willing . . . made her his. She *was* his. Dominic had known it for some time, but he had refused to recognize the feeling for what it was. But now she knew it too, had admitted it in deed if not in word. Sarah was not a promiscuous woman; she would give her body as she had given it today only to one man—the man she loved.

Love: the word was almost foreign to his vocabulary. He had loved only one other person in his life, and that love had caused him nothing but grief, and finally brought him,

chained and half-dead, to this godforsaken excuse for a
country. His train of thought halted abruptly, struck by
something that had just run through his head. He backtracked,
frowning, and found the nagging thought: he had loved
only one *other* person. . . . Other than whom? he demanded
of himself, knowing a faint flare of panic. Then the answer
came, so swift and pat that he could not believe he had not
realized it all along. Other than Sarah, of course.

He loved her. The realization was frightening, exhilarat-
ing, unreal. He had never thought to love a woman, had
been on guard against it, in fact. Loving a woman, in his
experience, brought heartache. But *Miss* Sarah, with her
man-sized courage and shrewish tongue, her pulled-back
hair and dowdy dresses and lion's heart, had slipped under
his guard. He had never expected to love her, had thought
that merely wanting her was an aberration. He had felt safe
in the knowledge that she was not his type. And so he had
not noticed when those huge golden eyes had wormed their
way into his heart.

Dominic shied from the knowledge, then returned
reluctantly to face it. He loved Sarah. That much was fact.
The question remained—what was he to do about it? When
a man found a woman he loved, the usual next step was to
marry her. . . . That idea he rejected violently. He had seen
enough of marriage to make him hate the institution like
the plague. But what else did one do with a lady like
Sarah? Set her up as his concubine?

"Dominic?" Her sleepy voice roused him from his
reverie. He blinked, then felt his heart jump with panic as
he found her eyes fixed on his face. Had she read his
thoughts? Sweet Jesus, he prayed she had not. He had to
have a little time to get used to the notion of being in love,
the idea of loving *her.* He needed time to decide what to do
about it.

"What?" The word was terse. He knew it but could not

help it. Her eyes clouded at his brusqueness. Dominic immediately felt like the swine that she had frequently called him before he had taught her less-decorous names.

"We should be going," she said stiffly, levering herself off his chest and sitting up, her back to him.

He looked at the swirling mass of tawny hair that hid from his view the fragile shoulders, the slender back, and the curving buttocks, and felt as if a hard fist had been rammed into his stomach at the realization that his curt response had hurt her. Lord God, was this what love did? Made a man willing to throw himself at his loved one's feet just to see her smile?

She was leaning forward, reaching for her shirt. He sat up, catching her by the shoulders, turning her around to face him. A single tear trembled in the corner of her eye; it stabbed him clear through to the heart.

"Sarah." His voice was gruff with emotion. He had to fight an urge to clear it, but he thought that might be too revealing. "Let's not go anywhere. Just for tonight."

Her eyes rose to his. He thought he read both hope and trepidation in her eyes.

"I need to get home. My family will be worried about me." But the words were uncertain.

"Will they?"

She chewed her lower lip. "No, not really. My father, perhaps; and Liza, a little. But . . ."

"But not so worried that one day more or less will make that much difference," he finished for her, catching her hands in his and bringing them one at a time to his lips. She was kneeling in front of him now, her long hair veiling her nakedness as it tumbled from her shoulders to her bent knees. Through its tangled thickness he caught tantalizing glimpses of rose-tipped breasts and glimmering, pale thighs. . . . "Let's stay here tonight, Sarah. Make camp near the creek, sleep out under the stars." His voice thickened on this last, telling her without words what else he wanted to do under the stars. Her lips parted; unconsciously, he thought, the small pink tip of her tongue flicked out to wet the lushness of her lower lip. Even that tiny movement sent a tightening through his groin. Dominic grinned a little, ruefully, as he contemplated what his body was giving every indication that it wished to do again. It had been years since he had felt the urge to make love three times in as many hours.

"If we're going to stay, we may as well get busy," she said, suddenly brisk as she pulled her hands from his and reached again for her shirt. "It's getting dark, and the horses need to be unsaddled and watered, and a fire made. If you'll see to the horses, I'll build a fire. I noticed last night that you're not particularly good at it." She was shrugging into her shirt as she spoke, then broke off as she noticed his broadening grin.

"What's so funny?" she asked suspiciously, eying him as he sprawled back on the blanket, his arms crossed beneath his head, unconcerned with his nakedness.

"Did anyone ever tell you that you're a very managing female?" he asked, still grinning. She flushed, looking suddenly very self-conscious—and very appealing. His groin tightened still more as he eyed her up and down. He was surprised that she seemed not to notice the rising evidence of his desire for her.

"Oh," she said in a tiny voice. "I guess I am used to—uh—sort of directing things."

"Giving orders," he corrected, charmed by her crest-fallen air. "Especially to me."

She looked over at him swiftly. He frowned in mock displeasure. She looked dismayed—and then her chin came up. "Yes," she said steadily.

He couldn't help it; he had to laugh. "Don't worry about it, my own," he advised, sitting up and reaching for his breeches and boots. "I find I'm getting used to being bossed around—by a particular managing female. Just be careful I don't beat you one of these days."

"You couldn't," she said, her nose in the air as she recognized his teasing for what it was. She was buttoning her shirt, then looking around for the rest of her clothes as he pulled on his breeches, stood up, and tugged on his boots.

"Why not?" he asked tranquilly, tossing her breeches and sandals to her as he found and pulled on his shirt. "I'm a deal bigger than you—and I owe you one."

He had meant to make light of what she had done, but she immediately tensed.

"I didn't tell Pa anything, Dominic. I give you my word."

Silently cursing himself for bringing up the subject, he left off buttoning his shirt to reach out and pull her to her feet.

"It's all right, Sarah," he said, his hands sliding beneath her shirttail to close on her still-bare buttocks and bring her against him.

"You believe me?" She did not seem to mind his touch, which just hours ago would have made her blush with shame. Her eyes searched his earnestly. Dominic wondered for the first time if perhaps she was telling the truth. Perhaps someone else had seen, and told. . . . It didn't matter, anyway. They were going to put that behind them, starting now.

"I believe you," he said, his hands tightening on her rounded little behind. Desire stirred uncomfortably in him at the feel of her silky firmness beneath his hands. He made a mental note to adjust his breeches the next time she turned her back.

"Oh, Dominic!" She smiled happily at him, her hands flying up to encircle his neck as she rose on her toes to plant her first spontaneous kiss on his mouth. Then Dominic returned her kiss with interest, and it ended up being quite some time later before they got around to making camp.

XXII

"Just for tonight" turned out to be two days, then three, then a week. Sarah and Dominic laughed and talked and made love, living off the provisions Dominic had grabbed as they had made their hurried exit from that other camp and whatever game either of them could shoot. Dominic was a far better shot than Sarah, which surprised her—she was very good. But she conceded with good grace his superiority in that area. She was by far the better organizer—it was she who organized the camp and their respective chores until she became aware of what she was doing, and guiltily stopped. She would not be persuaded to resume—which meant that they went disastrously short of salt when Dominic used it all to season a hare he was roasting instead of dividing it into careful portions as Sarah would have done—until Dominic convinced her that her "bossiness" appealed to him enormously. And by the time he finished convincing her, that particular hare was burned to a crisp. They dined instead on strips of dried mutton, and didn't care two pins. Much of the time they were scarcely aware of what they ate anyway. What interested them was the time they spent together in their bedroll, tucked up cozily under the stars, or brazenly uncovered beneath the blazing sun.

Their lovemaking was like nothing Sarah had ever imagined. It was wild and wanton, slow and tender, infinitely varied, always wonderful. Sarah could not get enough of his hands on her skin, or he enough of her body. He taught her to return kiss for kiss, caress for caress; he explored every curve and secret recess of her body with his hands and mouth, and encouraged her to gain similar intimate knowledge of his own. Sarah spent her days in a haze of bliss, sparkling with happiness, unaware that Dominic's lovemaking had brought a glow to her skin and hair and a softening to her features that made her for the first time in her life as truly beautiful as Dominic insisted she was. His eyes seldom left her; he made no effort to hide his need and desire for her. Sarah blossomed as night blended into day and day into night, taking care not to let thoughts of the future intrude on their idyll. For she knew, and she knew Dominic knew, that this could not go on forever. Decisions had to be made sometime, reality faced. But not yet. Not yet.

One night, while they lay in their bedroll, Sarah's head nestled in the crook of his arm and his head resting on the saddle that served as a pillow, she ventured to ask him how he had come to commit the crimes for which he had been transported. His arm went heavy beneath her head, and for a long moment she thought he wasn't going to answer. Then he turned his head to look at her, his eyes deeply blue even in the darkness under the cloud-covered night sky. She looked gravely back at him, loving the lean hard cheekbone that was faintly silvered in profile, the long straight nose, the firm chin.

"You don't have to tell me if you don't want to," she said, lifting her hand to trace the outline of his mouth. Touching him was something she did often. When she thought about it, she could hardly believe that it was she, Sarah Markham, plain, skinny, old-maid Sarah, who had never had a serious suitor, who was on such intimate terms with this gorgeous man. He caught her hand, pressing a soft kiss to the caressing finger, and smiled at her. His white teeth gleamed briefly at her through the darkness.

"No, I know I don't have to." His voice was husky. "But I want you to know. So you don't go thinking that you've got yourself mixed up with an inept thief." He was silent a moment longer, while Sarah waited patiently for him to tell her what he would. She could tell that he was debating with himself, probably wondering how much of his life story to tell her. In the end, she didn't think he kept anything back.

"For you to understand how I ended up here—not that there is anyplace that I'd rather be just at this moment—" This was said with another quick smile at her; Sarah smiled back, her body clad only in his too-big shirt as she nestled closer to his naked body beneath the blanket. "I have to go back a long way, thirty-some-odd years, to be exact. I was born on March eighth, 1804, to the only daughter of a wealthy Irish landowner. Her name was Maura Kathleen Gallagher, and though she was only eighteen at the time she had been married to the earl of Rule for nearly three years." Sarah started to ask him to repeat himself, because if she had understood him correctly he was the son of an *earl*, which was mind-boggling, but he held up a hand for silence. Sarah obediently subsided, her eyes huge as she waited for him to continue. "There was a huge celebration when I, their first child and heir to the earldom, was born. A week later, with much pomp and circumstance, I was christened John Dominic Frame. The earl was John Christopher Frame, you see." Again Sarah opened her mouth with a question, and again, with a gesture, he silenced her. "The earl was Irish only in domicile. His breeding, education, and inclination were English. I grew up in a castle overlooking the dark waters of Lough Der—the big black castle with the turrets and the battlements I told you about once; it is called Fonderleigh, and it has been the home of the earls of Rule since William the Conqueror. It's a beautiful place. I loved it as a boy, and I love it still. I had all the privileges and advantages that you might expect the only son of an earl to have, including a tutor who strictly oversaw my education whenever he could persuade, bribe, or force me to sit still long enough, a dancing master"—this elicited a quick smile from her, which he returned—"a fencing master, a boxing master, a shooting master, a music master, and an untold number of other masters until I was in danger of being mastered to death. I saw as much of my mother as most boys in such circumstances—which is to say, not a lot; they spent a good part of each year in London—and considerably less of the earl himself. At that time he was proud of me, I believe; despite all that mastering I still managed to be something of a hellion, which appealed to him. But he was not an affectionate man, even to my mother, who, looking back, I can see he loved as much as his nature would permit him to love anyone. She was very beautiful, my mother, with coal-black hair and perfect features and eyes as blue as the Irish sea." Like you, Sarah thought, but she didn't say anything; he was looking away from her, up at the dark canopy of clouds. Sarah watched that chiseled profile intently. "I adored my mother with the blind adoration of a child. I was convinced that she was an angel, and the thought that she could do wrong never even occurred to me. Which was why what happened came as such a shock to me.

"Three days before my seventh birthday, my mother's father died. My mother had been estranged from him for some time—since before my birth, in fact—but she cried copiously when told of his death. Then the letter came—a letter written on his deathbed by my staunchly Catholic grandfather to the earl of Rule. In brief, it said that the old man could not go to his reward peacefully if he kept his daughter's sinful secret any longer: it seemed that when Maura had come to visit him on his estate in County Cork in the summer of 1803—the earl had been in London—she had had an affair with an Irish peasant boy whose family lived in one of the hovels on the estate. When Maura's father found out, he immediately shipped the whole family off to the States, but it was too late: Maura had committed the unforgivable indiscretion and was with child. Me. I, John Dominic Frame, was not a Frame at all, but the son of that Irish peasant. After reading that, the earl sent for my mother, taxed her with it, and she collapsed in tears, admitting everything, and begging his forgiveness on her knees.

"Well, he forgave her, all right, as far as I know—at least she remained his wife until her death—but I, as the living symbol of her betrayal, became the focus of his hatred. The first inkling I had that change was in the wind was when he called me into his study, shut the door, and, in the iciest voice I have ever heard to this day, informed me that I was never again to call him Papa because I was not his son, but a nameless bastard who had been foisted on him by deception. I was stunned of course, and frightened. Even now I can remember the suffocating fear I felt when he told me that he and my mother were removing at once to London, never to return. I was to remain behind at Fonderleigh—I should be grateful for

that, he said; it was only his Christian charity that kept
him from throwing me out among the peasants who were
my real kin to make my own way. Neither he nor my
mother ever wanted to set eyes on me again as long as I
lived. When he dismissed me, after many more scathing
remarks about my person and ancestry, I was sobbing—
something that I, a very manly seven-year-old, rarely
did. I ran at once to my mother, who held me to her and
cried and told me that she was powerless to aid me. And
I suppose she was, unless she had a mind to jeopardize
her own position. In any event, the very next day they
left for London. Bewildered and scared to death, I
remained behind at Fonderleigh; but everything had
changed. I was no longer the earl's son, but a charity
case, though no one other than those immediately concerned knew it. I believe the earl was too proud to
acknowledge that his wife had betrayed him and that his
son and heir was not his own flesh. At any rate, the
servants and neighbors still regarded me as the earl's
son; only I knew differently. I felt like an inter-
loper. . . .

"My mother and the earl never returned, never wrote or
sent gifts or messages at Christmas or birthdays. I, who
had been hopelessly spoiled, was now abandoned. I will
pass over the next few years except to say I was very
lonely and very bitter. It galled me to no end to know that
the roof over my head, the bed I slept in, the clothes I
wore, the very food I ate, were grudgingly provided by a
man who hated me. I grew to loathe the very idea of being
beholden to anyone at all, and I still do. . . . Finally, on
my sixteenth birthday, I could stand it no longer. I left
Fonderleigh. Like the idealistic youth I was, I went immediately to see my mother. She and the earl lived in a
fashionable London townhouse, and I arrived on their
doorstep at the height of the season. Fortunately for her,

the earl was out when I arrived, shy and gangling as most boys are at that age; it was fortunate for me too, I suppose, because I considered myself very much a man and had half-formed the notion of drawing the earl's cork for him in defense of my mother's honor. He likely would have killed me on the spot. My mother was horrified to see me, though she hid it rather well, and quickly hustled me out of the house and into a lodgings in an out-of-the-way part of town. She made protestations of love but said she couldn't stay, as she and the earl were giving a dinner that night, but she would try to come by and see me again before I went home to Fonderleigh. Then she pressed a pound note in my hand and told me to buy myself a gift, and left.

"I tore the note up as soon as she had gone, and left myself, making my way to the waterfront where I signed on as crew for a merchantman leaving the next morning for Spain and then Africa. Luckily for me, three of their crew had jumped ship the day before—I was too naïve to realize what this said about the ship and her captain—or they would never have taken me on. I was a very bad sailor, who knew nothing about ships or the sea. I spent the voyage—a hellish trip, though not as bad as some I've had since—green with seasickness and disillusionment. I had idolized my mother, you see, and convinced myself that she had been forced to acquiesce to what had been done to me, that once she saw me again she would run away from my father and take me with her—you know, the sort of thing any adolescent might dream. She had shattered my illusions in about twenty minutes flat, and I thought I was nursing a broken heart. It took me a while to learn that hearts are sturdier than most people give them credit for being. . . . Anyway, by the time we reached Africa I was convinced that I was not a seaman. But there was still the return voyage.

"Two years had passed by the time the *Avery*—that was the ship's name, the *Avery*—returned to London. This time I didn't bother to visit my mother. I was eighteen, and a man.... I took my pay packet—precious little it was, too—and went home to Ireland. But not to Fonderleigh— that was not my home, it was *his*. To Dublin. And I parlayed that pay packet into quite a stake, thanks to obliging dice and fast horses. Luckily, I had the sense to quit before I lost all I'd won. Dublin had never appealed to me despite its obvious attractions, so I took the money and bought a farm near Galway. And I commenced breeding horses. My stud was beginning to acquire quite a reputa- tion when I learned, through gossipy neighbors who had no idea I was in any way connected with the family—since I had signed on the *Avery* I had been using the name Gallagher, which was the only one that was *mine*—that the countess of Rule was dying. I had long since thought that any love I had once felt for my mother was dead, but this hit me hard. I went home and brooded, and finally knew that I had to see her again. I drove to London and went straight to the earl's townhouse without even bothering to book a room or change clothes. The butler was loath to admit a stranger at such a time, but I was not taking 'no' for an answer. I forced my way past him and took myself up to my mother's bedchamber in the wake of a frightened chambermaid. My mother was lying in the middle of an enormous bed, alone except for a priest who was administering last rites, and her maid. I can still see the huge fire that blazed in the hearth, though the weather outside was mild....

"I won't bore you with the details of what passed between my mother and me, except to say that we reconciled. Just before she died she took my hand and slid the pearl-and-ruby ring that she had worn ever since I could remember onto my smallest finger. Her fingers were so delicate that, despite the fact that she had worn it on her ring finger, it would go only as far as my knuckle. The earl burst through the door just as she breathed her last. I almost felt sorry for him—he was too late to say good-bye, and it was easy to see that he was shattered. But then he turned from her bedside and saw me. And with a howl of rage attacked me with his cane. I merely wrested the cane from his grasp, but he was demented: he screamed for the servants, and every one of them in the house must have come running to his aid. Two burly footmen held me while the constable was fetched. I didn't struggle; after all, the whole thing was ridiculous, or so I thought. But when the constable came, he wouldn't listen to my side of the story, and I was hauled off to jail.

"I wasn't seriously alarmed—until I was moved to Newgate Prison, to await trial. To my amazement, I was told that the charge was robbery—my mother's ring, which I supposedly stole. I was still more amused than alarmed at such a flimsy charge—until the actual trial. I was not even permitted to appear. I was tried in proxy and found guilty. The judge sentenced me to be transported to Australia, there to serve a term of fifteen years at hard labor. Thus, I was as completely removed from the earl's world as if I had died—which I am certain he intended for me to do on the voyage. After all, as the legal if not actual son of his marriage, I was still heir to his title, and to the entailed portion of his estates.

"But then Captain Farley got greedy and arranged to sell me to your father. When your father refused to take me, I was convinced that I would be killed. And, sure enough, they had me strung up and would, I believe, have beaten me to death. But for a flashing-eyed virago who set them all on their ears." He slanted her a whimsical look.

Sarah smiled at him, appreciating his description of her

for the teasing it was, though her eyes were wet with tears
as she pictured the lonely, frightened, mistreated little boy
he had once been. In her opinion, his mother was the one
who deserved to be horsewhipped, but she wisely kept that
thought to herself. Just as she hoped that the darkness
would hide her tears. She had a feeling that he would
interpret them as pity, and she knew him well enough now
to know that he would hate that.

"I wanted to kiss the hem of that awful skirt you had on
when you told them to cut me down. And I hated you for
making me feel so beholden to you."

"Which was why you were so nasty to me that night at
the inn," she said, remembering. She cast him a mock-
chiding glance. Her tears were almost gone now. "I only
wanted to help you."

He shifted suddenly, his arm under her head pulling her
closer, his other arm fitting itself around her waist beneath
the shirt. She could feel the heat radiating from his
hair-roughened body as he hugged her to him, brushing
her cheek with the softest of kisses. Her own arms slid
around his neck. He held himself a little away from her,
looking down into her face. Her head was pillowed on the
hard muscles of his upper arm.

"I'm sorry," he said, sounding contrite. "I was a . . ."
His voice trailed off tantalizingly as he made her wait for
the description, which she was fairly certain would be too
pungent to be proper.

"Swine," she interjected firmly.

"Swine," he agreed, laughing. And then he kissed her
soundly on her eager mouth.

"You made me furious," she said against his mouth. "I
could never remember being quite that angry before."

"I shudder to think what would have happened to me if
that brute of an overseer of yours had not come along. If I
had known then what I know now, I would never have

chanced that temper of yours. You likely would have shot me, or clubbed me to death, or . . ."

"I don't have a temper. Usually," she temporized as he laughed again, delightedly.

"Oh, Sarah. How little you know yourself. You have a glorious temper, and I love you even more when you lose it. It's such a fascinating change, from prim lady to spitting hell-cat."

Sarah was silent for a moment, her eyes widening. Dominic stopped laughing suddenly, his body going very still as he met her eyes. If it hadn't been absurd, she would have sworn she saw trepidation in those blue depths.

"Dominic," she said faintly, after carefully replaying his words in her mind. "What did you say?"

He stared at her without answering, looking as if he was trying to make up his mind about how to reply. Then, with a grimace, he rolled onto his back and stared up at the cloudy night sky.

"I love you," he said, very gruff.

Sarah lay without moving for several heartbeats, her eyes wide as she stared at his averted face. Then it was she who rose to lean propped on her elbow as she looked down at him, her hair forming a trailing brown-gold curtain that shut them away from the world. He met her eyes reluctantly, his mouth taut and straight, his eyes defensive.

"Do you mean it?" she asked, scarcely breathing. He didn't say anything. "Dominic . . ."

His mouth twisted. "Yes, I mean it."

"Oh, Dominic!" It was a soft cry straight from the heart as she toppled onto him, her arms locking around his neck, her lips pressing a flurry of kisses all over his dark face. He suffered her onslaught for several seconds before catching her elbows and rolling with her so that their positions were reversed, with her lying flat on her back while he loomed over her.

"It would be nice to hear that my very flattering sentiments are reciprocated," he muttered, frowning down at her.

"What?" She grinned at him, delight shining from her huge golden eyes. He glared, then surrendered with a groan.

"Oh, hell, Sarah, do you love me?"

She stared up at him. Faint traces of starlight peeping through the black clouds illuminated his hard, handsome face and picked out the blue highlights in his midnight-black hair.

"Yes," she said, suddenly knowing that she did love him.

His face relaxed, he even managed a smile. Sarah reached up to kiss him, to press her lips to that lovely male mouth, to stake her claim in the most basic way of all, but he held her off.

"Uh-uh. Not till you say it."

"Dominic!" Looking at him, suddenly she felt absurdly shy.

"Say it, Sarah."

It came to her then that he was as vulnerable as she. Not his height and strength, nor his blatant masculinity, nor his dazzling good looks protected him from the insecurities of the heart. Like her, he had not expected to fall in love, and it had caught him by surprise. And also like her, he was frightened by it.

"I love you, Dominic." She had not meant them to be so, but the words were solemn, a pledge. Her lips trembled as his eyes searched her face, locked with her eyes. His expression was very grave.

"Again."

"I love you, Dominic."

He groaned, a guttural, animal sound, and lowered his head to capture her mouth with his. His kiss was such sweet torture that it made her want to cry. . . . He made love to her the same way, with a ferocious gentleness that had her crying out and clinging to him, locking him to her forever with her arms and legs and mouth as he whirled her away with him on a tempestuous floodtide of passion.

XXIII

Sarah woke the next morning to a sky so filled with heavy gray clouds that it seemed to be only inches away from her small nose. Safe in the shelter of Dominic's arms, she grimaced at the sky, knowing that she should be pleased, because the clouds meant rain at last. But she wasn't pleased: she was depressed, nervous, uneasy. Those lowering clouds warned of a terrific storm, and even ordinary storms in that part of Australia were devastating. Without shelter on the open range, they would be scourged by lightning, pelted by hail, drenched by rain. Their wisest course would be to head at once for Lowella, which was half a day's ride away, or less if they hurried. Which brought Sarah back to why she was feeling depressed— here was the "someday" she had been dreading. Today the future had to be faced.

"Dominic."

There was no point in delaying the inevitable, she thought as she gently shook his shoulder. They had to get moving if they hoped to miss the rain. The arm clasping her waist tightened as she said his name again. Slowly, reluctantly, one blue eye opened to slant a disgruntled look at her.

"Go back to sleep, *cuilin*."

"No, I . . . What's *cuilin?*" She was momentarily sidetracked by the unfamiliar word.

He sighed, releasing her to turn over onto his back, rubbing his face with his hands. Looking down at him, at the tousled black hair and unshaven jaw, at the wide, bare, bronzed shoulders and black-pelted chest, Sarah wondered suddenly if she hadn't been dreaming the night before. Surely such a splendid male could not be in love with *her*. . . . Then his hands dropped away from his face and she found him smiling tenderly at her, and she knew that, however unlikely, it was true.

"You—maid with the beautiful hair," he said, and reached out to pull a lock of the hair he praised. Sarah slapped his hand lightly in response; he caught her hand then instead of her hair and pulled her toward him. "It's Gaelic. Come here."

"No, Dominic," she said, resisting.

He saw that she was serious and let her go. Sarah sat up, unselfconscious at being clad only in the thin blue shirt that revealed the shape of her breasts and the outline of her nipples to him. He had seen her breasts, and indeed the rest of her, in far more intimate detail. And he himself was naked beneath the blanket drawn modestly—by accident rather than intent, she knew—up to his waist. She smiled to herself as she remembered how shocking she had once found his nakedness.

"What's the matter, my own?" He lounged back against the saddle, his arms crossing behind his head to reveal the luxuriant black forests of hair beneath each arm.

Sarah looked at him, feeling a queer little pang of pain

grip her heart. She loved him so much—it would be hard not to be able to touch him whenever she wished, to talk with him and kiss him and share his bed. . . .

"It's going to storm, Dominic." The words were harmless enough, but he seemed to sense that she was trying to say something more.

His blue eyes regarded her steadily. "Is it now?"

"We have to go back, Dominic. To Lowella. We can't put it off any longer."

He studied her for a long moment before he spoke. Then he seemed to choose his words with care.

"I can't go back there, Sarah."

She moistened her lips. "Of course you can. I'll tell Pa how you saved me from those bushrangers—"

"And how I abducted you," he interjected dryly.

She frowned. "I wouldn't tell him *that*."

"I know you wouldn't," he conceded. Then he sighed, and levered himself into a sitting position. He looked magnificent, sitting there bare to the waist, but Sarah was not in a mood to appreciate his appearance. "Let me put it another way: I *won't* go back to Lowella, Sarah. I'd have to be out of my mind if I did. What if you can't convince your father that my rescuing you outweighs everything else I've done? He ordered that buffoon of an overseer of yours to have me beaten to death the last time. If I go back, I'll be throwing myself on his mercy, and so far I haven't found him to be particularly merciful."

"I'll tell him—"

Dominic snorted, cutting her off. "Sarah, my love, you're fooling yourself if you think your father will welcome me with open arms. He was ready to have me killed even before I helped plan a raid on his station, participated in stealing his prized sheep, and abducted his daughter. How do you think he's going to feel about me now?"

"My father is a just man. I know that's hard for you to

believe in light of what was done to you, but that's something I still don't understand: ordering that you be whipped isn't like him. He would at least have given you the opportunity to speak.''

''Well, he did not.''

''Dominic . . .''

''I won't go back, Sarah. And that's my last word on the subject.''

Sarah looked at him, sighed, and recognized defeat. ''What will you do? Where will you go?''

He met her eyes very steadily. ''I mean to go back to Ireland. It's my home—though they sold my farm to pay the fine that was levied at my trial. But I can start again, and I mean to.''

''But what about me? About—about us?'' The question burst forth in an agony of pain.

''You could come with me.'' His eyes were suddenly very blue as they looked into hers.

Sarah stared back at him, conscious of a rising anger. ''As your camp follower? Your easy woman? Your mistress?'' Her lip curled. ''Do you really think . . . ?'' She was working herself up into a fine rage, fueled as much by her hurt at his refusal to consider returning to Lowella with her, for her, as by his suggestion.

''As my wife,'' he interrupted quietly. Sarah stared at him. ''I'm asking you to marry me, Sarah,'' he said when she, shocked into silence, didn't reply.

His wife, she was thinking, his wife! Her heart leaped at the idea. She would be Mrs. Dominic Gallagher. . . . Suddenly she faltered. Mrs. Dominic Gallagher—the wife of a convict. In Australia, that would be to put herself beyond the pale. Her family would disown her; she could never go into society again; her children, their children, would be tainted. . . .

''I can't marry you!'' she blurted. His eyes narrowed.

She had not meant to say the words, at least not that way. She needed more time to think. . . .

"Why not?" He wasn't giving her more time. His eyes were hard as they raked her face. "Why not, Sarah? Last night you said you loved me." His voice mocked her.

Still she couldn't say anything, though she sought desperately for words. He could not expect her to make a decision like that, now, here, without giving it careful consideration. He could not be aware of the enormity of what he was asking. If she married him, she would never be able to go home again, never see Lowella. . . .

"Is it because you're ashamed of me?" His eyes scorched her. "I'm good enough to be your lover but not your husband, is that it? Because I'm a *convict?*"

The words were savage. Sarah's eyes widened on his face as she sought desperately for a way to make him understand her position.

"Dominic, you don't understand. . . ."

"The bloody hell I don't!" He leaped to his feet, roaring, and began to pull on his breeches and then his boots while she watched helplessly. She stood, too, clad only in the blue shirt that left her long, slim legs bare, reaching automatically for his arm. He shook her off. The face he turned on her was so vicious that she recoiled.

"Dominic, if you'll just listen!" She was growing angry herself as he jerked on his shirt and began to throw some gear together.

"I've listened enough to be sick of myself and you. Stand aside, Sarah!"

His eyes flashed blue murder as she stepped in front of him, her hands going out to catch at his arms. As he had done before, he shook her off, then reached out to grasp her shoulders and lift her out of his way. That done, he stalked past her toward where the horses were tethered, his saddle and other gear over one arm.

"Dominic!" Angry or not, when he started to throw the saddle on Kilkenny she ran after him. "Dominic, wait!"

He had tightened the girth and was slipping the bridle over Kilkenny's head. Untying the tether, he swung himself into the saddle. Sarah stood watching him, one hand to her mouth, unable to understand how they had gone so quickly from being tender lovers to bitter enemies.

"Go home, Sarah," he told her harshly, raking her with one last hard glare. Then he was riding away.

"Dominic . . ." But it was too late. He was gone. Sarah stood there staring after him, feeling as though her heart would burst. Her anger was fading, to be replaced by a sickening knot in the pit of her stomach. She was very much afraid that she would never see him again. And she knew that she had made a terrible mistake. No matter how her father, Lydia, Liza, or their friends and neighbors, would view the union, she loved him and suddenly realized that she wanted very much to be his wife. Why hadn't she come to that conclusion while he was waiting for her answer? It had been such a surprise, of course. She had never expected him to suggest marriage. She didn't know what she had expected. That they would exist in their dream world forever and ever . . .

She saw now, with the wisdom of hindsight, that even if Dominic had agreed to return to Lowella with her, even if she had managed to persuade her father not to punish him, it wouldn't have worked. Dominic was a proud man, almost too proud. He could never have tolerated the notion that she owned him, when all was said and done. That she could, if she would, force her will upon him with whips and chains. He would soon have hated her. And she realized now that having Dominic hate her would break her heart. As would never seeing him again. She lifted her hand to her eyes, staring in the direction he had taken. He was already out of sight. Tears welled to her eyes and rolled unheeded down her cheeks. And for the first time in years, Sarah succumbed to a feminine weakness she had always despised. She sank to her knees, dropped her head to her hands, and cried.

The ominous rumbling of thunder roused her at last from her misery. She lifted her head, scrubbed at her swollen, tear-wet eyes with both hands, and stood up. As she had always suspected, crying had not done a bit of good. She still felt miserable, and Dominic was still gone, probably for good. Added to that were a stuffy nose and stinging eyes. . . . Those eyes widened as Sarah took in the sky. It was no longer a mass of soft, cottony gray rain clouds, but a solid ceiling of near black. At its center, tongues of lightning darted. It was going to be a bad one. Sarah knew that even before she became attuned to the nervous nickering of the horse behind her. He sensed the ferocity of the coming storm and was frightened.

Sarah did not stop even to gather up her gear. She quickly finished dressing, threw her saddle on the horse's back in record time, bridled him, then released him from the tether—being careful to keep a firm hold on his reins in case he should try to bolt—and swung into the saddle. The breeches made it easy for her to mount unaided and to ride astride. The horse—she was going to have to come up with a name for him, she thought distractedly—threw up his head and whinnyed as she kicked him into a canter. He was spooked, ready to take fright at the slightest provocation. Sarah clung to the saddle with her knees, wary of the beast's reaction to the storm. Some horses went wild. . . .

She stayed near the creek, knowing that, upset as she was, it would be fatally easy to let her mind wander so that she got lost in the bush. There was time enough to go overland when she was safely on station land. She was familiar enough with the station to chance it. The wind had changed direction, beginning to blow from the east. It was hot and fierce, whipping her hair, which she had not taken time to secure in a braid, around her head so that the ends stung her when they struck her face. The thunder was closer now, booming rather than rumbling. The black clouds roiled overhead, and the searching arms of lightning were getting terrifyingly near. The horse beneath her was whickering with fear, ready to bolt if she did not keep a firm grip on the reins. And maybe even if she did. There was an acrid smell on the wind, a smell that reminded her of something. . . . The night the stable burned. She looked around, eyes widening as she saw an orange glow lighting up the dark sky five or six miles behind her. A forest of dense tan and gray smoke was rising to join the ceiling of clouds. Bush fire! They were words to strike terror into the heart of any Australian, and they struck terror into Sarah's heart now. The tongues of lightning must have found their target in the dry trees and brush, and as a result the whole plain was on fire!

Sarah abandoned the steady canter to which she had been holding her horse and kicked him into a gallop. He spread out beneath her, as frightened as she by the raging inferno that was consuming miles of brushland at unbelievable speed. It would not take long for the flames to catch them up. Worse, bush fires were unpredictable—they could start in a dozen spots at once, and once started they moved fast. There could be more ahead of her, to the east or west, anywhere. Even at Lowella . . . Lowella could be burned to the ground. Sarah knew it, but still she headed for home. Her father would have all hands marshaled to save Lowella— it would be marginally safer than anywhere else, and it was where she wanted to be.

Her thoughts turned to Dominic. Would he recognize the significance of the orange glow in the air and head for safety? He was not familiar with the speed and ferocity of brush fires. But there was nothing she could do to aid him, no way she could warn him, because she had no idea where he was, so she tried to force all thoughts of him from her mind. Time enough to dredge up bittersweet memories when she was safe . . . She thought of Dominic trapped by a rushing outcropping of fire, surrounded. . . . Shuddering, she banished the image from her mind. And rode on.

The smell was worse now, and smoke was beginning to swirl in teasing little tendrils beneath her nose. There must be fire ahead of her as well as behind her. Instinctively she turned the horse, heading for the creek. It might be her only salvation.

The smoke was growing thicker, making Sarah's eyes water and her nostrils sting. The horse was stampeding now, running headlong for the water. Sarah made no move to check him. She was terribly afraid that the fire was dangerously close. . . .

She screamed as, without warning, a solitary gum to her left exploded with a loud boom. The heat had been too much for the volatile sap. The tree burned brightly, instantly consumed in flames, as the horse beneath her, maddened with fear, screamed, too, and reared and bucked in a frantic effort to escape. Sarah, her attention momentarily, disastrously distracted, felt herself flying through the air. She landed nose first in a gorse bush, and immediately, without even waiting to check for broken bones or other injuries, forced herself to her feet. It would need only a single spark from the living torch that had only seconds ago been a tree to set the brush alight. As she shook herself off, she saw her horse disappearing in the distance. Whether he was heading toward the fire she had no idea, but she thought not. In a situation like this, a horse's instincts were often better than a human's. She was on foot now, alone in the bush, and the bush was afire. There was no time to take further stock of the situation. A loud boom made her jump as another gum exploded behind her and burst immediately into flames. Thick smoke poured from the burning trees toward the sky; tendrils oily from the burning sap escaped to coil around her. Sarah coughed, choking. Showers of sparks were raising tiny flickers of fire in the grass. . . .

Sarah ran for the creek as the flames spread. The water, she knew, was her only hope. She thanked God that she was wearing breeches. A long, trailing skirt, impossible to hold off the ground altogether, might well have been the death of her. As it was, she might die anyway. Gum after gum was noisily exploding, until, as she reached the water's edge and cast one last, scared look behind her, it seemed as though the whole world was in flames.

She felt heat blistering her cheeks as she plunged into the creek and waded out to the center, which came no higher than mid-thigh. Sparks were swirling in the air around her as she sank to her knees, submerging herself up to her neck. She could only pray that the smoke wouldn't get too thick, or the fire heat the water to boiling. She shuddered at the idea of being boiled alive. . . .

The next thirty minutes, as the fire leaped the creek to rage ferociously on each bank and groves of gums and eucalyptus burst noisily into flames, seemed like as many hours. The water was crowded with animals that had flocked to escape the blaze. Koalas, dingoes, kangaroos, and other marsupials huddled in the creek along with snakes and hares, emus, kiwis, and other birds. In this time of emergency, none threatened the others, or Sarah. She didn't even shiver when a reptile some fifteen feet long slithered through the water right in front of her nose, closely followed by another of its kind. They were intent only on escaping the fire.

The heat grew so intense that she felt as if it was scorching her lungs. She held her head beneath the water for as long as she dared, surfacing only to draw a quick breath of the hot, smoke-thick air through the soaking tail of her shirt before submerging again. Sparks fell like rain to sizzle on the surface of the water; on the banks, flames raced through grass and up trees to leap for the sky.

The water was getting hotter and hotter. The animals restless shifting indicated that the fire was reaching its peak. Would they live or would they die? Sarah could only pray.

Then, as if her prayers were answered, a miracle happened. The heavens opened as though a giant hand had ripped out its bottom, and deluges of icy water descended to soak the earth. In minutes the fire was out. The earth steamed in silent relief.

It was some little while later before the animals, one by one, began to slink and waddle and hop from the river. Sarah followed cautiously on unsteady legs. Her face was sore from the heat, and the ends of her hair were singed. Her lungs ached with every breath she drew. Her throat and nostrils were raw. She shivered with chill as rain poured over her already soaked body, but after the deadly heat of the fire the cold was a welcome relief. She wanted to cry, laugh, sing. She was glad to be alive.

The ground felt hot beneath her feet as she went up the bank and along the creek. Tall, blackened corpses of what had once been trees stood smoldering, steam rising from their lifeless limbs as the rain doused the last remaining sparks. Ashes lay thick on the charred ground as she walked through the remains of what less than an hour before had been a living grove of ghost gums. An unnatural stillness lay over everything. There was absolutely no sound except for the slapping of the rain.

Then, from directly overhead, came a sharp crack.

Sarah glanced up to see a huge black branch hurtling like a bolt from heaven. She didn't have time to cry out before it struck her. And for her, the world ceased to exist.

XXIV

Sarah opened her eyes, winced, and promptly shut them again. Even that tiny movement caused blinding pain to stab through her head. She moaned. Immediately a cold cloth was pressed to her forehead, her eyes, and then wiped carefully over her face.

"It's all right, my lamb. It's all right."

Sarah knew that soothing voice. Despite the pain, she forced her eyes open to stare with amazement at Mrs. Abbott's homely face bent over her. Then her eyes went beyond Mrs. Abbott to the familiar peaches and creams and greens of the room: her room. The bedroom she had slept in since she was small, at Lowella.

"What happened?" Her voice was so faint that it alarmed her.

"You were caught out in that bush fire, and a limb fell and hit you on the head. But you're safe home now, Miss Sarah, and you're going to be all right. All you need is rest."

"But how did I get home?" She was too tired to talk, and her eyes were closing even as she said it.

Before Mrs. Abbott could attempt to answer, Sarah was asleep. When she woke again, she did not know how much later, Mrs. Abbott still sat beside her. After drinking thirstily from a glass of barley water the housekeeper held to her lips, Sarah determinedly repeated her question. Disjointed memories tugged at the edge of her consciousness; there was something important that she should recall. . . .

"How did I get home, Mrs. Abbott?"

"Miss Sarah, you shouldn't be talking."

"Then you talk, Mrs. Abbott. Tell me what happened. Please, I need to know."

Mrs. Abbott leaned nearer, concern and indecision plain in her plump face.

"You were carried home, Miss Sarah. Your pa's face lit up like a candle when 'e saw that you were safe. 'E was beside 'imself when we found you'd been taken, you know. 'E had all the men out looking for you, and was even ready to offer a reward for your safe return—and you know how 'e is about money. We were all sore afraid for you, Miss Sarah."

"But who carried me home?"

Mrs. Abbott moistened her lips, looking uncharacteristically nervous. "Miss Liza was sitting on the porch when she saw this man riding in with you 'eld in front of 'im in the saddle. Lord, she let out a scream that must near 'ave shattered the windows! And we all came running, thinking something awful 'ad 'appened to 'er. And we saw you. You looked like you were dead, Miss Sarah. It was near dinnertime, and your pa and Mr. Percival were in the 'ouse. Your pa snatched you down from the 'orse and carried you inside. 'E was yelling for Madeline to be brought to tend you—"

"But who was the man on the horse?" Sarah interrupted. She was beginning to feel considerably better. The pain in her head wasn't quite so acute, and her thought processes were clearing. And still that niggling memory nagged at her. . . .

Mrs. Abbott looked uncomfortable. "We can talk more when you're better, Miss Sarah." She stood up, brushing nervously at her skirt. "I'll go fetch you some more barley water."

"Mrs. Abbott!" Sarah's voice was sharp. Mrs. Abbott backed toward the door, looking hunted. "It was Dom— Gallagher, wasn't it?"

"Oh, my, oh, my! Lamb, don't get yourself upset! When you're better . . ."

"*Wasn't it?*" That was the memory that had plagued her. Dominic's strong arms around her, lifting her, carrying her . . . He had somehow found her and brought her home. When he had been so adamant that he would never return to Lowella.

"Miss Sarah . . ." Mrs. Abbott sounded really upset.

Sarah sat bolt upright in the bed, ignoring the throbbing in her head. "How long ago was that? *What's happened to him?*" A terrible fear was coiling in her belly. Had he been right about her father after all? Surely Dominic wasn't— they hadn't harmed him?

"Miss Sarah, you 'ave to lie down! All right, I'll tell you, though your pa will likely 'ave my 'ide. But you must lie down!" Mrs. Abbot was hovering anxiously over her now, her round face creased with worry. Sarah fixed her with smoldering eyes as she lay tensely back against the pillows.

"Tell me." Was that her voice, that near-toneless command?

"You've been 'ome near a week, Miss Sarah. Gallagher came riding up bold as brass with you across 'is saddle on

Tuesday last. Your pa grabbed you away from 'im, and 'e turned to ride out again. But Mr. Percival . . .'' She hesitated a moment, then went on, her voice clearly reluctant, '' 'E ordered 'im to stop. When Gallagher just kept riding, 'e shot 'im clean out of the saddle.'' At Sarah's alarmed sound, she continued hastily, '''E didn't kill 'im, or even 'urt 'im bad. Just caught 'im in the shoulder.''

''Dear God!'' Sarah was no longer concerned about concealing from Mrs. Abbott the secret of her love for Dominic. Besides, she guessed from the woman's reluctance to tell her what had happened to Dominic that Mrs. Abbott had shrewdly surmised much of how she felt. ''Where is he now?'' The question was a strangled croak.

Mrs. Abbott looked even more uncomfortable. ''Mr. Percival locked 'im up in one of the sheep byres. You know, that one nearest the house. Mr. Percival was all set to 'ang 'im, for escaping, but your pa said to wait. 'E said 'anging couldn't be undone just by wishing it. They argued for a bit, with Mr. Percival saying, 'ow did they know what the convict had done to you?—but still your pa said to wait. Until you were well enough to tell what 'appened. Then, if 'anging was deserved, Gallagher'd be 'anged.''

Sarah had sat up again as Mrs. Abbott spoke, ignoring the housekeeper's worried expression. Now she swung her legs determinedly over the side of the bed. Her head spun for a moment, making her close her eyes. When she opened them again, the room slowly settled into place.

''Miss Sarah, you can't get up! You'll do yourself an injury! Please, Miss Sarah!'' Mrs. Abbott's hands were on her shoulders, trying to push her gently back into the bed.

Sarah gritted her teeth and shrugged free of Mrs. Abbott's grip. In truth, she wanted nothing more than to give in and lie back on her soft nest of pillows; her head was throbbing so that made her wince. But Dominic was hurt, too, more badly than she, Sarah had no doubt. He had no soft nest of pillows to lie on. But she meant to remedy that without delay. And she didn't give a damn what her father, or anyone else for that matter, thought.

"Mrs. Abbott, you go tell Tess or Mary to fetch that chair with wheels that Pa had brought out from England for my mother. Tell them to have it waiting at the foot of the stairs. Then you help me get dressed. I may need you to help me downstairs, too, and out to the byre. Call Jagger or one of the other men—it doesn't matter who—to come along with us. If Dom—Gallagher is badly hurt, we'll need a man to push the chair with him in it. Hear?"

Mrs. Abbott protested mightily, insisting that she would go herself to check on Dominic—she was fond of the boy herself, she said. But Sarah was determined, and she had her way. They made a curious procession crossing the yard, Mrs. Abbott supporting Sarah on her arm while Jagger followed, pushing the invalid chair with one hand and holding a rifle in the other. The rifle was for insurance. She doubted that there was any need for it, but she meant to get Dominic out of that byre. No matter what—or who—stood in her way.

By the time they reached the byre—a small shed erected near where the stable, now a blackened ruin, had stood; it was used to house any sheep that might need to be kept close at hand, for, say, a difficult lambing—the skirt of Sarah's faded blue gingham dress was wet to the knees from brushing across the soggy ground. Mrs. Abbott's skirts were in a similar condition, while the invalid chair made tracks in the field, which was still muddy from the torrential downpour that had ended the drought.

Heart hammering, Sarah had Jagger remove the thick plank that had been used to wedge the byre door shut, then, still supported by Mrs. Abbott, she stepped inside. For a moment she could see nothing in the pitch-dark interior of the small shed. Her nose wrinkled as a pervading stench assailed her nostrils. Mrs. Abbott's arm beneath hers trembled as the woman was struck by the odor. Jagger, following them with the rifle, whistled softly in consternation. As Sarah's eyes became accustomed to the gloom, she saw why.

Dominic lay on his back on a heap of matted straw, his eyes closed, his body bare from the waist up except for a dirty, bloodied bandage that bound his shoulder. His beard was thick now, obscuring the lines of his jaw and chin. His hair, waving wildly around his head, was filthy. Chains linked his wrists and ankles, and more chains secured him to iron rings set into the wall. His feet were bare and as dirty as the rest of him; his breeches were torn and ragged. Dampness pervaded the air as noticeably as the stench, which to her horror Sarah began to perceive emanated from one corner, which he had used for his physical needs. The shed floor on which the thin layer of straw was strewn was cold, clammy earth.

"Dominic!" Uncaring of her audience, Sarah pulled free of Mrs. Abbott's hold to take two tottering steps forward and drop to her knees at Dominic's side.

His eyes opened as she said his name. They stared at her blankly for a moment, then filled with a terrible anger.

"Get the hell out of here, Sarah." The voice was hoarse and weak, but, accompanied by the glittering stare he raked her with, it had the impact of a shout.

Once, Sarah would have been affronted by that hostile growl. But now that she had come to know Dominic almost as well as she knew herself, she realized that his anger stemmed less from the quarrel they had had—he must have forgiven her for that, if he had been willing to jeopardize his safety to bring her home to be cared for—than from shame at having her see him in such a state.

"Don't be a fool, Dominic," she said quietly. And,

ignoring the vivid string of curses he flung at her, she calmly instructed Jagger to fit keys into the shackles until he found one that worked, and then to help Dominic to the house. Dominic could use the blue bedroom just along the hall from hers. . . .

"You can't be meaning to let 'im stay in the 'ouse. Think of what your pa will say!" Mrs. Abbott whispered, upon hearing this last.

But Sarah ignored her, and Jagger's equally alarmed face as he searched for and finally found a key that would work the lock on the shackles. When Dominic's arms and legs were free, he struggled into a sitting position, and would have stood up if his strength had permitted. It did not, so he fell back, leaning against the shed wall and glaring ferociously at Sarah. Eyes narrowing, he deliberately called her a string of names that would have made a saloonkeeper wince. Mrs. Abbott gasped, clapped her hands to her ears, and stared at him with horror. Jagger stepped back a pace, jerking the rifle to his shoulder and pointing it at Dominic's middle.

"You an' me is friends, Gallagher, an' I don't wanta shoot ya, but I will if you keep talkin' to Miss Sarah like that. She don't deserve it."

"It's all right, Jagger," Sarah assured him over her shoulder. Unconvinced, Jagger lowered the rifle with obvious reluctance. To Dominic, Sarah added calmly, "If you say another filthy word, I'll have you hog-tied, and gagged, and carried to the house that way." She fixed him with a long, cool look. He scowled back.

"Back to being a Good Samaritan, are we?" He was smiling nastily, hostility plain in his eyes. The hostility deepened as she reached to touch his bandage. As she suspected, it was damp.

"When necessary," she answered calmly, and smiled when his only reply was a gritting of his teeth.

He could not walk unassisted, and Jagger was too slight
a man to support Dominic's much greater weight for any
distance, so he ended up being transported to the house—
with some difficulty because of the mud, which in places
was inches deep—in the invalid chair that Sarah had
brought along for that purpose. Dominic maintained a
sullen, glaring silence throughout the short journey, which
was a relief to Sarah. Her family would be horrified
enough when they discovered what she meant to do,
without him being carted through the house cursing like a
sailor.

Lydia and Liza, the first tight-lipped, the latter wide-
eyed, were standing together on the porch as they returned
to the house. Sarah, with Mrs. Abbott supporting her with
an arm around her waist, was in the lead. She faltered only
slightly when she saw the reception committee that awaited
them, then walked steadily on. Jagger, pushing Dominic in
the chair, followed. As they neared the porch, Sarah spoke
over her shoulder, instructing Jagger to take Dominic in
and make him as comfortable as possible in the bedroom
she had designated. Mrs. Abbott could show him where it
was. Then she shrugged off Mrs. Abbott's support, finding
that as her battle-readiness mounted so did her physical
strength.

"What do you think you're doing?" Lydia said with icy
outrage as Sarah indicated with a gesture that Jagger
should help Dominic into the house. They had stopped just
below the porch, and Lydia and Liza were staring down at
them over the rail. Jagger helped Dominic from the chair
and up the stairs, while Sarah hovered at Dominic's other
side. Lydia moved to confront them as they reached the
top of the steps, an ugly expression on her softly dimpled
face. "You can't come in here!" she said to Dominic.
Then, to Jagger, who looked distinctly alarmed, she added
regally, "Take him elsewhere at once."

"Believe me, ma'am, I don't want to profane your sacred house any more than you want me to," Dominic growled at Lydia as Sarah, feeling stronger by the minute as her temper mounted, turned to confront her stepmother. In her unbecoming blue gingham dress, now muddied to the knees, and with her hair pulled back into a bun as she usually wore it, Sarah looked no different from the young woman who, before her abduction, had borne Lydia's airs and megrims and verbal attacks without retaliating. Except for her eyes, which were flashing golden fire, and the snap in her voice as she told Lydia to move out of the way.

"Or I will knock you on your backside!" Sarah promised.

Lydia gasped, one hand flying to her mouth. Liza's eyes seemed to bulge from their sockets. Jagger looked even more alarmed, Mrs. Abbott chortled and quickly turned it into a cough, and Sarah could have sworn that even Dominic's grim lips twitched a little. She ignored them all, fixing her stepmother with a menacing stare. That look said that she was no longer a motherless little girl to be bullied and broken and finally despised. She was a woman, ready to fight for herself if necessary—and for her man.

"Your father will have something to say about this!" Lydia hissed even as she retreated. It was defeat, and both she and Sarah knew it.

Sarah paid her no further mind, but gestured to Jagger to do as she had bidden him. He did, silent and scared— Sarah guessed he was hoping that he would not be blamed for this day's work. Dominic, tight-lipped, suffered himself to be helped upstairs and bestowed on the bed in the blue bedroom.

"And if you don't stay put I'll have you tied to the bed," she warned him, still feeling militant. He glared at her, mouthing an obscenity that should have shamed her into silence. But fortunately he was too weak for anything but talk. She ignored him, not even blushing as she turned to Mrs. Abbott and directed that Madeline be fetched to tend his wound. In the meantime, Jagger could help Dominic bathe and, if Mrs. Abbott would provide a nightshirt, get him into bed.

"If he gives you, or Madeline, any trouble, tie him to the bed," was Sarah's last instruction to Jagger before she left the room. Her strength was rapidly ebbing, her head was beginning to pound, and she knew that if she did not lie down again she would fall down. Dominic's curses echoed in her ears all the way back to her own bed.

As Lydia had prophesied, Edward did have something—many somethings, most of them nearly as profane as Dominic at his worst—to say about a convict in his house, being cared for and tended like a valued guest or a member of the family. Lydia must have greeted him at the door with her tale of his daughter's simultaneous recovery and perfidy, because he came bursting into her bedroom without even stopping to wash away the day's grime. He yelled and stomped and threatened, then yelled some more, while Sarah, ensconced in her bed with an ice pack on her head, listened calmly, only occasionally wincing as a particularly loud roar found its echo in her head. Finally, when he threatened to have Dominic shot where he lay, Sarah interrupted. She never raised her voice, but the cool determination in her eyes made him stop yelling and listen.

"If you harm him in any way, if you even refuse to have him in the house, I'll leave, Pa, and never come back. And if the thought of my leaving doesn't particularly bother you, let me remind you that I keep the books and pay the bills and run the house. And if I go, who will you get to do it? Lydia?" There was a distinct sneer as she suggested her stepmother, who both she and Edward knew would be horrified at the notion that she should assume such duties, which she considered distinctly beneath the lady of the house.

Her father stared at her without speaking for a moment. His hands, which had been clenched into fists as he ranted and raved, slowly relaxed. The red color that once would have alarmed her began to fade from his face.

"What do you mean, if the thought of your leaving doesn't bother me? Of course it bothers me! I'm your pa, girl!" This was said testily, while he looked her over with a frown.

"Then you will let Dom— Gallagher stay in the house until he's well, and then see about getting his sentence commuted? As a reward for saving my life, if you like. He is really not guilty, Pa."

"I suppose he told you that?"

"Yes. And I believe him."

Edward's frown deepened. "Just what is this man to you, daughter?" he asked, moving until he stood beside the bed looking down at her.

Sarah felt color rising in her cheeks as she considered confessing that she loved Dominic, but as she looked at her father she decided to wait. The belligerence had left his stocky body. His gray eyes looked tired, almost sad. Maybe she was being cowardly, but she thought such a traumatic announcement was best saved for another time. Maybe, after he got used to having Dominic in the house, he would be more amenable to the idea of her marrying him.

"He has put himself at considerable risk for me more than once," she said. Then she went on to describe, with careful editing, how Dominic had put his life on the line to protect her from the bushrangers—whom he had just happened to encounter after the raid on Lowella; she reminded him of that earlier incident with the escaped convict, and finally of how Dominic had jeopardized his own safety and freedom to bring her back to Lowella after she had been struck by that falling limb. When she finished, Edward ran a hand through his thinning red hair and tugged on his dusty, loosened cravat as if it had suddenly become too tight for him.

"Sarah—daughter, forgive me, but I must ask you: Did that convict touch you?"

There was no doubt of his meaning. Sarah did not want to lie, but on the other hand she was afraid the truth might send Edward into a towering rage, and Dominic would suffer the consequences far more than herself. Then it struck her: surely Edward knew what had happened between herself and Dominic that night in the orchard. If he did not, why—and by whose orders—had Dominic been punished? But if he did, why would he ask if Dominic had touched her? He would already know the answer.

"Pa, tell me something," she said slowly. "Did you give an order for Dominic to be whipped at any time?"

Edward ceased his nervous movements and stared back at her. "I don't see what that has to do with my question, but the answer is no. I had no reason to, to my knowledge."

"He *was* whipped, Pa. Brutally, just before he ran. And he was left to hang in a barn for days. If he hadn't managed to escape, he would probably have been allowed to die there."

Edward's gray eyes narrowed. "Did he tell you that, too?"

"Yes. And it's true. I saw the marks on his back."

The color was seeping from her father's face. He moistened his lips before answering. "I gave no such orders."

"It must have been Percival," Sarah said under her breath.

"What?"

Sarah repeated herself.

"If so, then he did it on his own initiative. Although I

can't believe he'd do such a thing without a good reason."
Her father paused and looked at her hard. "Did he have
such a reason, Sarah?"

Sarah hesitated. Then she decided to take the plunge.
"He may have thought I was growing too fond of Dominic,
Pa."

She watched him as she spoke. He closed his eyes for a
moment as if in pain. When he opened them again, he
looked suddenly old.

"And were you—are you?"

This time it was Sarah who moistened her lips. She
hesitated, then met his eyes with a calmness she didn't
feel.

"Yes, Pa."

Nervously she waited for his reaction. But he did not
bellow or roar, as she might have expected. Instead, he
seemed to wilt.

"Sarah, I know that since your mother died I've not
been the best of fathers to you. You look so like her, you
see, that it hurt me to look at you for a long time after she
went. Then I married Lydia, and . . . well, you know Lydia!
She can be difficult. It just seemed easiest not to fight her.
I know you haven't been as happy as you might have been,
and the fault for that is largely mine. What I'm trying to
say is that I love you, girl. I want what's best for you in
life. I'll let the convict stay in the house until he's
recovered if it will please you. And I'll even do my best to
get his sentence commuted."

"Oh, Pa!" she said, tears welling into her eyes as she
smiled up at him. He had not told her he loved her since
she was a tiny girl, and over the years she had come to
believe he no longer did. Because she was plain, and her
sex a disappointment to him, when she knew he would
have preferred that his only child had been a son. But just
now he had compared her to her beautiful mother, and

agreed to relax his long-standing prejudice against convicts for her sake, and told her he loved her. . . . Edward harrumphed loudly as the tears in her eyes glistened in the flickering light of the candles by the bed, then abruptly sat down on the mattress and pulled her into his arms. He hugged her quickly, while she hugged him back, the tears rolling unchecked down her cheeks.

"My girl Sarah," he said into her hair, sounding as if he too was close to tears. "I know you're a woman grown and capable of making your own decisions. But, daughter, take a word of advice from your father, who has lived a lot longer than you and has your best interests at heart. You admit you're fond of the man: he's attractive to women, I suppose, and I know you haven't had too many beaus, though I would have thought John . . . well, never mind that now. You know my feelings about *that*. But, Sarah, you listen to me, girl: never forget who you are and what he is. Don't get *too* fond of him. If you do, it will bring you nothing but heartache. There's no future for you with a convict. And I tell you this out of love."

He stood up as abruptly as he had sat down, and before she could say anything he stamped noisily from the room. Like her, he was not used to showing emotion, and it embarrassed him. Sarah stared after him, not knowing whether to laugh or cry or curse, and ended up doing a little bit of both. He loved her—but there was still a long, long way for him to go before he would accept the idea that she was going to marry Dominic. In a way, she almost wished he knew, as she had thought he must, that Dominic had been her lover. He might still suspect, but she rather thought he preferred not even to speculate on such an intimate subject concerning his daughter. But he had left her with considerable food for thought. And think Sarah did, mulling over all he had told her until at last she fell asleep.

It was the following afternoon before she felt well enough to leave her bed again. Yesterday's little jaunt and subsequent emotional scenes, when she was still so weak, had taken more out of her than she had realized. Upon wakening from a long and surprisingly restful sleep, her every instinct urged her to go to Dominic at once. But her body just would not obey. It obstinately insisted on remaining in bed, sipping tea and broth prepared by Mrs. Abbott and brought up by Tess, and nibbling on triangles of toast while it slowly regained its strength. Besides Tess, no one ventured into her bedchamber, which piqued Sarah a trifle. She would have thought that Liza at least would have popped her head in to inquire how she was doing. Despite their differences, which Sarah knew were mainly Lydia's doing, she was genuinely fond of her stepsister, and thought Liza was fond of her as well.

The afternoon sun was shining in through the open windows when Sarah at last swung her legs out of bed and attempted to stand. Her knees were a little wobbly at first, but she made it to the window and stood looking out for a moment while she waited for either Mary or Tess to respond to her summons. The rain had brought the lush colors of the countryside to vivid life again. The lawn was newly green, and while the tall eucalyptus trees guarding the house were still bare-limbed, they looked somehow refreshed. The wattle bushes had burst into glorious bloom; their sweet fragrance floated up to her nostrils as she stood drinking in the soft, clean air. In the distance, the mountains were a deep blue haze rising to touch the brighter blue of the cloudless sky. Sarah smiled at the beauty of it. Then a light knock heralded Tess's arrival, and Sarah turned back into the room.

Tess shyly complimented her on the new beauty of her skin as she helped her dress—an assistance that Sarah normally scorned but felt in need of today. When at last

her clothes were on and her hair was brushed and styled,
Sarah dismissed the girl, then with a critical eye regarded
her reflection in the cheval glass in one corner of the room.
Despite the soft shine of her hair and the glow to her skin
that Tess had praised, Sarah saw nothing new in the
mirror. She was still the same tall, skinny, plain Sarah. But
her father had said she resembled her lovely mother, and
Dominic had called her beautiful. Sarah eyed her angular
face—perhaps its too-prominent planes and resulting pronounced hollows could be softened by a new hair style,
one that was less old-maidish than her prim bun. And her
figure—dressed in feminine, fashionable apparel, would it
acquire the illusion of womanly curves? Sarah remembered
how fervently Dominic had insisted—and demonstrated—
that he liked her body just as it was, and blushed. She saw
how the rosy pink color flooding her cheeks emphasized
the guinea gold of her eyes, warmed her face, making it
look almost girlish, and even seemed to brighten the
brown-gold of her hair; and for the first time she saw her
own possibilities. With the right clothes and hair style ... But
Sarah thought glumly, she wouldn't know where to begin.
She imagined herself tricked out in the tiers of pastel
ruffles deemed fashionable by Lydia and Liza, and felt a
return of self-doubt. She would look ridiculous, she knew.
Worse, she was very much afraid she would look, as Mrs.
Grainger had once said about another old maid on the
catch for a husband, like mutton trying to pretend it was
lamb. Sarah sighed, turning away from the mirror. There
was no point in wishing she were something she was not.
She was a twenty-two-year-old spinster of uncertain looks
at best, in love with a man ten years her senior who had
undoubtedly made love to more women than he could
count. And he was gorgeous, too. But he had said he
loved her and wanted to marry her. Sarah clung to that.
   She made her way along the hall to the blue bedroom.

Before she reached it, she heard voices and laughter through the door, which was ajar. Sarah frowned, distinctly recognizing Dominic's lilt. She would know that voice in a dark cave in China. He sounded amused. Sarah's eyes widened as she thought she recognized the feminine voice talking to him. Surely it couldn't be . . .

She walked to the door and opened it, standing for a moment in the aperture as her eyes took in the scene. Dominic, clad in one of her father's old nightshirts, was sitting propped up in bed, freshly shaved, his hair black as midnight against the white pillows, his eyes, still with a grin lurking in their depths as he looked up to see her standing there, as blue as the lapis-lazuli brooch she owned that had once belonged to her mother. One of his hands was clasped between both of Liza's, as she perched on the side of his bed.

XXV

"Sarah!" Liza looked around, too, following Dominic's eyes. As soon as she saw her sister scowling at her from the doorway, she dropped Dominic's hand as if it had suddenly turned red hot and jumped to her feet. Her cream-colored dimity with its feminine flounces around the neck and hem fluttered around her as she moved. Sarah's scowl deepened. She knew that, next to Liza's soft prettiness, she must look severe, unattractive—in a word, old-maidish.

"What are you doing in here, Liza?" Knowing that it would be all too easy to snap at her young stepsister, Sarah carefully kept her voice even.

"I came to see Dominic." Liza's reply was truculent. Her lower lip thrust forward in a charming little pout, and her brown spaniel eyes as they met her sister's were challenging.

"Dominic?" Sarah echoed the name with raised brows, questioning Liza's use of it. On the surface, her objection was that it was not done to call a convict by his given name. Underneath, however, she knew that her objections were very different—and far more personal. Dominic himself said not a word. A slight frown darkened his handsome face as he sat, with arms crossed, listening to the girls' exchange.

"Why shouldn't I call him Dominic? You do." Liza was throwing down the gauntlet with a vengeance.

Sarah's eyes widened and went swiftly, involuntarily to Dominic, who returned her look blandly. Surely he could not have told Liza about their relationship. . . .

"You know that it's not proper for you to be in this room," Sarah said quietly, choosing not to reply directly to Liza's attack. She would be treading on very thin ice.

Liza snorted. "You're a fine one to be preaching propriety, sister. All these years you've set yourself up as such a lady—Mother told me differently, but I didn't believe her! But I'm no longer as ignorant as I used to be—you like handsome men every bit as well as I do! Your only problem is, unless they're convicts like Dominic here and have to, they won't pay any attention to you!"

"Liza!" Sarah was shocked.

"That's enough out of you, young lady!" The growl was Dominic's. He had abandoned his lazy posture against the pillows to sit bolt upright in the bed, fixing Liza with a fierce gleam in his blue eyes.

Liza looked at him, and her chin quivered. "How dare you talk to me like that, convict! Just because I flirted with you a little doesn't mean you can go beyond the line with *me!* I'm not like my sister here. She's an old maid, so it's not surprising that you can kiss her once and she'll let you be as familiar as you please! I'm a lady, and don't you forget it!"

"Would this tantrum have anything to do with the fact

that I was just gently refusing to kiss *you?*" Dominic asked, very polite.

Liza glared at him, crimsoning.

"Stay out of this, Dominic," Sarah intervened hastily, before Liza could go into screaming hysterics, as she gave every indication she was about to do. "Liza, suppose you explain yourself."

"Suppose you explain yourself, sister!" Liza retorted, whirling again to face Sarah, hands clenched at her sides, face crimsoning. "*You* just called him Dominic—is he your lover? Mother says he is!"

"Liza!"

"Be silent!"

The exclamations came from Sarah and Dominic respectively, the first shocked, the second furious. Liza glared at them both impartially.

"Why? You've kissed him at least. I know—I saw you."

Sarah fought to keep guilty color from creeping up her cheeks. Undoubtedly this was just another form of Liza's usual temper fit.

"If you speak to your sister again with such a lack of respect, I'll paddle your backside until you can't sit for a month." The threat was Dominic's, and even if Liza didn't know him well enough to recognize her danger, Sarah did.

"Don't you dare, Dominic!" she warned, sparing him a chastening glance before focusing her attention on Liza again. "Liza, I think you'd better go to your room and calm down. I'll send Mary to you with some fresh tea."

"Don't you take that patronizing tone with me, Sarah Markham. I know better! I tell you I saw you kissing him in the stable the day before he ran away."

Sarah's lips quivered with sudden memory. Of course, Dominic had kissed her in the stable the morning after he had first made love to her. A hard, brutal kiss it had been, too. . . . And Liza had seen. A sudden suspicion had Sarah's eyes focusing on Liza, narrowing.

"And who did you tell, Liza?" The words were soft, deadly.

Liza met her eyes defiantly for a moment before her lids fell to cover them. She looked suddenly very guilty.

"I—Mr. Percival," she said, all the anger draining out of her. "I was coming back from the stable just as he was leaving the house with something he'd forgotten that morning. He could see I was—upset. He asked me what was the matter and I told him. He got really furious—said that he would have the filthy b— uh, convict whipped. I told him Pa didn't permit such things, and he said that he didn't mean to tell Pa, and I shouldn't either, or he'd tell that I'd been—doing something I shouldn't. It's none of your business what." Liza looked suddenly at Sarah, a trace of defiance in her eyes again. "There's no need for you to look at me like that: No harm came of it. Dominic ran away before Mr. Percival could whip him. If he hadn't, if Mr. Percival had really started in on him, I would have told Pa. Really I would have, Sarah."

Liza looked very young suddenly, and very earnest. Sarah sighed, shook her head, and felt her anger dissipate. No matter what havoc her actions had wrought, Liza hadn't meant to do her or Dominic any harm.

"I know you would have, love," Sarah said, voice soft.

Liza smiled at her, shakily, then suddenly burst into tears and ran from the room.

"She really didn't mean any harm," Sarah said to Dominic, coming a couple of steps closer to where he sat propped against his pillows once more. He looked absolutely dumbfounded. "She's very young."

"A spoiled brat, is what you mean," Dominic muttered absently. He was silent for a moment, seeming intent on the pattern in the woven bedspread. Then he looked up.

"Your father stopped in here for a moment last night. He was surprisingly cordial, under what I thought were the circumstances. I was wary at first, expecting at any moment for him to pull out a hidden pistol and shoot me through the heart for a damned blackguard. But he merely thanked me for looking out for you in the bush and bringing you home again when you were hurt. He even apologized for what happened then—said if he'd known the whole story he would never have been so harsh. I've been wondering about it ever since—and now I begin to see. He doesn't know about us, does he?"

Sarah shook her head. "No. I asked him outright if he had had you beaten, and he denied it. Whatever else he is, my father is not a liar."

"So it was your damned overseer, acting on his own. . . . Now that I come to think about it, I never actually saw your father. Percival just kept saying that he was acting on Mr. Markham's orders."

"That's what I've decided, too."

Dominic was silent again, his eyes straying back to the coverlet as if fascinated by it.

"I owe you an apology," he said suddenly, looking up to meet her eyes.

"Yes, you do." She hid a smile, looking severe as she pronounced the words with a waiting air.

He scowled, then grinned reluctantly as he gave in to her air of silent expectation. "All right, you shrew, I'm sorry. I should have believed you when you told me you didn't go running to your father. And while I'm at it, I might as well apologize for the way I behaved yesterday, too. To tell the truth, I was damned glad to see you—and even gladder to get out of that hellhole."

Sarah frowned, as if considering. Then she smiled and took another step closer to the bed. "I shouldn't, but I suppose I forgive you. If you forgive me, that is."

He looked at her questioningly. She took another step. She was standing beside the bed now, so close that her skirt brushed the mattress. Her hands were clasped nervously in front of her. Now that the time was at hand, she felt very awkward. What if he had changed his mind and no longer wanted to marry her? What if he had merely been carried away by the circumstances when he had proposed, and, after recovering from his snit, had actually been relieved when she had not accepted? Why should he want to marry her, after all? She was plain. . . .

"For refusing to marry you," she said, forcing the words out through dry lips. Every instinct cried out for her to stop there, to leave the rest to him if he would, but, having said so much, she was determined to plunge ahead regardless of propriety. "Dominic, is—is the offer still open?"

"What offer?" He was starting to smile. That dimple that she had noticed before appeared suddenly to crease his right cheek, making him look so handsome that she clenched her fists. Impossible to believe that this beautiful man was really in love with her, really wanted to marry her. He had been flattering her, or temporarily mad. . . .

"Never mind," she muttered hastily, losing her nerve. She started to turn away, embarrassed at having so nearly made a fool of herself, not wanting to hear him try to be kind as he put her off.

Suddenly he yelped, lunging forward and stopping her with a yank on her skirts. She yelped too as she felt herself tumbling backward to land in an undignified sprawl across the bed, in his arms. A ripping sound was clearly audible as she fell. Half-laughing, half-struggling as Dominic pinned her to the bed, Sarah glanced down to find her plain white petticoat clearly visible through a tear in her skirt that split it from the waist almost to the hem.

"My dress—look what you've done!"

He was looming over her, his eyes caressing. She could feel his hard thighs against her back as she lay across his lap. The white linen of her father's nightshirt—he looked maddeningly attractive in the homely garment, she thought—made his skin and hair look very dark and his eyes very blue in contrast. Again she was conscious of a qualm—could he *really* love her?

"To hell with your dress—it's little better than a rag anyway. So are most of your clothes that I've seen. When you're my wife, you'll dress to show off your beauty, not hide it."

"Oh, Dominic," Sarah said, half-laughing. "Are you sure that your eyes are working properly? I fear I'm rather plain."

"I don't ever want to hear you say that again." He looked suddenly fierce. "I don't even want you to think it. Your bitch of a stepmother and that spoiled little stepsister have turned your thinking, Sarah. Sure, you don't look like they do. You shouldn't want to! They're pretty, Sarah, in a totally ordinary way. There are hundreds of women across the world just like them. But you—you're unique. You're beautiful, Sarah, if you weren't so afraid to show it. From now on, every morning when you get up, I want you to look in your mirror and say, 'Dominic says I'm beautiful.' Do you hear me?"

"I would think the whole house hears you." Her eyes were smiling at him. He smiled back, bending to drop a quick kiss on her nose before reaching beneath her head to begin pulling pins from her hair.

"What are you doing?"

"Starting the transformation with your hair. You have beautiful hair, Sarah. It's a crime to screw it back in this ugly bun. I won't have it."

"I'm not answerable to you, sir," she mocked him, smiling.

"Are you not, now? You will be—when you marry me." The words were smug.

Sarah looked up into the handsome face bent so closely over her own, not quite daring to believe that this wonderful thing could be true, that he could love her and want to marry her and that she could actually be planning to go against every prejudice she'd ever been taught and marry him, the most handsome, charming, wonderful man she had ever known—but a convict, nonetheless. . . . Her father would hit the roof, Sarah knew. It was possible that they would have to leave Lowella for good. But Sarah knew that if she was forced to choose between Lowella and Dominic, there was no longer a contest. She would choose Dominic every time, without regret.

"Will you marry me, Sarah?" The words, spoken in the tenderest of voices, were a formal proposal.

Sarah smiled radiantly, unaware of how that smile transformed her, making her golden eyes shine with happiness, parting her soft pink lips so that her teeth showed white between them, lending rosy color to her cheeks. Her hair, which he had loosened, framed her face like a tumbling golden mane. She was, in that moment, gloriously beautiful as she smiled up at the man she loved.

"Yes, Dominic," she whispered, and caught her breath as he lowered his head.

His lips were soft as they caught hers, infinitely gentle, loving, caring. . . . Sarah responded to them like flowers to the sun, opening up, stretching, reaching. Her arms went around his shoulders to clasp him to her. He winced, cursing, and immediately released her to probe his shoulder gingerly with his hand.

"Oh, Dominic, I'm sorry. Did I hurt you?" She was immediately concerned. Impossible to believe that she had so completely forgotten about his wound.

"Just a passing twinge. Nothing to concern yourself

about.'' He moved his shoulder once, experimentally. Then he was leaning over her again, clearly intending to take up where he had left off.

Sarah pushed him away with a hand on his chest, sitting up. The gaze she turned on him was determined. ''I came in here meaning to check on your wound, and with one thing and another I forgot. But I've remembered now.''

Dominic abandoned his attempt to kiss her for the moment, and leaned back against the mound of pillows, surveying her with a look of possession that nearly made her forget what she was about.

''Sarah, my own, the only way you're going to be able to see my wound is if I get out of this very peculiar garment. It—uh, has no top, you see. It is entirely in one piece.''

Sarah lifted her eyebrows at him. ''So, get out of it.''

His eyes widened in mock horror. ''But I have absolutely nothing on underneath.''

''It's a little late for modesty now, isn't it?'' she said to him as he had to her once before.

He grinned, showing her that he remembered, too. ''You're right about that. Well, if I must I must. But, Sarah—close the door first, will you, please? I don't fancy having the entire household gaping at me in the altogether.''

Sarah glanced over her shoulder, startled to find that the door to the hallway stood wide. Anyone could have seen her rolling on Dominic's bed. . . . She blushed. And got up to close the door.

When she came back, he was clad only in a neat white bandage wound crisscross fashion around his left shoulder. The contrast between his bronzed, hair-roughened masculinity and the soft white bed was riveting. It certainly riveted Sarah. It was all she could do to stop herself from staring at him.

''There's no need to worry yourself about it, my own. It

was naught but a flesh wound." He was sounding very Irish, which Sarah had noticed he did in moments of tenderness.

She smiled at him. "For a flesh wound, it left you awfully weak. Yesterday you could hardly walk."

"That was yesterday. Today, after a good meal and a night in a fine bed, I feel a new man."

"What a shame! Just as I was growing rather fond of the old one."

"Rather fond? Rather fond!" It was a fearsome growl. He caught her by the arms, pulling her down and turning until she was lying on her back on the bed while he, with the bedspread still covering him to the waist, leaned over her. "Admit it, woman. You love me madly."

"I love you madly," she said with an air of humoring a lunatic.

He grinned, the twist of his lips wolfish, and bent down to find and ravish her mouth with his. When he lifted his head at last, her blood was drumming in her ears.

"Now say it again," he ordered.

"I love you madly," she repeated obediently, but this time the words were breathless.

"Much better," he said with satisfaction, and bent to kiss her again.

Sarah's arms went around his neck, mindful of his shoulder this time as her eyes closed. She would allow him to kiss her for a few minutes only, then would see to his wound. . . . But her fingers found the silken hairs that curled at his nape and lingered, fascinated by the contrast between warm, hard skin and cool, soft hair. Her mouth was preoccupied, too, with the feel of his firm lips and searching tongue. She met that tongue with hers, stroked it, explored the inside of his mouth while he held back, letting her learn new ways to please him. Her hands began to move, stroking his hair, his neck, his back—she ran her

fingers along the faint trails left by the beatings he had
suffered. She could barely feel the scars. In time, she
thought, they would heal completely, and she was glad.
Dominic should not have to bear all his life the signs of his
enslavement. . . .

His fingers were searching behind her for the fastenings
of her dress. His fingers fumbled, tugged, and he cursed
under his breath. She reached behind her to still his hands.
His wrists under her fingers were hard and strong, and
roughened by hair.

"Let me," she whispered. He looked down at her for a
moment before releasing her to roll onto his back.

Sarah stood up, her eyes never leaving his as she
reached behind her back to feel, through the thick curtain
of her hair, for the tiny hooks. She found one, then
another, and loosened them while he watched her with
eyes so blue that they would have put sapphires to shame.
When the last was freed, she hesitated, then slowly slid the
dress down her arms and over her hips. When she straightened, she was clad only in her plain white linen chemise
and unadorned petticoat. He looked at her as if she were
dressed in the filmiest of silken underthings. She met his
eyes, and felt love and desire join forces within her to
make her as clay before this man, willing to do anything
and be anything to please him. And she knew that her
boldness pleased him. . . . Slipping out of her shoes, she
placed one foot deliberately on the edge of the bed. She
slid first the plain blue ribbon garter and then the sturdy
white cotton stocking down her leg with seductive slowness.
His eyes followed her every movement as she repeated the
deliberate provocation with the other leg, then he gazed
with open heat at the slender curves of her bare leg as it
poised for an instant before vanishing again beneath her
petticoat.

Sarah smiled to herself at the dark color that mounted to

his forehead as he stared. He wanted her—she had seen the signs often enough now to recognize them. But she meant to make him want her more. . . . Her hands moved to the tapes of her petticoat. She untied them one at a time, carefully smoothing each crumpled ribbon, watching him all the while. Tiny beads of sweat appeared one by one to adorn his upper lip.

"Sweet Jesus, Sarah, hurry," he whispered hoarsely.

She smiled and let the petticoat flutter to the ground. Standing there clad only in her chemise, with her long, curving legs bare beneath and her breasts pushing against the thin white linen so that the tiny hard buds of her nipples were clearly discernible, she no longer felt she bore any relationship to plain spinster Sarah. She was beautiful Sarah, beloved Sarah, Sarah who would soon be Dominic's bride. . . .

"Sarah, if you don't get that damned flimsy thing off and get into bed with me, you're liable to cripple me for life," Dominic warned in a thick voice.

"Am I now?" she whispered, smiling a little.

Then her hands were beneath the sensible shoulder straps, sliding the garment down. When she stepped out of it, she looked up to find his eyes as hot as the fiercest flame as he looked at her bare skin. Sarah trembled beneath that searing regard. Suddenly she was no longer in the mood to tease him, to play. . . . She joined him on the bed, melting into his arms, her own locking around his neck as she returned his kiss with the same ferocious abandon as he offered it. She was as quicksilver in his arms.

"Oh, Sarah, my Sarah, I ache with wanting you," he whispered into her ear as his hand found her swelling breast. She closed her eyes as tremors of passion curled her toes, and reached beneath the coverings to find and claim that most tangible evidence of his ardent desire. . . .

He groaned as her fingers closed around him; his eyes closed as she caressed him in the way he had taught her, her fingers tantalizingly cool and sweet against the swollen shaft that pulsed and burned in her hand. He tried to roll with her, so that he could cover her with his body, but Sarah was having none of that. Being the aggressor, she found, was a heady experience. She was suddenly consumed with the need to bring him to the same pitch of feverish delight he always evoked in her. Wriggling free of his possessing arms, she pushed him back against the mattress with one hand against his chest.

"Sarah?" Her name was a hoarse question. He was lying obediently back against the mattress, his skin very dark against the white sheets. She was kneeling over him, naked, her breasts pink and swollen with need, her unbound hair falling down over her shoulders to mix with the black curling wedge of hair on his chest.

"Sarah!" This time it was an urgent demand, punctuated by his hands as he reached for her.

Again she eluded him, trailing provocative fingers down over his hard abdomen to slide beneath the blankets and just brush the hardness of him before dancing away. He clenched his teeth, his eyes open again as he watched her. Watching dark color suffuse his face, nearly giddy with the knowledge that she could excite him as he always so effortlessly excited her, Sarah's eyes widened as a sudden inspiration occurred to her. She loved the feel of him under her hands, the way he pulsed and hardened. She wanted to know him better, to know him every way there was to know him, as intimately as he knew her. . . .

The blankets were tangled around his hips. Dominic drew in his breath as she pulled them away. He was completely naked now, his long length sprawled darkly across the bed, his eyes a smoky sapphire as they stared at her.

"Sarah, what the hell . . . ?" His voice was hoarse, and he made no further effort to reach for her.

Sarah looked at him for a long moment, her eyes as hot as his, then turned her attention from his face to other, more immediately interesting parts of him. Her hand came out to rub over his belly. The muscles tightened under her soft caress; then she bent her head and replaced her hands with her lips, nibbling and licking and biting. The thick, soft mat of hair on his belly tickled her nose; beneath her lips she felt his stomach tighten. With the corners of her eyes she saw his hands clench into fists on either side of his hips as she followed the beckoning arrow of hair downward.

When the moment came, she hesitated fractionally. Could she really go through with this? He did not move, seemed not even to be breathing. His hands were clenched so tightly at his sides that his knuckles were white. A fleeting glance upward showed her that his face was hard, intent, his lips slightly parted, his eyes aflame.

When she kissed him, he groaned as if in mortal agony. Encouraged, she ran her lips over the length of him, her tongue coming out to savor and taste. He was salty, and faintly musky, and scalding hot. . . .

"Jesus, Sarah!" The thick mutter came as he jack-knifed upright, his hands catching her waist and dragging her up with him. He was breathing hard, his face a dark red, his hands trembling where they held her.

"Didn't you—like it?" she whispered, staring at him, thinking that, in her inexperience, she had done something wrong. Or, was it something that men did only to ladies?

"Like it?" He groaned the question, twisting with her so that she was flat on her back on the bed and he was looming over her. He seemed to be having trouble speaking.

"You do it to me," she pointed out in a barely audible whisper.

"Christ!" The word was explosive. His legs slid between hers, his long thighs trembling, and then he came into her so fast that she cried out. He bent his head, drowning her cry with his mouth, taking her with hard, urgent strokes as his broken mutters gave her to understand that he liked her innovation very much indeed.

XXVI

Sarah spent the next few days trying to work up the nerve to break the news to her father. He would not be pleased —to put it mildly— that his daughter was planning to wed a convict. She hoped that she could persuade him to accept the situation with a modicum of grace, but she feared he would not. Her father's prejudice against convicts was deeply ingrained. His staunchly exclusionist beliefs would, she knew, be outraged. And Lydia wouldn't help matters any. Her stepmother's attitude had been positively malevolent every time Sarah had crossed her path. Lydia would never forgive her for having forced her to back down, or, Sarah thought, for the improvement in her appearance. At Dominic's request, Sarah had taken to wearing her hair in a loose roll, which was vastly becoming. In addition, also at Dominic's request, she had taken a few of her mother's old gowns from the attic. With only minor alterations, they fit Sarah as if they had been made for her. Although they were out of fashion, the high-waisted empire styles, with their fitted bodices tied beneath the breasts to fall into a long, slim skirt, somehow managed to transform her boyish figure into a graceful elegance that was very feminine indeed. Every time Sarah caught a glimpse of herself in a mirror, she marveled at how much difference these dresses made in her appearance. She was having less and less trouble believing Dominic when he insisted that she was beautiful.

Dominic's wound was much improved. He could walk without difficulty, and had very little trouble moving his arm. Although he was eager to move back into the bunkhouse—he did not feel comfortable in the big house, where he knew he was tolerated at best—Sarah so far had managed to talk him out of going. Her reasons were twofold: first, she usually managed to creep into Dominic's bed sometime during the night when the rest of the family were sleeping. These sessions had of necessity to be very quiet, but what they might have lacked in sound they certainly made up for in fury. The wanton pleasures her body was capable of were as constant a source of amazement to Sarah as was her changed appearance. She had supposed that as she grew accustomed to Dominic's love-making, the sharp, spiraling excitement would be progressively dulled. Instead, it increased.

Her other reason for wanting Dominic to remain in the house was very much her secret. She hoped to get him accustomed to her family, and her family accustomed to him, so that when they married they might stay on Lowella. The thought of leaving—her father more than the land itself, probably never to return—brought an ache to her heart. But Dominic was determined to return to Ireland, which he loved more fiercely than she loved Lowella. And she was prepared to go with Dominic to the ends of the earth if necessary. She only wished it would not be necessary.

About a week after Dominic had come to stay in the

house, Sarah woke with a queasiness in her stomach that
had been plaguing her for several days. She lay with her
head resting back against the pillow, idly contemplating the
scene outside her window, and wishing very much that she
and Dominic were already married so that she could wake
up in his arms. She hated leaving him every night, hated
sneaking about the house like a thief. But it would not be
for much longer. Sarah meant to find a way to break the
news to her father before another day had passed. And if
her stomach did another peculiar flip-flop at the mere idea,
then that was just too bad. It had to be done; she had put it
off long enough.

Her stomach ailment had not caused her much concern
at first. But this was the third morning in a row that she
had lifted her head from the pillow only to be overwhelmed
with nausea, and she was beginning to wonder if perhaps
her head injury, which she had nearly forgotten, had been
more serious than she had realized. She was rarely ill. Her
constant, hearty good health was another of those unfeminine
traits that Lydia was always making snide remarks about.
But fortunately this ailment—whatever it was—did not
seem particularly severe. If she stayed abed for an extra
quarter-hour, it passed and she felt fine for the rest of the
day.

The more Sarah thought about that, the more peculiar it
seemed. And the more alarming. She had heard of such
symptoms from the women in their social circle. Whenever they got together, the talk was always of courtships,
weddings, and babies. Lizzie Warren, who had been three
months' gone at the time of Liza's birthday ball, had gone
into her various physical miseries in excrutiatingly boring
detail. Sarah had barely listened. Now she regretted it—
because a dreadful suspicion was beginning to take possession of her. She was not ignorant; she knew precisely how
babies were made. One could not live on a sheep station,

watching life and death and birth among the animal and human populations, without acquiring comprehensive knowledge on the subject. But somehow she had never thought to connect what she and Dominic did together with babies. . . . Sarah thought back to when she had last been visited by her monthly time. It had been months ago, shortly before Liza's ball. . . . She shut her eyes in instinctive denial, then slowly opened them as she forced herself to face facts: she was with child.

The knowledge was horrifying. If Dominic and she had already been wed, it would have made her feel better, but it would not have eliminated all the difficulties that she now confronted. As she had told herself once before, when she had instinctively turned down Dominic's proposal, this child that was even now living in her womb would not be welcome among the friends and neighbors that she had known from childhood. Her own family—her father—might even disown it. The more she thought about it, the more she realized that he probably would. Because the child would also be the offspring of a convict. It would be a child of tainted blood. . . . The only worse stigma was to be oneself a convict. Her child would be scorned by everyone who was anyone. He would have to earn his living in some menial way; or, if it was a girl, she would be forced to marry either a convict or a man with the same tainted blood as herself. No boy from a decent family would have her.

Sarah felt sick, and not just at her stomach. What had she done? It was one thing to choose, deliberately, to forsake the society, friends, and family that were her own birthright. It was another thing to bring into the world an innocent child who could never, no matter how he or she tried, be accepted. The thought made Sarah furious, and her anger made her feel better. She was surprised that she already felt so fiercely protective of this fruit of her womb. . . . Somehow, she would see to it that her child was not stigmatized. There had to be a solution, if only she could find it.

Sarah could lie abed no longer. Agitated by her thoughts, and by the realization that she—she, spinster Sarah!—would in a few months be the mother of a child, she had to be up and doing. For now, she decided as she dressed, she would keep her secret to herself. She would not even tell Dominic until she had decided what was best to be done. Undoubtedly he would be as appalled as herself; just as undoubtedly he would try to take charge of the situation, and Sarah was not yet settled enough in her own mind to allow herself to be taken charge of.

The dress she chose was of amber muslin, a fine, floaty material that moved easily about her legs as she descended the stairs. It was trimmed with satin ribbons in a dull gold color that brightened her hair and brought out the color of her eyes. Beneath it she wore her plain underthings right down to her practical cotton stockings. She still could not feel at ease wearing filmy, feminine frivolities where no one could see. Then Dominic's darkly handsome face appeared in her mind's eye. Perhaps she would have to give feminine underwear a chance, too, when her body had returned to its normal shape after the baby was born.

As Sarah busied herself about the house, directing the maids on a cleaning spree of the sort that usually occurred only once a year, she thought of little but the changes that were in store for her body—and her life. Unbelievable to think that in just a few months she would be a wife and mother. How her life had changed—would change! And all because of a devilishly handsome Irish convict who had come into her life by merest chance and stayed to utterly consume it. Sarah shook her head, marveling at the vagaries of fate. The miraculous had occurred: she had fallen in love, and was expecting her lover's baby.

"Miss Sarah, it's almost dinnertime." Mary's voice brought Sarah out of her rapt contemplation. She looked at the maids, both of whom were drooping with weariness, then out the window of the front parlor which had just been thoroughly cleaned. Through the sparkling glass she saw that the sun was low, sending long feelers of bright pink and orange shooting across the darkening sky. It was indeed almost time for dinner. The men would soon be returning to the house, and Mrs. Abbott would have ready Dominic's tray, which Sarah would carry up to him and remain to share.

"You girls go on and wash up. I'll just finish here." Sarah sent the maids on their way with a smile and a wave of the feather duster she held. When they were gone, she continued to wield the duster over the collection of glass ornaments on the mantel. Looking down at the grate, black and cold now, she was reminded that it would soon be winter. By the time the first snow fell, she would be Mrs. Dominic Gallagher, and her stomach would be big with child.

"Miss Sarah!" The resonant male voice made her jump. Turning with a faint frown on her face at having been jolted from her thoughts, she saw that Percival had entered the room and stood, dusty hat in hand, smiling at her. If he was home, then her father must be, too.

"Oh, good afternoon, Mr. Percival," Sarah replied vaguely, as she set down the feather duster and reached up to untie the scarf that had protected her hair. This was not the first time she had seen Percival since learning of what he had nearly succeeded in doing to Dominic. But, for her father's sake, she had swallowed her animosity and been, if not cordial, at least civil. She had to force herself not to remember the healing weals on Dominic's back. . . . Percival watched her movements with deepening interest, though Sarah was barely conscious of the expression in his eyes.

"Please excuse me. I must wash my hands and face before dinner. I'm afraid I forgot the time." She moved toward him as she spoke, intending to go straight up to her bedroom.

"Sarah, wait." He stopped her with his hand on her arm. Sarah stared down at that stubby hand with some surprise as it rested on her bare skin, and tried to shake it off. He released her at once, but still stood in front of her, blocking her path.

Sarah's eyes moved to his ruddy face. She gave him a darkening frown. "What is it you want of me, Mr. Percival? I've already told you that I'm late." Her tone was cool.

"Sarah . . ." Her face tightened at the familiar address, which she had often forbidden to him, but she decided for the sake of family harmony not to make an issue out of it. He continued, his voice thickening, "I haven't told you— you're looking very good lately. Very pretty."

"Why, thank you." Sarah smiled, relaxing a little. Compliments were still so new to her that she considered every one a delightful present. Percival smiled back at her, which did not improve his coarse features. His eyes were a darker hazel than usual as they ran over her. Sarah shifted impatiently, eager to be on her way. Dominic would be growing hungry. . . .

Percival cleared his throat. "Sarah," he began in a low, intimate tone. "I just wanted to assure you that your infatuation with that convict makes no difference to things between us. I know he's kissed you, maybe done even more, and I just wanted to tell you that I won't hold it against you. I won't be constantly throwing your indiscretion in your face when you're my wife, I promise you."

"Why, that's very generous of you, Mr. Percival." Despite herself, Sarah had to laugh at the absurdity of it. "But, as I've told you before—many times before—I have not the slightest intention of becoming your wife. Ever.''

Percival stiffened. His eyes narrowed, darkened still further. His hand came back up to grasp her arm. Sarah tried to shake him off again, but this time he refused to release her.

''I know what it is, it's that convict,'' he gritted. ''But there's no future for you with him, no matter how much you might be enjoying his bed. *I* can marry you, give you children. You'll be glad to settle for that in the end.''

''I don't have to settle for anything,'' Sarah replied icily. Then she hesitated. But she had to break the news of her wedding plans soon—in fact, immediately, in light of recent developments—and who better to begin with than this man whom for years she had been longing to take down a peg or two? She smiled in anticipation, ''You see, I'm going to have just exactly what I've always wanted. I'm going to marry Dominic.''

Percival looked stunned. Shock momentarily silenced him. Then angry color began to mount in his face. Sarah was tugging at her arm, trying to wrench free of him, but his fingers tightened so fiercely that she gave an involuntary gasp.

''You'd choose that *convict*—over me?'' he sounded as if he would choke. The words were fierce, his voice guttural. ''You'd marry him—a convict—over me? Oh no you won't! I've been too gentle with you, you haughty little bitch, but I see my mistake now. That prissy air of yours was always an act, wasn't it? The truth is, as that convict found out, you like men. Well, I'm more man than he is! As you're going to find out!''

''Let me go!'' The words were shrill with outrage and growing alarm as Percival hauled her against him, his arms wrapping around her like thick vines, locking her to his body, which was muscular despite his stockiness.

Sarah writhed frantically, trying to get free, but he only laughed low in his throat and caught her head with his hand in her hair, his fingers digging hurtfully into her scalp as he held her still for his kiss. The touch of those thick lips on hers, the greedy rape of his mouth, was nauseating. Sarah fought like a wild thing, her sharp, shrill cries escaping into his mouth as she kicked him and beat at his head with her fists. He only held her tighter, kissing her with a kind of insulting ferocity that filled her suddenly with fear. Dear God, did he mean to rape her? Even as she had the thought, one of his arms slid all the way around her body so that his hand could grapple clumsily for her breast. Sarah's heart seemed to stop with horror. Then she kicked at him furiously, managing to tear her mouth away from his long enough to scream. . . .

"What the bloody hell?" the angry growl was Dominic's. Sarah had barely registered that before Percival was being torn away from her and sent crashing across the room by Dominic's fist against his jaw.

Percival crashed into a small table, overturning it so that the delicate china figurines on it were dashed to pieces on the floor, and fell heavily atop the shards.

"Are you all right? Did he hurt you, the bloody bastard?" Dominic's voice was still thick with fury as he turned to Sarah. His handsome face was dark with rage, and a muscle twitched at the corner of his mouth. His hands clenched and unclenched at his sides. "If he did, I'll kill him."

Sarah saw with alarm that he meant it, and grabbed at his arm. "Dominic, no! I'm all right! He didn't . . ."

She never got to finish. A roar from behind her interrupted, causing her eyes to widen as she turned instinctively to seek the sound's source. Dominic thrust her aside just as she realized that Percival was back on his feet and charging Dominic. . . .

Dominic, an ugly snarl twisting his face, caught him with the same uppercut that had felled Minger all those weeks ago in the bush. It had the same effect on Percival. The burly overseer went hurtling backwards . . . .

"What's going on in here? Sarah! John! What's happening?" This new voice was her father's. Sarah turned to him with blatant relief. Surely, now that he was here, Percival would not press his attack any further.

"That damned convict attacked me!" Percival got his say in first from his half-sitting, half-prone position on the floor. The remains of a flower arrangement peeked incongruously from beneath the seat of his dusty brown breeches.

"He did not! He . . . !" Sarah came hotly to Dominic's defense. Dominic frowned at her, but since Sarah knew him well enough to know that he would say nothing in his own defense unless asked directly, she was determined to present to her father the truth of what had happened. "Percival . . . !"

But Percival's enraged bellow drowned out her voice. "Damn you to hell, Markham, I told you that convict was nothing but trouble! I told you that I was right to beat him for daring to touch Sa— Miss Sarah. But you wouldn't listen, would you? And now you know what's come of it? Have you heard her plans?" He laughed, the sound nasty. "She says she's going to marry that damned *convict*!"

Sarah saw Dominic stiffen, and stepped hastily to his side to place a restraining hand on his arm. It would be best if he stayed silent, let her handle her father. . . . Edward's head swiveled around so that he was staring at her. His face was suddenly gray, his eyes bulging at her.

"Is that so, daughter?" His voice was hoarse, his breathing labored. Groping behind him, he rested his hand on a polished tabletop as if he needed its support. Sarah felt sorry for him, but the moment could not be put off any longer.

"Yes, Pa. I'm going to marry him." Dominic's eyes touched her face in a brief caress before shifting to fasten again on her father. Edward was staring at her, his lips pale.

"I won't permit it."

Sarah's lips tightened and her chin came up. Dominic would have spoken, intervening between father and daughter to draw the onus on himself, but Sarah's fingers tightening around his arm stayed him.

"You can't stop me, Pa."

He closed his eyes, visibly wincing. Then he opened them again to regard her with pain.

"Sarah, Sarah, I am thinking only of your good. I won't allow you to marry this—man. I'll take whatever measures I have to, to prevent such a disgrace from befalling you."

"It won't be a disgrace, Pa, but a blessing. And there's nothing you can do to stop me, short of locking me away in chains."

"If I have to." Edward sounded infinitely tired.

Sarah shook her head. "If you do, Pa, you'll only be letting me—and yourself—in for worse disgrace." Sarah hesitated, swallowed, shooting a lightning glance from her father's ashen face to Dominic's watchful one. Then she plunged ahead. "Because I'm with child, Pa. Dominic's child."

Three pairs of male eyes seemed to burn holes in her face.

XXVII

It should have been a happy occasion. Usually brides were married amid lace and flowers, smiles and kisses. But Sarah's wedding more nearly resembled a wake.

She wore a simple silk dress that had once been her mother's. Jane Markham's wedding dress was stored in the attic, wrapped carefully in clean sheets, but under the circumstances, Sarah had not wanted to wear it. She felt that it would have hurt her father too much. But Dominic had insisted that the color of her gown be white—after all, as he reminded her in one of their few exchanges since that dreadful scene in the front parlor, she had been a virgin when she first came to him, and that was what counted.

Her father seemed to turn into an old man before her eyes as he watched her become Mrs. Dominic Gallagher. He _was_ old, Sarah realized as she glanced at him over her shoulder as the priest spoke the words that would bind her to Dominic forever. Her father was nearing sixty. . . .

Lydia was present, a spitefully amused light in her eyes as she witnessed what she regarded as her step-daughter's ultimate fall from grace. Liza stood beside her mother near the hearth in the front parlor, her eyes huge and a little fearful as she watched Sarah wed a convict. Both ladies were dressed in mauve—the color of light mourning, though Sarah was determined to think that it was not a deliberate choice, at least on Liza's part.

Dominic was dressed in a black frock coat and gray breeches. His cravat was snowy white, and he looked so handsome that his appearance was the one bright spot in Sarah's day. The clothes had belonged to Sarah's father, and Mrs. Abbott had labored prodigiously to alter them to fit. She did not witness the ceremony—Lydia and Liza had said pointedly that they would find business elsewhere if the woman stood in the front parlor with the family—but Sarah knew that she was in the kitchen even as the vows were being said, putting the final touches on a towering white cake that Sarah hadn't the heart to tell her no one wanted.

Since the scene that had occurred in the very room in which they were now being wed, Dominic had been unlike himself. He seldom smiled and never laughed. His eyes were very dark, almost brooding. Sarah had tried to get him to talk to her, to tell her what was wrong—she was afraid that he was unhappy about the baby—but he would not. He would merely look at her out of those hooded eyes and ignore her question. Sarah didn't know whether to shake him, throw something at him, or burst into tears at his feet. In the end, she did nothing. After the ceremony there would be time enough to get to the bottom of what ailed him.

"Do you, Sarah Jane Elizabeth Markham . . ." The priest was addressing her now, intoning the age-old words of the marriage service. Sarah's hands were icy cold as she gripped the Bible that she held instead of flowers; when it came time to respond, her voice was equally cold and clear. The crystalline pureness of her words surprised her. Inside, she was a trembling mass of nerves.

The priest turned to Dominic. Without so much as a glance at his bride, Dominic said the words that would make her his wife. Sarah stared at his profile as he did so, suddenly not sure that she knew this tall, black-haired, incredibly handsome stranger. With his hair neatly brushed, and his fashionable clothes, he looked impossibly remote, not at all like the man she had fought with, bedded, and loved. Until the priest pronounced them man and wife, that is, and he turned to look at her at last. Even after a thousand years had passed Sarah thought she could not mistake those Irish blue eyes.

His lips as they touched hers in the obligatory kiss were as cool and remote as his manner. He smiled afterward when Edward, with the determined air of one who has made up his mind to make the best of a bad situation, offered a toast to the newlyweds' health. Sarah smiled too, as mirthlessly as Dominic, as the priest added his congratulations. The cake was brought out and cut, another toast was drunk, and the wedding was over. And Sarah's new husband had not spoken a word to her.

Mrs. Abbott had returned to the kitchen after bringing in the cake, Liza and Lydia had drifted off to their rooms for the afternoon naps so necessary to their beauty, and the priest had taken himself off in Mrs. Abbott's wake, lured by the promise of a hot meal. Left alone with his daughter and new son-in-law, Edward swallowed the wine left in his glass in a single gulp, set the glass down with a purposeful click on a polished sideboard, and crossed the room to where Dominic stood.

"Gallagher, you know that I don't like the idea of my daughter being married to you. I think it very possible that the silly puss has ruined her life." During this speech, Dominic's eyes rose from their contemplation of his wine-glass to regard his father-in-law with a darkening frown. Edward continued, "But, be that as it may, what's done is done and you and Sarah are married now. And about to make me a grandfather, I guess. So..." He held up a hand as Dominic, his dark face hard, started to speak. Dominic obligingly held his tongue while the older man finished. "So I want you to know that as far as I am concerned we're starting with a clean slate. As my daughter's husband, you are welcome to remain with her on Lowella for as long as you will."

"Thank you, sir, but..." Dominic's face had changed, become less shuttered as Edward completed his speech, but the negative attitude was clearly there in his look. Sarah, coming up to them with a package that Tess had just given her, heard the last part of her father's words and the beginning of Dominic's reply. He was going to refuse, she knew. But Edward waved him into silence.

"I know there's a lot still between us, but I think for the sake of my daughter and grandchild, your wife and child, we could work it out. All I ask is that you think about it. You would be a free man, of course. I've already had my man in Canberra petition our new governor, Sir George Gipps, for commutation of your sentence. I have every reason to believe that it will be speedily granted. And with Percival leaving as he did—no, I'm not blaming you for that, but there's no denying that he left because you were marrying elsewhere—" This aside was addressed to Sarah, who had been looking guilty; she knew as well as anyone how much Edward had depended on Percival. Edward's gaze shifted back to Dominic. "I need an overseer. If you want it, the job is yours."

"Thank you, sir. I'll think about it." Dominic's words were formal, but his expression had warmed.

Sarah felt hope rise inside her. Maybe they could stay on Lowella after all, if only Dominic's colossal pride did not stand in their way. She watched wide-eyed as her father looked at Dominic, hesitated, then thrust out his hand.

"Welcome to the family, Gallagher."

Dominic looked at that outstretched hand for a moment in silence. Then he smiled, crookedly, and clasped Edward's hand with his own.

"I'm honored, sir."

Sarah looked at those joined hands, the one short and wide, with splayed fingers spattered with freckles, the other brown as teak, long-fingered and, as she knew from experience, strong, and felt a lump rise in her throat. These two men whom she loved more than anyone else in the world . . . she wanted to hug them both. Instead, she smiled mistily as her father harrumphed and disengaged his hand, turning away. Then she gave in to the urge to plant a kiss on his weathered cheek. Whatever else happened, she could not but be grateful for the events that had restored her father to her. For the first time since she was a tiny child, Sarah felt secure in his love.

"Be happy, daughter," he said gruffly, his eyes almost as misty as hers. Before either of them could fall further under the sway of their emotions, he stepped away from her, his attention shifting to the flat brown parcel in her hand.

"What is that you have?"

Sarah looked down at the package, remembering it for the first time since Tess had called her into the hall to give it to her.

"It's addressed to you, Pa."

"Ahhh. I've been expecting this." He took the package

from her and tore it open, a satisfied expression on his face as he inspected the governor's seal. "Your papers have arrived," Edward continued, addressing Dominic, who still looked brooding. "As of this moment, you're a free man."

"I thank you for your efforts on my behalf."

"No thanks necessary. You're a member of the family now, and I do for you what I'd do for Sarah or Lydia or that girl of hers."

"Still, I appreciate the effort."

Edward nodded his head once in acknowledgment, and signaled to his daughter with his eyes that she could escort him to the door.

"He's a proud man, Sarah, and you may have trouble with him yet. I doubt he'll be willing to stay on at Lowella—under the circumstances, I don't think I would myself, so I can't blame him overmuch." He sighed. Sarah noticed that his face was gray beneath its sunburned ruddiness. A twinge of concern pierced her.

"Pa . . ." she began, her hand coming up to catch his arm as he staggered a little before grasping the edge of the doorjamb to steady himself. "Are you all right?"

"Must have had too much wine," he muttered, not looking at her. Then he thrust the papers into her hand. "You keep these by you, Sarah. I don't want to give them to *him*. I've had dealings with that kind of damn-your-eyes Irishman before: liable to take offense at the drop of a hat. And we don't want that. I'm looking forward to seeing my grandchild."

Sarah laughed a little unsteadily. Her father was taking that aspect of the situation—indeed, every aspect of it—far better than she had expected.

"Don't worry, Pa, you will. I'll see to it."

"Planning to rule the roost, are you, girl?" He chuckled, pinching her chin. Sarah was relieved to see that he was standing without support now, and the normal ruddy color had returned to his cheeks. "You two should have some bang-up battles. I only wish I could be around to see them."

Sarah frowned quickly. "What do you mean, Pa?" Something about his tone made her uneasy. Was he ill, and not telling her? It would be like him, she thought.

"Why, what do you think I mean? Just that like all married women, you'll likely be going to a home of your own, if not now then in the future. And I won't get to witness the taming of the shrew."

"Or vice versa," Sarah said, smiling. Edward chuckled again in response.

"Or vice versa," he agreed, grinning at her. Then, with a look over her shoulder: "You'd best be getting back to your husband. He's looking a mite serious. And I'm going upstairs to lie down for a bit."

This was so unlike her father—he was far more likely to leave his daughter's wedding directly for the breeding pens—that Sarah's earlier concerns were roused once more.

"Pa, don't you feel well?"

"I feel fine. Oh, you're wondering about me lying down?" His grin widened, and he winked at her roguishly. "Now that you're a respectable married woman, I guess I can tell you: it has to do with Lydia. She's taking a nap, don't you know."

"Ahhh." Sarah nodded, returning his grin.

Where once such an obvious reference to what went on between a husband and wife would have shocked her to her toes, now she didn't feel so much as a quiver of unease. Probably because she was possessed by a similar urge to get her new husband upstairs. . . . Her father pinched her chin again and left the room. Sarah turned back to Dominic, who had poured himself another glass of wine and stood staring out the window at the front lawn.

"That went rather well, considering," she ventured, speaking to his broad back.

He turned his head to regard her steadily over his shoulder. "Yes, it did, *considering*," he said, his lip curling. "Considering that you disgraced yourself by marrying a convict, and your father buried his prejudice and resentment and, out of love for you, offered me the charity of his home, and . . ."

Sarah was staring at him, hurt and startled. It took her a moment to gather her wits for a reply.

"Dominic, what is the matter with you? You've hardly spoken to me for the past week." The fear that had kept recurring but that she had tried to hold at bay surfaced and had to be expressed. "Do you—you do want children, don't you? Or is it me? Did you not want to get married after all?" Her voice faltered over this last. Despite her best efforts, her eyes were very wide and vulnerable as they met his.

He laughed, harshly, setting aside his glass before coming to catch her by the shoulders.

"Tell me something, Sarah: just when did you find out that you were with child? Before or after you decided to sink yourself below reproach by marrying me?"

Sarah blinked up at him as the import of his question sank in. He suspected that she had married him, despite his convict status, only because of the coming child.

"After, Dominic," she said with quiet force.

He stared down at her, his blue eyes searching her face. She met his gaze steadily, hoping to convince him by sheer force of will where words, she knew, would not suffice.

"Sarah . . ." Whatever he had been going to say was cut short by Liza, who was looking both confused and excited as she entered, bringing with her a man who, despite his dusty traveling clothes, had the precise look of a lawyer or other businessman.

"I'm sorry to interrupt," Liza said breathlessly, her eyes agog as they moved from Sarah to Dominic and back again. "But this gentleman—he says he's come all the way from England, looking for the earl of Rule!"

XXVIII

It was the dead of winter. Sarah, clad in a longsleeved, loose-waisted wool dress of unrelieved black, clutched her voluminous cape closer about her as the wind nipped at her pinkened cheeks. The orchard was bare now of fruit, the trees stripped of leaves. Sarah stood beneath the interlocking gray branches, looking east at the distant blue haze of the mountains, white capped now with snow. A single tear rolled from her eye to trickle forlornly down her cheek. She wiped it away with an impatient finger. No matter how she tried, she couldn't seem to shake the black depression that had been her constant companion for weeks. And she did try. She very much feared that such unrelenting misery was bad for her unborn child.

It had been more than four months since her wedding, and in that time her world had changed so much that it was no longer recognizable. Dominic had gone back to England with that man who had come to inform him that the earl of Rule had died. As the earl's legal if not natural son,

Dominic had inherited the title and entailed property.
Which meant that, to Lydia's chagrin, Liza's excitement,
and her father's thigh-slapping pride, Sarah was now a
countess. And, she thought bitterly, much good it did her.

She should have gone with Dominic, she acknowledged
now. He had asked her, just once, and she had refused.
The thought of leaving Lowella, and her father, to journey
to a strange and frightening land with a man who was
scarcely more familiar had suddenly terrified her. Her
child would be born on alien soil, would never know the
blistering heatwaves and frigid winters of New South
Wales, would never see Lowella. . . . And her father—how
could she leave her father, never to see him again? Because she didn't fool herself that they would one day return
for a visit. And even if they did, she had had the strangest
certainty that her father would no longer be waiting. . . . She
had tried to explain all this to Dominic, but the words had
tumbled out in a confused jumble and he had gotten angry
and stalked away. And the next day he had gone. Though
she had longed to, she had not asked him to stay. He had
to go; according to the man who had come to find him—a
representative of the old earl's bank—there was considerable question as to whether John Dominic Frame was
alive. If so, he was heir to the title, but if he was dead, a
nephew of the old earl's, who had been willed the unentailed
property, got everything, including the title and Fonderleigh.
The nephew had already filed a claim, and if Dominic did
not appear in person the bank very much feared that the
nephew—a known spendthrift—would win. If it had been
only the title, Sarah thought, Dominic would not have
cared, would not have gone, but for Fonderleigh. . . .

Sarah's heart ached as that lean, dark face rose in her
mind's eye as clearly as though he stood before her. Would
she ever see those Irish blue eyes again? Honesty forced
her to admit that she probably would not. Ireland was so

far away, and by now she and their unborn child were in all likelihood only dim memories, if he thought of them at all. After all, as Lydia took some pains to point out, Dominic was an earl now. With his new title, the wealth that had been entailed on him, and his dazzling looks, he would be able to take his pick of women. Why should he remember a sharp-tongued, bossy female whose looks could most charitably be described as passable and who was well past the first blush of youth? Because of the child she carried? As Lydia also gloried in reminding Sarah, a man could father a passel of children by many different women. What did she think was so special about hers? Every time Lydia said that, Sarah mentally hugged the unborn infant who was as yet only a cumbersome bulge where she had once been so slim. Whether or not Dominic, or Lydia, or anyone else thought so, this child *was* special, to her at least. Boy or girl, she loved it. Its presence inside her had been the one talisman that she had clung to during the past dark days.

Even if she could have, Sarah thought, staring sightlessly at a soaring hawk as it winged into the distance, would she really have done any different? If she had, she would not have been with her father when he died.

Her instincts concerning Edward had been right. He had been dying for some time, of a wasting disease, and had known it and told no one. Even when he heard that Dominic was returning to Ireland and thought that Sarah might be going with him, he had held his peace. But Sarah wondered now if she had not known even then, on some subconscious level. If that had not been part of her reluctance to leave.

Two months ago, Edward had collapsed at the breeding pens. Two aborigine workers had carried him home and put him to bed. He had never left it. Sarah, Liza, and Lydia, to the woman's credit, had nursed him devotedly, making sure that one of them was always with him and that he was never left alone. Though the doctor they summoned from Melbourne had told them bluntly at the outset that he was going to die, they had all refused to believe it until the very end. Only six weeks ago, when Edward had been scarcely more than a flesh-covered skeleton with staring gray eyes, had Sarah accepted the inevitable. And a week after that, Edward had breathed his last.

At the end, Sarah and Lydia had held his hands while Liza cried copious tears in the background. It was near dawn, and they had sat that way all through the night, the two women who were not friends sitting on either side of the man who had played such a major role in their lives, a frail shadow of himself. As crimson feelers of dawn crept past the horizon to bathe the world in a pink glow, he pressed a kiss to his wife's hand and smiled at his daughter.

"I would have liked to have seen my grandchild," he whispered. And died.

Remembering, Sarah dashed more tears from her cheeks, and started walking again, her movements purposefully vigorous as she took deep gulps of air. Even in the winter chill, walking about outdoors—riding was forbidden her for the duration of her pregnancy—was the highlight of her day. It was the only way to escape the oppression of the house.

It was late afternoon when Sarah decided, reluctantly, that she must go back inside. It would not do for her to make herself ill by exposing herself to the elements for too long a period. She had to think of the child. So, with dragging feet, she returned to the house. Entering through the kitchen—Mrs. Abbott, who had shed a deal of weight in the past arduous weeks, could always be counted on to try to cheer her with a smile—Sarah found Tess hard at work peeling vegetables, while Mrs. Abbott poured juice over roasting meat. Mary was nowhere in sight. Sarah guessed that she was busy waiting on Lydia. Now that Lydia was part owner of Lowella, she had decided that she needed the services of a personal maid, which, as she had never let anyone forget in all the years she had lived on Lowella, she had enjoyed in England. And Mary, as the more graceful and self-effacing of the maids, had been selected. Which left Mrs. Abbott and Tess to do the work that had previously been done by three. Sarah supposed that she should protest the new arrangement. As Lowella's co-owner according to the terms of her father's will, she had the authority to do so. But so far it hadn't seemed worth the inevitable quarrel.

"Can I get you something to eat, lamb?" Mrs. Abbott turned from what she was doing to look at Sarah with concern. Sarah knew that her increasing thinness, apart from her swelling belly, worried the older woman.

"Just a piece of bread and butter, I think." Sarah wasn't hungry, but for the baby's sake she forced herself to eat regularly, "Don't bother yourself, Mrs. Abbott, I'll get it."

She loosened her cloak, hanging it on a peg inside the door, and walked over to the table to cut herself a slice of just-baked bread. She slathered the thick slab liberally with butter, poured herself a glass of milk, and with a wave of her hand left the kitchen. Today she just didn't feel like company; she would take the bread and milk to her room and eat it there.

Lydia's voice floated to her from the front parlor as she passed its open door, stopping her in her tracks.

"I think crimson brocade, don't you, dear? I've ever liked crimson brocade window hangings. Be sure you get the measurements right, girl."

This last, said in an entirely different tone, was clearly addressed to Mary, who, as Sarah saw as she came to stand in the door, was stretching string the length and breadth of the wide windows overlooking the front lawn. Lydia's earlier remark had just as clearly been meant for Liza.

Watching the two dark heads close together as mother and daughter sat side by side on the somewhat shabby gold settee, pouring over a book with illustrated furnishings, Sarah sighed. There was no getting around it. She would have to acquaint Lydia with a few hard facts before she bankrupted them all.

"I've told you before, there's no money to redo the house."

Lydia and Liza looked up simultaneously. Both were dressed in the same sober black as Sarah wore, and neither looked particularly well in it. Their faintly olive complexions called for brighter colors.

"I believe I may spend my money as I please."

Sarah barely managed to stifle one of Dominic's more descriptive oaths. Unlike its creator, it had stayed with her, although she tried her best to banish it from her mind.

"Lydia, please try to understand. There *is* no money. Not until after shearing."

"I don't believe you."

"Lydia . . ."

"You've been crying again, haven't you?" Lydia changed the subject with a taunt. "Poor Sarah, you really do have something to cry about: deserted by your husband, and you huge with child. But you really shouldn't, you know. It makes you look even worse than usual. Sort of pink-eyed, like a rabbit."

"Mother!" That was Liza, getting to her feet and frowning down at Lydia in the first display of defiance against her mother's authority that Sarah had ever witnessed. "Why are you always so unkind to Sarah? Why can't you just leave her alone?"

"Liza!" After a moment's stunned silence, Lydia too

rose to her feet as her voice swelled with outrage. "How dare you speak to me in such a fashion! Let me remind you, young lady, *I am your mother.*"

"And Sarah is my sister!" Liza said determinedly.

Mother and daughter glared at each other. Sarah hurried to intervene before a full-scale war could develop.

"Liza, dear, thank you very much for your championship, but it really isn't needed. I'm quite accustomed to your mother's ill humors. Lydia, if . . ."

Mary, who had gotten very busy indeed at the window as this interchange developed, interrupted.

"Miss Sarah . . ."

"Hush, girl, haven't you learned not to speak unless you are addressed *yet?*" Lydia shook her head with disgust. Then she added under her breath, "Really, these natives! There's no teaching them anything!"

"I'm sorry, ma'am, but, Miss Sarah . . ." Mary was determined to speak, and this was so unlike her that Sarah stared at her with amazement. Mary beckoned urgently. Intrigued, Sarah forgot what she had been going to say and joined her at the window. Lydia and Liza, the former with a petulant frown, followed.

"Look, Miss Sarah!" Mary was pointing out the window in the direction of the drive. Sarah followed the direction of her pointing finger, and froze. A man was cantering a big bay up the curving drive. . . .

"Dominic!" The word was scarcely a breath. She felt as though her heart had stopped as she stared and stared, sure her eyes must be playing her false. But the horse and rider kept coming, and there was no doubt.

"Dominic!" This time it was a full-throated cry. Leaving the other three staring out the window, Sarah picked up her skirts and went flying out of the house. She ran across the porch and down the drive, her eyes shining as Dominic, seeing her coming, reined in the horse and dismounted.

"Dominic!"

He was holding out his arms to her, and she ran into them, scarcely noticing that her big belly kept him from holding her as close as she would have wished. "Oh Dominic, what are you doing here? I thought you would be halfway to England by now."

He put her a little away from him, his eyes sweeping her up and down, widening a little as they rested on the visible evidence of their growing child.

"I would have been—except I jumped ship when we stopped to take on fresh water at the Mascarene Islands. There was another ship in the harbor, bound for Sydney. I brought me back. I decided to wait until we could go together."

Sarah smiled at him, scarcely able to believe that he was real. He smiled back at her, the twist of his lips faintly crooked.

"Oh, Dominic. Welcome home."

He laughed a little, unsteadily. Sarah stared up into that handsome face and felt her heart turn over inside her. His hands on her arms felt so good, so right.

"Home," he said, musing, his voice a low rasp as his eyes ran over her again. "That's what I learned when I left. Home for me is anywhere you are, my Sarah."

Then he pulled her into his arms again, and, belly and all, held her tight.

Epilogue

It was exactly one year later, except that in Ireland it was summer, not winter. Lush green grass grew thickly over the rolling hills. Sunlight sparkled and ducks played in the blue waters of the lough. The mist that had hovered over the countryside that morning had largely dissipated now, leaving behind only a few drifting veils to mark its passing. In the distance stood a very big castle with battlements and turrets, made of stone as black as the devil's heart. The sun glistened on the black stone, making it shine like thousands of diamonds.

Down by the lough, Sarah was laughing as she clung to the trouser seat of her year-old son. The boy, having lately mastered the art of walking, was delighted with it. He was bound and determined to toddle straight into the water. Sarah had been showing him how to feed the ducks, and his chubby fists were full of bread crumbs. Though a flock of the white birds quacked and pecked at his feet and

Sarah's skirts, he had his eye on the large swan that floated in the water, just out of reach.

"Edward, no!" Sarah repeated for what must have been the dozenth time.

Her son, determination in every line of his solid little body, quite properly ignored that, his legs churning as he fought to get to the swan despite his mother's grip on his pants.

"I can see he takes after his mother. A fighter to the end." This light-hearted remark made Sarah turn her head and smile at the tall, black-haired man who himself was smiling as he watched them.

"I thought you were going to be busy with your estate agent all afternoon."

"I was—but I happened to glance out the window and saw you and Ned down here by the water. So I decided to join you. You're looking very lovely today, Countess."

"Thank you, my lord." Sarah smiled with mock coquettishness up into her husband's handsome face. It seemed so strange to call him that, and to be called countess herself. She wasn't sure she would ever get used to it. A brief shadow must have crossed her face, because he searched it with his eyes.

"Sorry you left Australia?" he asked softly.

Sarah looked at him, at the black castle looming behind him, and shook her head.

"How could I be sorry? I love Fonderleigh, and Ned, and you. . . ."

"Not in that order, I hope." He was grinning at her. Sarah wrinkled her nose at him impishly. Then he sobered, "I'm serious, Sarah. Do you ever miss Lowella?"

She thought about that. Her life had changed so much in the last year. She was no longer uncertain of herself, or of him, and it showed. Her clothes were stylish yet simple, like the bronze-green walking dress she had on at the moment. As did all her new clothes, it played up her quiet beauty, bringing it to the forefront so that one noticed it now instead of overlooking it. Her tawny hair was worn in a soft upsweep that made an effective frame for her golden eyes. Her mirror told her that she looked a totally different woman from the one he had fallen in love with in Australia. She no longer had trouble believing him when he called her beautiful, and he called her that a dozen times a day.

"Sarah?" he prompted softly.

"Oh, sometimes I miss the heat, when the chill gets into my bones. But that's all, I think."

"You're not homesick?"

She shook her head. "How could I be homesick? You and Ned are my home."

He smiled, remembering. Their son chose that moment to lunge again for freedom. With his mother's attention distracted, he made good his escape.

"Edward Dominic!"

Both parents lunged for him before he could fall headlong into the lough, but it was Dominic who caught him. He hauled his protesting son into his arms, then swung him to his shoulder, while Sarah shook her head at the child and tried to look severe. He beamed at her, his chubby face splitting into such a wide smile that she had to smile back.

"He's a little rogue," Sarah said to her husband.

Dominic grinned. "I told you, he takes after his mother."

"His father, more like," she retorted, eyeing both her maddeningly handsome males. And smiled again at the expressions in two sets of identical Irish blue eyes.